A da

Kos retired to the edge of society for some well-earned rest. But on the fringes, the Guildpact is fraying. The guilds rip each other apart, a terrible plague runs rampant, and someone has a secret worth killing for. Kos must uncover the secret before it destroys the Guildpact he's spent his life protecting.

Cory J. Herndon continues the intricate tale of murder, conspiracy, and adventure he first began in *Ravnica*.

"Cory Herndon's Guildpact is rousing tale of high (and low) adventure in Ravnica, the city that fills an entire world. The novel is much like Ravnica itself, immense in its scope, incredibly detailed, and churning with both political intrigue and magical danger. Featuring a large cast of unique and engaging characters (that includes everything from a humble goblin test pilot to the most feared and respected of elite wizards), the story's momentum never lets up and the surprises keep coming as retired constable Agrus Kos continues to dig up Ravnica's greatest secrets. Herndon has expertly crafted a sharp and fast-paced tale of good old-fashioned detective work set against a world of magic, madness, and monsters."

—*Scott McGough, author of*
Guardian: Saviors of Kamigawa

EXPERIENCE THE MAGIC

Ravnica Cycle · Book II

Cory J. Herndon

Ravnica Cycle, Book II
GUILDPACT

©2006 Wizards of the Coast, Inc.

All characters in this book are fictitious. Any resemblance to actual persons, living or dead, is purely coincidental.

This book is protected under the copyright laws of the United States of America. Any reproduction or unauthorized use of the material or artwork contained herein is prohibited without the express written permission of Wizards of the Coast, Inc.

Published by Wizards of the Coast, Inc. MAGIC: THE GATHERING, WIZARDS OF THE COAST, and their respective logos are trademarks of Wizards of the Coast, Inc., in the U.S.A. and other countries.

Printed in the U.S.A.

The sale of this book without its cover has not been authorized by the publisher. If you purchased this book without a cover, you should be aware that neither the author nor the publisher has received payment for this "stripped book."

Cover art by Todd Lockwood
First Printing: January 2006
Library of Congress Catalog Card Number: 2005928110

9 8 7 6 5 4 3 2 1

ISBN-10: 0-7869-3989-3
ISBN-13: 978-0-7869-3989-3
620-95471740-001-EN

U.S., CANADA,
ASIA, PACIFIC, & LATIN AMERICA
Wizards of the Coast, Inc.
P.O. Box 707
Renton, WA 98057-0707
+1-800-324-6496

EUROPEAN HEADQUARTERS
Hasbro UK Ltd
Caswell Way
Newport, Gwent NP9 0YH
GREAT BRITAIN
Save this address for your records.

Visit our web site at www.wizards.com

Dedication

For Dad, who taught me everything there is to know about bam-sticks.

Acknowledgements

The following signatories made *Guildpact* possible:
Susan J. Morris, the editor;
Brady Dommermuth, of the *Magic* creative team;
the artists, writers, editors, freelancers, and other
professional folk who create and produce
Magic: The Gathering games and books;
and the past and present residents of Kari Jo Lane and
Cunningham Road.

Special thanks to
S.P. Miskowski, beloved heroine of Alligator Point.

CHAPTER 1

Die trying.

—Motto of the Izzet Observation Corps

15 Mokosh 9965 Z.C.

Observer Kaluzax was not a betting goblin, but before he set foot inside the mizzium-plated vessel that was designed to carry him to his doom (and perhaps a bit beyond) he put his life savings—all 5,732 zinos of it—on the chance that he would survive Observation Expedition Nine. The odds against him when he'd placed the bet were enough to make him the wealthiest goblin in the history of Ravnica, and he intended to collect. Observer Kaluzax was not a betting goblin, but he was certainly a lucky one.

He settled into the lizardskin acceleration chair; slotted the traditional ignition offerings of sulfur, saltpeter, and coal into slot atop the brazier mounted near his right foot; and said, "Glory to Niv-Mizzet. Ignite!"

The darkened, powerless observosphere rumbled to life and the interior lamps flashed to life. The rusty glow revealed a simple set of controls and a glowing scrying pool that would record everything Kaluzax saw—and much more—from ignition until he returned to the floating Dragonfire Base. The base was currently high over his head, nestled atop the back of an enormous zeppelid that had been bred from the rarely domesticated high altitude variety. The observosphere was clamped to its underbelly, ready to launch. One day the creature might be eight hundred feet long, big enough for its shadow to black out the sun, but after sixty years it was less than half that size. Kaluzax's observosphere hung at the front of a row of six, though his was the only one occupied. The corps had not decided to send more than one observer on this particular mission, nor had the magelord ordered more than that—if he had, the corp's wishes would certainly have been cast aside.

Observer Kaluzax had earned every syllable of his name, and the title he bore testified he was elite among the goblins in the Izzet League and the members of Zomaj Hauc's colloquy. No mere lackeys or lab assistants, goblin observers bore witness to the grandest of experiments. They were the eyepieces of the magelords, the stalwart recorders of every major advance in the magical and alchemical sciences since pre-Guildpact days, and their unique vessels were designed to record every angle of an experiment for posterity. Observers, not surprisingly, had a much higher mortality rate than the average Ravnican goblin, and that came with the territory despite the sturdy observospheres they flew. Major advances in the magical and alchemical sciences usually required an explosion or two.

The odds against his survival on most missions were astronomical, but Observer Kaluzax guessed that the bookmakers had needed all the stars in the sky to calculate the chances of surviving this particular jaunt. With those odds, Observer Kaluzax's life savings, meager as they were, could win him a stake impressive enough to establish his own academy. He muttered a curse—the observer had uncanny luck, but there was no need to push it with such jinx-worthy thoughts.

It was not easy to keep away from such thoughts. After eight successful flights aboard the observosphere, never once had fortune failed him. Kaluzax had ridden the eruption of a geothermic dome at the southern pole, escaped the gullet of a titanic bat-bird, and even been shot from a cannon—twice. After the collision with Xalvhar's fortress it had taken a month and a half of precision 'drop treatments to get his bones set properly, but he had lived and returned crucial information on a competing magelord's experiments. His master had been pleased and had begun to take notice. Such achievements, no doubt, were why Hauc had personally chosen him for this mission.

Observer Kaluzax had even seen two previous iterations of the current experiment, an Orzhov-commissioned enhancement of the Orzhov's own project. The magelord called it a mana-compression singularity bomb, and had explained—personally, which counted for quite a lot in Kaluzax's opinion—that the bomb's purpose was to remove life. That meant all life from the plague-stricken Utvara Valley, from the biggest zeppelid to the inscrutinizable worms beneath the flats. If it worked properly, the effect would accomplish the task without harming any artificial structure, inorganic object, or goblin observers protected by forged mizzium. The first two iterations had met with limited success and had caused some trouble for his master with the other guilds, but this time the Orzhov had secured an area specifically for the magelord's practice that could only be improved by the removal of every living thing: the Utvara Valley. By getting rid of any potential plague carriers, the new lords of Utvara would shave centuries off of the process of reclamation.

Kaluzax doubted his master had any intention of disappointing those owners. No one, not even powerful magelords of Izzet, made a habit of disappointing the Orzhov. A pyromancer could set you on fire today, but a patriarch could set you on fire every day, now and for the rest of your afterlife.

Observer Kaluzax was a lucky goblin, as well as a skilled one, but he was not truly as skilled as most thought and was luckier than most suspected. He was clever enough to make sure his bosses mistook fortune for ability every chance he got. Perhaps his luck was supernatural, as his mother had always claimed—a result of some explosive astronomical event the night of his birth. Perhaps it was mere coincidence. Either way no goblin lived forever, but a very few lived rich. A love of gambling was one of the many reasons the entire Izzet tribe was perpetually indentured to the Magewrights, and though Kaluzax had never before succumbed to his people's celebrated predilection for games of chance, he figured his luck owed him a big win this time. He pulled a rip cord that cut the observosphere loose from its moorings and involuntarily grinned. "Dragonfire, 9477 is airborne," he announced.

Goblin and 'sphere dropped, spewing flames and magic, into the darkening sky over the City of Ravnica.

His destination was miles away, but it took a little time for the vessel to pick up speed. Once he and the observosphere reached the elementally balanced velocity of 58.6 miles per hour, the pyromanic flare-pods would kick into overcharge and send him to the Utvara region before you could say "Niv-Mizzet."

Kaluzax flicked a silver switch on his panel to activate an hour's worth of recording ribbon for the archives. "This is observosphere *Peripatetic Eye of Niv-Mizzet 9477,* calling Dragonfire Base," he barked into the pneumanatic tube. His voice entered a magically charged glass cylinder and shot along an invisible network of aerial leylines to emerge, unseen to the goblin pilot, from a glass sphere set into the wall of a dimly lit control room atop the zeppelid he'd just departed. A second later, the slightly fuzzy voice of Observer Kaluzax's boss emerged from the smaller, fist-sized sphere set into the simple controls in front of his pilot's seat.

"9477, we have you on scrying pools now," Chief Observer

Vazozav replied. "You're hanging a little low over those spires. Destruction of public property has not, repeat, has not been authorized for this maneuver. Pull that 'sphere up out of traffic, the last thing I need is wojeks filing complaints."

"You won't get any on my account, Base," Observer Kaluzax replied. "Beginning counter-ascent. Don't want to damage the City of Guilds, do we?"

"What we want isn't an issue, Observer," Vazozav chuckled through the crackling static. "I for one would love to see what they'd do if you burned off a pod over Vito Grazi or whatever they call that place."

"Dragonfire Base, have you no respect for history? For the majesty of the Selesnyan Conclave?" Observer Kaluzax said, affecting a nasal sneer in a goblin approximation of a dryad accent. "For the little flowers and the dancing centaurs, lithely flitting through the dryad's grove?"

"I respect things that explode, Observer," the older goblin said. "Why don't you go find us one?"

"Understood. Estimating elemental balance velocity in fifteen," the pilot said. "Initiating unauthorized roll over the center."

"Get an eyeful," said the chief observer.

Observosphere pilots were as superstitious as any other goblins, and Observer Kaluzax had made a roll like this on his first successful expedition. It was part of the subtle manipulation of luck, which expected to be honored with repetition. Observer Kaluzax goggled at an urban landscape that spread from horizon to horizon. Few goblins ever saw this view more than once, and most that did were in the clutches of something winged that planned to eat them.

The City of Ravnica was always a shocking sight from the air, and for a mathematically minded Izzet, the careful design and geometric beauty of the central metropolis could only really be appreciated from this angle. Kaluzax squinted against dawn. Sunlight, blindingly bright, bounced off the spires that covered the radial wheel of the city's ten sections. He flipped two fingers against his brow in a silent, private salute to the ancient stone titans that watched over the City of Ravnica.

He flew within a bamshot of the face of the tenth and largest titan, sky-grazing Zobor, standing astride the gates to the wojek headquarters known as Centerfort. He would have gone closer, but it was best not to alarm the wojeks stationed atop the titan's head—more than one aerial accident had been caused by such foolish behavior.

Like most every Izzet goblin, Kaluzax had been taught that the City of Ravnica—the central metropolis from which had grown a civilization that covered the entire world—had been meticulously planned with Izzet precision after the ancient Guildpact signing, the Magewrights' gift to the other guilds. One ready-made city that would serve to inspire the world.

The City of Ravnica was also, secretly, an offering to Niv-Mizzet the Firemind, Izzet parun and guildmaster. According to the stories he'd learned as a young goblin, the plan would have created a giant, city-sized power sigil that would have given the magelords ultimate dominion over the entire plane of Ravnica. But Izzet goblins had intentionally (so it was said) fumbled the design just enough to prevent the sigil from working as it had been meant to.

In the old days, the goblins had been a bit more rebellious, but most goblin theologians believed the goblins simply wanted to show off to the boss. They did make an impression. The cleverness of those ancient goblins' actions had so impressed the magelords that the Izzet League purchased the entire tribe outright, gave them the name they now carried, and indentured Kaluzax's people for the next thousand millennia. Over thousands of years, the slight imperfection in the layout of the city had spread—weathered, beaten, and reshaped by millions of denizens. The power sigil would never work now. But from this vantage point the goblin touch was clear—even inspirational.

No one knew what the Izzet goblin tribe used to be called before the Izzet League bought them, and no one, least of all the goblins, seemed to care. Compared to the primitive, short, violent lives experienced by their kin in other guilds, life as an Izzet goblin was paradise. Even being *near* the power that magelords like Zomaj Hauc could wield was an honor. And though it hadn't happened in a generation, every once in a while a goblin gained the gift of Niv-Mizzet, was touched by the Firemind, and became a magelord too. True, every goblin magelord in history had been killed by his or her human peers within a week of receiving that gift, but the point was that a goblin could really *be* someone in the Izzet League. This was rarely the case in the Gruul Clans or the Cult of Rakdos.

Observer Kaluzax spared one contemplative look through the invizomizzium viewplate—tempted, as always, to clip off the tip of the holy Selesnyan Unity Tree as it passed only a few yards below the observosphere. Then he leveled the glittering machine with the horizon and placed a hand on a simple, red lever set into the floor. With the other he turned a small, black knob in the control panel precisely ninety degrees to the right, which sent additional pyromana to the belly-bursters and lifted the observosphere above normal air traffic such as transport zeppelids, rocs, bats, and other flying mounts. This gave him plenty of open sky to burn so long as he kept his trained eyes open. The only other things that flew as high as an Izzet observosphere were wild zeppelids, the angelic fortress of Parhelion, and the great Niv-Mizzet himself. All those obstacles were large enough they could be easily avoided. Anything smaller wasn't any threat to his vessel.

The chief interrupted Kaluzax's focus only briefly when he signaled the start of the mission's next stage. "Begin pod firing countdown on my mark," the fuzzy voice scratched out through the console, then waited a beat. "Mark."

"Ten, nine, eight," Observer Kaluzax counted down, his heart pounding in time with the pulsing sound of the charging flame-pods, "seven, six, five, four, three, two, one."

"Engage flame-pods!" the chief observer shouted with vicarious glee.

"Engaging flame-pods," Observer Kaluzax replied and yanked the red lever back with all his might. With an explosion that would have been deafening to one without sturdy goblin ears and excellent mizzium sound baffling, the observosphere went from a brisk 58.6 miles per hour to precisely thirteen times that speed in seconds.

Observer Kaluzax felt like a giant's hand flattened him against the pilot's seat, and indeed the forces of acceleration would have suffocated the goblin and crushed his insides if not for protective enchantments.

Now there was little to look at below but clouds and the occasional glimpse of grid or highway that flashed past too quickly to make out details. Within minutes, he'd crossed the terminator and found himself beneath a dazzling, star-filled sky that stayed eerily still even as the world screamed by. An observer should always be observing, as the ancient codes said, so Kaluzax mentally catalogued star forms. Modern Izzet goblins rarely even saw the sky unless they were in the corps, and few learned the old star forms or cared about them, but for Kaluzax it was an excellent hobby that kept his fast-working mind occupied between jobs.

He'd made it all the way to Qeeto the Cat-Thief, rising in the east, when he felt deceleration begin, just less than halfway to his final destination. He could not yet see Utvara, still over the horizon.

Utvara had been a vibrant section of the world thousands of years ago, with a free zone that was said to rival the central metropolis of Ravnica. Before that it had been part of the ancient hunting range of Niz-Mizzet himself. Now Utvara was a name synonymous with disease and death where only the desperate dared try to survive. And "desperate" invariably meant "Gruul." Kaluzax had trouble pitying them. Even the lowest Izzet goblin was better than a mangy Gruul.

Observer Kaluzax heard the first thump a few seconds after clearing the bottom of the cloud layer and emerging once more over the planewide metropolis. The sound wasn't loud, and a quick check of his instruments showed he was still on course. Probably just a surprised flock of aquatic birds migrating to a new sky reservoir, he reasoned. Nothing for him to worry about.

Then again, no sky reservoirs were on his naviglass or his well-studied mental map of the plane.

"Speaking of mangy Gruul . . ." he muttered.

He took hold of the twin steering rods and spun the observosphere cockpit module, which floated on magnetomanic fields inside the secondary invizomizzium hull. This let Kaluzax see where he'd just been through the transparent viewplate on the inner sphere. The gyroscopic cockpit's globe-within-a-globe design allowed the flame-pods to fire in one direction while the pilot looked in any direction he pleased, but it took experience to handle it well. One-shots usually became one-shots when they hit the cockpit release before they were ready for the dizzying sensation of spinning in midair without leaving the flight path.

Kaluzax had not struck a flock of aquatic birds, though his

pursuers were indeed winged creatures. At least, some of them were. The others rode the ones with the wings. Three humanoid figures atop reptilian pterros were catching up to the slowing observosphere. The scaly, bat-winged mounts strained against the air currents. They bore strange, organic markings on their leathery flight membranes that Kaluzax recognized as the tribal brands of the Utvar Gruul. So far, they only seemed to be following him, but that didn't explain the thumps. They were falling behind but wouldn't be for long—the belly-bursters were slowing the 'sphere at a considerable rate.

Out of the corner of his eye he caught a glimpse of a wild zeppelid feeding on the upper reaches of a smoggy cloud. There was little the pursuers could do to the observosphere no matter how much they thumped, but a high-speed run-in with the giant lizard's gas-bladders could ruin visibility. With no visibility, an observer observed nothing but failure. With a nauseating whirl, he swung the cockpit around to face front once more.

"Dragonfire Base, it looks like the scouts were right," Observer Kaluzax said. "I've got Gruul in pursuit. No damage so far and none anticipated. I don't think they're looking forward to the experiment. From the look of it, their mounts might give out before they catch up."

"Let them follow," came the reply. "The more test subjects, the better, the magelord says."

"My thoughts exactly," Kaluzax said. "Do you suppose many stayed behind on the ground?"

"Not even the Gruul are that stupid."

"Yes," Kaluzax said, "but they might be that stubborn. Who knows how these primitives really think?"

"Looking for a job in neuristics? Don't worry about what they think, 9477. Just worry about how they die," his boss said.

Another series of thumps struck the rear of the goblin's craft, this time shaking the 'sphere enough that he actually had to manually to correct a slight drift ten degrees to the east. The last one was accompanied by a high-pitched ping that reverberated on the hull. A series of numbers began to flash from red to blue and back again in midair before his eyes.

"Base, the warning light shows I've got a small power loss in flame-pod six. Can you track what they're hitting me with? Should I be concerned?"

"Negative, 9477. Stay on course," said Chief Observer Vazozav, "but feel free to burn off a little extra pyromana at your discretion. The magelord grants you leave to kill them if you wish. Further analysis supports a little leeway to teach ignorant savages to stay out of Izzet business. We can afford it."

"You've been spending too much time with those Orzhov accountants," Observer Kaluzax said. "Remember, 'The study of mathematics is but the first step to understanding the macrocosmic.'"

"Save the proverbs, 9477. Burn something."

"With pleasure, Dragonfire."

To the casual eye, or the primitive one, an observosphere appeared to be unarmed, and technically Kaluzax supposed that was true in the case of the *Peripatetic Eye of Niv-Mizzet 9477*. But he had ways to fight if need be. His innards wrenched violently upward, then down, as he rolled 180 degrees back to again face his ill-advised pursuers. At this altitude, the long-nosed, batlike reptiles were already showing the stress of hard, prolonged flight. Kaluzax adjusted the flame output to slow the observosphere even more, drawing the trio of pterro riders close enough that he could make out the species of the three humanoids. Two were viashino, a race of bipedal lizards that took to flight as naturally as a goblin took to burrowing. The third—the leader, or at least the point of the riders' arrowhead formation—was a broad-shouldered human with dark, reddish skin covered by ritual scarring that matched the pattern on the wings of his mount. The human raised what looked like a spear and pointed one end at Kaluzax's viewplate. The "spear" glowed orange, a color matched by the three small spheres that clung to the side of the weapon like salamander eggs. In fact, they *were* salamander eggs, of a sort—artificially created by Izzet magic and sold in licensed weapons emporiums all over Ravnica.

It was not a weapon a Gruul was supposed to be carrying.

"Looks like the primitives are trying to move up," the observer muttered.

"Repeat, 9477."

"Nothing much, Base," Kaluzax replied, "at least, nothing mizzium plating can't handle." I hope, he added silently.

The primitive tribesman had gotten hold of a goblin bam-stick somewhere, which explained the thumps against the observosphere's hull. With the flick of a thumb the Gruul launched another eyeball-sized projectile of blazing, concentrated mana, this time aimed directly at the center of the observosphere's viewplate. The human probably expected Kaluzax to at least flinch, but the goblin did not. He did blink when the tiny, white-hot pellet of energy struck the invizomizzium, but only at the loud *spang*! sound it made as it ricocheted harmlessly off the flame-proof material.

"Wrong target, Gruul," Kaluzax said as the human raised the bam-stick again. Kaluzax gave the flame-pod alignment a last-second tweak that left all six pointing at the center of the formation, then wrenched the red lever back halfway while slamming the emergency-braking switch to compensate for what otherwise would have been another rapid-acceleration maneuver.

It was not a full blast, and odds were Kaluzax would have to perform a tricky deceleration to stay on target—belly-bursters could only compensate so much—but the results were more than enough to make up for the inconvenience. Six fiery columns of magical immolation met at a single point. Specifically, they met at a spot just north of the lead rider's navel. The concentrated flame burned the human's flesh away in seconds and kept going to flash-cook the pterro as well. The creature's hollow bones, packed with the same gasses that kept zeppelids afloat, ruptured violently from within. As the creature exploded, it set off the remaining ammunition spheres on the bam-stick and obliterated what was left in a spectacular flash.

Observer Kaluzax pressed the red lever forward again and brought the engines down to a tenth of normal as the small shock-wave created by the leader's destruction knocked the two viashino wingmen off course. One mount clipped the other, and the panicked creatures snapped at each other while their equally panicked riders fought the pterros' instincts to no avail. As they rapidly shrank behind him, Observer Kaluzax saw one beast succeed in slicing through the membranous wing of its kin, which crumpled and fell from the sky like a stone. Then distance—and the impending arrival of duty—forced the goblin to swing the cockpit around to forward configuration so he could get to work.

"That got them, Dragonfire Base," Kaluzax reported. "Estimate I shaved a few minutes off my travel time with that blast."

"Correct, 9477," the chief observer replied. "In fact, you may need to hitch a ride or stop off at a guild academy for refueling before you get home, especially if I'm reading these pools right. Pod six isn't just losing power, it's draining pyromana from the other pods, and the bursters."

"Repeat that, Dragonfi—" before Observer Kaluzax could

finish, a rapid-fire series of bells and shrieking whistles sounded in the tiny observosphere. "Oh, dromapples."

"It wasn't that bad at first, just a small leak, but your targeted blast blew it open," Vazozav said, an apologetic tone creeping into his voice. "I was not aware of that when I gave you leave to—"

"Not your fault, Base. It takes more than a little exploding pod to take out ol' 9477," Kaluzax said.

"I was not about to apologize," the chief observer replied.

"All right, my gauges are showing the leak now," Kaluzax said, ignoring him. "Looks like a bad one. Where did primitives get a weapon like—" The question never made it out of his mouth because the observosphere rocked with an explosion from the stern. "That's it, pod six just went!" he shouted. Kaluzax gripped the steering levers as the sphere lurched into a counterclockwise roll.

"Looks like the projectile entered through the exhaust—*that* was a lucky shot. 9477, can you keep it in the air?" the chief observer shouted back, with enough volume to rise above the sudden chorus of alarms. "We're showing pod six has increased in temperature four hundred—no, six hundred percent. Seven . . . eight . . ."

"I'm cutting the pod loose," Kaluzax said. Sweat pooled on his knobby brow and ran down either side of his face as even the mizzium plating grew hot and threatened to turn the 'sphere into an oven. He tugged a length of cable that hung over his head like a clothesline, careful to make sure he pulled the one labeled "6."

The expected clang of releasing clamps did not reach the goblin's ears. "Dragonfire, I'm pretty sure the fire has melted the pod releases."

"That's impossible!" Vazozav replied. "Those are mizzium alloy!"

"Next time, let's get pure," Kaluzax said, "The alloy can't take the heat. It's getting to the next two pods."

"Observer," said a new voice. It was not one Kaluzax had ever heard come over the pneumanatic cylinder, though of course he knew the speaker's identity immediately.

"My lord," Kaluzax said. "You honor me with your words."

"This experiment must go forward, brave Observer," the voice of Zomaj Hauc boomed, somehow drowning out the cacophony in the observosphere with ease. It was as if he heard the voice in his bones as well as his ears. "I will not lie to you. Your vessel will be destroyed. This was, as you know, likely in any event, but now it is certain. Your records will survive and will bring greater glory to the colloquy and, indeed, to all the Izzet."

"I never expected to go any other way, my lord," Kaluzax said. He was surprised to find that his heart did not sink with the realization he truly was doomed—indeed, he felt more exhilarated than ever. Cocky. "I will not fail you. 'Power is knowledge, and knowledge is costly.' Your words, my lord, and I hope to honor them. And you."

"Die trying, Observer," his lord replied. "And farewell."

Kaluzax's heart swelled with pride.

Another loud thump sounded at the rear of the vessel, and for a moment Kaluzax thought the Gruul had returned. Another set of bells told him that no, it wasn't Gruul, but two of the five remaining flame-pods exploding almost simultaneously. He twisted another set of knobs to force the pyromanic flow into the belly-bursters as *Peripatetic Eye of Niv-Mizzet 9477* steadily lost more and more altitude. The auxiliary thrust would be enough to keep him in the air and would help relieve the rising pyromanic pressure, but for how long?

The proximity warning cut through the din as easily as the magelord's voice with a single, clear whistle that rose in pitch until it disappeared beyond the upper realms of even goblin hearing. Kaluzax pulled out a cluster of metal tubes beneath the control panel with his bare hands and tossed them on either side of his chair to cut the alarms off completely. He ignored the burns and cuts, but wiped the blood from his palms before taking the control sticks again.

At least the bookmakers would not be able to come looking for him after this was over. Observer Kaluzax's luck had taken a different form today. It had gotten him to the experiment right on time. His 'sphere was in flames, and he was now certain he would not live out the day, let alone the next hour or perhaps even the next few minutes, but he'd kept his appointment.

Fighting nausea, burning pain, and the steering levers, he managed to slow the ball-shaped craft's meteoric descent before he deployed the witness orbs. Six of them popped into being around the vessel and immediately moved into their predetermined viewing angles. The orbs were intended to supply telemetry, backup data, and clear visuals not obscured by invizomizzium refraction and of course recorded it all for posterity. Usually, Observer Kaluzax would return with the bulk of the data himself. But if an observosphere did not survive a given experiment, the witness orbs ensured the magelord lost nothing more important than a goblin and the data stored in the vessel's memory.

Inside the 'sphere, anything not made of mizzium began to cook. The leather straps holding Kaluzax into the seat ignited briefly and were soon mere ashes dusting his fireproof salamander-skin flight suit. He could feel his ears and the back of his head blistering, every nerve screaming that he should be, well, screaming.

Kaluzax did not scream. Instead he focused on a singular proverb that seemed quite appropriate: luck was a fickle mistress, and didn't like to be pushed.

With both hands, the observer grabbed the remaining cutoff cables dangling overhead and pulled downward. The pods sputtered and fell silent. Another dial told him he had maybe four minutes before the belly-bursters gave out and the *Peripatetic Eye of Niv-Mizzet 9477* dropped like a mizzium egg. Fortunately for Observer Kaluzax—whose only concern now was to finish his life the way he'd lived it—and even more fortunately for Hauc and his colloquy theorists, the experiment took place in a little more than two.

The goblin wiped sweat from his eyes with a blistered hand and saw it come away bloody, his leathery skin cracking. He was glad the scryers couldn't see inside the mizzium observosphere. His colleagues didn't need to see him slowly burst open like a roast dromad. Kaluzax forced the pain into another part of his brain—which didn't help as much as it normally would have since his entire head was also in physical agony, and there was no place to shunt *that*—and turned the observosphere to face the zero point of the experiment. He hit the delayed return switch that would automatically pull the orbs inside the 'sphere one minute after the effect was triggered, an automatic reflex that he knew was pointless since there would probably be nothing to return to at that time.

His last task completed, Kaluzax began to giggle uncontrollably for no discernible reason, and one part of his simmering mind realized that another part was seeping through his right ear, unable to take the pressure. The randomly firing, half-fried synapses in the goblin's brain shifted from laughing to singing for the remaining minute, an old metallurgical ballad he'd learned in childhood. He sang "drop the baby on the anvil" just as his master's experiment began, and so those were his last words.

The experiment was powerful, but not flashy. In mere moments, a tiny point of light in the sky drew in and devoured every living thing in the Utvara province.

In the time it took to blink, the zero point once again had no depth, width, or height, though its mass had increased considerably.

The witness orbs finally recorded the observosphere as it appeared to stretch into infinity, then it was gone. The stretching was all too literal for Observer Kaluzax's body to take, and his life ended with more rending and less immolation than he had ever expected.

The goblin's fleeing spirit snagged on an event horizon. It wasn't long before the fragments of identity and memory coalesced once more into a mind, a mind with a distinct feeling of an elusive identity called Kaluzax. The mind became preoccupied with one question:

Why am I still in this observosphere?

* * * * *

Chief Observer Vazozav tugged at a dangling gold chain he had wrapped absentmindedly around his left ear. His right ear was mostly gone. His excellent eyes, as young as they'd ever been, peered out between centenarian lids at the scrying pool that filled most of the floor space at Dragonfire Base. It displayed in seven dimensions a colorful, accurate map of the Utvara area and the sky above it. The chief observer's boss and magelord had ordered Dragonfire to get close enough to gain visual images from Observer 9477's collection orbs, which were unliving and therefore immune to the mana-compression singularity bomb's effects.

The seven-dimensional image showed a sort of crease in the sky five miles above a now-empty ghost town.

No, that wasn't accurate, Vazozav thought. This wasn't a ghost town—there were no ghosts at all. The scrying pool map was certainly on a scale large enough to display individual specters and phantoms that should have remained. Vazozav had seen the Gruul with his own eyes before the loss of Kaluzax's 'sphere, they were far too close to have survived. Even at the standard and measurable average rate of ectoplasmic dissipation, ghosts—by definition *not* living things—should have been all over the place. Yet Gruul spirits were nowhere to be seen.

Seconds passed, and the crease appeared to fold in on itself, then fracture, finally settling into a shape that his eyes had trouble comprehending. Vazozav could only see it by looking for what wasn't there—blue sky or a cloud of any kind. It was just—a fractal *nothing*.

Chief Observer Vazozav let another ten seconds pass and finally decided it was his place to speak first. And if Hauc struck him down in anger, it would only be right.

"My lord," Vazozav turned to the scarlet-skinned human who stood at his shoulder. He drove his claw tips into his palm to force himself to meet Zomaj Hauc's fiery gaze, "The graviticular effect was a masterful success."

"Yes, it was."

"But . . ."

"Spit it out, Chief Observer, before I cut it out."

"Shouldn't it," the goblin stammered, "shouldn't the bomb have exploded by now?"

"Patience," the magelord said. "Not all explosions are quick."

CHAPTER 2

The Ghostfather: Why are the best Orzhov advokists women, Mubb?

Mubb the Hapless: If you have to ask, you've been dead too long, Ghostfather.

The Ghostfather: Insolent fool! To the pits with you!

Mubb the Hapless: Hooray! Torture again! You are too kind, Ghostfather.

—Rembic Wezescu,
The Amusing Punishment of Mubb the Hapless

14 Paujal 10012 Z.C.

Teysa Karlov rested her cane against the polished surface of the lectern and stood.

Like much of the Orzhov advokist's routine, the placement of the cane was a minor influential affectation she no longer even consciously thought about, though she did actually require it if she was walking any great distance. The cane was of a piece with the look she gave the assembled jurists, the one that carefully expressed surprise she did not truly feel and only a hint of the incredulity she certainly did. She topped it off with an arched eyebrow that few males could resist, for a variety of reasons.

"Doctor Zlovol, could you repeat that? I want to make sure the jurists—and myself, I admit—heard you correctly."

"I said," the vedalken in the hot seat snarled, "that the fatality count was well within the expected parameters covered under the contract. An *Orzhov* contract, advokist. The loss of life was not unexpected, and our own lawmages inspected the contract

20

thoroughly to ensure that we were, indeed, protected from proceedings like this one." Dr. Zlovol actually smiled a bit, something vedalken were not known for. The vedalken was putting on confidence, but his raised voice belied a flicker of doubt. Teysa knew he was thinking hard about whether he really trusted Azorius lawmages doing contract-inspection duty for a Simic viromancer. He was wondering why Teysa had made him repeat the answer. And he was terrified she knew far more than was in the official report on the incident.

"Doctor, you sound like a man with a guilty conscience," she said amiably.

Arrogant types like Zlovol could never resist that bait. The need to point out their superiority inevitably made them come off as defensive.

"Far from it," the vedalken said. "I am a seeker of knowledge. I am proud of what I have achieved, and you all are better off for what I have learned in my studies. I have nothing to feel guilty about, of that I assure you."

There you go, Doctor, Teysa thought. It's all true. I'll give you that.

"What did the deaths of more than a hundred people teach you, Doctor?" The vedalken's lips remained tightly together, and he gave her the evil eye. Teysa's smile disappeared as she sharpened her blades, metaphorically speaking. Not that bloodshed was unknown in Ravnican courts, but by definition it was not generally accepted in a modern court of law in the city itself. "Forgive me. That may have seemed melodramatic. But I consider myself something of a truth seeker as well. I'm curious. You must have learned much from one hundred fourteen dead bodies. Was that enough? Were one hundred forten corpses enough to give you the knowledge you sought?" The pale vedalken looked like he might turn purple.

She smiled genuine smile number thirty-two and added with a hint of apology, "Doctor, I digress. Give us your answer. I'm sure your fellow Simic on the jury are eager to learn how, statistically, one hundred fourteen corpses provided a proper sampling that could truly tell you the full effects of your—I'm sorry, I'm no viromancer, what was it called again?"

The vedalken squirmed. That was something Teysa *had* seen before, not just on a vedalken but also on many other witnesses and defendants who found themselves under her gaze in the verity circle. Dr. Zlovol could not tell a falsehood while within the circle, though he could be as circumspect as he liked. That's why a good advokist threw in specific questions as often as possible. Teysa was much better than good.

"It is called," Dr. Zlovol said, "the Zlovol contagion."

"Very modest of you," Teysa said, though she looked at the jurist chairman as she said it. The vedalken smirked along with her. "And I'm still hoping you can tell us how such a small sample gave you confirmation that this Zlòvol contraction—"

"Contagion!" Zlovol snapped. "The Zlovol contagion!"

"Yes, the Zlovol contagion," Teysa said. "And my question still stands, Doctor. Please answer it."

"You know perfectly well how," the vedalken said. "The one hundred fourteen were the recorded deaths. The rest were guildless and therefore did not need to be officially recorded." As soon as the words were out of his mouth, his eyes grew wide. Whatever he'd started to say, the verity circle had turned it into the truth.

"And how many guildless died when your so-called 'plague apes' spread the combustion—"

"Contagion!"

"Contagion, sorry. But how many, Doctor?"

"Six hundred seventy-seven."

"And how many plague apes died of the contagion they carried?"

"All of them, as intended. It worked perfectly. None remained to infect the general population, as required by the Statutes." Pride crept back into the vedalken's voice. "To do otherwise would leave a virulent plague inside a lethal delivery system. What kind of monster do you think I am?"

"I'm not sure what kind of monster you are, sir. That's what we're all trying to learn," Teysa said. "How many apes, exactly?"

"There were thirty plague apes," the vedalken said as if explaining the movement of the sun to an infant. "Therefore, we recorded thirty. Seven hundred seven unofficial, one hundred fourteen official, one hundred fourteen recorded. Are you satisfied?"

"Nearly. Thank you, doctor," Teysa said. She snapped her fingers, and one of her thrull clerks stepped forward with a single sheet of cosmetically yellowed parchment that she thrust in the doctor's face. "And this is a copy of your contract with the Orzhov upon whose property you performed this test, is that correct?"

The vedalken barely looked at the parchment. "Yes," Zlovol said. "As you have already noted, the terms are clear."

"I agree," Teysa said. "And, as you can see, this copy bears the Orzhov seal, which makes it for all intents and purposes the same as the original. And Doctor, it is clear, very clear. Especially this line here. Would you be so kind as to read this section aloud?"

"No, I will not," the vedalken said. Honest to a fault, this one. "Do it yourself."

"Very well," Teysa said and began to read. " 'In the event of deaths associated with this enterprise, the First Party'—that's you, Doctor—'the First Party shall hand over any and all recorded spiritual and physical residue to the Second Party'—and that, as you know, is the assurance firm of Garn, Yortabod, and Fraszek.

Did you collect and return that residue, that is, corpses, ghosts, and the like, to the Second Party, Doctor?"

"We turned over all officially recorded 'residue,' as you call it, to the appropriate—"

"Yes, Doctor, but that is not what I asked, nor is it what this contract lays out. 'Any and all recorded,' not *officially* recorded.' "

"This is the same rote contract I've signed a dozen times with you people!" Zlovol said, catching the looks passing between the jurists. "This has never become an issue before!"

"With all due respect, sir, you may wish to refrain from confessing further violations of contractual obligations until we have finished dealing with this one. Thank you for putting that information on the official record, however. It will certainly make my job easier in the long run should my clients choose to pursue these additional potential grievances. Now, as to this current incident—"

"This is nonsense! Everyone knows—that is, everyone—" the vedalken fought with the magic of the verity circle and lost, as did all who tried to lie under its influence. He finally changed course. "*I* was given to understand that it was assumed."

"Assumptions are dangerous, Doctor, as I'm sure anyone working in your field would agree," Teysa said. "By your own testimony you have shown that you did indeed record the exact numbers of fatalities amongst apes and guildless. And, beings of the jury, I would not presume to assume that what you have just witnessed is enough to prove to you that the good doctor is in violation of his contract and convince you to find that he has reneged on his agreement and must pay the appropriate penalties." She cocked her head to one side and smiled. "I *predict,* however, that this will be the case. The facts are clear, as is this contract. Jurists, I have nothing more for this witness." She watched the faces of the small assembly as they mentally conferred and quickly reached the same opinion. As one, they nodded to the vedalken jury chairman.

"But I—" Dr. Zlovol began.

"Silence," the chairman of the jury said. In a higher court a single judge would have made that order, but for a simple contractual lawsuit like this one the chairman took the judge's place. "This jury does not need further time to deliberate," he continued. One of the benefits of a vedalken jury chairman was the vedalken's telepathic ability. It made them popular choices for the position. "We find you in violation of contract, Doctor Zlovol. There will be no need for additional testimony."

The chairman nodded to the bailiff, a hulking troll in the ill-fitting uniform of a first-tier wojek guard. The bailiff's one good eye had never left the doctor during the entire exchange. Though the doctor had not said so, Teysa knew that more than eighty percent of the "officially unrecorded" guildless who had died were trolls. She suspected the doctor would have an interesting walk down to the processing chamber, where he would either meet the terms of his contract or pay penalties in zinos and pain.

The doctor's own expensive advokist didn't even offer to shake Teysa's hand. She merely sniffed, took up a stack of parchments and scrolls, and shuffled out the door without saying a word. Teysa made a mental note to send the advokist a consolation letter. The woman had built a solid case until Teysa taunted Dr. Zlovol into offering testimony. Teysa might want to hire the opposing advokist, or perhaps have her killed.

Teysa turned back to her beaming client. Hundreds of ghostly slaves and valuable corpses were now the property of Zacco Garn and his associates. A thrull scampered over and passed her a copy of the settlement. Not a huge payoff, but a bit more than Teysa herself had expected. Vedalken sometimes shaved a few points off of the damages when passing a sentence on one of their own. To balance the books, she'd counted on their instinctive repulsion at Zlovol's act—specifically, the fact that he had failed to report his findings accurately. The additional monetary penalties they'd piled on, quite unbidden by Teysa, would bring even more wealth into the coffers of the assurance firm and another fat percentage.

Garn rose to shake her hand, his beady eyes shining. "Wonderful!" the assuror said. "This could not have turned out better! And now, we will pursue these other violations, as you said, and—"

"Congratulations, Mr. Garn. I will have someone from my office contact you," Teysa said through bright teeth and sincere, generous grin number twenty, which combined 'It's been pleasant,' 'Good luck', and 'Good-bye'. "Now that the heavy lifting is out of the way, this is a job for one of our less senior advokists."

"Of course, of course," Garn said, no doubt already counting the zinos he was going to save by going with the second string. Teysa didn't bother to point out that she intended to add a surcharge to each case, since, as she said, the heavy lifting had been done here. The percentage she'd get next time would be even bigger, or he'd have to go with another advokist. If he did that, she'd have Garn in the verity circle when she sued for breaching their contract and verbal agreements.

Teysa turned and nodded to the thrull, who scurried off to fetch her cane. After the diminutive servant handed it to her, the creature began to dance impatiently in place. It could not speak—few thrulls could—but it squeaked and pointed to the rear of the courtroom, where those assembled to watch the proceedings were also congratulating each other. Most had lost relatives or friends to the Zlovol contagion and were happy enough that justice had been served to the doctor, even if they would never see a penny in compensation. That was *not* part of the contract. Justice would have to be enough.

In only a few years of law practice in the City of Guilds, Teysa had been doing this long enough to know that there was punishment, and there was compensation, but justice for justice's sake? It was fiction—a fiction she exploited well.

Teysa finally spotted what had the chirping thrull—a relatively new one she hadn't named yet—so excited. A tall, bald, tattooed man in ornate gold, black, and white robes had entered the courtroom, holding a staff topped by a pale mask before his face. He nodded when she caught his eye. She gathered her files and notes, tucked them into a leather satchel, and handed it to the thrull, who accepted it with glee.

"Meet me at my chambers," she told the thrull. "Be there when I arrive and you'll get an extra box of rats."

The thrull nodded, turned, and bounded on froglike legs into the noisy crowd before vanishing into a thrull-sized exit cut into the wall. The courts in the City of Ravnica were riddled with such passages and tunnels to expedite the workings of the law—a testament to the power the Orzhov had within the legal system. Judgment was the domain of the Azorius Senate, but advokists paid dues to the Guild of Deals.

Leaning with well-concealed relief on her cane, Teysa made her way through the crowd to the tall man who had come to meet her. Once she got there, the two stepped through the double doors and into the less-crowded hall.

"He wants to see you," the man said without preamble. His name was Melisk, and he was probably the highest-ranking member of the Karlov hierarchy who actually had no Karlov blood. Melisk rarely came down to meet her personally at the court these days.

"What does he want?" Teysa said.

"I just told you, my lady," Melisk replied. "He wants to see you. He did not explain further, and it is not my place to ask such things unless by such inaction I might endanger the life of the patriarch. It is my place to serve."

"You've changed. I remember a time when you didn't require so much prodding," Teysa said. "Serve me by walking me to his chambers and telling me what he *didn't* say about what he wants."

* * * * *

There was very little actual walking involved in their short journey from the halls of judgment to the Orzhov mansion district. Teysa's infirmity, which had crippled her right leg at a young age and resisted all forms of medical treatment, made truly long walks uncomfortable at best, so they made use of a private teleportation station. The Izzet-run platforms were prohibitively expensive for most, and thanks to some clever legal maneuvering were off-limits to wojeks or other city servants who might have wanted to make use of them. Even better legal maneuvering meant that as an Orzhov of a great family, Teysa technically owned them and didn't need to pay the fees, though a hefty tip to the switchgoblin was customary.

Teysa Karlov was merely an advokist for now, but she had plans for the long term. She was not immune to greed and ambition. Indeed, she embraced them. They were two of the holiest motivations written in *The Book of Orzhov*. Teysa did not consider herself devout, but that, at least, she agreed with.

The pair stepped onto the platform and winked out of existence for a moment, then reappeared at the edge of a long, elevated path the color of polished ivory. The Bone Walk had been made from the femur of an ancient stone giant in the days before the Guildpact united Ravnica's people under a single governing document. The path led over black, still water that was not as deep as it looked but was deep enough to hold mysteries that made falling in perilous. The things beneath that placid surface didn't care what family you belonged to, but the Bone Walk's protective enchantments and magically infused material kept them at bay.

"What is this all about, Melisk?" Teysa asked as the pair made their way across the Bone Walk toward the arched portals that marked the entrance level of the Karlov Cathedral. "Enough of the ominous silence. I'm not buying it. You know more than you're letting on, and I know you're not frightened of repercussions."

"I thank you for the assessment, my lady," Melisk said. His words supplicated, but his tone was as bored and impenetrable as ever. "I'm not sure how many ways I can say I know nothing more."

"Melisk," Teysa sighed, "I'm not in the mood for this round-about nonsense. Don't play games with me. I don't find it endearing any more."

Without blinking, Melisk nodded. He hardly ever blinked. His necrotized, enhanced eyes required little in the way of moisture. But he tried. "I did overhear a name. 'Utvara.' That is all I have for you, my lady. I have now violated an oath I made to—"

"Utvara," Teysa said.

"Yes."

"The reclamation zone?" Teysa asked, "The one where that plague got out of control back in . . . what was it, '60? '65?"

"Ninety-nine sixty-five," Melisk confirmed. "It is Karlov property."

"I thought it was a public-works write-off," Teysa said. "The Izzet are running an operation out there, I believe." She scowled. "I don't like Izzet clients, if that's what's so urgent. I don't care what they're paying. They have ways of bending the verity field that throw off my rhythm. It's irritating."

"Surely the patriarch will make everything clear."

"Or the exact opposite," Teysa muttered.

They approached the pair of masked guards who flanked the central archway, and Teysa nodded to each in turn. In response, the tall thrull soldiers faced each other and brought their pike blades together to form a smaller arch that Teysa and Melisk slipped beneath single file. The thrulls had been grown from ogres, from the look of them, with troll thrown in around the edges, and were covered from head to toe in polished, golden armor rimmed with obsidian. Teysa stopped to drop a few large coins into each of the guard's collection plates and continued with her attendant up the long steps.

With the kind of internal logic that springs up in all huge metropolises, the Orzhov district was not considered part of the "undercity" section of Ravnica, like the Golgari and Rakdos territories were. This was true even though the mansion district spread both upward and downward to encompass several vertically adjacent areas of the City of Guilds. The district's own towering, interlocked structures prevented daylight from ever reaching any but the uppermost spires, casting the entire area in perpetual darkness cut only by the glowspheres that hung everywhere—but never close enough to each other to prevent a few stretches of permanent night.

It was typically busy inside the cathedral. Spectral messengers floated to and fro, indentured to serve the patriarchs beyond death by ironclad Orzhov contracts. Clusters of statues celebrating the achievements and wealth of the guild, especially those linked to the family Karlov, gave the place the feel of both a museum and a tomb. Few actual Orzhov were there. However, mansion-district residents enjoyed an extremely sedentary lifestyle. More active types like Teysa tended to live in the city proper.

The lifestyle in the mansion district would not have been possible if not for the thrulls, gargoyles, and other semi-intelligent (and sometimes fiercely intelligent) servant races employed by the Orzhov. But creatures like the one Teysa and Melisk now approached were the primary reason the Orzhov had been able to stay so well protected in their mansions and estates.

The creature was an intelligent golem that had slaughtered its creator, a wizard whose name had been lost to history and that the guardian would not repeat. Its body was composed of stone, bone, and raw elemental magic in the form of an enormous scorpionlike creature, long extinct, called a solifuge. The guardian usually stood in a perpetual state of attack: all eight primary limbs bent at the first joint and jammed down into the granitelike stone pillars, each one twice as tall as Teysa. Its forelimbs were raised to the sky like horns, and its eight crystalline eyes took in all angles. One could only enter the mansion on foot by walking beneath the guardian, and the guardian could impale someone with both fangs before he cleared the second set of limbs. The huge arachnid was working off a vengeance contract that the Orzhov had fulfilled their end of several millennia ago. It would be working off the contract for several thousand years to come, as well.

The creature, ancient beyond reckoning, had wanted a *lot* of vengeance.

"Hello, Pazapatru," Teysa said, and extended her arm, hand out, palm up. "How are you?" Her robe slipped away from her forearm and exposed a set of three black stones set into her skin. The stone solifuge's mammoth head creaked and scraped until it faced the advokist. Its forward set of eyes shone red for a few seconds, and the stones in her wrist reflected the light.

Pazapatru spoke, a sizzling series of hisses and clicks that Teysa's Orzhov blood let her understand as easily as if the ancient creature had been speaking common Ravi. "Teysa. I am well and look forward to my freedom in precisely 2,281 years, nine months, eleven days, two hours, forty-four minutes, and . . . ten seconds. On that day I will destroy you all."

"I don't doubt you will, but I hope to be a ghost by then."

"That would be wise. Only one guest?"

"Yes," Teysa said. "One attendant guest. Don't eat him, please. I look forward to your vengeance as always, old friend."

Click-scrape-grind-screech. "Enjoy your visit, Teysa. Eventual death to you and your attendant guest."

"And to you," Teysa said. The guardian reared up on its four hind legs, Teysa nodded to Melisk, and they headed inside.

By the time they'd reached the entrance to Uncle's chambers, the welcoming glowspheres of home no longer seemed inviting, since this was only home to her now in the sense that it was her place of origin. The old patriarch had better have had a good reason for calling her all the way back here. She'd forgotten how long and monotonous the halls could be in this place: wing after wing of statues, paintings, glowing mana sculpture, and chiseled-stone likenesses, all depicting the pure Orzhov greatness of the house of Karlov. It was all gaudily lit, all overdone, all, in general, nauseating to any being that possessed a modicum of taste—especially when every single piece of "art" in the halls depicted the same person: the patriarch she called Uncle.

Teysa had long wondered why there were no matriarchs but privately suspected it was because no woman in her right mind would want to spend a life of near-immortality with the patriarchy.

A pair of bald, statuesque angels flanked the gold-leafed doors to his chambers. They were not Boros angels, of course, but angels of a darker hue, more suited to Orzhov needs, and, from the look of it, fighting was only one of the needs they'd been built to answer.

Teysa had it on good authority that the angels' blind devotion to the patriarchs—a devotion carved into their very beings at the time of their creation—often led to scenes that the advokist would rather not consider for too long. Their black, feathered wings flared as they spotted the newcomers, and their solid-white eyes glowed softly in recognition of Teysa's Orzhov blood.

Uncle was unusual in some respects. Unlike most other patriarchs, he preferred not to use an elaborate and impressive-sounding name to bolster his authority. He was simply "Uncle" to anyone with Orzhov blood, "Patriarch" to all others. And unlike his fellows, he had left the district in the last twenty years, a firsthand witness to the bizarre events at the Decamillennial convocation more than a decade ago. His angels of despair had accompanied him and, by Uncle's personal account, had saved his life from the onslaught of the Selesnyan quietmen. Teysa could believe that. Though useless in long, subtle, more effective campaigns, the Orzhov angels were deadly in swift, straightforward combat.

Uncle's angels slapped the flat of their sword blades against opposing shoulders and took a precise sidestep that revealed identical golden collections plates mounted on small pedestals. Teysa placed enough zinos in each to buy a small starter mansion—this offering was not just to the Orzhov, it was to her personal patriarch, and in those cases the "offering" was more like a tribute. As each coin dropped atop its fellows, she spoke ancient words that praised Uncle's longevity and health.

When the clinking of coins stopped a few seconds later, a panel in the right door slid aside like clockwork to reveal the sallow face of Mr. Yigor, Uncle's personal doorman. His face could hardly have been more skeletal if one had gone through the trouble of skinning it. For a long time Teysa had thought that Mr. Yigor was some kind of thrull or zombie, but he was actually just a very old, very overworked human with an attitude and independence spawned from countless faithful years at Uncle's side.

"Yes?" Mr. Yigor said.

"Don't act surprised. We've been sent for."

"And?" the doorman said.

"And you should open the door before I remove your eyes, servant," Melisk said in a slightly muffled voice from behind his mask.

"Very well," Mr. Yigor said. He never did anything until threatened, as was the custom when a personal servant was dealing with anyone but the one to whom he, she, or it was indentured. Teysa suspected Mr. Yigor also enjoyed the ever-so-tiny opportunity to give a little guff back to his betters, if the old creature could be said to enjoy anything.

Melisk took up his staff and readied the mask, a superficially beatific representation of Uncle's face. Teysa reached inside her robes and produced a slim, fragile mask of her own that bore a face almost identical to the one Melisk was using. Teysa's was an heirloom, a brittle-looking shell of painted mother-of-pearl, nine hundred years old. It had been a gift from Uncle. She pressed the heirloom to her face and felt it affix to her skin—it would come off whenever she actively willed it to do so, but for now it would stay put.

Uncle's chamber was as opulent as it was old, packed with the gaudiest décor yet. Aside from Mr. Yigor, Uncle was the only truly living thing beneath the vaulted ceilings, but that didn't mean the place was empty. Thrulls and gargoyles lined the walls and hung from the ceiling, many of them cackling or calling out to the new arrivals like a flock of caged birds in a coop—all but the tallest thrull, which stood tall, silent, and filled with quiet menace behind Uncle's left shoulder. His bulbous eyes flicked from Teysa to Melisk before they resettled on Uncle and stayed there.

Garish tapestries hung over sections of the windowless walls, partially concealing ancient but continually revised murals. Both hangings and paintings depicted lascivious and salacious entertainments that had been Uncle's primary pastime in his younger days, including, as expected, extensive scenes that included the very angels they'd just passed. Teysa could not imagine Uncle had ever had younger days. Most others who had shared such times with him had been dead for years, some by his hand. A few sat on the Obzedat, the ghostly council that led the Orzhov. Uncle fully expected to join them someday, he'd often said, but not any sooner than necessary.

"The Lady Teysa Karlov," Mr. Yigor announced with reliable tardiness and waved in Teysa's general direction, "with an attendant," he finished. He bowed and slipped back to his corner near the door, joining the shadows there as easily as a fin-snake slipping into the placid water beneath the Bone Walk.

Uncle, facing away from them in his enormous, high-backed floating throne, spun slowly in midair and smiled a corpulent smile at his great-great-great-great-grandniece. He did not acknowledge Melisk—a mere attendant deserved no such attention, especially one without Orzhov blood. The smile cut horizontally above four rolls of chin that sunk to the middle of his mercifully concealed belly. His eyes were tiny pits in the wrinkled sacks that made up his cheeks and wide mouth.

Teysa fought back a shudder. She hadn't seen him in two years, but in that time, the patriarch's own blood-related infirmities had begun to run rampant.

Naturally, he was eating. Keeping a human body alive for more than a millennium required energy. His robes were a mess, and it wasn't all because Uncle had become a particularly sloppy eater in the last two years. His condition had seriously deteriorated, due to both to his Orzhov blood and his age. The blood extended an Orzhov's lifespan by centuries, but it exacted a toll in the form of random deformities and inherited diseases. Some were apparent at birth, like Teysa's crippled leg. Others, like Uncle's necrotic decomposition, manifested very late in life.

"Uncle, it is good to see you well," she lied. "You look like a million zinos."

The patriarch laughed and raised a tankard of wine in her direction. His laughter erupted like a cross between a belch and an earthquake, causing his entire glistening form to launch itself in different directions, jiggling. After the nearest imps and gargoyles were thoroughly showered in mucus, his laughter subsided enough for him to speak. His voice wheezed like a dying animal, but there was still power in its depths.

"Don't insult your Uncle with faint little lies," the patriarch said. He took a gulp of the wine that mostly went into his mouth, and a few more wheezing breaths, before he continued. "I taught you how to lie, Teysa. Don't forget that."

"As if you'd ever let me get away with it," Teysa said and shrugged. "But do you want me to tell you what you really look like?"

"You're too honest for someone who works in a courtroom," Uncle said. "I'm fully aware of how I look. It is nothing like those sweet, beautiful faces you and your attendant hold to my eyes. When I take my place on the Obzedat, all masks of my likeness must be burned along with my body. Eternity looking back at that face for all time does not appeal to me."

"I will see to it personally, Uncle," Teysa said, "though I do not believe you intend to leave us anytime soon for that august body."

"And why do you say that?" Uncle replied. "Look at *my* 'august body.' My skin rots through. My robes—soaked with infection. I am decomposing, child. I'm already dead, but my body, it's taking some time to get the point, I think."

"Is that why you summoned me? You really think this might be the end?" There was little hint of anything but concern when she spoke, though Uncle would have been gravely insulted had she not also included a dash of expectancy and perhaps even anticipation. "Where is your physician?"

"He spoke out of turn one too many times," Uncle said and rumbled out another wet, messy laugh that he washed away with another half-missed drink from the tankard.

"He was a fool. You are as alert and scheming as ever," Teysa said.

"Perhaps you are right," Uncle replied. "But my condition is not why I summoned you here. It is your condition, or disposition I should say, that is of concern to me. Of concern to this family."

"Mine?" Teysa said, eyes flicking momentarily to the cane in her hand. "What about my condition?"

"Not that deformity. That's nothing. I've seen lungs growing outside bodies. Arms lined with blind, dry eyes. Teeth and tongues growing from foreheads. That leg of yours, that is but a peck on the cheek from the family blood. You are a lucky young woman."

"I'm not that young," Teysa said, allowing indignity to creep into her voice. "I also have cases to work on."

"What you should be working on is your patience," Uncle said. "I speak to you now of your status. You are a scion of this family, and you know you have always been especially dear to this house and to my own shriveled heart. You have been at your practice long enough."

"I've barely gotten established," Teysa said, struggling to control her voice. Fortunately, the mask obscured her face. She doubted even someone as well trained as she was could hide the look of anger and disbelief etched upon it. "Practicing law is an honored profession, Uncle, and if I'm going to—"

"Going to become another in a long line of famous con artists? You're better than that, and it's time we set you on another path."

"No," Teysa said. "No convent. I would find a way to escape it." She looked sidelong at Melisk, whose mask concealed what, if anything, he thought of this development. She wondered how long it had been since someone had given Uncle a flat refusal like this, for his eyes widened even more, and his wheezing became ever so slightly faster.

"You doubt the wisdom of your elder," Uncle rumbled. "And you should not presume to know my mind. Child, in your first three years, you've won more cases than your mother or aunt ever did. You're a prodigy, my dear."

"I wouldn't say that," Teysa said with knee-jerk modesty. "I've received cases that, when you looked at the details, were obviously in favor of my clients."

"That attention to the details is why you're here," Uncle said. "It's why you are a successful advokist and why you will also be successful where we're going."

"Going?" Teysa said.

"Oh yes," Uncle said. "You know of a place called Utvara, I take it?"

"Utvara?" Teysa said.

"A place Melisk already mentioned to you," Uncle said. "Do not waste our time, please. It makes my back ache."

"Utvara, then," Teysa said. "But what of it? I have cases, Uncle."

"That must wait until we are on our way," the patriarch said. He waved a hand in the air at the arched ceilings and gargoyle-lined pillars. "This place is filled with ears—you know that. But I will tell you about Utvara. It is a curious place. I purchased it many years ago, not long before you were born."

"Why?"

"An investment in the future. What do you know if it?"

"Only the name," Teysa admitted. She didn't like where this was leading. She was due in court in two days on another suit, to say nothing of her distaste for the hinterlands. To a city girl like Teysa, anything beyond the gates of Ravnica was hinterland, no matter how densely it was populated.

Utvara was also a curious type of investment. Curious enough to pique her interest.

"All right. Utvara. What about it?" she asked.

"It is your inheritance," Uncle said, "Baroness."

"Inheritance?" Teysa asked. "But how am I to inherit anything if you're—"

"Knew there'd be a catch, didn't you?" Uncle replied.

CHAPTER 3

*Freedom from the mortal connection to crude coinage and
simple riches allows the members of the Obzedat to pursue true
and holy power, unshackled by worldly concerns. So why do they
still pursue the coin with as much fervor as ever?*

—Anonymous,
The Generational Manifesto for Orzhov's Future (4582 Z.C.)

30 Paujal 10012 Z.C.

Forty-seven years after the *Peripatetic Eye of Niv-Mizzet 9477*
soared into the Izzet history books, another pair of eyes beheld
the ostensibly lifeless Utvara region from a slightly less elevated
viewpoint. The eyes belonged to a Gruul bandit chieftain, a viashino
named Aun Yom, a reptile who knew his prey would soon walk
right into his trap. Aun Yom knew this because the new arrivals
could not have made their invasion of the Gruul's territory more
blatant. He tracked the Orzhov caravan as it broke around the edge
of the ruins and entered the long canyon leading into the bowl-
shaped center of Utvara.

The word "caravan" was something of a misnomer, as it
consisted primarily of a single vehicle but one that did the work
of many more. Six long carriage cars sat atop the flat back of a
gigantic, segmented lokopede. Six mounted guards moving along
at the same pace rode watchfully on skeletal mounts off each flank,
the Orzhov sigils emblazoned on their shields glowing brightly
enough to illuminate the immediate area but not much more. The
guards had forsaken torches, it seemed, to keep their profile low
in this dangerous night passage, but the sigils more than made

up for it from a hunter's perspective. The entire party moved over stone and earth, as if eager to keep their passage secret. Therefore they had no support from the air and would have no warning of his attack.

Aun Yom wondered again at how a people who refused to consider practicality over affectation had risen to such power in the world while his own people scrabbled for bits and scraps at the feet of those like the Orzhov. The Orzhov had even found a way to rob the Gruul of the ghosts of their ancestors, who no longer lingered to give advice and guidance.

The lokopede's body consisted of alternating segments of black and white plates that reflected the thin, silver light of the crescent moon like cold obsidian. If the bandit's ears were correct, the thing had a separate set of legs for each of its more than two thousand individual sections. The lokopede was a fast-moving tube on legs, easy to control, and difficult to spook or hurt. Aun Yom's attack would require storming the carriage cars but only after sending in some leg breakers on catback. A well-aimed strike from their sweeper scythes should be able to take out a dozen legs at once. The eyeless creature followed the guidance of a single crouching figure, some kind of foul, impish coachman, with another posted atop the second car back.

The sets of feet carried the lokopede forward without a chance of jostling the riders inside the cars, but the smoothness of the transport was countered by its relatively slow speed compared to a typical dromad-drawn coach. That gave the bandits an edge. The skeleton-mounted guards would be easiest of all to knock out, thanks to Aun Yom's new weapon and their ridiculously bright shields. Aun Yom was the best shot in his gang. The second-best shot—his sister Illati—was taking up a position much like his on the facing cliff side.

The Izzet goblin had not even asked for zinos when he gave the Gruul the power orbs that fed the miraculous bam-sticks, the same ones Aun Yom's ancestors had used to destroy the *kuga mot*, though they failed to stop the *kuga* plague itself. The heirloom weapons had not worked for decades, exhausted from hunting long before they ever saw another like the plague bringer. Until the goblin came.

The Izzet had also told them when and where the Orzhov caravan would approach. It reeked of a willing deception, but Aun Yom didn't have the luxury of turning down the offer. Such power was too tempting. Aun Yom had considered interrogating the creature before eating him but had lost the coin toss to Illati.

Neither of them had given much more thought to *why* the Izzet wanted them to have arms and advanced knowledge of an Orzhov caravan. The goblin had to have known he would be killed and cooked and had walked into the camp alone and bearing ridiculously generous gifts. It was obviously a setup, but the brother and sister bandits had great faith in their own ability to improvise.

The *kuga* plague winds that lingered in Utvara made air transportation by zeppelid virtually impossible for an Orzhov—the creatures fed off of the pollutants in the air generated by ten thousand years of unending civilization, but their immune systems had little defense against infectious diseases as dangerous as the *kuga*. Few creatures did. And flying birds, bats, and insects didn't come in the sizes needed to move the possessions and passengers that accompanied so much as a single patriarch, at least not in the style to which the Orzhov seemed to be accustomed.

Ground transportation through the Husk was the only alternative to flight that was reasonable, provided one moved quickly, reached the safety of the reclamation zone within a day or two, and reached the plague-free area in time. The hated ledev guardians had given up on this particular route years ago, after the disaster at the Decamillennial had forced them to call many of their number home to Vitu Ghazi, so this pass through the hills was one of the few stretches of road on the entire plane that had no protectors.

The Gruul, of course, had developed some resistance to the plague but at a painful cost—one that Aun Yom was reminded of as he scratched the thick, knotted patch of fungal growth on his left shoulder. Many more like it grew on his back, ribs, legs, arms, and face. They itched constantly, though fortunately for his sanity never all at once. The antigen fungus kept the *kuga* from killing him quickly but not from shortening his lifespan by decades. Gruul life expectancy had never been high; in the forty-seven years since the *kuga mot*'s golden sphere had turned the ancient, dormant plague into a ravenous, airborne killer, it had been sliced in half.

And it was getting worse. Aun Yom himself would never have been a gang chief forty-seven years ago. He hadn't even been *born* forty-seven years ago. The rest of his band was even younger, including Illati.

Aun Yom signaled his brethren to move into position and continued to watch the new arrivals as they followed the winding route through the crumbling ruins. With a sharp twist he brought the goblin weapon to life and crouched against the cracked remnants of a ruined wall to steady his aim. He raised the cylinder to his eye and brought the sight level with the head of the lokopede driver.

He'd placed his thumb against the firing stud but hadn't yet pushed hard enough to fire when he realized he hadn't heard or seen any of his gang take the positions he'd told them to take when planning this ambush.

In fact, he didn't see them at all, in or out of position. So enamored of the weapon and its potential had he been that their disappearance had gone unnoticed.

"Foolish, Aun Yom," the bandit chief whispered. "You knew there'd be a catch."

Aun Yom of the Utvar Gruul never did find out where they had gone or who, exactly, had betrayed the gang. No sooner did he open his jaws to call out to Illati in warning than a thin, silver stiletto blade entered his neck just below the base of the skull. By the time Aun Yom saw the tip, it ran red with his own blood and protruded a few inches beyond his chin. He did manage a brief, strangled gurgle before he hit the ground. The blade was removed swiftly and cleanly from the dead Gruul, though the wielder could have decapitated the corpse with little effort.

His ghost did not linger to get a final look at his attacker. It tried but fell too quickly into a crack in the sky. A few seconds later, his body got back to its feet, but Aun Yom was no longer in control.

* * * * *

Inside the front car atop the giant lokopede, Teysa Karlov rode in luxury and comfort. The lokopede swayed mildly from side to side, causing the fresh wall hangings inside the gold-and-platinum-appointed cabin she shared with Melisk and Uncle to follow suit. The only other occupants of the car were Uncle's thrull bodyguard, one of his two dark angels, and some mute thrull servants. The five cars behind them contained an assortment of servants, slaves, courtiers, and other hangers-on, along with supplies that would allow her to live in the manner she, and all others with the true blood of Orzhov in their veins, deserved. There were also a few non-Orzhov passengers who had paid ridiculously large sums to the Karlov coffers for one of the only safe ways into Utvara, including a female goblin that had paid in shiny zinos and refused to name any destination but "the Utvara region."

Uncle had allowed Teysa and Melisk to forego their masks, and he wore a traveling mask of his own. Teysa had been forced to sell her law practice, though she retained forty percent and had left a qualified advokist—her second cousin Dahlya—in charge. Teysa hadn't told Uncle, but in case the old patriarch's plan didn't work out she had also included a clause that gave her the right to buy back a controlling interest in the firm whenever she chose, at fair market value.

The walls glittered with indigo silks and woven strands of precious metals that, among other things, conveniently regulated the temperature and humidity within the car. Unfortunately, Uncle had refused to relinquish control over the woven sigils and was keeping this car at near-freezing temperatures. Uncle was decidedly uncomfortable in hot weather.

Teysa was not, by nature, a patient young woman, but while studying law, she had also devoted herself fervently to side studies of the alchemical and sociological sciences with the finest tutors the Karlov fortune could offer—brilliant Simic manabiologists, cunning Orzhov lawmages, foolishly noble but well-informed Azorian archivists, and many others. Teysa's mind had absorbed all this information and more, confined as she often was to the tower in which she'd grown up. She had cast aside all other considerations to make herself the most indispensable young Orzhov advokist she could be. But grand estates were run by patriarchs, not matriarchs. As an advokist she had examined the will when Uncle had finally produced it. She'd also pored over all the appropriate laws involving inheritance. Sure enough, there was nothing that stated a Baroness—the word "matriarch" was apparently still verboten—could not be awarded ultimate control of an estate if and *only* if she was the closest blood relative of the deceased.

That, certainly, was true. There were cousins, nieces, nephews, even other uncles and aunts, but Teysa was both a niece and a direct descendant of Uncle. The disgusting old creature had, it seemed, been quite familiar with his brother's wife long ago, as she had learned only days earlier.

Now Teysa was poised to become the first Karlov baron*ess* in at least ten generations.

She was more than ready to take control of the Utvara reclamation zone. All that remained was for Uncle to die already and officially hand over the estate, which comprised the surrounding Husk area, a central township, a treasure-ridden waste known as the flats, and acres of abandoned architecture awaiting development and exploitation. She had hoped the transfer would take place back in the Orzhov territories, but Uncle had refused. He demanded a certain drama to these things, and he'd been insistent. What she could not fathom was how Uncle seemed so certain his death was imminent. The obvious answer—taking out an assassination contract on his own life—was forbidden to those who would take their place on the Obzedat. Yet the old patriarch seemed positive he would soon be on his way out.

Teysa's patience was stretching thin, but soon the waiting would be over. Reclamation zones were a curious investment that the Orzhov did not usually make. Most were the result of plagues or disease, unfortunately common occurrences in places where populations grew faster than the cityscape's ability to accommodate them. If a plague was lethal, such a place was quarantined for a suitable period, as determined by the Simic Combine, whose knowledge of diseases was frightening. Then a minimum of four hundred years of abandonment was required, to ensure that whatever had wiped out the population was gone. For these reasons and more, reclamation zones rarely made the financial return a great family expected on an investment, and the laws of the

Guildpact—enforced by millennia-old enchantments that had a sometimes frustratingly mysterious way of working—demanded that reclamation zones had to attain a certain level of civilization in the year after their mandatory four-hundred-year fallow period. Once the fallow time ended, if there were not some form of local government, law enforcement, and public works available (and the definitions of these were relatively broad) then the reclamation zone reverted to the control of the guildmasters, who invariably handed it over to the Selesnyan Conclave.

The Selesnyans had their rackets too, Uncle often said. But this time he'd challenged Teysa to beat them at their own game.

Utvara was an unusual reclamation, to be sure. It had been part of the ancient hunting range of old Niv-Mizzet, the legendary dragon parun of the Izzet Magewrights' guild, who these days rarely left his majestic aerie in the City of Guilds. Supposedly, Niv-Mizzet's first lair was down there somewhere, and, even if it wasn't, the city had been wealthy. The crumbling structures and caved-in buildings contained an untold amount of lost treasure just waiting to be found, and the landlord—whether it was Uncle or Teysa—was entitled to a substantial percentage.

The other thing that made Utvara different was that Uncle had won special dispensation from the Guildpact Council to end the fallow period early. He'd hired an Izzet to aid in crafting a device that would eliminate all life in Utvara, and apparently it had worked. It had also left a floating distortion of reality in the sky called the Schism, about which little was truly known. "Just don't fly anywhere near it and you'll be fine," Uncle had told her. As if Teysa had any intention of flying at all—ever since her youth, heights had given her unsettling vertigo she'd rather not experience any more than necessary.

The now-ubiquitous Utvaran treasure prospectors had provided the rest of the reason for the short fallow period. They'd invited members of the Selesnyan Conclave to plant a disease-fighting Vitar Yescu in the center of what was rapidly becoming a small squatter's town among the ruins. Essentially a giant tree in a state of perpetual flower, the Vitar Yescu filled the air around the town with a pollen-carried antigen to the new plague, which had mutated when the Schism was created. Now the locals called it the *kuga*.

A strange series of special circumstances to be sure, and so Uncle had been given reign to do things his way. Uncle's lawmages had easily been able to prove in court the place was livable because people he hadn't invited were already living there. They were technically his property too, or at least a percentage of them were.

Soon they would be hers.

The "foothills" of the Husk rose around their lokopede caravan as they entered the eastern canyon road that would take them to the heart of town. Like most of the seemingly geological features on Ravnica's surface, the foothills were derived from ancient architecture that had been rebuilt and reused over thousands of years by millions of individuals. Unlike most, the foothills of the Husk had been allowed to decay to the point where they almost looked like paintings of the ancient natural rock formations that had once stood here, now deep beneath layer upon layer of advancing civilization. Her studies of the region over the last couple of weeks indicated that the foothills were filled with dangerous sinkholes and, of course, the Utvar Gruul that somehow clung to existence despite the *kuga* plague winds.

She let her bored gaze leave the hulking, greasy, perpetually sweating shape of Uncle, snoozing in his massive seat beneath his pale mask, and exchanged a glance with her trusted attendant. Melisk, his pale-white skin now covered only in a light traveler's suit, still displayed a few magically inscribed tattoos that testified to his high rank within the Orzhov servant class—there were many so-called Orzhov "nobles" who possessed nowhere near the prestige and influence her "servant" did. Melisk smiled humorlessly and returned to staring out the window. He seemed distracted.

Teysa leaned forward and prodded Uncle with her cane. His beady, black eyes flickered open beneath the mask, somehow taking in Teysa and Melisk through layers of surrounding fat and scraggly eyebrows that dangled like jungle moss.

"Uncle, we draw close to our destination," she said.

"Ah! Yes," Uncle rumbled, and absentmindedly picked up a half-eaten piece of his most recent meal—a double-roasted ratclops—to chew on. His eyes shot to the landscape outside, and he nodded into his rolling chins in satisfaction. "Lovely. Right on time, right on time." He noisily slurped marrow from a shinbone.

"Why must we approach under cover of darkness, Uncle?" Teysa asked.

"The Gruul do not strike by day," he rumbled between long wheezing breaths. "And I find it more fitting this way. Your inheritance, this grand gift, is wrapped in the blanket of night."

Teysa sighed and turned back to the window. The darkened shapes of crumbling towers against the gray night sky revealed nothing but shadows moving in shadow.

She'd made a good start with her advokism, but Uncle was right. Now that she was prepared for it, the potential she saw in Utvara was enormous. An entire system of laws built from scratch but bound to the Guildpact, and they were hers to create. The size of the place had surprised her, as had the already-developing township that she would take over, assuming Uncle's predictions of his own demise proved accurate.

She found herself actively wishing for that demise.

The Orzhov scion's sigh triggered an unexpected reaction

from one of the Grugg brothers. "Need somethin', do ya?" Bephel piped up. The diminutive thrull was on his shift inside the cabin, while brother Phleeb drove the lokopede and brother Elbeph stood lookout. "Need someone killed, do ya? Do ya?" His head was shaped like two fat, stacked arrowheads, and his three rows of teeth clacked as he spoke. His bulbous, black eyes protruded out from either side, taking in 360 degrees at once. Of the three, he was the only one she had granted the power of speech.

"Not right now, thanks," Teysa said.

"Suit yourself," the thrull said and squatted back into his corner. Bephel's source corpse had been a reptilian viashino, and he still vaguely resembled a crouching lizard but without the scales and with a much longer, barbed tail lined with metallic needles. The only skin the thrull had, in fact, was almost translucent, a gray, thin epidermis that showed more of Bephel's innards than anyone really needed to see. The Grugg brothers had been her personal bodyguards for several years now, almost as long as Melisk had served as her attendant. Bephel, in particular, was always more than ready to tear apart anyone or anything that could conceivably threaten his charge, but such opportunities to prove his loyalty were rare.

Ahead lay open road with no sign of the life churchers and their meddling "protection," filled with hundreds of Gruul that could be slaughtered with impunity if Teysa cut the Grugg brothers loose and really let them get to it. The thrulls were incapable of betraying her, even if they weren't the brightest of traveling companions. Their fervor to kill was admirable, and their talent for it was indispensable.

As boredom gave way to weariness, Teysa stood and stretched, her cape and robe splayed like wings, and yawned. Her less-than-useful right leg almost buckled, but she caught her weight on the cane before she lost composure or bearing.

"Perhaps you should move back to a sleeping cabin," Uncle said.

"I think not," Teysa said. "I just need to stretch this useless limb now and then."

"Of course, of course," Uncle said. "Perhaps you are right. And perhaps . . . I should sleep some more. Just a quick nap before we arrive?"

"You do look tired, Uncle," Teysa said. Was Uncle planning to wake up? She dared not ask, but his tone carried a strange air of finality.

"My favorite niece, you have grown into a cunning and beautiful young oligarch," Uncle said, leering at her in a way that she'd long ago gotten used to and even learned to use to her advantage. The Orzhov had a very exclusive family, and many uncles had married their nieces to keep the bloodlines going. Not that Teysa would ever go through with such a thing.

"Thank you, Uncle," Teysa said, belying no hint of her lingering physical repulsion. "I have always strived to please you and impress you."

"As you should, as you should," Uncle replied, "and I assure you it has paid off. Good night, for now. I will see you again . . . when we arrive." Within seconds, the old creature's beady eyes had closed, his head lolled to one side, and he began to snore wetly.

The next second a miniscule pellet of concentrated pyromana shattered the glass near Melisk's head and left through the opposite window—but not before it incinerated a significant portion of Bephel's head and both his eyes along the way. The faithful thrull flopped over sideways and twitched pitiably as blood and brains pooled around the smoldering hole in his wedge-shaped skull.

"Gruul!" Melisk shouted, loudly enough for the guards stationed outside the patriarch's car to hear.

The patriarch continued to sleep, unaware and happily unconscious.

*   *   *   *   *

Crix fiddled with the trigger and firing assembly of a disassembled bam-stick to pass the time as the lokopede continued the long trip to Utvara. The goblin acolyte was one of only a very few non-Orzhov on the lokopede's back tonight, and none of the others—prospectors who'd given the Guild of Deals their life savings for a chance to reach Utvara—wanted anything to do with her. Crix wouldn't have been there at all if her master had not insisted on sending her to deliver a set of personal instructions to the overseer of the Izzet-run Cauldron power project. She'd requested and been granted permission to make her own report upon her return, and Crix intended to have something impressive to show the magelord Zomaj Hauc when the time came. If time allowed—and at this point, it most likely would—she also hoped to get in some anthropological studies of the locals, who might make good expendable labor once the Cauldron was running at full steam.

The goblin did not kid herself. She was almost as high up in the echelons of the Izzet hierarchy as most of her kind could ever expect to reach. But Crix figured it could never hurt to be well-rounded, just in case that ever changed. She knew hers was an uncommon intelligence among her kind—a gift from the magelord who had claimed her as an infant and used magic and alchemy to enhance her abilities. Crix was always looking for ways to thank him and show him that the enhancements had not been in vain.

She didn't mind the work or the long journey, but the absence of other goblins onboard made her antsy. She was surrounded by what she took to be the typical Orzhov retinue of ghostly servitors, ghoulish but more or less human retainers, and the less intelligent imps and thrulls that moved among them. They were all in some way part of the Orzhov helot slave class but still treated Crix as much less than an equal.

Three in particular had harassed her at the departure station and had found time to pester her for the rest of the trip. The trio of thrulls who bore the serpentine ouroboros symbol of House Karlov on their thin, gray skin had been the only ones to give her trouble, though she'd expected more. The Orzhov, in general, were longtime business associates of the Izzet, but the two guilds rarely socialized, largely because the individual members could barely stand each other. Crix had never had a problem with them, but those three sure had a problem with her. They seemed to take every chance they could to "accidentally" trip her as she passed from her car to the dining coach or "mistakenly" slough off their skin while standing near her soup. When they'd departed for the patriarch's parlor car, she'd been relieved.

It was at times like these she wished she carried an entire bam-stick with her instead of just the lucky mechanism that her biological sire, a great observer in the corps, had taken from the body of a Gruul savage. This weapon component, he'd said, had survived the heat of a thousand suns and was a testament to the Izzet goblins' skills with metals and magic. He'd given it to her just before he'd left for one final observation flight that had ended in his fiery death.

Booking passage on the Orzhov lokopede had been surprisingly easy with the help of the magelord. Zomaj Hauc had a way of getting cooperation out of people. In fact, he had several ways, many of which Crix had never seen personally, to her relief. This time he'd simply contacted the fat old patriarch who owned the thing and told him he needed transportation for a courier. Then

Crix was on the next zeppelid to the Orzhov territories. Flying directly to her destination was not impossible, but Crix wasn't keen to ride a giant bird that would have just as soon eaten her as given her a lift.

The lokopede offered an amazingly smooth ride and was capable of more speed than she'd been led to expect. A quick wave of a sensory crystal confirmed the creature had been heavily enchanted to enhance performance, and with a little focus the crystal had told her how much of each elemental force the enchantments had required. Her notes on the subject would please his lordship. Crix did a quick calculation in her head, multiplying the levels of mana required times the number of legs a goblin would need to keep pace.

"Now that's strange," Crix said to no one in particular. The crystal was sensing more than just the lokopede, the various enchantments worn by it, and the beings along its back. There was a cluster, several tiny nodes of energy that formed a sort of cloud at this distance, off in the hills. She peered out the window to see if her eyes could confirm what the crystal was telling her.

There was nothing there. Strange indeed. What could that cloud of energy be?

Intrigued, or at least diverted, by a new puzzle, Crix was still fumbling for her pocket abacus when the entire car lurched to one side. The jerking motion knocked Orzhov retainers, servants, and her lucky bam-stick mechanism to the floor. Crix dived after the ornate little piece of metal and caught it before it slid into a pile of ice that one of the servants had dumped across the gold-weave marble tiles. Cries of surprise gave way to shouts of alarm, many of them including the word "Gruul."

"Oh, dear," Crix said. "Guess that explains that, eh?" A hunched old man in a white apron struggling to gather all of the ice cubes back into a bucket thought she spoke to him.

"Don't need explanations," the miserable helot said. "Just don't kick that ice, huh?"

"Er, right," Crix said. She pocketed the lucky assembly and gingerly stepped through the ice and the babbling passengers to the door that led, eventually, to the private carriage of the patriarch himself, two cars ahead. She noticed she was the only one not clamoring for a look out the windows, but then she'd already heard what she needed to know. The Gruul were savages in the best of cases, but what she'd heard of these Utvar Gruul was worse: cannibals, at the very least.

The master would never forgive her if she didn't warn the patriarch and his retinue and do all she could to protect him. Crix was an extraordinary goblin in many ways. More than just her intelligence had been augmented by the magelord. And Zomaj Hauc took business partnerships very seriously. He never betrayed a trust unless he could get away with it. Since Hauc was the master of the Cauldron, and the Cauldron sat within Utvara, he and the patriarch were by default partners. Crix's goal was clear.

Besides, if something happened to the patriarch, she doubted she'd get to the Cauldron at all.

The guard usually stationed at the door had joined the crowd around the window, so she slid the door aside without asking permission. She found the next carriage, the dining car, to be equally chaotic and covered in dangerous, slippery foodstuffs. There wasn't much that could knock a goblin off her feet. Crix's people had uncanny balance, and her own was even better, thanks to Hauc. Without much trouble, she maneuvered through the car until she reached a door that *did* still have its guard. Two of them, in fact.

"Hello," Crix said amiably and favored the pair of helmeted, pale-skinned humans with her toothiest smile. "I must warn your masters of this impending danger. May I pass?"

"No." The helmets, which only showed twin sets of unnaturally golden eyes, concealed which one had said it. "Can't imagine they don't know, goblin."

"The name is Crix. Surely their safety is of the utmost importance," she said. The guard was probably right, but even so the appearance of giving warning would still serve both her master's and her purposes. "Perhaps the two of you could at least ask—"

"No one goes in, goblin," said the one on the left. Her ears told her what her eyes couldn't. "Attendant's orders."

"Really," Crix said. She chose a different tack. "Surely this attendant would reward your initiative if you made an exception in this case." The car lurched again as if to emphasis her point.

"Attendant don't like initiative," said the right guard. "Had a cousin, got flayed for showin' initiative. Just stay put, Crix, before we use you for spear practice."

Crix opened her mouth to apologize but caught herself. Debating these guards was pointless. Time to bring out the big bam-sticks. She raised one hand, palm facing the guards, and let her sleeve slide down to her elbow. The golden eyes widened appropriately when the Orzhov lackeys recognized the glowing, tattooed name of Zomaj Hauc.

"You recognize this," she said. "Good. Would you like to—" a sound of shattering windows rang out from what sounded like three cars back, and she flinched. "Reconsider?" Crix finished.

"Goblin's got a point, Grubber," said the guard on the left.

"A good point," said the guard on the right. "Lots of good points. Good goblin."

"Patronizing me will get you nowhere," Crix said, "but opening that door will keep your names out of my report to my master."

"Grubber, you idiot, open the door."

"Right."

Grubber, the one on the right, gave a light knock and shouted through the door, "Message for you, marked urgent!" he called. Without awaiting a reply, the second guard pressed the door release, let the golden panel slide to the side, and shoved Crix through.

"Thank you," Crix managed as she stumbled over the threshold. A tiny vestibule separated the two cars. A second sliding door—this one unguarded—was just a few feet ahead of her. As the door behind her clicked shut, the one in front of her slid quickly aside to reveal the luxuriously appointed patriarch's car.

The name, Crix guessed, would probably be less than accurate soon, though the more accurate "bloody-massacre car" probably wasn't about to catch on.

The patriarch inside appeared quite dead. Crix could see his bloated, exposed heart, raw after what looked like lots of vigorous, deranged slashing through layer after layer of human blubber. What looked like an angel with black wings lay bleeding on the carpeted floor, and pieces of gray-skinned thrull were everywhere. The only two survivors—a tall, bald man in expensive robes and a younger human woman dressed in similar attire—stood over the patriarch's corpse. The woman's face was twisted with shock. The man was bloodied but appeared impassive—until he saw the goblin, that is.

"I am a message bearer," Crix began, raising her marked arm. "I am to deliver a message of utmost importance to—"

"Another one!" the young woman cried. "Don't just stand there, Melisk, kill it!"

Crix looked from the somber man to the gore-covered young woman and back to her own wrist. It was time to use a little of the independent strategizing all couriers had to fall back on now and again. She was through the door before Melisk took his second step and was legging for the sixth car as fast as her feet could carry her.

The guards who had let her in, Grubber and the other one, must have received some kind of silent signal from Melisk. Or maybe, Crix supposed, they were the types to give chase to anyone who came bursting out of the patriarch's car as fast as she did, leaving bloody footprints. Whatever the reason, they shouted warnings and orders to halt as she half-ran, half-careened through the chaos in the car. Out of the corner of her eye, she realized she couldn't see any Gruul who had made it inside yet. So far, they were just attacking windows, from the look of it, doing plenty of damage to the occupants and the lokopede from a distance. Too bad. She could have used the confusion to escape more easily.

She didn't have any further time for analysis of Gruul strategy though. She needed to start forming her own. The guards with their much longer legs would catch up to her soon if she didn't figure out a way to slow them down. Crix pushed the door to the third car open and was once again in a vestibule. The noise of shouting and metal striking chitin echoed inside, and she had a moment to be glad for the lack of windows in the connecting chamber.

Crix reached into a pocket and produced a small lump of pliant, silvery metal, then pressed the metal and her marked palm against the edge of the door she'd just left. Sometimes the quick and dirty spells worked best. She rushed through the words to a simple but effective welding spell.

The power of the pyromana almost melted the metal doorframe. There would be no sliding that one aside unless the guards knew a spell that could shatter magically fused steel.

Crix took a deep breath and did her best to compose herself in her temporary refuge. She went to the sliding door that led into the third car and pressed the release just as Grubber and his nameless partner used the universal door-opening spell on her seal—a pair of heavy boots. The metal door, its edges still glowing red-hot, clattered noisily into the vestibule just as the goblin slid the door shut behind her.

"Simplicity works both ways," Crix muttered and bolted back through the car she'd started in.

There they were. This next car was filled with Gruul, who must have struck just as food service began. The Gruul tore into the Orzhov servants and cooking staff, scattering food, wine, cooking utensils, and body parts over the slick floor. Crix slipped on what she hoped was some kind of meringue and crashed into—no, *through*—a shrieking ghost, one of many confused and angry specters who weren't happy to find their journey to Utvara cut short. Her wild slide through the gore and foodstuffs ended at two tree-trunk legs wearing lizardskin sandals, wiry hair, and chunks of something resembling fungus. She wiped gelatinized dessert (if that's what it was) from her eyes and looked up into the seething face of the bandit.

He was human, he was ugly, and he was very, very angry from the look of it. What looked like a fresh wound showed on his throat, but it didn't seem to be slowing the savage down. The Gruul raised a bloody club lined with jagged pieces of stone and roared, which gave Crix just enough warning to roll to one side when he brought the weapon crashing into the marble floor. Now on her belly, the goblin scrambled between the human's legs and pulled herself to the next door back.

"Stop that goblin!" she heard one of the Orzhov guards shout as she fumbled for the door release. The Gruul who had just about smashed her to a pulp saw the new arrivals and flashed ritually sharpened teeth in a wide, bloodthirsty smile.

"Er, actually, I don't think we need to stop that goblin anymore, Grubber. We're probably needed back in car one."

"I think you're right."

Crix didn't hear whether her pursuers survived her Gruul

attacker because she'd made it to yet another vestibule. Something slammed into the door behind, and she hoped it was the Gruul. Sure, the guards were trying to catch her on the orders of a murderous Orzhov, but they seemed like decent fellows. The Gruul she'd seen was a monster.

Before blindly heading into another car that was no doubt already filling with bandit attackers, she considered her situation. She was in a tiny room of her own, which was helpful. No one seemed to be attacking this linking vestibule between cars three and four. That meant, she hoped, no one was watching them from the outside either.

She hoped even more that if she managed to get out, she could get to the Utvara township before the plague killed her. But one problem at a time.

The "walls" of the connecting vestibule were little more than accordioned leather, she saw upon closer inspection. It was thick—the hide of some large grazer from the look of it. The important thing was it was organic, which meant it would almost certainly burn. The goblin pushed up her right sleeve and debated with herself briefly just how much power she could spare—the magic of the tattoos would not last forever without recharging, but she wouldn't last three seconds in a physical showdown with one of those Gruul.

With her right index finger, Crix drew a roughly goblin-shaped outline on the vestibule interior. Then she drew her hand back into a fist, counted to three, and threw what could generously have been called a punch right where the sketched goblin's heart would have been.

The invisible outline she'd traced glowed orange, then white. Then the entire shape fell away like a pastry popping out of a mold.

"Oh, this is going to hurt," Crix said as she tracked the rocky landscape flashing past her and the daunting drop from the side of the lokopede. Then she took a deep breath, put one forearm over her face, and leaped through the hastily made exit one step ahead of the roaring creature that bashed through the door and into the vestibule behind her. She flew through open space, cold air rushing into her face—

—only to stop short when four cold, viselike fingers latched around her ankle.

"What do you think you're doing?" Grubber snarled. "You want to drop? You want to face *them?*"

Grubber spun Crix by the ankle, and she got a good look at the attackers still outside the lokopede. She could see at least a dozen, all savage roars and flashing blades, atop scaly riding beasts and dromad-sized Husk-cats that were easily keeping up with the besieged caravan. The nearest one was only a few yards away, and as Crix yelped involuntarily, the Gruul, a viashino with wild eyes, raised a glowing bam-stick and drew a bead on her.

"All right! All right! Just don't leave me hanging—" she managed as the end of the bam-stick flashed. She had just enough time to see the projectile vault from the end of the weapon straight at her, before Grubber pulled her back inside. With a faint pop, the bam-stick punctured a tiny, sizzling hole in the leather binding just over Grubber's head.

Crix felt herself swing around involuntarily to face the Orzhov guard, whose looks hadn't improved in the interim. He was now sporting what looked like pieces of skin that weren't his and a nasty cut across his brow. The bone of his skull was exposed, and blood streamed out of the small head wound.

"Well, what are you going to do now?" Crix demanded. "I'm a licensed courier, you know. You can't—" The goblin stopped. Grubber's expression had begun to change, stretching from an angry scowl to a look of disbelief. Together he and the goblin looked down and noted the silver spear tip protruding from his chest. With a wet slurp, the weapon disappeared and Grubber's last breath finally gave out.

A second later, they hit the floor, one dead and bleeding, the other alive but pinned beneath Grubber's meaty, lifeless arm. Crix managed to roll onto her back and gazed up at another Gruul. There was something strange about him from this angle, like bits of him were simply . . . not there. Wounds showed clearly on his arms and chest, but instead of flesh underneath, there appeared to be something that glowed from within.

The parts that *were* there lifted an axe overhead and roared, a leonine sound that should not have been able to emerge from a human mouth. The rusty blade traveled in an arc directly at Crix's face as she struggled to free herself from Grubber's body. Just before the axe struck, she stopped trying to push the arm upward and satisfied herself with rolling beneath it to the side. The axe severed Grubber's arm above the elbow, spattering the goblin with bits of bone and gore but freeing her from her immediate predicament. She managed to push herself to her feet and boldly faced the Gruul warrior, her right forearm exposed.

"Do you *see* this? Do you have any idea what the penalty for attacking a licensed courier is under Guildpact—"

The Gruul scooped up Grubber's arm, tore a hunk of graying flesh off the bone with a set of large, apelike teeth, and swallowed it in one gulp.

"No, I don't imagine you do," Crix finished.

She was cornered. The Gruul had maneuvered between her and the goblin-sized exit, and the warrior, blood running from the edges of his mouth, took one step, then another, pushing her back, back—into the door to the next car. She felt the latch slap against her hand as the Gruul raised his bloody axe again and flashed a wide smile of berserker glee.

"No!" Crix shouted and slapped the latch. It slid aside, and she rolled through just as the axe came down again. Sparks from the blade striking metal struck her legs, and she instinctively crawled back in pain.

Yes, Crix was an extraordinary goblin, but many of the things that made her extraordinary were not technically hers to use without express permission of her magelord. She had been given no such dispensation on this mission. Therefore, she would have to get out of this like any other goblin would—by scrambling and running.

This car must have been one of the first hit, she now saw as she regained her footing. There wasn't anyone left alive in here, and not even ghosts remained. The only living things other than herself and her pursuer appeared to be a pair of horse-sized brutes that looked like brutal crosses between wolves and hyenas. The monstrous beasts fed upon the remains of what looked like still more helot servants.

The beasts growled as soon as she stood and continued to do so the nearer she got to their food. The pursuing Gruul wasn't giving her any other avenue to escape, however, and through the shattered, cracked windows she saw the Gruul riders now much closer. The Orzhov guards were long gone.

Until now, Crix had been pretty sure that even with the attack, the powerful lokopede and the Karlov security forces would be able to fight their way through and on to Utvara proper. Now she was much less certain, and concern for her mission took complete control. She had to get out of here, even if it meant walking all the way to the Cauldron. If she could somehow get word to her master and permission to use some of her more unique abilities—

One of the beasts roared through bloody jaws, interrupting her train of thought. They closed in slowly, mirroring the movement of the snarling Gruul warrior, all three circling her like a tiny prize. A courier's legal protections meant nothing in this circumstance. She felt the back of her head brush against something she thought at first might be an intestine but turned out to be a single, simple length of rope with a heavy weight on the end. She followed the rope up to the roof of the car, where it ended with a knot tied to some kind of emergency hatch. The roped was twisted like a spring, as if it had spent a very long time wrapped around the edge of that hatch waiting for someone to come along and pull it.

Goblins were natural burrowers and, by extension, natural climbers. True, usually the climb was up a cliff face or a mining tunnel that had taken a turn for the vertical, but a rope was just a very, very small vertical surface. At least that's what she told herself as she leaped up and grabbed hold of the thing.

The fibers cut into her skin, but it was enough to let her pull her legs out of the way when the Gruul's inevitable axe strike sliced beneath her. One of the wolf-hyenas leaped up, snapping its jaws at her, but came away with the rope in its mouth instead. The thing's fangs clamped tight, and it kept barreling through the air, forcing Crix to hold on even more tightly to the painful rope as the creature inadvertently yanked open the hatch over her head. The fibers digging into her palms kept her in place, and she crawled up the rest of the way in a few seconds.

Crix pulled herself through the hatch and rolled onto the bouncing, shaking roof of the car. She managed to slam the exit shut just as the beast thumped against it from the interior.

"Well, at least I'm outside," Crix said. She rolled onto all fours and thought better of standing when the car lurched again and forced her to dig in with her claws to stay onboard.

The goblin could see more of the howling Gruul riders and their various mounts and attack beasts. Some of the warriors bore torches, others spears, and a few packed bam-sticks like the one that had almost killed her a few minutes earlier. They lined either side of the lokopede, but she couldn't tell if they also followed along behind. She saw no firelight coming from that direction, and there didn't appear to be anyone else sharing her roof, so she proceeded back the way she'd been going while inside the car—toward the hind end of the lokopede.

She'd made it over the accordion-leather gap between the fourth and fifth cars when something screeching and leathery piled into the small of her back and knocked her flat on her face. The thing hissed something that sounded like "Sssstop!"

Crix pushed onto her back and started to crawl away from the thrull, who stood over her with hunched batwings and glowing, red eyes. His thin, membranous skin was wrapped tight around a roughly humanoid frame topped by a toothy head. The batwings spread from the tips of his fingers to his ankles, and as the moonlight caught the thing's tattoo, Crix realized why the screech had sounded familiar—it was one of the trio who had been tormenting her the entire trip.

"Gruul sssspy," the thrull hissed. "Gonna kill ya now."

"Spy?" Crix shouted. "Are you crazy?"

The thrull merely advanced and repeated, "Gonna kill ya, gonna kill ya," over and over.

The goblin patted her belt, feeling around for some trick that would keep the thrull off of her, but a cursory search revealed nothing. And in a situation where it seemed like a courier might be in danger of losing her life despite the many edicts against harming messengers, fighting was not the rule. Crix turned and ran toward the lokopede's tail.

She cleared the gap between the fifth and six cars easily, running on adrenaline and panic. The thrull spread his wings but continued to follow her on foot. An orange flash streaked overhead, reminding her that the Gruul weren't all that far away, and they were well-armed. Now that she thought about it, she wouldn't have been too eager to take to the air either.

The thrull cleared the gap just as Crix reached the end of the line, the edge of the last car. She'd guessed right—there were no Gruul directly behind the lokopede, where there were no windows and the creature's natural armor was toughest. The attackers seemed happy to enter through the easily shattered glass.

Crix gazed at the dirt road fleeing away behind them and back at the thrull. Her message had to get to the Cauldron in Utvara. That was the important thing. If it took a little extra time, so be it, but if she was killed here the message would never make it. That was simply not acceptable.

"Going to have to find someone else to kick around, thrull," Crix said and vaulted backward off the rear of the lokopede. She landed hard and didn't stop rolling until she struck a pair of legs. The legs were covered in clumps of bristly, white fungus, as were the arms that scooped her up and carried her away from the scene of the attack. When she finally opened her eyes again, they were deep into the Husk, and the burning lokopede was out of sight.

CHAPTER 4

Tired of lawlessness? Looking to make a difference and a little extra pay in this unforgiving world? If you want to do your part for justice and earn a guaranteed bumbat ration daily, contact your local Haazda recruiter today!

— League of Haazda recruitment poster

30 Paujal 10012 Z.C.

"Why didn't *you* join the Haazda anyway?" the off-duty deputy asked. His fifth mug of bumbat helped the middle-aged man—still only half the age of the man he challenged—stretch the "z" in "Haazda" until it threatened to become its own word. "You, sir, would have been a natural. Natural command material. Got a lot of former 'jeks, too, you know. You're wasting your—you're wasting your *abilities* here, pal. You could make a *difference* in this place. A *difference.*" He signaled the bartender for another round. "What you—what you drinkin' there, sir?"

"Dindin juice."

"*Dindin* juice?" the deputy asked. He added an exaggerated layer of disbelief that, had he not been alone at the bar—the last patron to leave, in fact, as usual—might have scored a rousing round of laughter from his fellow volunteer officers. The much older man sitting next to him at the bar simply nodded. Had the deputy been sober, he might have noticed the nod said a lot more in a simple motion than the taciturn fellow had said with words in the last two hours. Had the deputy been sober, he might not have chosen to press the issue.

"I got a—got an aunt, she drinks that stuff," the deputy

volunteered, making an admirable effort to come off amiably and defuse the situation. "Supposed to be good for the digestion and the heart. 'Specially if you're eldelell—ellelly—if you're *old.*"

"Don't need to remind me of that, friend. You might want to try a glass yourself. You're not getting any younger." The old dindin drinker waved the barkeep over and indicated the listing deputy, who was momentarily distracted by concerted efforts to stay on his barstool.

The barkeep, an imp no more than chest height, put down the glass he'd been polishing and ambled over, leathery wings folded against his shoulder blades and a friendly host's grin on his face. He hopped up, balanced effortlessly on a brass rail bolted behind the bar, and let his wings flair once before he tucked them back to his side.

"Bartender," the sober one of the two said, "this fellow wants a dindin juice. That recipe I cooked up?" Because the bartender was the sort whose sensibilities demanded it, he waggled his brow. "Can you *help* him *out?*"

"Certainly, certainly, my friend," the imp replied. "I am here to serve. An excellent choice, if I may say," the imp added and turned to the inebriated Haazda before launching into a sales pitch. "The dindin plant contains a natural stimulant that should prepare you for continued drinking of our more potent spirits as you enjoy the refreshing atmosphere that only the Imp Wing Hotel and Bar can offer you."

"You're not so bad for a—for a—what're you 'gain?" the deputy managed.

"I am Pivlic!" the imp declared, improbably squaring his knuckles on his hips, his wings spread like a stylized eagle. "I am the owner of this establishment, friend Vodotro, and your host. Would you like anything to add enhancement to your beverage?

Will you be booking time in the hourly suites this evening before setting off to a dangerous life of crime-fighting and derring-do that could, conceivably, end your life before you next experience the joys of—"

"Juice, Pivlic, then this fellow's going home," the older man said. "We've got few enough lawmen around here, even if they are volunteers. Half of them are still recovering from your last 'civic-awards ceremony.' "

"And you care because . . . ?" the imp said. "Every day since you came to work for your old friend Pivlic you have brought up these issues, but the fact is—friend Kos, dear *old* friend Kos—you are my employee. I have masters of my own, as well you know. It is time you accepted you are not in the Tenth anymore. This is a different place. Can you not, at long last, get used to it? The ogres would appreciate it, and so would I. I make good zinos off of ogres, and not one has set foot in this establishment the entire month." Pivlic tsked as he pulled a pair of fresh dindins from behind the counter and tossed them into the juicer. "Kos, you've been here almost twelve years. You're not a 'jek anymore. You don't have to police the whole township, my friend, just my place. And you do have additional help for that."

"I know," Agrus Kos said, not looking directly at the imp or the drunk. "Gave 'em the night off. Just doing my job, Pivlic. Watching your place. That's all I'm doing. And you could be a little more civic yourself when you're yammering on about my employment situation."

"Oh, now you're ashamed of me, are you?" Pivlic said, hopping from the rail to the bar. "Kos, please. How long have you worked for me?"

"Twelve years," Kos said through gritted teeth. I have this one taken care of now, Pivlic. Get off it.

The imp was no telepath, but he seemed to get the message the teeth sent. "And twelve years should be enough time to acclimatize." Pivlic didn't elaborate and didn't need to. The drunk, on the other hand, saw an opening and dived into it.

"That'sh what I'm shaying," Vodotro slurred. "You, you need to join up. You're an *Orzhov* now, Kos. Think about that for a shecond. But the Haazda, we're . . . we're . . . well, we're volunteers, you know, but we pay dues to the Borosh just like 'jeks. I mean, you could even keep this job. You could do the noble shervice in your off hours. I myself am responshible for inshpecting shtructures for poshibilty of fire. As my day job." He picked up the glass of liquid Pivlic put before him and took a pull that emptied half of it into his mouth, a quarter into his moustache, and the rest somewhere onto the table. That should easily do it, Kos reckoned.

Kos nodded but said nothing and finished his glass of juice. He set it down hard on the table and pushed back from the bar. Kos made a mental note to check in with that goblin foreman out at the Cauldron and see about getting Pivlic to "civically" purchase the services of a few emergency hydromancers. He rarely mentioned it in front of others, but the imp was very much of the same mind as Kos when it came to that sort of thing. And the fact that this deputy was, apparently, somehow responsible for the safety of the township in case of fire was bad news for anyone. Having a few hydros around might not hurt.

"Thanks for the thought, Vodotro," Kos said, "but I think it's about time I showed you the door." He hooked one arm around the sloppy drunk, whose balance seemed to have gone. That would be the special recipe kicking in.

Kos didn't want drunks sobering up in Pivlic's place, they just got angry. There was a lot of anger in Utvara: prospectors showing up to find the streets not exactly paved with gold, people trying to start a new life only to find that their new life was confined to five square miles around the Vitar Yescu, and plenty of people who, in this remote town of squatters, were just plain mean. The Utvara township was a semilegal establishment, but when the fallow period ended it would likely see a big population increase. From what Pivlic said, the fat Orzhov who owned the whole thing was due any day now. The retired wojek imagined even more anger would be forthcoming, though fortunately not directed at him. Kos was just Pivlic's security man while Pivlic was acting as the owner's agent in this township.

Kos was getting too old to deal with politics or violence. Unfortunately, they kept bumping into his life even when he dragged his aging carcass out to this remote reclamation zone.

Then there were the Haazda. Overall security for the Imp Wing was something Kos and a small staff hired by Pivlic could handle without too much trouble. Pivlic had an unbelievable number of cousins, nephews, and nieces who needed just a few months of toughening up before they could break up most any typical Imp Wing brawl at Kos's order. He didn't have to get involved directly with, well, anything. The township didn't have much in the way of government, but it had a way of policing itself: Most of the small population was only interested in getting out to the flats and hunting for their fortune, and if someone did something that merited absolute punishment, they simply cleared it with the imp, who acted as agent for the Orzhov owners. The Haazda were largely unnecessary. And they never ventured into the Husk. Nobody with any sense did, and the Haazda might be a bunch of drunks and wojek wannabes, but they did have enough sense to steer clear of the Gruul.

Kos wasn't getting any younger, and the angry types weren't getting happier. He couldn't bring himself to join those Haazda volunteers. Their lack of any real authority was the main reason. By and large, the volunteers were frustrated, barely trained, and looking to lash out.

And when a member of the Haazda got out of hand, it was much easier to slip them Kos's dindin special than to lay into one of them simply because the Haazda was frustrated and drunk. One glass of juice, liberally mixed with a narcotic sleeping powder. Harmless, but it knocked them out and let them sober up somewhere Kos didn't have to look at them.

As if on cue, the argumentative deputy's head slumped against Kos's shoulder, and the Haazda started to snore loudly.

"Checking out for the night, boss," Kos said. Pivlic nodded and whispered he'd lock up, careful not to wake the slumbering drunk on Kos's shoulder. The imp still had preparations to make for the incoming Orzhov bigwigs, no doubt, and Kos expected he wanted time to hatch his plans and perhaps a few poisonous spiders. That was to say nothing of the new décor that would no doubt be in place an hour before dawn.

Kos half-carried, half-dragged the snoozing man past several sets of empty tables, around the presently unoccupied fighting pit—a lone echo of Pivlic's old arena-eatery establishment in the city but one that didn't see much use in the small township—and heaved Vodotro across his shoulders with no small amount of popping joints. Kos pushed one of the swinging double doors open with his foot.

"Ooof!" the door said, and Kos blinked. No, it wasn't the door but a tall, bald man covered in tattoos and wearing a black and gold Orzhov-tailored suit. The man grabbed the edge of the door before it could swing back. Behind the man's right shoulder stood another Orzhov, a young woman with striking features who momentarily reminded Kos of his second ex-wife and also reminded him of just how old he was getting. The woman stood at the head of three thrulls that supported a huge, fat, apparently dead man between them. All of them were covered in fresh blood, and the thrulls displayed fresh patches of necrotized skin that still had a silvery sheen.

The fat man was a patriarch. Kos had never been so close to one before, but he didn't even have to ask. The clothing, the almost palpable aura of power, and the corpulence said it all. The blood-covered corpse sat atop a floating chair of some kind or the thrulls would never have been able to get him this far.

From the look of the patriarch and the enormous sigil that adorned his vile robes, this wasn't just any patriarch, either. This was *Pivlic*'s patriarch, the one Kos's boss had been expecting to arrive the next day. The ouroboros symbol of house Karlov was unmistakable. It matched the one over the bar.

The patriarch's clothing was even more ornate and expensive-looking than that worn by the bald man or the young woman, but, most notably, the bulky creature did not appear to be breathing. Oozing, yes, but not breathing. Though it was hard to tell with a mask covering the patriarch's face.

Kos stood there for a second with his jaw hanging open, uncertain what to say. It had taken him three seconds to notice the old man was dead—one expected a patriarch to look half-rotten, but he should have paid more attention to the urgency across the faces of the two living Orzhov travelers. Fortunately, Pivlic jumped to his rescue.

"Attendant Melisk! Lady Karlov! It's good to see you again, my friends," the imp said. He hopped over the bar and soared over the tables, landing next to Kos. "We did not expect you to arrive until dawn. My apologies for the state of—"

"Shut up, Pivlic," the woman said, "and help me get him into a saferoom. We haven't seen a ghost yet."

Kos took one look at the imp, another at the young woman, and adjusted the Haazda he carried. He nodded to the newcomers. "Good evening, Madam. Sir." As he slipped past the pair of Orzhov and their grisly burden, he turned back and called to Pivlic. "You need a hand, boss?"

"He can take it from here," the bald man said, and Kos heard Pivlic concur.

"All right then," Kos said and left Pivlic to take care of the unusual situation.

Kos didn't believe in gods, but he'd been known to buy into the concept of lucky streaks. Of late, he hadn't had any. But the fact that he knew with absolute certainty that he would not have to be witness in any way to the patriarch's necrotopsy seemed to indicate that his luck, such as it was, was getting better. He wondered if Pivlic would perform it himself.

* * * * *

"You call this safe, imp?" Melisk demanded.

"As safe as anything in these parts," Pivlic said with just enough obsequiousness to avoid a slap from the attendant or an unkind word from her ladyship Teysa Karlov, soon to be declared Baroness of Utvara.

"Boys, Uncle is getting heavy," Teysa said.

"The thrulls and the throne are—*oof*—Sorry, *were* taking quite a bit of the load," Pivlic croaked as Uncle's weight shifted.

"Is that your ectochair?" Melisk said. "Why, I didn't know that model even existed anymore."

"It will do the—Do you mind *pushing* instead of pulling, friend thrull? There you are," Pivlic said. "That is it, yes, and it will do the job. Please, no offense intended, honored attendant, but the thrulls seem to be bickering. If you wouldn't mind lending me a hand?"

"Certainly," Melisk said. He lifted the staff and let his head loll ever so slightly backward. He hummed a low dirge, and the mask atop the staff glowed fiercely. Uncle's corpse rose upward to hover in the white light, spun into an appropriately seated angle, and settled—with only a little guidance from Pivlic, who struggled to hold on, into one of Pivlic's oldest and most valued possessions.

The ectochair had been a gift from this very patriarch over two hundred years ago. That was clear from the Orzhov script lining the back of the seat and the tiny, stylized sigils painted in red upon the skullclamps. Teysa doubted the imp was the original owner, though Pivlic's name had been carefully inscribed into the chair as well.

"An excellent forgery, imp," Teysa said, gesturing to the chair.

"Pardon?" the imp said, looking up from the power nodes along the left armrest.

"You expect me to believe that Uncle gave you this antique?" she demanded.

"Believe what you will, my lady," Pivlic said.

"That will be 'Baroness' soon enough," Teysa said. "Just so long as the thing does what it's supposed to do."

"One moment, Baroness-intended," Pivlic said. "We must ensure the nodes are properly grounded, then retrieve the mirror from above the bar."

"You stored it above the bar?" Teysa said, a little aghast but not truly surprised.

"It seemed a good place to keep an eye on it," Pivlic said. He turned the three nodes clockwise a full rotation and said, "Attendant, I fear my last employee left before I thought to retrieve the mirror, but you seem handy with telekinesis. Would you mind?"

Melisk scowled at the imp, but Teysa scowled harder at Melisk. Her attendant turned, grumbling, and tromped down the hall outside the saferoom. She'd have to sit him down for a nice, long talk soon. Ever since their brief partnership, he'd been entirely too impudent at all the wrong times.

"My lady," Pivlic asked as soon as Melisk was around the corner. "May I ask—Was there an attack?"

"Yes. Gruul. What else would it have been?" Teysa said. "Is this contraption ready?"

"Yes, Baroness-elect," Pivlic said. "And it appears Uncle is ready as well."

"Good," Teysa said. "When this is finished, I will expect you to—"

A crash from direction of the bar was followed by Melisk's voice.

"Those were only glasses, my lady!" the attendant bellowed.

"As I said, we will finish this ceremony as quickly as possible. The official induction will be at the end of the year, after he serves his probationary period."

"Amazing that one so great should even need to serve a probationary period," Pivlic said.

"We'll get along a lot better if you cut out the unnecessary fawning, barkeeper," Teysa said. "Have you ever been in a court of law?"

"Why do you ask?"

"Imp . . ."

"Occasionally, but fortunately I pay my dues like any other loyal guild member in good standing," Pivlic said, his mouth left hanging at the beginning of a self-censored "my lady," Teysa guessed.

"Then understand that I was, until very recently, an advokist," Teysa said. "As you might suppose, that means I have spent a lot of time listening to people get to the point in the most roundabout way possible. Now I didn't plan on taking over Utvara," she saw Pivlic's eyes widen slightly. Good, no objection, though definitely a little surprise. "But we're going to make it work, and we're going to be recognized by the Guildpact. We're going to do it with efficiency, we're going to do it with confidence, and we're going to do it with diplomacy. Then I'm moving back to the city, and my appointed agent will take over here in my stead."

Pivlic nodded. More efficient by the second, she noted.

"You have been Uncle's agent here for, what is it?"

"Twelve years," Pivlic said. No wasted syllables. The imp learned quickly.

"And he told me personally you could be trusted," Teysa said. "That makes me want to distrust you. Does that surprise you?"

"Not at all," Pivlic said. "I would be insulted if it were otherwise."

"My lady," Melisk said, carrying the heavy mirror into the room over one shoulder. "I do not mean to interrupt, but where would you like me to put this?"

"In front of Uncle, of course," Teysa said. "How else will he be able to admire himself?"

"Of course," Melisk smirked and moved the silvery glass into place. The large mirror rested against a set of legs that folded out from the back. It was quite simple-looking, but sometimes the simplest-looking things had the greatest power.

"What do you think, imp?" Teysa said.

"Pivlic," Pivlic said.

"What do you think, Pivlic?" Teysa said.

"It appears to be in place, and the connections are sound," Pivlic said. "I admit I have not yet had the opportunity to see the chair used on one as auspicious as—"

"Efficiency," Teysa warned.

"But it will certainly work for your purposes," Pivlic finished.

"Wonderful," Teysa said. "Turn it on."

* * * * *

Kos stopped a moment to stretch and pop his back into alignment. Vodotro had been eating too may roundcakes and drinking too much bumbat. But that, at least, wasn't so different from some wojeks Kos had known. Borca, to name just one. He'd never had to drag Borca anywhere though. He hadn't planned to carry Vodotro all the way to the Haazda guardhouse, but leaving the man in the street seemed a little too cruel. Kos had given him the sleep-inducing narcotic, after all, and anything that happened to the drunken deputy would have been on the old 'jek's conscience. His conscience carried plenty, and he was tired of adding to the weight.

He sometimes missed his irritable old partner Bell Borca and half-expected the fat 'jek sergeant's ghost to be floating in his doorway every time he made it home. It had never happened, but he wouldn't put it past Borca to have made some kind of arrangement for it, if only to see the look on Kos's face.

That, at least, was one thing Utvara had over the city, and it was one of the reasons Kos stuck around. He had never seen a ghost in Utvara that lasted longer than a few seconds. He wasn't quite as curious as he'd been in his younger days, when he might have independently decided to investigate the reason for the region's lack of residual souls. These days, he just knew there were no ghosts in Utvara, and that was enough to satisfy.

The air had barely cooled even though the sun had been down for almost eight hours and already threatened to return.

Kos found himself still sweating from the exertion of packing an overweight, drunken Haazda half a mile. Then the real reason for the sudden sweats kicked in, and he felt his heart begin to race in his chest. He stopped, leaned against a glowpost, and willed the troublesome muscle to slow down. Kos closed his eyes and forced his breath in through his nose and slowly, so slowly, out from his mouth.

Eventually, it worked, but it was an exhilarating and terrifying couple of minutes.

In the last few months, random and sudden panic episodes like this had become more frequent. This one was only a week after the last, the closest they'd ever been together. Twelve years ago a physician had told him that heavy use of medicinal magic—specifically, the teardrops that were standard issue for peacekeepers in the City of Guilds—had taken their toll on his system. At Kos's advanced age, one more 'drop could be the death of him. As it was, he felt like his heart was just waiting for the right time to finish him off, 'drops or no 'drops. It seemed almost anything could set it off. Last time he'd just been sitting at the bar drinking juice when the attack hit.

Once the pounding stopped, Kos straightened and went on his way, grateful he had not been seen. His gratitude soured somewhat when Kos spotted a gang of four street toughs harassing an old centaur at the mouth of a narrow alley. Kos knew the centaur well and recognized the thugs too—they had once been hired labor, long since released from indenture by a prospector who had made his fortune and left. Like so many without a guild to call their own, they had formed a small pack and now roamed the streets by night, picking up what they could with street crime.

You don't need to get involved in this, a voice not unlike Pivlic's sounded in Kos's brain. Just walk by and get home. You're old.

You've already been on the verge of a heart attack once tonight. Leave it be.

Younger Kos, he suspected, might well have hated the man his older self had become. But what was cowardice to the young was common sense to the old. At least, that's what Kos kept telling the nagging voice in the back of his head that wouldn't stop telling him he'd become a sad, cowardly, old fool.

One of the thugs, a wiry sort with a scraggly beard, spotted Kos and pointed at him. The other three, all human like the apparent leader, turned from the centaur and stepped out into the thoroughfare.

"Guess they're not going to let it be," Kos muttered and pulled a silver baton off of his belt. *That* shut the little voice up. Just because he tried to avoid trouble didn't make him a coward. Then, more loudly and in his best 'jek's voice, he called, "Evening, boys! Out for a little fun tonight?"

"What do you want, Kos?" the bearded one replied. "This isn't any of your business."

"Yeah, people keep telling me that," Kos said. "But you're wrong. That centaur owes me zinos. Leave him alone." With a loud click, Kos turned the hilt of the baton ninety degrees, and the weapon hummed audibly.

"Orubo, is that what I think it is?" one of the others said to the leader.

"Shut up, Vurk," Orubo said. "He's no 'jek. Not anymore."

"Maybe not," Kos said and gave the baton a flashy-looking twirl, "but they did let me take a few things from the armory as keepsakes. Want to see how we handle street trash like you in the City of Guilds?"

"Orubo, I don't know," another said. "The centaur was one thing, but this guy—He's famous."

"Heard of me, have you?" Kos said. The old 'jek wasn't fond of his celebrity, but at times it did come in handy. "Then you probably know who I work for now too. Now I know I can beat every one of you within a whisper of your lives. And on a word from me, you'll be sent to the Cauldron or, better yet, the Husk. That's assuming they don't ship you off to the mansion district and the entertainment pits. You don't look like Gruul to me, but I'm sure I can convince Pivlic that you want to be."

"Pivlic?" repeated the only thug who had yet to speak. "That's the Orzhov, isn't it? Orubo, maybe we should think about—"

"Shut it!" the leader snapped, but he was spending more time watching Kos's baton than he was looking at his potential victim now. "There's one of you, Kos. There are four of us." His words were bold, but even at this distance Kos could read the uncertainty in his eyes.

"You're not dealing with a Haazda here," Kos added. He brought the baton up and aimed it like a bam-stick at the thug leader's chest. "Now I know you boys don't get out to the big city much, but I'm sure you know that I can drop all four of you before you even get within an arm's reach of me?" The baton hummed in agreement.

"Orubo, I think maybe we should—"

"Quiet," the leader said, then called down the thoroughfare to Kos. "All right, 'jek," he said, "but we're going to remember this."

"I certainly hope so," Kos said. "I'd hate to have to teach you all over again. If the four of you leg it down to the hostel, I imagine they'll let you get some sleep on the steps. You all look like you could use a little. I mean, why else would you accost someone in the middle of the thoroughfare?" He took a step toward them, the baton still aimed squarely at Orubo. One more step, and the gang leader turned, beckoning his fellows to follow him.

"Watch your back, 'jek," Orubo called over his shoulder before the group rounded a corner that led to the local prospector's hostel, a boardinghouse that most prospectors preferred to the more expensive hourly rooms at the Imp Wing.

Kos turned the hilt of the baton and the humming stopped. He gave it another experimental twirl and replaced it on his belt. The old 'jek-issue baton had gotten him out of quite a few scrapes in this way, even though it would never be able to fire a submission blast again. Kos had long ago run out of the powerful crystals the League used back in the city. The League didn't hand out crystals to retirees, no matter how honored, so the best he could get were cheap Orzhov knockoffs that could make the baton hum and little else. Fortunately, the hum was usually enough warning to get thugs like Orubo to back down. Fortunate, because despite his bravado, there was no way Kos could have taken all four of the much younger gang members. His heart was racing—not a real attack, but fast enough that he doubted he would have lasted long.

Eventually, someone would call him on his bluff, but no one had done so for twelve years. He supposed he was lucky.

"They're gone," he said aloud.

The elderly potential victim emerged from a nearby alley, his hooves clopping against the dry stone. The old centaur beggar's forelimbs creaked as Trijiro stepped like a cautious foal from what had probably been the safest place he could find to sleep that night—outside a livery stocked with riding dromads for rent. Kos could hear the nervous dromads shuffling and whinnying inside, reacting instinctively to the scene outside their stables that they could no doubt hear, if not see.

"Good evening, Officer," Trijiro chuckled. His voice was as deep and sturdy as his body was ancient and tired.

"Good evening, Chief," Kos said.

"Don't call me that. You know full well I was thrown out by my tribe," Trijiro objected. He might have convinced a Haazda that he was sincere, but Kos had known too many liars. Besides, it wasn't the first time they'd had this exchange, nor was it the first time Kos had been forced to rescue the old Gruul from thugs.

"And I quit the 'jeks a long time ago. It's 'Mr. Kos,' if it's anything. What keeps you up this late?"

"These old bones. The ache, it comes and goes—when it pleases, not when I do." Trijiro winked. "I suspect I'm not the only one feeling the pangs of age this evening, Mr.-not-Officer Kos?"

"No, Trijiro," Kos said, "you are most certainly not. Saw that little performance, did you?"

"Indeed I did," Trijiro said. He swung a satchel around his shoulder and flipped open the top, poking a hand inside. "Perhaps I could offer you a genuine tonic of yarbulb extract, with remarkable healing properties? Only two zibs and a real bargain at that."

Kos raised his hand in objection. "No, Chief. But I can spare a couple of zibs if you need them." Trijiro, of course, knew that Kos would not accept any medical aid, but the offer of a sale gave him honorable cover to accept charity. Kos placed a pair of coins in the centaur's open hand, and Trijiro dropped them into the satchel where they clinked against a few others.

Then Kos let the old curiosity finally take control. There was something that had been bothering him ever since he'd left the Imp Wing.

"Trijiro, you didn't happen to see an odd-looking group come down the thoroughfare, say, maybe an hour ago? Headed toward Pivlic's place? There would have been a man, a woman, and some thrulls carrying a big, fat fellow on a floating chair. If they came this way, you couldn't have missed them."

"I did see an odd-looking group, but you just chased them away."

"Trijiro . . ." Kos said.

"Yes, yes, perhaps I did, not-Officer Kos."

Two more zibs went into the centaur's satchel, and Kos arched an eyebrow. "Did you say 'Did not, Officer,' or 'Did, not-Officer'?"

"Yes, I saw them," Trijiro said, his deep voice now a whisper. "Did they murder him?"

"Murder who?"

"The big, fat fellow," Trijiro said. "He was talking about how the other two would benefit from his death."

"Wait, the big, fat—the big fellow was *alive* when you saw them?"

"Most certainly," Trijiro said, "at least, there were three voices. I never did actually see the big one's mouth move, but his face was covered in a mask. I assumed the wheezing voice was his."

A mask. The patriarch had been wearing a mask when Kos had opened the Imp Wing's doors to the attendant's face.

"Not-Officer, you seem intrigued," the centaur said. "Would you like to hear more?"

I *am* intrigued, Kos thought. But that's not my job anymore. I work at a place where, on the good days, the patrons beat each other up for fun and, on really good days, the patrons kill and eat each other in the pits. Intrigue was no good for Pivlic's business, and like it or not the imp was right. Kos *did* work for him, and frankly the old 'jek was lucky Pivlic had taken him on. You couldn't eat fame or live under the roof of celebrity.

"Trijiro, if you're as sharp as I suspect you are, you know the answer to that," Kos finally said. "But I'm still going to say no. It's been a long day."

"Then why did you ask about those hurried, secretive Orzhov travelers?" Trijiro said.

"Because I like you, you old coot, and I thought you should know—that fat bastard was murdered by Gruul. At least, that's the story the other two gave my boss," Kos said.

"I would agree that was the most likely thing," the centaur said, "if not for the fact that I heard a third voice speaking. And it was not thrulls. Your patriarch was not killed by Gruul. He was alive."

"Not anymore, I'd guess. The point is that however the old guy ended up dead he's dead now, and the ones who are going to make that news public are saying it's your people," Kos said, irritation creeping into his voice. "I know they 'threw you out,' but I suspect you still see them from time to time?"

"Beggars passing beggars, yes," Trijiro said. "It happens. And you believe these new arrivals mean the Utvar Gruul harm?"

"Count on it," Kos said, turning to go.

"Kos!" the old centaur said, stopping the retired wojek in his tracks with a commanding tone Kos wasn't sure he liked. He turned back to face Trijiro slowly.

"Yes?"

"From what you tell me, my people may be in danger," Trijiro said.

"Sounds like it," Kos said. "That just now sunk in?"

"And yet you go back to work for those that would endanger us," the centaur said. "Despite the fact that you just saved my life. You make a curious Orzhov, my friend."

"Look, I warned you," Kos said, even more irritated now. "Go warn them. Beyond that, it's not my business and you didn't hear it from me." He scowled and added, "And I'm not an Orzhov. I don't have a guild anymore."

"But even if this were the work of Gruul, you know, the Utvar

Gruul is made up of many tribes, and just because one has committed a crime does not mean all should pay," Trijiro said. "You, perhaps, could get this through to them. What about justice, Kos? What if they are lying?"

"Everybody lies," Kos said. "And I don't do justice anymore. I just don't like street thugs getting in my way. Good night, Chief."

After half a minute, Kos heard brisk hoofbeats headed in the opposite direction, toward a road that led into the heart of the Husk.

* * * * *

Crix had suspected the Husk would be an unpleasant place, and she was not disappointed. The long-fallow area had degenerated into something like a landscape instead of a cityscape. It looked dusty, dangerous, and diseased. She had a long time to take in her surroundings while riding, strapped tight as she was to the back of a hulking Gruul that her nose said was human but her eyes told her had to be ogre or troll. The brute's furry back was making the goblin itch like mad, but there was no way to reach it. Nor did it do any good to try to use the straps against the Gruul as a garrote. Tugging on one arm just made another strap wrench her leg around sideways. She was more or less a goblin backpack.

Crix thanked the magelord that she'd taken an inoculation against the plague. At least her physical proximity to the bandit chief, or whatever he was, wouldn't pose much risk of the *kuga* infection. For a time. A week of protection remained at most, she estimated. The lokopede ride itself had taken almost a week, and the shot was good for two.

After the first hour of painful, bouncing travel pinned to this creature, she'd begged to be allowed to walk. The Gruul ignored her. She'd continued for another hour, pleading, trying to reason, appealing to fear, responsibility, to *decency*. The Gruul spoke, but only to bark orders to others in a guttural tongue that the multilingual goblin could not quite place. All couriers had to be conversant in numerous languages, and she definitely heard some immediately familiar sounds, if not full words, in the orders. Maybe it was some kind of dialect run wild in this wasteland, or a code language perhaps. A few of the words were Ogrish in origin, others Centaur, some definitely a variant of Goblin.

The Gruul hadn't said much, but what he had said she picked apart and analyzed as the small raiding party made its way through the rusty, ruined hills. It kept her from dwelling on the many gaping sinkholes and jagged edges that lined the path. The Husk was not a place to walk without an able guide, from the look of it. She wondered at first why there were no warnings or signs around the bigger sinkholes, but on second thought it made sense—the Gruul knew right where they were, and the rough and dangerous landscape made an excellent natural defense against intrusion. It was a wonder the road the lokopede had taken existed at all.

The first order the bandit leader barked had been to a small, agile scout who rode a wiry Husk-cat. Crix could make out a word close to Centaur for "tell" or "teach." There was something like *ghrak*, the common Goblin word for "prisoner." That would be her, presumably. Then "ask," "kill," and "courier." Was it possible they recognized her station by the tattoos on her arms?

Crix had just worked out the first order—definitely "Tell the shaman (or perhaps chief) that the prisoner is a courier"—when she heard growling off to the left, and the bandit carrying her froze and raised a fist to bring the entire gang to a stop. Though the straps cut into her wrists and ankles, she wrenched her head and body to the left to get a better look at where the sound had come from—no doubt from somewhere near the seven sets of glowing, canine eyes obscured by thick shadows.

This had gone on long enough. She was entitled to study this strange Utvar Gruul subculture, so long cut off from the rest of Ravnica by the fallow quarantine over the Husk and everything it encircled. She guessed that on foot the Gruul couldn't possibly be making more than five or six miles every hour. But to study the tribe, they'd have to last long enough to get her to their camp, village, tents, caves, or wherever these primitives called home. She could tolerate a little discomfort, and the show of begging and pleading had been an act, mostly. But if Crix didn't speak now, a pack of wild *somethings* was going to strike their flank without warning.

She didn't dare try the barking Gruul tongue yet, though she was pretty sure she could follow along. Instead she tried common Ravi, which even these isolated barbarians should have been able to comprehend in some small way.

"I think—" she began.

The bandit carrying her whistled, and the pack of hulking, black dog-lizards emerged into the dim moonlight. Their scaly heads were roughly canine in shape, with forward-facing binocular vision—though she suspected things tended to look reddish through their glowing, scarlet orbs—and a slobbering muzzle filled with the teeth of a mammalian predator. From the neck down, they were more reptilian, with squat, wide legs and long, whiplike tails lined with tiny barbed quills. Not counting the tail, each one was easily a horse's length from snout to hindquarters, and the tail added the body's length again. Their hides reflected shades of indigo, blue, and green in blotchy patterns, each one marred by a branding scar in the shape of a **V**.

The reflection of light off the creatures made her wish she'd gone ahead and freed herself. She'd love to get a reading on their auras. Even her unaided eyes could see that they seethed with inner fire that her magelord might well be able to use. Something to catalog for the report. The magelord had given her a fair amount of time to deliver the message, trusting her to get it there, and now she could use those months to better her studies. Surely this would please Zomaj Hauc, who valued information as much as he valued loyalty.

Might as well keep hanging around, Crix mused. Freeing herself would give away much of the extent of her own abilities, and she preferred to let these Gruul know as little as possible. They were fascinating, and she did not fear them exactly. But she definitely did not trust them.

Despite the addition of more than a half-dozen giant lizard-dogs to the raiding party, the group was moving even more quietly now. The beasts were curiously attentive. To Crix's dismay she felt a trickle of nervous sweat run down her captor's neck and onto her head. From there it tortured her all the way down to the back of her own neck, and somehow she fought the urge to scream.

When the threat finally came, it came not from the reptilian canines.

A rank, overgrown junkpile to her right stood up and flattened two of the lizard-dogs with one swipe of an arm as big as a loko-pede car. The bandit chief turned to face this new danger, which spun the goblin around to face the rest of the gang. Whatever was under the junkpile was now behind her, and all Crix saw were more Gruul. They looked over her shoulder at something casting a shadow over the entire group, blocking what light the predawn sky provided.

The Gruul looked terrified. And considering how terrifying she found the Gruul, Crix considered herself fortunate to be looking the other way.

CHAPTER 5

You demean your family when you negotiate in good faith with the lieutenants of one who dares to oppose you. You demean yourself when you accept the word of lackeys, for it means your family accepts the word of lackeys. If the opposing party does not respect you enough to show you his throat, find it and cut it out.

—Patriarch Xil Xaxosz
(b. 3882, d. 4211 Z.C., Obzedat member 4211–present)

31 Paujal 10012 Z.C.

Teysa's first instinct had been to summon the local guild representatives—or their equivalents—as soon as the business with the mirror had been completed. Melisk had counseled her to wait until at least dawn, and she'd reluctantly agreed. In the few hours before the first light of morning broke through the corroded skyline of the Husk, she set about adjusting Pivlic's saferoom into an office. The imp's second saferoom, which he'd foolishly tried to conceal from Melisk, would serve as her living quarters until she had her own residence in place. Two Grugg brothers stood watch outside the door, while Bephel, the smartest and the one who had been given leave to speak, monitored the reception line for assassins and weapons their mistress would want to know about. His replacement head had grown in quickly, though he tended to veer a little to the left when he walked.

She invited the head of the local slave unions first. Not technically a guild, though many of the workers in the area were captured and tamed Gruul, the slave unions had enough pull that their collective owner, a fat half-demon who called himself "Wageboss

Aradoz," had earned a face-to-face with the new ruler of Utvara. For Teysa, he would serve as a test subject for the way she intended to handle the local luminaries, such as they were.

The slave boss leered at Teysa across the table. He favored his human half, though his demonic ancestry was hard to miss. He was of average height and bore a pronounced hump on his right shoulder. Small ram's horns curled about either ear. Teysa's carefully chosen attire made him lean to the side and a little bit forward.

Teysa had tuned Pivlic's saferoom décor enchantments to create a simple wood-paneled office, with a dining table that would do until she had a proper desk. She sat in an approximation of her Uncle's favorite chair, facing three smaller chairs that were designed with the comfort of the user in mind. Beneath it all, only the table was unaltered by the enchantments, though the office, chairs, and occupants were all real enough. She'd considered something more intimidating, but she decided to use a generally neutral backdrop for these initial meetings. In her practice it had never served her wrong. A neutral background ensured you kept the client focused. This would serve until Teysa had a better handle on how she was going to, well, handle these people.

Wageboss Aradoz barely qualified as "people," at least in her hastily forming opinion. When his leer drew no response, he leaned further forward to pick at a blister on the inside of his big toe and grab a lingering look at her décolletage. After a few seconds she reached across the table, grabbed him by his left ram's horn, and twisted. The wageboss squealed a distinctly unramlike squeal.

"Wageboss, we will get along better if you keep your eyes on the future," Teysa said, then shoved the half-demon back into his seat, driving the horn into Aradoz's forehead in what she hoped was a moderately painful way. She sat back in her own chair and waved a hand over one shoulder at Melisk, who stood patiently by. "This is Melisk. Do you like your eyes the way they are? I imagine Melisk could get you an amazing deal on necrotic surgery."

The half-demon scowled, growled, and massaged his skull.

"I think at the very least you like them in your head and not in tonight's soup. We've hired a local chef. I hear he likes to experiment," Teysa said.

"All right!" Aradoz said.

"Splendid," Teysa said. "Now let's talk about how the unions are going to pay their dues this year. I was thinking we might start with a proper mansion. Have you ever built a seat of power, Wageboss? It's a bit of an honor, don't you think?"

"Yes, Mistress—"

" 'Baroness,' or some other suitable honorific will do, Wageboss, but certainly not that vulgar term," Teysa said. She snapped her fingers, and Melisk produced a tightly bound roll of parchment that Teysa handed to the sputtering wageboss. He took it and placed his thumb against the seal, but the new baroness raised her hand. "Not yet. I do not have time to hold your hand through this process. Take those blueprints and build it."

"Where?" the wageboss managed.

Teysa sighed but kept Melisk at bay. She stood and leaned across the table, snatched the roll of blueprints, and snapped the seal with her thumb. She bid Aradoz to pin down the opposite corners and circled a rough area in the southwest quarter of the ovoid Utvara area with her index finger.

"What's here?" she said.

"That is—Let me see . . ." A corner of the map curled up when he reached into his pocket and slipped a blue monocle over his eye. Melisk waved a hand, and the entire thing flattened out against the table and glowed faintly.

"Thank you, Melisk," Teysa said. "That quarter—what's there?"

"A small beggar's warren. That's Gruul country, of course. That there is a zombie colony—Golgari labor mostly. And those are guildless slums," Aradoz said. He pointed at three distinct blocks of the quarter. "There, there, and there. Well, the slums are pretty much everywhere between those two areas."

"Zombies?" Teysa asked.

"Yes," the half-demon replied. "Workers for the northern farms."

"They yours?"

"As a matter of fact, they are. I have a Devkarin overseer out there, but I take care of the details with labor."

"Then move them closer to the fields."

"But Baroness," the wageboss said, "the Selesnyans will never allow the undead so near the Vitar Yescu. They interfere with its life energy or some such nonsense."

"Then put them in the flats," Teysa said. "They're undead, right? The *kuga* can't be too hard on them."

"Perhaps," the half-demon replied, "but there are essential services, especially climate control, that those types require."

"What do you mean?"

"They dry out, Baroness."

Teysa examined the map. Utvara was roughly the shape of an egg, if one counted the fringes of the Husk region. Inside that shape a rectangular township filled the southern two thirds of the egg—the township proper, sliced by the wide thoroughfare and numerous alleys and byways. The Vitar Yescu sat north of center, bordering the farmlands, and there were several other Selesnyan-looking structures nearby. North of the farmlands were the flats, which included the Cauldron project.

The flats that filled the northern third of the Utvara region, or rather what was under them, were the main reason this township had sprung up even before the end of the fallow period. The flats had been some kind of ceremonial square long before disease hit the area. No records of its construction existed. Whatever it had been, it had become a huge, flat dead zone where nothing could grow and where the plague winds blew unimpeded. Roughly twenty years ago, a bold, destitute explorer braved the plague in a homemade survival suit and broke through the bricks of the old square to find miles of lifeless, buried city—abandoned, cold, and technically unclaimed. The township formed then, despite Guild-pact law, with a little help from Uncle. It was little more than a boomtown outpost, and the life churchers were expanding like a healthy tree, thanks to their, well, healthy tree.

"Wageboss, you're a local," she said. "What is the range of the Vitar Yescu's effects? Where can you go without contracting the disease? Assuming one is not undead, of course."

"The safe zone extends maybe a quarter mile into the flats," Aradoz said. "Beyond that, you need a sphere helmet and a miner's suit, at the very least."

"Perfect," Teysa said with a smile. "I want you to go to a few of these enclaves, or whatever they are, clear them out, and house at least some of your deadwalkers there. Quarter the Selesnyans in that area of the flats that's still within range of the Vitar Yescu, and see about moving a few Rakdos up there too. Give the 'churchers a reason to proselytize. Everybody's happy."

"Well, I—That is, very well," the wageboss said. "But what if the undead somehow affect the behavior of the Vitar Yescu? We all rely on that."

"Oh, let the life churchers shoot any zombie that gets too close. Maybe give them an enclave between the tree and the deadwalkers. Fair enough?"

"And the guildless?"

"Why not hire them too?" Teysa said. "This is just the first of many projects I have planned. I'll let you in on a little secret, Wageboss. I'm not happy that this Izzet Cauldron was built on my property. The deal wasn't a good one. It's not smart to rely on unproven methods, and frankly I'm annoyed that the biggest structure in town is, at the moment, the property of the Magewrights." She effortlessly flowed from scowl number six to ingratiation number eleven. "Therefore, I'm going to keep you employed for a long time making the *rest* of this place into an Orzhov barony. The plague is nothing compared to what I have in mind."

The wageboss's jowls dropped. "Baroness," he managed, "with what shall I purchase materials? All these new workers? I serve the Orzhov and the Karlov family without reservation, but—"

"I'm sure the union's coffers have some petty cash available. Once my new home is built, we can discuss your fees for future projects, which I'm sure you'll find more than generous."

"But I am merely a union man. What you're asking would require an army, Baroness," Aradoz said. He waved at the plans on the table. "I'm just supposed to *do* this?"

"If you don't, I'm sure I can find someone ambitious enough to do it," Teysa said. "Perhaps he will let you stay on as hired labor, if you're still alive." She nodded to her attendant, who produced small broach set with a ball of onyx bearing the Karlov ouroboros. She stepped around the table and pinned the jewelry to the wageboss's chest. "This should help you get things done. Don't let me down."

"Is that—?" The half-demon gaped at the sudden turn of events and at Teysa's employment of smile number fifteen. "I won't let you down," he parroted.

"Melisk, we are finished here," Teysa said. "Please escort the wageboss to the door. Oh, and Aradoz?"

"Yes?"

"If ground has not broken on the mansion by sundown, Melisk is going to kill you and replace you with someone who can do the job."

"You can't do that!" Aradoz shouted. "I'm in charge of—"

"Nothing," Teysa said. "I, meanwhile, am in charge of everything. That pin won't come off, Wageboss. One would think someone in your position would wish to ingratiate himself to one such as me. The rewards should be obvious—leaving here with your life, for example."

The wageboss opened his mouth to speak, thought better of it, and nodded. Teysa knew that Melisk's gaze could intimidate a bull ogre and didn't have to look to see her attendant was giving Aradoz maybe sixty percent of his maximum glare. She was impressed by the wageboss, who had obviously earned his position at the top. Most opposing parties couldn't handle a quarter of the full Melisk.

Teysa tapped the corners of the map, and the image flickered, swirled, and coalesced back into the plans for her new mansion.

"There you are," Teysa said. "Do you require any more of my valuable time?"

The half-demon shook his head.

When the wageboss had gone, walking backward until he cleared the door that the thrulls shut behind him, Teysa swiveled in her chair and smirked at Melisk. "Who's been waiting longest?"

Melisk closed his eyes for a moment and communed with Phleeb, standing watch at the door. A moment later he said, "First Acolyte Wrizfar Barkfeather of the Selesnyan Conclave, Holy Protector of the Vitar Yescu, Knight of—"

"Ah, hoped so," Teysa said. Her smirk broke into a grin. "We'll see him last. Send in that doctor next. The Simic. And remember, I will ask for your opinion when I desire it."

"Yes Baroness."

* * * * *

The towering shape that blocked out the moon was roughly humanoid, with a blunted head made from concrete and stone, arms of wiry metal bars with scrap-iron knuckles that grazed the ground, and a skeleton of girders rusted together by time and fused by magic. The monster reeked of dead rats and tangy corrosion—a cloud of rank odor that washed over the spread-eagle goblin as the Gruul bandit she was strapped to thought better of this challenge and barked a retreat.

The Gruul called it a "nephilim," a word with elements of the ancient Draconic tongue implying godlike power. Crix found it hard to argue with the assessment. Her vantage point let her see how painfully easy it was for the rusting nephilim to keep up with them—the junk creature would be on top of them in seconds. Fortunately, she'd been able to pick out her personal captor's name among the Gruul chatter.

"Excuse me, Golozar," she shouted over her pinned shoulder. "I feel compelled to tell you that I have a way of stopping this creature. Will you consider untying me?"

The Gruul spun around, realized the speaker was on his back, and cocked his head to one side. "What makes you think we can't handle this?" Golozar then switched to guttural Gruul. "Beast-wards, strike the hind legs. Wait for the rest of us to strike the right forelimb first. I'm going for the head."

"Are you insane?" Crix screamed.

"I've seen your kind before, goblin. Learned types, studying us like animals, never bothering to *help* unless you, too, are in trouble. And now you offer to humiliate me in front of my people?" Golozar said. "I would not recommend that. Shut up and watch."

Aren't I facing the wrong way for that? Crix thought, but she didn't say it. She wasn't really in immediate danger, not yet, even if her limbs were going numb. Numb or not, the tattoo could burn through the straps with a single thought. Couriers were protected by special magic, and couriers that lasted as long as they knew when and how to use it.

The Gruul started jogging toward the junk-covered behemoth, circling around and scanning the area. The smell became unbearable, and finally caused her to shout.

"Are you crazy?" Crix said. "What are you people doing? You can't—You can't fight that! We've got to run!"

"Quiet," the Gruul behind her snarled. "You don't know *what* the Gruul can do, goblin."

Crix was baffled but kept her mouth shut. They had indeed been running, but the small raid party had stopped short at an area that was even more riddled with crevices and cracks than the sections of the Husk they'd already crossed. As the Gruul turned left and right, obviously scanning the area, she saw even more fissures—this area was filled with them.

The whole place was a deadfall for something as huge as the lumbering creature that even now closed in. She couldn't see the nephilim, but she could see its shadow and hear its thudding approach. Out of the corner of her eye, she spotted other members of the Gruul raiding party splitting up and spreading out.

"That thing is made of junk," Crix muttered. "How is a fall going to kill it?"

She must have muttered more loudly than she thought, because the Gruul behind her answered, "Killing it is impossible. Things like it have been lurking in these hills forever. But we can get rid of it for a while."

"You sure speak good Ravi for an ignorant savage," Crix said.

"You expose your own ignorance with your words," the Gruul replied. "Education is not reserved for brainy goblins."

Crix readied a response but didn't get a chance to give it—the rusty ground behind her was beginning to creak and groan as though it were a living thing. It sounded hungry.

* * * * *

"I don't want any trouble, Baroness . . . Baroness . . . Baroness. . . ?" the vedalken stuttered.

" 'Baroness' will do," Teysa said. "I can't imagine what kind of trouble you mean, Doctor Nebun."

"Why ask *me* about the *kuga* plague?" the vedalken asked, exuding paranoia.

"I'm told you represent local Simic Combine interests, in their entirety," Teysa replied and pressed her fingertips together with her elbows on the table to rest her chin.

"The Simic did not create the plague!" the doctor said, coming out of his seat. For a vedalken, it was the equivalent of blind human fury. "Do you know what I have to put up with in this town? Everyone thinks that just because it's a disease, it must have been created by one of us. As if that's *all* the Simic Combine does. And even if I *did* have something to do with it—"

Teysa grabbed one of the vedalken's flailing hands in her own and slammed it down onto the table. "Doctor! *Listen.*"

The vedalken nodded.

"Listening?"

The vedalken nodded again.

"Good," Teysa said. "I don't care who invented the plague. All I want to know is what it is, how it works, and how to get rid of it when I need to."

"Oh, is that all," Dr. Nebun blurted and covered his mouth.

"I don't like Selesnyans, Doctor," Teysa said, "so that means you get the job. I want a cure, and I don't want anything that will put me in debt to the Conclave. You're not to base *any* of your work on their Vitar Yescu or any of their tricks. Do you understand me? There will be no quietmen or hive-minds controlling Utvara as long as I'm here."

"But why me?" the doctor said.

"I don't explain myself, Doctor," Teysa said. She pushed back from the table and rested her hands behind her head, a neutral smile gracing her face. "It doesn't have to happen right away. You'll find I'm quite reasonable."

"It would take weeks just to gather my notes," the doctor said.

"Reasonable, not stupid," Teysa said. "Begin experimenting and find me something that doesn't come from the Selesnyan Conclave in any way within, say, a week. After that, we'll start talking about charges."

"Charges?" the doctor stuttered. "Of course, I couldn't be expected to do this for free, I will—"

"Melisk," Teysa said. The attendant handed her a small but thick ledger bound with satin ribbon. "This is the first volume. In your time in this township, you've violated Guildpact laws I didn't even know existed, and, in case you hadn't heard, I'm an advokist. I believe you would call me a 'lawmage.' Now before we get too far, I just want you to know—your light at the end of this tunnel is the destruction of those records. No charges will be filed. Now what do you say?"

The doctor rose, this time to bow deeply. "I will do it."

"Of course you will," Teysa said. She handed the ledger back to Melisk, who tucked it into his pocket. "Now, before you go, tell me about the *kuga* plague."

"It's deadly. It rots the skin and devours the lungs."

"It is painful?" Teysa asked.

"What do you think?" the doctor said.

"But it's not the *original* plague," Teysa said.

"No, but as I said, no one, least of all the Simic Combine, has any knowledge whatsoever of the origin of the plague, or why—"

"Doctor, do that one more time and you'll be getting around your laboratory on stumps," Teysa said pleasantly. "Information, not protestation. You're a vedalken. I'm sure you don't need notes to give me the gist."

"All right, all right," the doctor said. He sat back in his seat and his face shifted to a thoughtful scowl of concentration. "According to records I found in the public domain and my own independent research—which as I said had nothing, nothing to do with the creation of this dread disease—the original plague was spread mostly through physical contact. Simple touching, nothing else was needed."

"So to clear out the population and finish off the disease, the place was declared fallow," Teysa said.

"Yes," the doctor nodded. "But a tribe of Gruul who had lived in the region and been the prime carriers of the original plague developed strong immunity. The fallow period was an ineffective means of clearing out the area for reclamation."

"You sound as if you know of this original plague firsthand, Doctor. Are you an original settler of the township, by any chance?"

"Why?"

"Just wondering."

"Yes, actually," the doctor said. "May I continue?"

"Go ahead," Teysa said.

"The Gruul immunity eventually robbed the disease of any means of spreading, though it remained in their blood," the doctor continued. "Even so, to ensure the plague was truly gone and to satisfy Guildpact Statutes, the fallow period needed to continue. That was when your family decided to speed things up, I believe, by bringing in the Izzet." Nebun spat the name of the magewrights' guild.

"The mana-compression device, as I remember," Teysa said. "Effective enhancement, from the look of it."

"If you don't mind holes in your sky," the doctor said.

"The Schism."

"Of course the Schism. And a mutated, wind-born plague. The energy that thing used, it devoured every living thing all right. But the plague wasn't living, exactly. It was waiting. So the energy that ate everything else caused a mutation that was built into the original plague as a reaction to such—oh, dear."

"You are in a verity circle," Teysa said. "Little admissions like that will happen. The plague was built. Interesting. But strangely, you also were telling the truth when you said the Simic Combine had nothing to do with creating the plague. We'll talk about that more at a later time, I think. Now let's go on."

"The mutation turned the plague airborne, as I said, but the peculiar history and geography of the Utvara region kept it more or less confined to this area."

"Almost as if the plague wanted to stay here, eh?" Teysa said.

"I did not say that," the doctor said.

"So why are my foothills still packed with Gruul, Doctor?" Teysa said. "Why did a Gruul raiding party attack and murder a patriarch—a *patriarch*, Nebun—before my very eyes?"

"The mutation was not enough to completely overcome the immunity they carry in their blood," the doctor confessed.

"But they're all different species," Teysa said. "Centaur, human, goblin, viashino—and that's just counting the four types I saw coming after our lokopede. How do they pass this down through generations?"

"Those are descendants of the original Utvar Gruul," the doctor said. "I have run blood comparison studies on many of them, as your ledger no doubt tells you." The vedalken's voice became tinged with pride. "The humans have been interbreeding with the other humanoids too."

"Not sure I like the way you say that, Doctor," Teysa said. "You have a problem with humans?"

"Only that they keep mucking up otherwise orderly bloodlines," the doctor said.

"Charming," Teysa replied. "So what does the *kuga* do to these new-and-improved super-Gruul?"

"Just Gruul, I believe," the doctor said, obliviously. "It shortens the Gruul lifespan, and it *should* kill them after a few years. There's some chieftain out there though. He's the one who keeps them as cohesive as they are. According to my Gruul test subjects, he is the one who found a wild fungus that shared many properties with the Vitar Yescu. The Gruul wear it all over their bodies."

"Which you had nothing to do with, of course," Teysa said.

"I—I am a doctor."

"Yes, you are. And a cytoplastician in addition to your other talents, I believe. Don't worry, I won't press you on that either. This does explain some of their more charming physical features, doesn't it?" Teysa said. Smile number two: I know what you mean. "And the Vitar Yescu—why doesn't it protect them the way it protects the township?"

"That overgrown dandelion is terribly inefficient," the doctor said. "And the pollen causes allergies in a small percentage of the population. It uses the same distribution method as the disease—the wind. And since that normally blows from the north, it leaves much of the flats under plague watch and never reaches the Husk, for the most part, before getting blown back down into the valley. I'm told that once the Cauldron is running at full power, the Vitar Yescu will be able to wipe out the plague completely. Pyromanic windmills, or some such infernal nonsense."

"Do you think that will work?" Teysa asked.

"It is certainly a possibility," the doctor said, "though I feel that it may still take years. One does not change the wind with ease."

"This tree is interesting but reeks too much of the Conclave. I prefer my own cure. So feel free to get to work, Doctor," Teysa said. "You've shared more than enough with me. I thank you for your candor and for the information, and I look forward to seeing your progress in a few days."

"Days? But I—"

Melisk cleared his throat.

"Ah yes, Melisk. Thanks," Teysa said good-naturedly. She took the Karlov sigil pin from the attendant and stood.

When the doctor had left, Teysa sat down again. "I feel well-armed, Melisk. I think it's time you sent in the Izzet magelord. What's his name? Hauc?"

"About that—" Melisk began.

"What now?" Teysa asked.

"The magelord isn't coming. The foreman brings his apologies."

"Well, send *him* in then."

* * * * *

Crix slid from Golozar's back like a dead fish and flopped onto the ground sideways. Every muscle she had buzzed as blood returned and her nerve endings all demanded her attention at once. The leather straps that had kept her bound to the Gruul were still attached to her wrists, but she could not manipulate her hands well enough to even consider trying to make use of the four lengths of leather.

A few seconds later, the junk elemental crashed through the not-so-solid ground not far away. The impact jarred the goblin enough to force her eyes open in time to see the thing's limbs—all four of them—disappear into the new chasm that had appeared under its feet. A quick head count revealed all of the Gruul raiding party had survived, none the worse for wear but covered in reddish dust.

Crix coughed and tried to spit, but her mouth was utterly dry, and her tongue felt scaly. "Decided . . . to let me . . . go?" she croaked to Golozar. The bandit chief looked back over one shoulder as he signaled the Gruul party to gather and prepare to move on.

"You were getting in my way," the bandit said. "You're not going anywhere." He turned back to his gang and barked a few more orders.

In most circumstances, it was not easy to insult Crix. She was a courier and a servant of a great magelord, and insults came with the territory. But outright dismissal by this savage, who had just put her in repeated peril as far as he knew, pushed her over a brink she didn't know she had. She closed her eyes and drew on the warmth of the morning sun; the heat of the distant Cauldron; the cool, clean water in their floating reservoirs; and the ice of the polar regions. All of them combined to soothe her aches, get her blood flowing with a minimum of discomfort, and most importantly allow her to stand, the straps hanging at her sides.

"Gruul," Crix said, "I believe I have learned enough for now. I should be getting back to my mission, my mission as a courier. A courier, I might add, who is protected by the Guildpact. To further impede me could and most likely will bring the wrath of the Guildpact down upon you—"

"Shut up," Golozar barked. He snarled a few words that were outside Crix's working Utvar vocabulary, and the whiplike cords tied to her wrists began to writhe like snakes. As she yelped in surprise the leather wrapped itself around her entire body of its own volition, pinning her arms to her sides and turning her short legs into a single trunk. As a final insult, a strap that she believe ended at her left ankle wrapped around her jaw like a sling and clamped her jaws together.

All right, she thought. *Now* I might be in trouble.

* * * * *

"What a charming surprise," Teysa said. "The weapon, I mean." She placed the loaded bam-stick on the table so that the business end pointed squarely at the goblin foreman's chest.

"A token, Baroness," the goblin said gruffly but with a veneer of diplomacy that showed he'd had more schooling than most. "A gift, but also a display of trust and goodwill to our allies in the Guild of Deals, the great Orzhov families, and their vast holdings."

The foreman of the Cauldron power project was a counterpart of Aradoz. Where the wageboss used what labor he could buy or steal wherever he could find it, the Izzet foreman oversaw his guild's most important presence in the township and only used loyal Izzet labor—usually goblins such as him—to do the job.

She hadn't expected trouble from the Izzet and didn't seem to be getting any from this particular goblin. But the foreman's veneer was just that—a veneer. Something was bothering him. The fact that Teysa had been expecting to sit across from the real Izzet power in Utvara had to be irritating to say the least.

"I accept this token and add the gratitude of my ancestors to my own," she said. "You begin our talk by giving me an immediate way to kill you. This, I feel, is an even greater token, one of respect. Respect for me is respect for the Karlov and the Orzhov. Nicely done, Foreman . . . ?"

"Babolax," the goblin said. He somehow gave each syllable more emphasis than the other, in that typical Izzet way. She wondered how they justified using as many syllables in their own names as the Great Dragon had in his. Izzet belief systems were, to an Orzhov, an obvious scam on most of the believers.

"How long have you been running things over there, Babolax?" Teysa said. She effortlessly mimicked the goblin's pronunciation, to his obvious pleasure.

"Seven months," the foreman said with pride. "Since old Fala-zavax had that accident."

"Who are your lieutenants? Shiftbosses, I think you call them?" Teysa asked.

"Dexawik runs days, Jybezax nights. A new fellow, Rawoniq, has been filling in for them and running the new half-and-again shifts we instituted in the last month," Babolax said.

"So, working hard, are you?" Teysa said.

"Very," the goblin agreed.

"Why, then, has your power output not increased appreciably since you added these half-and-again shifts, Babolax?" Teysa asked. "You wouldn't be hoarding it, would you? And where are these 'windmills' I've heard spoken of?"

Babolax looked at his feet. Had he looked more closely and been more familiar with magic common in the courts of Ravnica he might have recognized the crudely drawn verity circle around him, but Teysa could see the goblin was baffled at the compulsion to tell the truth that came over him.

"It's for, it's for . . . the power . . . it's for the magelord, Baroness," the foreman said, his eyes widening as he revealed what he'd obviously been ordered not to share.

"What does he want with the extra power?" Teysa said.

"That I don't know!" the goblin said. He bit the tip of his tongue but couldn't stop the facts from coming out. "He's the boss of bosses at the Cauldron, Baroness. Please, don't ask me any more. He'll kill me!"

"I doubt it," Teysa said. "You will deliver a message for me, Babolax?"

"Of course," the foreman said. "Just don't make me break my oath any more. I don't want to—I've seen what happens to people who disappoint him. I can't face that."

"Very good, then," Teysa said. She picked up the bam-stick with one hand, pressed the end to Babolax's forehead, and thumbed the firing stud. One loud, bright, pungent, but small explosion later, the former foreman's headless corpse slid sideways off of the seat and settled into a smoldering puddle.

"Get me the day and night shiftbosses, Melisk," Teysa said. "We'll work them into the parade later this evening, and they can deliver this message to Zomaj Hauc for me. The magelord needs to learn I don't deal with underlings and that his Cauldron exists at my pleasure, even if he has got contracts and agreements that say otherwise. I've never met a contract I couldn't turn upside down."

"Shall I remove the corpse?" Melisk asked.

"No, leave it there for now," Teysa said. "Should help speed things along with the rest of them." She turned to the mirror that hung on the wall directly to her right. "Don't you think so?" she said.

"Well done, child," the mirror said. "I am curious what that cut-rate pyromancer is keeping from us."

"What does the Obzedat say?" Teysa asked.

"Patience," the mirror replied. "You're doing well. Don't rush this."

"Easy for you to say," Teysa said. "Melisk, turn him around, will you? I don't like people watching over my shoulder. Even you, Uncle."

CHAPTER 6

The Gruul might once have been a guild, even a force to reckon with, but they now are a guild in name only. Scattered and scarred as they are, it would take a miracle to unite them now. The Guild-pact bound the rest of us, just as it fractured the clans. And yet you say there is no injustice in this document?

—Ambassador St. Bayul, address to the Guildpact Council
(22 Mokosh, 9997 Z.C.)

1 Cizarm 10012 Z.C.

Kos slept in for a few hours on the first of what Pivlic had promised would be several days off. He bathed, shaved, ate a boiled egg, and took a cup of ogrish coffee to the top of his private tower about an hour before noon. He was lucky that his home had running water. Not many in Utvara did, even after a relatively long period of reoccupation. This was the hour he set aside every day to look, in vain it seemed, for a missing friend.

He brought along a goblin spotting scope—a mundane instrument of crystal and wood that let one see great distances with a single eye—and settled with practiced ease into the canvas chair. Normally, he would have completed this ritual and headed in to work at the Imp Wing, but with the place closed (temporarily, of course) he could afford the time. Time to make sure there were still no angels on Ravnica, that is.

When he'd arrived with Pivlic twelve years ago, Kos had not expected to stay long. He'd bought this small tower—one of many that had survived the fallow period unscathed and relatively stable—from the Orzhov themselves with Pivlic as an intermediary.

It had cost most of his pension, but then at his age and with his assortment of old-man maladies, keeping those zinos in the bank did him little good. Kos had meant to sell the tower and move on after a few months, making what should have been a lot of zinos on the deal, but for a long time no buyers were interested. After a while the inertia of comfortable solitude and a good, steady salary had kicked in. He'd settled into the tower for good. In retrospect he couldn't think of anything else that gave him this view. He could search for Feather and Parhelion just as well from here as he could anywhere else in the world, provided he looked at the right time of day.

Kos checked the sun's position in the sky—still an hour before it would cross in front of the Schism and a sort of mirage effect that would give him a clear, 360-degree view of the world, from horizon to horizon. The Schism, Pivlic had told him, was a semi-failed experiment the Orzhov had hired the Izzet magelord Zomaj Hauc to perform. The Izzet had successfully triggered the thing, which wiped out all remaining life that hadn't made it to the Husk. As Pivlic explained it, the thing the Schism had been before it was the Schism—some kind of magic life-crusher—was then supposed to explode, burning away the dormant plague entirely. The thing never went off, however, and now Utvara faced the *kuga* every day. The Schism formed a bizarre spiderweb crack in the sky some five miles overhead as the sun drew closer.

For the few minutes the sun's orb passed behind the Schism every day, the fractured sky became clear as glass, and light from all over the plane somehow found its way to the old 'jek's spotting scope. Kos didn't understand it much beyond that. It was magic, never his favorite topic. With the help of the scope, Kos could even see the heads of three of the stone titans of Ravnica, even though they were almost halfway around the globe. As far as Kos knew, there was no place else he could see so much of his world and her sky at once, and that more than anything had kept him bound to Utvara.

As usual, today's hope failed to ignite, as scheduled. The sun passed behind the Schism, and Kos scanned the entire horizon in two minutes. His body was old, but his eyes were sharp as ever. His heart skipped a dangerous beat when he spotted movement against the ruined Husk but calmed as soon as he saw the telltale round shape of the *kuga mot,* floating in for an uncommon but not unheard of daytime appearance. As far as he knew, a daytime appearance was less ominous than a nighttime showing, but any appearance of the *kuga mot* tended to rile the Gruul a bit.

He made a mental note to make sure Trijiro had warned his people to stay clear of the township for a while. The glowing sphere of the *kuga mot*—"plague herald" in Utvar Gruul—floated upward into the glassy sky and faded from sight within seconds. The ghost, or apparition, or illusion, or whatever it was never stuck around for long. In Kos's experience, its reputation as an omen of good or ill was overrated. He'd seen it on several occasions and suffered no notable ill effects. Not even an increased heart rate.

Don't think about it, Kos, he told himself. That just leads to anxiety, and that—

Kos looked at his coffee, now two-thirds full, and dumped it out. Now why had he even made coffee? He couldn't handle it any more. The new arrivals had shaken him up, and so had the messenger bat Pivlic had sent that morning. He didn't mind an unexpected day off, but it bugged his still-keen lawman's instincts that he wasn't privy to whatever Pivlic and the new arrivals were no doubt discussing.

As the sun moved a few degrees past the Schism, the long-distance sight it granted Kos flickered and faded as well. He still had an excellent view of immediate Utvara, and turned the spotting scope on a few places that seemed to be magnets for disturbances.

There were the smoke and steam clouds over the Cauldron, the massive dome-shaped . . . thing that rested north of the township, looming over the flats and the Vitar Yescu. It resembled a domed mesa, but the mad assembly of tubes and ducts around its base also gave it a weird sort of root structure that constantly crackled with light. The Izzet who worked the power station weren't quite prisoners, but most lived there anyway. Kos had not been out to the place in all his time there. He'd never gotten an invitation and didn't feel like catching a fireball in the face for paying a friendly hello—even from here the scope revealed a pair of hydropyric weirds, their liquid bodies of pure flame leaving smoking footprints as they patrolled the station.

Pivlic knew plenty about the place, though, and had given him a simple, wojek-friendly version: The Cauldron was probably at one time some kind of arena but one that nobody could find in the history books. The Cauldron sat over a geothermic dome, burning its way up through layer after layer of Ravnican history, crushing buried architecture from below while occasionally rumbling the surface. The sky reservoirs that ringed the dome of the Cauldron drew water from the Ravnican air and poured it into the fire pits below, where pyromancers, hydromancers, and hundreds of goblin workers turned it into the energy that kept the township alive—and this still left plenty of water for the township itself too. Pivlic had tried to explain the technicalities, but Kos hadn't grasped most of the details. The steam-power angle made sense, but beyond that it became too arcane and academic, usually both at the same time. All Kos needed to understand was that the geothermic dome was power. Power for the glowposts, the water supply, temperature control, and most importantly keeping the Vitar Yescu healthy.

Kos understood geothermic domes, at least. He and his third wife had honeymooned at the northwest pole, where most of Ravnica's fresh water came from the reaction of fire and ice. It had been an appropriate honeymoon location, as it turned out.

The exhaust clouds the Cauldron cast sent whirling, foggy shadows over the Vitar Yescu. The giant tree, with its slender willowlike branches shimmering with pollen-laced white flowers that regularly fluttered off on the wind, had grown prodigiously in the time Kos had been in Utvara—so quickly that the Selesnyans had to dismantle at least three nearby structures to accommodate its bulk. The Conclave had built into the side of the tree's trunk, but it wasn't a living monastery like the Unity Tree that graced the Center of Ravnica. These were just a few lookouts and platforms where Selesnyan acolytes could bless the Vitar Yescu, which Kos guessed couldn't hurt. Though the tree took up more space these days, the area it protected hadn't grown with it. Kos didn't know why, and he didn't get many more invitations to the Vitar Yescu than he did to the Cauldron. He had plenty of contacts within the Conclave but hadn't seen any of those people for almost a decade. They were all back in the city.

Kos scanned the flats, that once-pristine surface now dotted with mining claims and wandering prospectors in bubble-headed sphere suits. He tracked the scope on up to the Husk and in the general direction of Trijiro's last known camp.

There was a small, smokeless fire and a few lookouts posted on jagged towers. A pair of pterro riders flapped overhead. Around the fire Kos could just make out the shape of a big human—Vor Golozar, from the look of it. Golozar was pacing before the fire, occasionally barking at other Gruul or in the direction of a lumpy object on the ground. A prisoner?

The Gruul had attacked the Orzhov lokopede caravan, hadn't they? Pivlic had told him that, anyway. Seemed eager to get the word out, in fact. So why hadn't Pivlic told him anything about a prisoner?

"Trijiro," Kos said aloud, "get home soon or someone's going to do something they'll regret." Silently, he added, and if he doesn't, what are *you* going to do about it, old man?

* * * * *

Even if her mouth hadn't been shut firmly by the magical bonds, Crix would have been unable to free herself. She had tried, of course. Ordinary leather should have burned away easily, but this was no ordinary leather. The magic of the living lashes was strong and resistant even to her abilities. She had to console herself with the fact that had she tried to free herself from Golozar earlier, she would certainly have failed. The Gruul didn't kid around when they bound their prisoners.

She wanted to study the lashes more closely, but her head was tied at the wrong angle to get a good look. She suspected they might not be leather at all but perhaps some kind of snake or worm. Intriguing, if frustrating.

Crix could always continue her studies in other ways. Her eyes had been blindfolded for much of the trip between the junk nephilim's deadfall—where Golozar had left it to burrow down into the ground in frustration—and the Gruul camp, but the bandit had quietly removed the blindfold once they arrived, if not the other bonds. For the last twenty hours or so, she'd been completely unable to sleep and barely able to close her eyes. The entire camp, all their daily activities, were laid out before the inquisitive goblin. And since none of them, even Golozar, seemed interested in speaking to her, she continued to study their language as well as their customs from afar.

The camp appeared to be home to some four to five hundred individuals. An accurate head count was stymied by the frequent departures and arrivals of small raiding parties that often shared members and wore heavy battle helmets that sometimes prevented proper identification. Not only that, but most of the tents and temporary homes were scattered in and around jagged, rocky ruins that didn't allow Crix the full view of the place, tied as she was to a post not far from a large central cooking fire she sincerely hoped wasn't for her. She somehow doubted it. From what she'd seen so far, these Gruul were nothing like the creatures that had attacked the lokopede. Those *had* been savage and definitely cannibalistic, as Crix could personally attest. But she hadn't seen any of *these* Gruul do anything like that.

And the mix of species! Crix had never seen anything quite like it. Centaurs, goblins, half-demons, ogres, trolls, a few elves, and of course humans—a lot of humans, but there always were, it seemed, no matter where Crix went. And that meant half-ogres, half-trolls, half-elves, quarter-everythings—humans always managed to get into the broader mix if you gave them enough time. There appeared to be nothing in the way of real cultural differences between the species. They were all Gruul, all spoke the barking Gruul language with a patois of Ravi thrown in, and they all gathered at the same time at dawn to pray with the same goblin priestess, at least the ones who weren't sharpening blades or pacing back and forth in front of her.

Not all the Gruul here were warriors. Far from it. Most of the ones she'd seen over the last day, night, and morning were parents and children attending to the daily activities that kept this small clan alive. The children, when they were not playing games or helping their parents, formed small hunting parties of their own and brought back game—rabbits; birds; fat, green lizards; and the like. Just before dawn on her first full day in the Gruul camp, one of the children bravely brought Crix a piece of roast rabbit and a skin of water. Crix thanked the boy—a young centaur—in the Gruul tongue. The youthful hunter and his friends seemed to find this absolutely hilarious.

She definitely needed to find someone with whom to practice this new language. Crix learned a couple of hours later that she'd mixed up the distressingly similar words for "thanks" and "flatulence" in one of her few stabs at speaking Gruul.

Though activity abounded in the camp, there seemed to be little in the way of central organization other than that priestess. There was no one leader to whom all deferred, at least none who seemed to be present. Different Gruul at different tents handed out food and water, others simply worked and lived. Leatherworkers and weavers made clothing, blankets, and baskets. Blacksmiths pounded away at hunks of metal that would almost certainly be weapons. Raiders returned, empty-handed in this case except for her. Golozar seemed to be the most important Gruul present, or at least the most feared by the others (if fear was the right word), but she could tell the others did not treat him as the real leader. In a tribal system like Gruul society, there had to be a chief, or at least a council of chiefs, running things. Crix wondered where that leadership was.

So immersed was Crix in the barking Gruul tongue that the sudden sound of a calm voice speaking lightly accented Ravi gave her a start. "Golozar, what is that doing here?" the centaur demanded as he ambled into the camp. The aging creature cocked his bearded chin at Crix and pointed. "Where did it come from?"

"Fell off the back of that lokopede Aun Yom's people hit, and we took it," the bandit growled. He switched to Gruul, which

Crix followed as best she could. "It is a goblin. Aun Yom left no quarter and refused to share the kill. We must talk about that, you and I."

"Later. I can see it is a goblin. Can you see it is a courier? The Gruul have enough enemies."

"So what is one more then? We tire of hiding from these interlopers. Utvara is ours, is it not? I tire of intrusion, greatest Zuriv."

"Zuriv. Zuriv. Greatest . . . shaman, I presume?" Crix whispered. "Greatest shaman-chief? Chief greatest priest?" She tried it in Gruul, then in Ravi, and ultimately decided to wait. He would no doubt speak to her directly soon enough.

"Aun Yom is bold, perhaps too bold, but until I speak to him, that is your problem. You want blood. Perhaps you will be allowed to challenge Aun Yom for his. But attack the township, and we will be through. The ghost-thieves will bring another plague bomb." Crix blinked. Had she translated that correctly?

"Ghost-thief?" she murmured. Did the chief mean the Izzet, the Orzhov, or neither?

Stranger perhaps was that they knew about the bomb. Well, she thought, gazing up at the Schism that hung high over the township, it *was* rather hard to miss the effects. And even if the members of this clan each had an overall shortened lifespan, they obviously had a spoken historical tradition. The Gruul did not strike her as especially stupid, despite their status as "primitives." They used bam-sticks easily enough. It seemed the Gruul were better educated than most of the Izzet, at least most of her goblin undercolloquy, on the subject of Utvara. Which made sense, she had to admit. She stifled a cough and wondered if her throat was dry or if this was the *kuga* beginning to work its way around her temporary defenses. And speaking of education, she wondered if perhaps this centaur had been the one to teach Golozar his Ravi.

"They cannot do that again," the bandit Golozar said. "Their own people are here now, in that town. They would never—"

"You think this number matters to them at all? It is a large world, Vor Golozar, and you have not seen as much of it as you like to think. Of course they would sacrifice this town if we caused them enough trouble. This small alliance is fragile and rare among our people. Even people like Aun Yom. This complaining is not like you. It does not befit a raid captain."

"He and his sister have gone mad, Greatest One," Golozar said. "The viciousness of their attack—it humbled me. We have been too long at bay here in this camp. We are not farmers or hunters. We are raiders. We take what we please! We are Utvar Gruul, Trijiro! What would you have us be?"

"So you hope to be the same as he?" The centaur stamped a hoof. "Impulsive, foolish, and suicidal? If you do not slay Aun Yom, my friend, the ghost-thieves and their servants will. I've received a warning. Now is not the time to increase our raids. Give these newcomers the chance to show us their colors and we will then decide what to do. If there is an attack to be led on the township, you will lead it, I promise you. But not now."

"This warning—it is from your 'trusted friend' who works for the ghost-thieves, Zuriv?"

"Kos is a good man, and there aren't many in that town," the centaur said. "If he says we should lie low, we should lie low. If this clan does not stay united, the greater clans will move in. We must remain strong. Borborygmos is ultimately the only enemy we should truly worry about, and a fractured Utvar Gruul would only serve him should we draw his notice. I have other sources of information, Golozar, beyond that old lawman. The cyclops king is surely aware of the treasures of the flats, and if he ever chose to go after them, we would be crushed without unity."

"Trijiro—" Golozar said.

"Zuriv Trijiro," the centaur said firmly. "And your zuriv wants to maintain peaceful relations with our neighbors, the fire-takers. Only a fool makes an enemy of the entire world." All right, Crix thought. The fire-takers had to be the Izzet, which would make the ghost-thieves the Orzhov. If the shroud fit. . . .

"And how do you propose we do that?" Golozar demanded. "Send another raiding party to be enslaved in their fire pits? An envoy for their weirds to burn alive?"

"Do not push your luck," the centaur said. "If you want to see someone burned alive, I can arrange that for you. But I speak of a simple, friendly delivery. I want you to deliver something. To the Cauldron."

The bandit bowed his head, seething but humbled before the centaur, who obviously had power Crix had not yet seen if he could so easily cow the brutish raid-captain. "You are the zuriv," he said.

As she listened intently to the bandit, flash-interpreting his words with the practiced, flexible mind of an able multilinguist, Crix realized several seconds had passed, and the old centaur had not answered.

Probably because he was staring right at her with a somewhat bemused but mildly irritated expression.

"I would have you watch your tongue," the centaur Trijiro said without losing eye contact with the goblin. "That one is listening more closely than you think."

Crix smiled tentatively, the smile of a cornered criminal found with a bloody knife, a dead body, and all the loot. She would have raised a hand in greeting had they not been tied behind her back.

"Hail to the . . . chief?" she ventured in Gruul.

"Would you prefer we speak your language, Izzet?" Trijiro said.

"If you wouldn't mind, though I would enjoy a few attempts at conversation in your own, if you have the time later," Crix said. "Are you in charge here, Mr. Trijiro?"

"How do you know our language, creature?" Golozar demanded in accented, snarling Ravi.

"I could ask you the same thing," Crix said, feeling curiously unintimidated.

"Release this goblin," Trijiro said.

"Greatest One—"

"Now, raid-captain. Unless you wish to challenge me?"

"No good will come of this. It was a curiosity. Now I should kill it."

"I prefer 'her,' if you don't mind," Crix said.

The centaur turned back to her as the ogrelike human bandit moved to the post to which Crix had been bound. He whispered a few words similar to an ancient Troll dialect from the Towerscar period, and her bindings—her constant nemeses for more than twenty-four hours—fell away to the ground and coiled themselves obediently. Golozar came around the post to pick up the lashes but stopped at a cough from Trijiro. Golozar scowled and instead offered the goblin a hand up.

"Thank you," Crix managed. Every muscle she had was in agony, but she forced herself to stand all the same. She channeled a bit of power from her arm into her bloodstream to improve her circulation and relax her cramped joints. "So you are in charge here."

"I am the one others go to for advice," the old centaur said. "I speak for this clan, and the others trust my wisdom in other matters. And you are a courier for," Trijiro looked her up and down, "Zomaj Hauc, of course. I recognize that brand on your ear and the tattoo work."

"I do have the honor of serving the great magelord Zomaj Hauc in this capacity, yes," Crix said. "I have a message to deliver to the Cauldron, and I fear I'm running out of time. Will you allow me passage?"

"I'll do better than that," the centaur said with a conspiratorial smile. "Our friend Golozar just volunteered to guide you there."

CHAPTER 7

The touch of the Firemind is not granted lightly. Have I been disappointed in some of those who accepted it? Of course. But without disappointment, there is no pride in those who exceed even my expectations. Next question, mortal.

—Niv-Mizzet, last recorded public statement
(4 Paujal 7425 Z.C.)

2 CIZARM 10012 Z.C.

Zomaj Hauc had many ways to get around, but his personal flight sphere was definitely his favorite. The forged mizzium shell, the belching flame-pods, the smooth lines of the controls, all had been personally designed by the magelord and assembled by his hands. No other being had ever sat inside the sphere's cockpit in flight or touched the interior, and except for power maintenance performed by his handpicked engineers, no other being *ever* made contact with the *Pyraquin.*

Unfortunately, this trip hadn't been as pleasant as most. The words of the Great Dragon still echoed in his mind, words that drove him to pour just a little more pyromana into the pods as he cleared a flock of wild birds. The avians were incinerated instantly, but Hauc could not even take joy in that simple pleasure. Niv-Mizzet was displeased, and for the dragon lord of the Izzet to take enough interest in the mortal world to show displeasure was a rare thing indeed. To be the object of that displeasure was terrifying, and Hauc doubted many magelords had ever weathered such fury and lived.

The plan was not the problem. It was the execution—several executions, actually—which had slowed down production at the

Cauldron while Hauc had been engaged in other matters, matters which, if Niv-Mizzet knew of them, might cause even further displeasure. Hauc knew he had pushed the dragon's patience to the limit and was grateful that the magic of his secret Orzhov contact kept their meetings from the dragon's attention. The other Orzhov, however, were causing trouble for him. This new Utvara baroness had callously murdered the foreman of the work crews—not truly any great loss. It hurt morale, though, which hurt production. The old goblin had been popular, and goblins with low morale worked slowly. Then an entire work crew stationed at a remote power node was butchered by roving Gruul.

Then there was the missing messenger. Niv-Mizzet knew nothing about Crix and his other secretly enhanced servants, and Hauc aimed to keep it that way. But it was difficult. The dragon's gift gave Niv-Mizzet ways to find out secrets, if he wanted to bother. That was why Hauc had sent the courier in the first place: to keep the information her message contained a secret. The Orzhov were just supposed to grab her and bring her to him, but no, they'd managed to lose her entirely.

The tragedy was that had he known what Hauc really wanted to do, Niv-Mizzet might have gone along willingly. But without certainty of that fact, Hauc hadn't dared bring him in on the plan. It was not easy being as brilliant as Zomaj Hauc.

Niv-Mizzet's displeasure had been burning a long time, ever since the mana-compression bomb had formed the Schism instead of wiping Utvara from the face of Ravnica. Hauc had convinced the dragon that the process was a lengthy one, and the dragon had accepted that. And indeed it was, though the result might end up being different than the dragon lord expected. The Schism would not exist forever, indeed, at the rate it was absorbing ectoplasma and other forms of energy, it might not last the week. Hauc had to find the messenger before then or Hauc's chance for real power on Ravnica would be forever lost.

Zomaj Hauc scowled as he broke through the cloud cover and bright sunlight streamed through invizomizzium plating. It was stressful deceiving the most powerful being in the world, but he must not crack under that stress. The rewards would be far too great.

There was no other option now. He had to risk communication with his Orzhov contact before he reached the Cauldron, where Niv-Mizzet would have more eyes on him. The flight sphere was Hauc's favorite not because of the freedom it allowed or the beauty of its design. It was the privacy. The Firemind could do many things, but only with extreme effort and concentration could Niv-Mizzet's fiery attentions pierce the flameproof substance. If he focused, of course he could do it. But if that happened Hauc would have a little warning. Not much, but enough to switch to less traitorous matters than what he had planned.

Traitor. They would call him a traitor for what he was doing, when he succeeded. In time, they would learn the truth. What he was going to do, he did for the good of the plane as well as the good—and power—of Zomaj Hauc.

The magelord turned a blue crystal dial on the control board, and a glass cylinder mounted next to it hummed to life. In the air above the cylinder a silvery-blue vertical pane appeared, like a tiny magical window made of water. Hauc's *Pyraquin* was the first flight sphere to use this Hauc-designed improvement over the old voice-only crystals, but they were now common within his colloquy, and he was looking into providing them for others in the guild as well—provided those others could afford them.

The face of a white mask appeared in the placid, vertical pool, and a voice sent visible ripples out from the center of the liquid-mana surface.

"What is it?" the mask demanded. "This is not the best time."

"I need a favor," Hauc said. "I've lost something important, and I think you can get it for me."

"The new baroness is wondering where you've been," the mask said. "I do not believe she will overstep, but her ambition was unexpected. If you don't get back soon, she may begin to catch on. She's liable to go to the Cauldron herself."

"Can't be helped. Tell her I'll be back at the Cauldron in a few hours," Hauc said. "I will meet with her if she wishes, wherever she wishes. If she wants to leave instructions, contact Chief Observer Vazozav, and ask her to please refrain from shooting him if she would be so kind. Do not let her get there before I do."

"Fine, a few hours," the mask replied. "Now tell me what you've lost."

* * * * *

"Are you sure we're not lost?" Crix asked the burly leader of the small band. The party of five Gruul and one nervous Izzet courier picked their way around a rotted, rusting tower that had fallen over at some point—recently, from the look of the cracks in the caked rust—and now effectively blocked what little path she'd been able to find.

"Of course I'm not lost," Golozar said in his accented Ravi, then barked to the others in Gruul. "Find a way around this. Now."

"I can understand you, you know," Crix said, sitting down on a hunk of rubble that seemed to be the least dangerous element of the surrounding landscape. "Was this unexpected? It looks fresh."

"What makes you say that?" the Gruul bandit said.

"Just look at it," Crix said, "It looks like a tree blown over in the wind. I thought you knew this country around the Husk. Maybe that nephilim of yours is still after us. You said yourself it was not dead."

"As far as I'm concerned, you're still my prisoner until we deliver you to the Cauldron," Golozar said with finality. "The nephilim will do what the nephilim do, and if they do it I will deal with it. Just sit there, would you?" He directed the two viashino in the party around the "root ball" of the toppled structure to see if they could find a safe path, then sent the other two—both big, ogrelike humans like him—to see if there was any way to clear the other side by walking under the gap between it and what passed for ground in these hills. Golozar himself scanned the higher hills behind them, looking for something but giving no indication to Crix exactly what.

She settled in to wait. The goblin was surprised that they had not encountered any large wildlife in the Husk yet. She'd heard that many creatures made their homes here and had hoped to catch a look at a saurian or two—from a distance, if possible. So far there had been only tiny lizards, dog-sized beetles, a few scraggly birds, and of course the Gruul themselves. The lack of large game did explain the general thinness of the Utvar Gruul. Golozar was big, but he had a wiriness to him that made him look poorly fed. The fires she'd seen had not been cooking anything large—game birds, rabbits, even a few rats. These people were in bad shape, and Crix couldn't help but feel sympathy for them even after the way she'd been treated.

Crix coughed, something that had become more frequent since they'd left the camp. Her inoculation seemed to be holding, but with raw exposure to the *kuga* she wasn't sure how long it would be before she began to develop symptoms. The fungus that clung to the Gruul was not something she was quite ready to try out, but if they continued to make excruciatingly slow progress she might have to.

Crix caught Golozar scanning the hills again and finally asked, "What are you looking for?"

Golozar scowled at her and shrugged. "You understand our language, so you can probably guess. No, it is not the nephilim, before you suggest it. But I think there may be another group tracking us."

"Would that be this Aun Yom character I heard you and that old centaur fellow talking about?" Crix said. She wasn't particularly nervous, but the look that passed over Golozar's lantern-jawed face when she said the name of the other bandit raider made her reconsider whether she should be a bit more nervous.

"It may be," Golozar said. "Though to track another raiding party, one from your own clan, is unheard of."

"Forgive me, I'm a mere courier. Why is that unheard of?"

"You ask questions like an ambitious Haazda," Golozar replied.

"A curious courier," the goblin said. "I'm not going to be delivering messages my whole life, you know."

"Curious courier, you're not afraid of me, are you?" Golozar said, switching gears. Crix considered the question. The hulking human, scarlet-skinned and adorned with ritual marks, was indeed intimidating. The loaded bam-stick slung on his back and the heavy, hooked blade sword on his waist made it clear he could and would kill, if he wished. And yet. . . .

"No, not really," Crix said. "I think you are a—" she searched for the right words, and finally settled on two simple ones. "I think you are a good man. I think you're cautious. I *know* you're more educated than the rest of them, though I'm not sure how. And I am glad you agreed to get me to the Cauldron. I don't think you're out here just to kill me. Why else would you all be working on finding a path? If you meant me harm, you could slaughter me here and tell your zuriv—that's some kind of priest-chieftain, right?—you could tell your zuriv I fell through a rusted hole. Seems to be a common enough occurrence. But you haven't done that. So no, I don't fear you."

"Figures," the Gruul said, and his scowl remained despite a creeping smirk threatening to break on one side of his mouth. "You should learn to fear more, goblin. A healthy sense of terror is the only way you'll survive in the Husk."

"I don't exactly intend to settle down here," Crix said. "The goblins in your clan didn't seem to want anything to do with me."

"I doubt they even recognized you as a goblin," Golozar said. He turned over his shoulder to shout in Gruul at the men getting ready to knock aside a stone pillar that blocked the easiest path under the leaning tower. "Not that one! That's load-bearing, you idiots!" The two Gruul backed off from the pillar and exchanged mutually accusatory looks.

Crix looked down at her own body, her arms and legs, and wondered whether Golozar was right. Hauc had taken her as an infant, and his experiments had given her greater intelligence than the average goblin, along with other hidden powers—the ones that she still didn't have Hauc's permission to use. But did she really look that different?

It was a discomfiting idea, so she focused on the matter at hand.

"Golozar, no offense, but you are what they'd call 'well-spoken' in the city. Is that where you were schooled? Your Ravi is sharp."

"And your Gruul is already starting to bother me," Golozar said. His eyes stopped tracking along the skyline, and he squinted against the light. "It's Aun Yom, all right. Strange, it's hard to make him out against the sun."

Crix stood and looked in the same direction, but all she got was a ray of sunlight in both eyes for her trouble. She blinked and cocked her ears and thought she could make out the clack of a piece of gravel rolling down a slope and a couple of shuffling footsteps where Golozar said this Aun Yom—the one who had apparently launched the attack on the Orzhov lokopede, sending Crix into Golozar's clutches—stood. As she tried to focus her eyes despite the glare, her ears picked up another distant noise that soon drowned out whatever sounds Aun Yom's group was making. It was a harmonic whistling sound, increasing in pitch every millisecond and growing in volume just as quickly. It was a sound Crix recognized immediately, and she smiled even as she had to put a palm before either ear to prevent the noise from causing her physical pain.

Zomaj Hauc's personal flight sphere, the *Pyraquin,* shot over the crest of the Husk and, for the briefest of moments, blocked out the sun. Just as the vessel cleared the ridge, Crix saw movement when the sun was blotted out—at least a dozen Gruul, pale and hungry looking. They ducked in surprise. A few scattered. They were perhaps a half mile away. The one that had to be Aun Yom never moved except to incline his head slightly and look straight at Crix. She took an involuntary step backward.

Golozar tensed but did not run, nor did his underlings, but like Crix, they followed the streaking *Pyraquin* as it left a glowing vapor trail in the sky overhead. It was a wondrous sight, and for the Gruul it was obviously rare. Crix wasn't much of an alchemical engineering enthusiast—her studies tended more toward the sociological, symbolic kinds of fire and ice—yet she still marveled at the magelord's personal coach. Unlike the smaller observospheres upon which the design was based, the *Pyraquin*'s entire frame and triple hull was pure, dragon-forged invizomizzium, which gave Zomaj Hauc a clear view at any time he wished. The sphere, which had an inner diameter of twenty-five paces and an outer diameter of thirty, carried a sextet of underslung, lift-providing belly-bursters and Hauc-designed megapyromanic flame-pods, just one of which could have moved a single observosphere around Ravnica five times without needing additional fuel.

The *Pyraquin* disappeared into a fog bank that had yet to burn off of the flats this morning. Before it occurred to Crix that perhaps she should have tried to signal the magelord, the vessel cracked the sound barrier and sent a staggering shockwave that shook the rusted, leaning tower that blocked their way with a palpable fist of sonic energy.

"Hey, get out of there!" Crix shouted at the two Gruul still trying to clear a path beneath the tower. "That tower can't take the—"

"They can't understand you!" Golozar shouted and started to run toward the Gruul, waving them back. "Get back, all of you!" the bandit shouted in Gruul. The two viashino on the other side had their hands full getting away from a rapidly widening gap in the ground at the tower's tilted base, but they were agile, and Crix couldn't get to them anyway. She charged after Golozar. She whispered as loudly as she could in Gruul and did her best to say, "Quiet! It's not fallen yet! Not too much shouting! No heavy footsteps!"

It must have been close enough because all the Gruul shut their mouths and Golozar slowed, then stopped. The tower was still humming and creaking like a listing sailing ship, and small fractures were appearing in the rust and calcified growth that had kept it precariously in place. The two Gruul beneath it looked upward, then at Golozar. The raid captain raised a hand, palm out. *Stop.* Two fingers up, then a slash. Index finger up, then crooked toward palm. *Not two. One at a time.*

They might have made it if one of the viashino hadn't been

forced to leap over the new fissure. The reptilian kicked a hunk of metallic stone against the tower's rusted medal frame, and it rang like a gong.

That was all it took for the fractured mishmash keeping the leaning structure in place to crumble away, and it collapsed with a final, resounding crunch that knocked Crix and Golozar onto their backs. Before the goblin went over she had a nauseatingly good look at the two humans crushed to a pulp beneath the tower, and once she struck the iron ground her ears could make out the rapidly descending screeches of both viashino plummeting into an underground cavern that had opened to the sky. In seconds, their group of six had been cut to two.

Despite a lifetime of service and devotion to Zomaj Hauc, an angry and rebellious voice in the back of her head—an ancient goblin voice—wanted to find the magelord and burn his skin off. She wondered if the plague was beginning to dig into her mind, for such thoughts were punishable by immolation.

* * * * *

Teysa awoke with the peculiar sensation she'd been engulfed, ever so briefly, in flames. When it passed, she realized with sudden dread that it had been more of an icy feeling of numbness. She'd had another spell and had fallen in a position that made her legs more useless than usual, one arm pinned beneath her side, and her neck wouldn't feel right for weeks.

At least she'd been alone. Or had she? With her one useful limb she pulled herself up by the edge of the table, then remained leaning there, willing her circulation to return. What had she been doing before it happened?

She'd been talking to Melisk, making arrangements to go

personally meet a few of the local guild reps who hadn't seen fit to accept her gracious invitation in a timely manner—the first acolyte, who had stormed out after being put off the day before; the centaur who was supposed to be the local leader of a beggars collective (which probably meant Gruul connections); and Zomaj Hauc, who'd dared to send an underling instead of coming to meet her himself. Along the way she intended to check in on the site where her new mansion was to be and perhaps make some surprise appearances just to let townsfolk know she didn't intend to stay in the Imp Wing permanently.

Then . . . Melisk had gone, hadn't he? And the mirror, it had been moved to the adjoining antechamber in what was rapidly becoming her floor of the Imp Wing. Yes. They'd gone. No one had been here. No one had seen her. She was alone, because. . . .

Teysa could have kicked herself if her legs had been operational. While going over recent events, she'd been staring at her toppled bowl of soup as it dried on the table and just hadn't brought it into focus. Yes. She'd been eating when another of her less-than-endearing "gifts" of the Orzhov blood had kicked in. Or more precisely, knocked her out.

Back in the city, Teysa had possessed access to a steady supply of pharmacological agents prescribed by her personal Simic physicians. There'd been a huge supply on the lokopede, but the lokopede and everything on it had been burned. They'd made their escape on foot.

Yes. They'd walked the rest of the way. All the way to the Imp Wing. That was what she remembered.

So why didn't that feel any truer than the idea she'd been alone eating soup?

It had to be the missing medication. She'd been taking it to stem the narcolepsy for years. Obviously, her body had become acclimated to it. The lack of it was making her distrust her own memory.

All right, add a visit to that Simic doctor too. Should have brought that up yesterday. Surely he'll have something to replace what was lost.

Lost. The lokopede had been lost. Of course it had. She remembered it going up in flames and the Gruul tearing apart what was left as they fled.

Teysa shook her head, which helped straighten out her neck a bit. She stood unsteadily and leaned one hip against the table as she tapped one of the black stones set in her wrist. A few seconds later a door swung aside and Melisk ducked into the room. The tall attendant was not having an easy time with the imp's doorframes and had a bruise over one eye to prove it.

"Yes, Baroness," Melisk said. "Shall I have the imp send up someone to tidy the room? Bring you some more food?"

"You don't seem surprised to see this mess," Teysa said. "Why?"

"This is the third spell you've suffered since our arrival, my lady," Melisk said. "It seemed apparent what had happened. I'm sorry. Are you injured?"

"No, I'm just—No," Teysa said.

"It is fortuitous you summoned me. I was about to request entry," Melisk said, oblivious to her concerns. "I have received word from Zomaj Hauc."

"About time," Teysa said. "Where's that magelord been?"

"In an audience with the dragon, or so he claims," Melisk said. "He apologizes for not meeting you sooner and wishes to meet you either here or at the Cauldron at your earliest convenience. There is also another small matter he hopes we may be able to assist him with."

"He wants my assistance?" Teysa asked incredulously. "He's

pushing the limits of my patience as it is. I assume you turned him down?" Her mind was already feeling sharper, focusing on Hauc.

"No, my lady," Melisk said. "I thought you might be interested in helping for different reasons."

"Explain," Teysa said, starting to pace, working the kinks out of her leg.

"He's lost a messenger," Melisk said, "a messenger who, I'm told, carries part of a spell that will bring the Cauldron up to peak efficiency."

"Why does this messenger carry this spell? Why doesn't the magelord have it himself?" Teysa asked. "This defies logic."

"Logic is not necessarily the Izzet way," Melisk said magnanimously. "It is custom, apparently, to use protected couriers in this way to keep secrets from other magelords. It's their way," Melisk said. "They are a paranoid, competitive guild. It does not surprise me that ambition drives them this far. Curious, however, that the courier was not better protected."

"What do you mean?" Teysa asked.

"She was traveling alone," Melisk said. "Hauc said he had no reason to believe she could possibly come to harm on an Orzhov lokopede."

"Loko—Oh, no," Teysa said. "The Gruul nabbed her on the train? After they killed Uncle?"

"Yes," Melisk said, "after the Gruul killed Uncle."

A moment of dizziness washed over Teysa and she put a palm to her brow.

"Are you all right, Baroness?" Melisk asked.

"Fine," Teysa said. "So you're saying . . . you're saying . . ."

"I am saying," the attendant replied, "that she is still out there, in the hands of the Gruul, and that she holds a crucial component to the entire Cauldron project."

"But the Cauldron project is already running!" Teysa said. "Why don't I trust any of this?"

"It keeps this township going, but there is not enough to feed the Vitar Yescu or to power the devices that should spread the pollen around the area. If this town is ever to become a new city of Utvara rather than a mere township—there are many more things to do," Melisk said. "The population here now is largely transient, with few true settlements. But I'm digressing."

"You certainly are," Teysa agreed. "The Vitar Yescu may not be needed if that vedalken doctor manages to come up with something, but I guess it doesn't hurt to be prepared. I'd rather the Selesnyans weren't here at all, but—but—" She felt faint for a moment again, then it passed. "What's the bottom line?" Damn this dizziness, which was already threatening to become a full-on headache. A spell right now would have been a blessing but none came.

"We lost the goblin, so Hauc says the goblin is our responsibility."

"Is it?"

"Izzet?"

"Is. It. The goblin. Is it our responsibility, Melisk?"

"Surely there could be some way to legally maneuver around it," the attendant said, "though it might be just as useful to help. We all want the township to become a city, do we not?"

"Right," Teysa said, still a little dizzy. "So how do we do it? I've already sent for more staff, but they're at least a week away. Send the brothers?"

"I doubt they have the mental capacity to succeed in such a job," Melisk said. "They are just as likely to kill the goblin we send them to save."

"What about the Gruul?" Teysa said. "Maybe we can negotiate there."

"That is possible," Melisk said. "There is a leader, one whose name has reached my ears over the last day, called Aun Yom. He is something of a rebel and is likely the one who raided our caravan and . . . killed Uncle."

"Killed—No," Teysa said. "We'll find another way. Bring Pivlic up here and we'll see about—"

There was a light knock on another door, the one that led to the hall connecting her to the rest of Pivlic's place. Melisk strode to the door and slid aside the lookout panel. He pulled back as a wrinkled, leathery, black face filled the empty space with a toothy grin.

"My la—Baroness!" Pivlic said over Melisk's shoulder. "You must let me in. I have urgent news!"

"Let him in, Melisk," Teysa said, wishing she'd gotten around to cleaning up the soup. She unfurled a silk napkin and laid it over the bowl, then positioned herself on the other side of the table, standing as steadily as she could.

Melisk opened the door to reveal not just the imp, flapping impatiently in the air, but the old man Pivlic employed as his chief of security. Teysa had only seen him once, two nights ago, but she didn't trust the way the fellow scanned the room in an instant. He was entirely too attentive. Probably a former wojek. He had the bearing of a real lawman—not one of those useless Haazda.

"Well?" Teysa said. "Are you coming in?"

"Yes," the imp said. He prodded the old human, whose dark brown skin was nearly as wrinkled as Pivlic's, to step forward, which the security chief did with obvious reluctance. "Go on, Kos. Tell her what you saw."

"Kos?" Teysa asked, now alert. "Agrus Kos?"

The old man heaved a sigh when she repeated his name. "Yes," he said, eyes still turned down to his feet like a truant schoolboy. "The very same."

"My uncle told me he saw you arrest a mythical vampire, Kos," Teysa said. "Is it true?"

"Your Uncle? I—Yes, I suppose it's true," Kos replied. "Except the 'mythical' part. That vampire was real." He finally looked up to meet her eye to eye, and Teysa was struck by the depth of those eyes. Kos himself was an old man, but whatever he'd seen over the course of his life had rendered his eyes positively ancient. "It's not something I like to talk about, Baroness."

"Nor is it the reason you're here, I'm sure," Teysa said as Pivlic hopped impatiently from foot to foot. "What, pray tell, is?"

"There's some trouble in the Husk," Kos said. "I think the Gruul took a prisoner from your caravan. Is anyone missing?"

Teysa shot Melisk a glance. The attendant's eyebrow arched, but otherwise he didn't respond.

"As a matter of fact, Agrus Kos, there is someone missing," Teysa said. "Tell me more."

CHAPTER 8

The Utvara Flats are not to be traveled lightly. The Husk is not to be traveled at all, but if you do for Krokt's sake stick to the roads.

     —M. Pivlichinos, *Utvara: A Visitor's Guide* (10004 Z.C.)

2 Cizarm 10012 Z.C.

Deep beneath the towers of the Orzhov mansion district, the Obzedat was in conference. The Obzedat was always in conference, but today they conferred with vigor and argument.

"This had better work."

"It will work."

"You are on probation. If you fail in this, you will die."

"I already died."

"For good this time. We did not make this pact without trepidation, and you were trusted—"

"And that trust, my friends, had not been misplaced. You wanted a secret pact. It is secret. Our hot-tempered ally is content that things are going as they should. My niece is more than capable enough to manage, and she won't get in the way when the agreement is fulfilled."

"Her mind is not her own."

"Untrue. She just doesn't know what she doesn't need to know."

"The repercussions will extend to your entire family if we default on this agreement. The dragon drives a hard bargain, even with us."

"I know. But think of the rewards that will extend to my family—all our families—when we succeed."

"We will wait and see."

"That's all I ask."

* * * * *

"Well I certainly feel ridiculous," Pivlic said. "This is no job for a successful and prominent merchant."

"Hard for me to say at the moment, but I imagine you do look ridiculous," Kos said. He gripped the reins of the hearty Utvaran dromad and gave the beast a mild kick to the flanks that brought it from a walk to a trot. Its hooves clopped along against the hard stone ground, and it snorted now and again. The dromad's thick legs couldn't possibly be getting tired yet, but he didn't want to push it too hard. He scratched the dromad on the back of the neck, ruffling its bushy mane. "And I don't know why it had to be the two of us either." This was not entirely true, nor was it entirely true that Kos had to be coerced. Odds were, if Teysa Karlov had not sent them on this journey, he would have attempted it himself. He had the sneaking suspicion that the new baroness meant the Gruul harm, and while Kos was no longer the idealist he once was, he could not bring himself to allow a slaughter to happen that he could prevent. If they could retrieve the messenger themselves, the Gruul might be allowed to go about their lives. His conscience, what remained of it, demanded that he try.

"Oh, I know why, but I don't have to like it. You haven't been an Orzhov long enough, my friend. When the baroness asks, we go. It wasn't like she was allowing me to open my doors anyway. Ow!" Pivlic said, and Kos felt him try to shift in the saddle without letting go of the old wojek's waist but with no luck. "Must we go so fast?"

"I'm not an Orzhov. Why does everyone keep saying that I am?

Besides, we're barely moving," Kos said, scanning the thoroughfare for the road that branched off into the flats, then up into the
Husk in the direction of Trijiro's camp. "It's going to get worse
before it gets better."

"You work for me, you're Orzhov enough," Pivlic said. He
sighed. "I should be flying."

"You're the one who wanted the full suit," Kos said. "At least
you were able to have a new one made. Mine still smells like wet
prospector. I think the former owner might have died in here."

"If this is leading to a request for a raise—"

"Pivlic, for this, I'm *getting* a raise, and you're setting me up
with a real pension."

"Ridiculous!" the imp said. "You already get paid most fairly,
my friend, and—"

"Had you going there for a second, didn't I?" Kos said. "Let's
say a bonus then."

"For what?" Pivlic objected. "You are my employee!"

"I don't know that riding into the Husk dromaback, with *you* for
company, qualifies as keeping the Imp Wing secure," Kos said.

"Actually," the imp said, and there was a flash as he summoned
Kos's employment contract, now more than twelve years old.
"You are not only responsible for the Imp Wing but for my own
personal safety."

"What?" Kos said and considered bringing the dromad to a
halt. The beast was beginning to build up steam, muscles tense
beneath the crusts of antigen fungus embedded in its hide, its
thick, heavy tail now sticking straight out. He'd bought the beast
from the Utvar Gruul, who were the main source of dromads, as
the valley-raised dromads came with their own antigen fungus.
"Where does it say that?"

"You should look more closely at what you sign," Pivlic said.

"But fear not. I have not abused your services before, I'm sure even you would agree, and I will personally see to it that you get a bonus. It may take a while for the paperwork to go through, you understand." There was another flash and the contract vanished from the corner of Kos's eye.

After a few moments of silence, the gregarious imp could not help but resume the conversation. "Well, this is not how I expected to spend today."

"I can't believe either one of us is out here," Kos said. "I must be out of my mind."

"Admit it, you are bored," Pivlic said. "I, on the other hand, am beholden to a higher power."

"That girl?"

"That 'girl' has more power in her little finger—real power, power over beings that has nothing to do with magic—than I ever will have," Pivlic said, "by right of her birth and of course by her position. She has the blood."

"Orzhov blood?" Kos said. "Explains that leg of hers."

"Yes," Pivlic said. "But I would not recommend asking her about it."

"Wouldn't think of it," Kos said.

The thoroughfare began to slope downward as they rode past the Vitar Yescu, around the cluster of stalls and huts that made up the bazaar, and out of the township proper. They veered east on the path to skirt the Cauldron, there was no need to draw any more attention to themselves. An old man and an imp, both armed with swords and fully loaded bam-sticks across their backs, did not make the most likely prospectors in any case. To go near the Cauldron was such unprospectorlike behavior that they'd be immediately spotted. Kos wasn't sure that was such a bad thing at first—weren't they helping the magelord out here?—until Pivlic reminded him that it was very unlikely the guard weirds, patrol drake, and heavily armored defenders that ringed the power station would think to check with Zomaj Hauc before taking out a couple of foolish trespassers. To reach their destination, the stretch of Husk known as the Huskvold, they'd first have to cross through the flats and past several different mining claims.

The dromad was strong and sturdy and seemed to take to the pair of strange riders easily enough. Kos was no riding expert, but in his twelve years in Utvara—and during the brief period of his wojek tenure that the Tenth had experimented with mounted dromaback patrols—he'd picked up enough to be capable, and he hoped the dromad sensed that. But capable rider or not, prospectors tended to get defensive when people got too close to their claims. The flats were a treasure trove waiting to be uncovered, but those who found specific access points under the surface guarded them as jealously as the Izzet protected their Cauldron. To say nothing of the Husk, which was almost as dangerous as the Gruul who inhabited it—filled with rusty, jagged sinkholes; chunks of towering metal that could topple in a strong wind; hideous subterranean monsters; and of course the *kuga* plague.

"What about them?" Kos asked, jerking a thumb over one shoulder at the pair of thrulls that bounded along a few paces behind them on Kos's right side. "Why are they here?"

"The Grugg brothers are the Baroness's personal servants, bodyguards, and all-around lackeys," Pivlic said.

"Yes, but why are they here?" Kos said. "We can handle this."

"That's brave of you to say, my friend, but I for one admit I don't mind their tagging along. And don't worry about them—thrulls can survive more than you'd think. The baroness told me that this one here, Bephel, had his head blown off by a Gruul bamshot. Now look at him."

Kos did look at Bephel, straining his neck to do so. Bephel was the one with the arrowhead skull and the viashinolike body, and he was indeed none the worse for wear. The other, Elbeph, was something like an ape crossed with a frog, hopping along on long arms and splayed hands while his dexterous feet picked at the teeth in his wide mouth.

"Just so long as they don't draw too much attention," Kos said. "Are they linked to the baroness somehow? Are they telepathic?"

"That I cannot say," Pivlic said.

"Cannot say or don't know?" Kos asked.

"I suspect there is something like what you describe, but the secrets of thrull control are not ones handed out, willy-nilly, to just any old faithful Orzhov servant," Pivlic said. His face, however, said, *Of course she can hear us. That's why they're here.*

"All right," Kos said. "Just wanted to know where we stand. Or ride, as the case may be."

They made it past the first few mining claims without major incident—fortunately there was enough open space between them that they didn't draw attention. After an hour of riding through the flats, however, the path grew narrower. Here, portions of the old surface had buckled, from heat or perhaps due to pressure released from the depths of the buried undercity. These ripples forced them to follow a trail that passed by a large mining operation guarded by a pair of ogre mercenaries in bulky miners' suits and several helmeted and armored swords-for-hire who probably didn't answer to any one guild. The mining rig itself was a contraption made from Izzet arcanery and Simic biomanalogical know-how, a half-living thing that aided the prospectors exploring the depths and also brought found loot and raw materials to the surface. The rig resembled a gigantic metal mosquito. The storage hut next to it reminded Kos of a giant egg sac.

As they drew closer, one of the ogres raised a halberd and roared.

"Intruder on the trail!"

Dromads were not known for their ability or willingness to walk backward. With the rough, rocky folds of the flats rising on either side of them, they had nowhere to go but forward. "Hold on, Pivlic. Gruggs! Follow us, and do not attack these miners! We're only trying to get past them!"

The prospectors were only doing what prospectors did. There was no reason to harm them, and Kos didn't intend to let anyone harm them on his behalf either. He would defend himself if necessary, but talking was not likely to help matters, and a direct attack would be both unprovoked and extremely foolish. They had to get through and get through fast, with a minimum of violence.

Kos kicked the dromad in the flanks and charged.

* * * * *

"Melisk?" Teysa said. "Do you believe those two can find Hauc's messenger?"

"Surely," the attendant said. "I consulted the sources, and made offerings and prayers. It was the right call. How could it be any other way, Baroness?"

"Don't patronize me, Melisk. We're far beyond that," Teysa said. "I wasn't asking for oracular pronouncements, just some advice."

"In that case, may I be honest?"

"Please do," Teysa said. "I'm not Uncle."

"We have few resources, and those two strike me as capable, at least the imp, and he vouches for the human as well. And you know, he *did* save the plane from Szadek's return, or so it's been said."

"He's so old, Melisk," Teysa said. "He looked like he might drop dead before they even get to the Husk."

"And the Grugg brothers are with them," Melisk said. "If Pivlic and Kos fail, there's always the more direct approach."

Teysa pinched her forehead between her thumb and finger, belying just a fraction of the stress she felt herself under. The Cauldron had to be up and running soon, very soon, or there would never be enough infrastructure in place to declare Utvara independent within a year. That power, energy, water—all of it was necessary. And either the Selesnyan tree would finish the plague—and she had her doubts about that—or Dr. Nebun would come up with something. Surely it would work.

If only she could get rid of this headache. She sifted through the sheaves of parchment on her desk and decided sitting here waiting for news was probably not going to do her headache, or anything else, any good. Maybe she should check in with the doctor, too, as well as those who had spurned her summons.

"Melisk," she said, "summon Phleeb from his guard post and seal up the mirror room. We're going for a stroll."

"A stroll?" Melisk said.

"Yes," Teysa said. "It's time I got to know a few more of the locals."

"Certainly," Melisk said, but a touch of annoyance crept into his voice. That annoyance was nothing compared to what flared in Teysa at that moment. She'd been dragged from her practice to this place, and she intended to make her fortune here. She'd gotten over that. She would use her taj assassins, held in reserve until now, to wipe out these Gruul once Hauc's courier turned up. To do otherwise risked the almost certain death of that messenger. The taj were thorough. And soon Hauc's Cauldron would bring in enough power to make Utvara into a city. But she'd also been in close quarters with the attendant for weeks on end, first on the lokopede, now here. And for reasons she couldn't quite place, she wanted to be out from under his steely gaze for a few hours. Maybe she just needed a break, but there was something in those black eyes that gave her pause, ever so briefly.

"On second thought," Teysa said, "I'd appreciate it if you could organize this paperwork for me, and while you're at it, have Phleeb poke through Pivlic's stores and prepare something decent for us to eat tonight."

"But Baroness—alone? Without even a guardian?"

"Yes, alone," Teysa said. "I am the baroness here, yes? You have an objection?"

"No, but—" Melisk's face again became an impassive mask. "Very well, Baroness. I would urge you to at least take the thrull."

"No, no thrulls," Teysa said. "I'm never going to get this place into shape if I'm never seen. People need to see that I'm involved and, more importantly, that I'm not relying on someone—you or the thrulls or anyone—to enforce my will. It will keep them honest, if nothing else. And if you demand any more explanation from me, I *will* begin looking for a new attendant."

"That will not be necessary," Melisk said. "But please, use caution. Your condition—"

Teysa's headache flared briefly on the word "condition," but she fought it away from her face. "It's a town of what, three, four thousand people at the most? And three quarters of them are out there taking treasure from my property. I'm sure I'll be fine. When you're through with the paperwork, you can begin plans for assessing our cuts—with interest and back payments—on all that loot they're finding on the flats."

"When should we expect your return?"

"A few hours," Teysa said. "Even with this leg, it can't take more than that to walk the length and breadth of my 'empire.' "

As soon as she'd closed the door behind her, the headache began to fade. By the time she stepped out the front door and into the noonday sun, it had disappeared entirely.

* * * * *

"Watch where you're going!" Pivlic shouted over Kos's shoulder. "Are you mad?"

"I'm a little angry!" Kos shouted back. "But 'insane' mad? No. Just trying to get us through this mess."

The dromad whinnied and jerked to one side, narrowly dodging the blade at the end of the ogre's halberd. It crashed into reddish, polished, ancient stone and left a radial crack like broken glass.

"How are the thrulls?" Kos asked.

He felt Pivlic twist around in his seat, checking on the Grugg brothers' progress. "Just like you told them," Pivlic replied over the roaring ogre. "They're not attacking. Look." The imp pointed over Kos's left shoulder, and sure enough the old 'jek saw the two faithful thrulls bounding along the rocky folds of a pressure fissure, keeping pace easily with the panicked, galloping dromad and staying well clear of the mine guards.

Kos should have kept his eyes on the path ahead. The second ogre had moved around to flank them on the other side and swung his halberd at the level of the dromad's knees.

"Hey!" Kos shouted and pulled up on the reins, giving the dromad another kick. The beast's hooves cleared the blade by a hand's breadth but escaped unscathed. This ogre was quicker than the other, however, and simply dropped the halberd when his strike missed and brought up a fist that slammed into Kos's protective sphere helmet like a hunk of stone. The sphere did not shatter, which was extremely lucky—it surely would have blinded Kos, if not killed him—but a web of cracks formed dead center, completely obscuring Kos's view.

Kos swore, swinging his head left and right in a vain effort to see where he was going with his peripheral vision. "Pivlic, I can't see anything! Where are we headed?"

There was no answer.

"Pivlic?" Kos repeated and reached back to see if the imp was still there.

He wasn't.

Kos swore. Less than an hour into their rescue mission and already they needed rescuing themselves. From *prospectors,* of all people.

Blind, he couldn't even be sure he'd be heading in the right direction if he went back. If he took off the helmet, the exposure to the *kuga* plague could kill him. Not immediately—Kos had a healthy dose of antigen pollen in his system like anyone else in the township—but he'd surely begin to contract symptoms within a day.

"All right," Kos said aloud, "then we just get back before the day is done."

He wound the reins around the pommel of the saddle and gripped the dromad with both legs. Then Kos reached up, placed both gloved palms against the cracked crystal sphere, and twisted it with all his might. The helmet turned left a half spin and clicked. There was a hiss of air as the seal on the suit was broken, and he pulled it straight up.

The hazy air, thick with plague and dust, stung his eyes, and the glare of the sun bouncing off the flats blinded him the rest of the way, but he managed to squint through it.

He'd cleared the mining claim completely. There was an open flat before him, and he could make out the branching path that led to the Husk. He was home free.

"Heeeeelp!" a tiny voice shouted distantly behind him. "Help! Get back here right now or you're fired!"

Kos pulled back hard on the reins, harder still, and eventually convinced the spooked mount to stop and wheel around.

The first ogre had moved faster than Kos thought possible and held Pivlic suspended in the air by the helmet, which it clutched in a meaty palm.

"You forget something, raider scu—" the ogre said. Then it froze and blinked in disbelief. "Kos?"

"Garulsz?" Kos said. "What are you doing here?"

* * * * *

"What brings you here, Baroness?" Dr. Nebun asked. "I would think you would know better than to show up uninvited at a Combine laboratory."

"And I would think that you—ow—that you would know better than to leave an Orzhov baroness hanging upside down any longer than you have to!"

"What? Oh, yes, yes," the vedalken said. "My apologies. Uvulung, release her. Gently, please."

"Yeth, Mathtuh," the frog aberration said from its perch over the Simic's doorway. She'd meant to go directly to the doctor's laboratory, but it turned out his home was attached to the place—part of it, really—and so she'd knocked on the door. When that didn't work, she'd pulled what she thought was a bell rope, and the next thing she knew her ankles were bound together and she was hanging—indignant, red-faced, and upside-down—before the entry way.

The frog aberration relaxed its vile tongue and she slid down into the vedalken's hands. He helped spin her around and get back to her feet without much effort. He was stronger than he looked.

But strong or not, he was now the focus of all her embarrassed anger. "I sent word I was coming," Teysa snapped. "There had better be a good reason for that."

"There is," the doctor said. "It keeps people from walking in unannounced."

Teysa didn't respond but looked up at the frog aberration, clinging to the doorway. With speed she could see the doctor found surprising, she whipped her cane upward and drove one end into the aberration's open mouth, twirled the end so that the creature's tongue wrapped around it, and pulled down hard. She whipped Uvulung against the stone street with a heavy, crunching thud.

The Orzhov baroness gave the cane a twist and released the aberration's tongue, then pushed it over with her foot. Its bulbous eyes blinked, and its whip-tongue hung in a limp coil beside its head, but the creature was alive. Dazed but alive. That was good. Teysa hadn't intended to kill it. "Aberration," she said. "Uvulung. Do you see me?"

"Yeth."

"I am the Baroness Teysa Karlov. I am announcing my presence. I will not announce it again, so consider me permanently announced. Then what just happened won't happen to you anymore. Do you understand?"

"Yeth! Mathtuh, a Baroneth Teytha Karlof to thee you."

"Would you like to step inside, Baroness?" the doctor said without skipping a beat.

"If you don't mind," Teysa said.

Dr. Nebun guided her past huge specimen jars filled with things that looked like amalgamations of amalgamations—distorted, redesigned, pulled-apart-and-put-back-together creatures that, she sensed, were somehow still alive. Tubes and beakers bubbled with rank-smelling things that lingered in the air. From there, he led her to into an adjoining chamber that bore an uncomfortable resemblance to a medical examination room one might have found in the city. The primary difference was an incongruous fireplace in one corner and a wall filled with thick tomes bearing titles like *Diseases of the Golgari Tombs* and *Cursed Reagents*. She was not surprised when he took the chair and gestured she should take the long couch.

"I'll stand, if that's all right," Teysa said. "I tend to pace. Lawmage, you know."

"Suit yourself," Dr. Nebun said. "Do you mind if I take notes?"

"I'd be shocked if you didn't, Doctor," Teysa said. "You seem to have assumed I'm here for treatment. Why have you taken us here?"

"You were alone," the doctor said, "and your message did not mention what we discussed yesterday."

"True," Teysa said and strolled around the doctor's chair, dragging her cane a bit as she went. "Yes, I am here for treatment. And if anything we discuss here becomes public, it will be the death of you, I promise."

"Before I continue, may I assume you will pay my regular hourly rate for this consultation?" Dr. Nebun asked without batting an eyelash. Vedalken didn't have eyelashes.

"Yes."

"I take your word as your verbal contract and hereby assure you of complete confidentiality."

"Good," Teysa said. "Does it surprise you that I walk with a cane, Doctor? What does that tell you?"

"It tells me you are a true Orzhov, as does, quite obviously, your title," the doctor said.

"Very good," Teysa said. "You know the Orzhov blood comes with certain . . . perks. Abilities that others do not possess. But with a price."

"Of course," the vedalken replied. "The more powerful the abilities, generally, the more debilitating the so-called 'conditions' that come with them, yes?"

"Yes. And so it would not surprise you to learn further, then, that my leg is but one of the conditions I am afflicted with." Teysa came around the chair and kept pacing, dragging the cane, until she stood facing him again.

"You do seem capable, and savvy. You obviously have power, though I have not seen it physically manifested in any way yet," the doctor said.

"Interesting you should say that," the baroness replied, "and irrelevant. You're jumping ahead. No, I'm merely here for treatment of the condition you have not seen. I am afflicted with fainting spells. A form of narcolepsy, the family physicians called it. I simply drop into unconsciousness."

"How frequently?" Dr. Nebun asked.

"It comes and it goes," Teysa said. "Usually, episodes come in groups, maybe a few days, sometimes a few hours apart. Then they might not reappear for months, sometimes years."

"So you've had these all your life," the vedalken said.

"No, but Orzhov conditions do not arrive on a schedule," Teysa said. "And to make a long story short, the supplies of medicine I brought to keep it under control were lost when my lokopede was attacked by the Gruul."

"Do you think I am a simple pharmacist?" the doctor said indignantly. "I have created viruses that destroyed thousands! I—" the vedalken's mouth clamped shut. "Oh, dear, you've done it to me again, haven't you?"

"I'm sure I don't know what you're talking about," Teysa said but rapped the silver handle of her cane against the armrest of the doctor's chair to punctuate the verity circle she'd just created in her turn around the room. "I do believe you when you say you have created viruses. I believe you are being truthful, and let's leave it at that. No, Doctor, I do not think you a pharmacist or any other kind of simple medicinal peddler. But I do think you have a whole lot of things out there the likes of which I've never seen, in jars, and tubes, and tanks, and who knows what else. Now tell me, do you have something that will stave off any such attacks?"

"Well, I—That is," the vedalken fought the power of Teysa's hastily cane-drawn verity circle and lost, as he must. "Yes."

"Nice to know," she said. "You will take fair market prices for the lot? And either concoct or request from your Combine fellows a regular supply for all the time I am in this township as your baroness?"

"Who sets these fair market prices?" the doctor demanded.

"The market, doctor, which as you probably know is something we Orzhov are familiar with," Teysa explained, as if to a child. "But," she added as she stepped inside her own circle, "they *will* be fair."

"Fair enough," the vedalken said. Teysa nodded and stepped back out to resume her cane-assisted pacing.

"Now for my next question, Doctor," she said. "Let's call it a follow-up from yesterday. I asked if you could develop a cure for this *kuga* plague. You said you thought you could. After consideration of the length of time you've been here and the things I've seen in just a small portion of your laboratory, it occurs to me I may have been asking the wrong question."

"But those are just for show!" the doctor said and made a move to get out of his seat. Teysa pressed the end of the cane against the center of the vedalken's chest, pinning him to the chair with ease.

"The—the real laboratory you haven't seen yet," he finished, with an odd tone of embarrassment and shame.

"I thought as much," she said, then closed in for the kill—the reason she'd truly drawn that circle. "Dr. Nebun, do you *already* have a cure to the *kuga* plague?"

"I—I can't—" the doctor struggled, then cursed. "Yes, I do. I have enough to cure every man, woman, and child of every sentient race in this valley."

"Where?" Teysa said.

The vedalken set down his notebook and pulled aside his robe to reveal some twenty small glass tubes hanging in leather pouches. "Right here. Each one of these could cure several hundred people before running out. But only if you do it all within a few hours."

"Wonderful," Teysa said. "I'll take them all. How does a million zinos sound?"

CHAPTER 9

A successful bartender never forgets a face, a name, or a drink. Know each one of these and you will have their patronage for life.

—"Muck" Mukoz, Founder, Publicans' Union,
The Care and Feeding of Patrons, Third Edition

2 Cizarm 10012 Z.C.

The ogress—the only way to tell it had been an ogress was her voice, as the bulky prospecting suit she wore erased any traces of gender that her ogre heritage didn't—placed Pivlic down gently on his feet, and the imp wobbled a bit. Kos calmed the dromad while the ogress signaled her fellow prospectors to stand down. She turned the imp to get a good look at his face through the helmet. The ogre herself wore a much larger helmet, tinted slightly, and she had to squint, but finally she exclaimed, "This is that imp!"

"Yes," Pivlic said, "Pivlic the imp, owner and proprietor of the Imp Wing Hotel and Bar, member in good standing of the Orzhov Guild and servant of the Karlov family." The imp made the self-introduction sound like a threat. "And you are. . . ?"

"Pivlic, this is Garulsz," he said, slipping off the dromad without releasing the reins. "You two probably never met, now that I think about it."

"The name sounds familiar," Pivlic admitted, "but no, I can't place the face. And I never forget a face. Especially not one like that."

"Garulsz. Used to run the Backwater, back in city," Garulsz said. "Pleased to meet you. Any friend of Kos, friend of Garulsz. Kos good man, good 'jek. Paid his tab before leaving town."

"Ah," Pivlic replied. "The Backwater. I seem to remember we were in a running competition for Kos's liver. I'm afraid we both lost that one, my ogre friend. He's switched to the dindin full time."

"Let's try to stay focused here, Pivlic," Kos said gruffly. "Garulsz, we're looking for a goblin. We're on a job. We're not prospecting. Though I do hope you've had some luck?" It felt good to say that. On a job. On a *case,* he'd almost said, but close enough. He'd spent too long at Pivlic's, breaking up bar fights and getting drunks out the door. He belonged on a *job*. He half expected his heart to begin racing at the thought, but its beat stayed regular.

That brief fight was the most fun he'd had in years. So he couldn't handle teardrops, so what? The trick to not using a 'drop was not getting injured. Kos, old man, you've been too cautious.

Either that, or the beginnings of *kuga* infection were making him delusional. Whatever it was, it was exhilarating, and his heart hadn't acted up once.

"Some luck," Garulsz said proudly. "Oh, who me kid? You Kos! You see right through Garulsz, you good 'jek! Yes, we doing quite well. You can see big digger, bigger than lot of others? We hit a vein. Some kind of—" Suddenly the ogress looked at Pivlic suspiciously, then back at Kos. "You sure you vouch for imp?"

"Pivlic's my boss, now, believe it or not," Kos said. "I wouldn't work for him if I couldn't vouch for him."

"Quite magnanimous," Pivlic said dryly.

"And if he in any way tries to take advantage of anything you tell us, I'll tell you where he keeps his lockboxes," Kos said.

"You wouldn't!" Pivlic gasped.

"And the combinations," Kos added.

"We are going to talk," Pivlic muttered under his breath.

"Heh. All right," the ogress said. "We think we found old bank of some kind. It huge vein of treasure, and it what Garulsz and her cousin and her employees," she waved a warty hand at the other ogre and the armed guards, "use to buy big mining rig to get out even more."

"Sounds like you're set for life," Kos said, "with a little hard work. A bank?"

"If you've found a bank, ogress, you should notify the Orzhov," Pivlic said. "No doubt there are records of its loss in the archives."

"Pivlic, cut it out. I vouched—" something felt like it caught in his throat, and he began to cough. After a few seconds, it passed, but Kos felt a little dizzy. "Sorry," he said, pointing at his bare, bald head. "No helmet."

"Oh no!" Garulsz said. "This all Garulsz's fault! Let me get you new one."

"Don't worry about it," Kos said. "I doubt you have any that would fit," he added, eyeing the pair of viashino and the other ogre, who was looking at both Kos and the imp skeptically despite Garulsz's stand-down order. They obviously understood Ravi because they had been paying special attention to Pivlic ever since he brought up the Orzhov archives. "Besides, I won't be out here long. You could help me most by letting me know where the Utvar Gruul are setting up camp these days. I spotted them a few days ago, but then—the camp, well, it moved." No need to add everything he'd seen—the captive, for example, or what looked like a raging argument between Trijiro the centaur and the raid captain Vor Golozar. He knew Golozar from the bandit's few forays into the township. He didn't strike Kos as an evil man, but he had certainly been confrontational during his one visit to the Imp Wing. Best not to mention that to Garulsz. The ogress had always been somewhat protective and would probably want to come along. If she did, he doubted they'd ever find the camp. Ogres had a way of standing out.

"Oh, sure," Garulsz said. "We keep eye on them. They head north. You don't want to take the usual path up into Husk." She brought Kos into the crook of one arm jovially and pointed toward a spot in the Husk so far north it was hazed over with plague winds. "You'll need to ride straight through, then. You see that little trail up the side?"

"Yes."

"They not far from there," the ogress explained. "Moved just a few days ago. But me see other Gruul than that."

"What other Gruul?" Pivlic said. "The Utvar Gruul are savages, but last I checked they were something of a united clan, were they not?"

"You talk long sentences, imp," Garulsz said. "But you not know as much as Garulsz." She turned east a bit and pointed to an area not far from the camp Kos had seen through his spotting scope. "They not camping, just raiding. And . . . what word for it . . . stalking. Stalking the other Gruul."

"Why would they do that?" Kos asked.

"Not know," Garulsz said. "Me miner now. Gave up city life but not 'frontier' enough to go into Husk. You think me crazy?"

"Some ogre," Pivlic muttered.

"What that, little imp?" Garulsz said, scowling.

"Some more," Pivlic said, louder. "Tell us some more."

"Right," Garulsz replied, oblivious. The ogre sense of smell was surprisingly sharp, but ogre hearing was less so, especially under an invizomizzium helmet. Kos wished he'd had the zinos to shell out for the invizomizzium himself but had gone with the cheaper crystal, and now he had no helmet at all. He coughed again but stifled it before it got out of hand. He willed his heart not to start racing and seemed to meet with some success there, at least.

"Do you recognize any in the other group?" Kos asked, trying to get the ogress back on track.

"No, but no ogres," Garulsz replied. "You go up there, you be careful. You Garulsz's favorite 'jek."

"I'll bet I financed half this operation with the bumbat I bought alone," Kos said. "Feels like I should ask for a cut."

"Ha!" Garulsz said, a sound that rang against the metallic mining rig behind her. "Good one, Kos." Kos started coughing again, and she added, "You shouldn't dawdle with no helmet. You not getting any younger."

"Thanks," Kos managed when he had wrested the hacking under control. "Come on, Pivlic." He hoisted himself into the dromad's saddle, and, without asking, Garulsz picked up the imp and set him behind the retired 'jek. The dromad's thick tail swished happily. It knew they were about to get moving again.

"Take care, Kos," Garulsz said. "Come out and visit any time."

"And you feel free to swing by the Imp Wing any time," Kos said. "I'm usually there."

"When we're open, at least," Pivlic said.

"See you later, Garulsz," Kos said with a wave. "Hey, you thrulls coming?" The Grugg brothers growled the affirmative and jogged up to join the dromad riders, chirping excitedly.

"What now, Kos?" Pivlic asked. "What do we do about those other Gruul?"

"Now, we ride," Kos said and patted the bam-stick slung across his back. "We worry about the rest when we get there."

"Have I mentioned I'm not cut out for this?" Pivlic said.

"I got that feeling," Kos said. He forced down another cough. With the tiniest motion of his heels, he spurred the dromad onward, leaving a cloud of reddish dust hanging in the air behind them.

* * * * *

Melisk was gone when Teysa returned. He did not respond to her shouted calls as she went from room to room on the second floor of the Imp Wing. She pulled up her sleeve and touched the middle stone, the one that helped her keep track of those sworn to serve her. "Melisk," she whispered and felt compelled to look at the southeastern wall, beyond which lay the slums where she intended to build a mansion. "You'd better be on some important paperwork-organizing mission, attendant," Teysa said. "You're starting to worry me."

That was when she heard a muffled voice from the antechamber adjoining her makeshift office. She couldn't make out what was being said, but the intensity, tone, and identity of the speaker was clear. She strode across the room and flung open the door to the side chamber where she'd taken to keeping the mirror.

"He's gone," the mirror said as soon as she opened the door. "Your contractor, that half-demon, came by and had some questions about the plans for the new mansion, and he went personally to set them straight."

"Why don't I believe you, Uncle?" Teysa said.

"I can't imagine, unless it's my immortal reputation," the mirror replied. "Yet I tell the truth. That is what happened."

Teysa wished it was possible to put a ghost in a verity circle, but even if Uncle had been here in person, it would not have worked. And since his ghost, murdered by the Gruul, had magically materialized in the Obzedat back in the City of Guilds, there was little chance she'd have the opportunity to try anyway. Teysa decided to let it drop. She could talk to Melisk about this later. Or confirm the story with the half-demon Aradoz.

"All right," she began. "My apologies. I don't feel quite myself. I have received a new medication to regulate my fainting spells."

"Ah, the Simic was good for something after all, eh?" Uncle's face in the mirror was covered with a white mask, but he still managed to smile and give a little chuckle. "Good to know. I was concerned that vicious Gruul attack would cost you more than the rest of us."

"It cost you your life," Teysa said.

"My mortal life only," Uncle replied. "But a new one stretches before me. This Simic, do you trust him?"

"The Simic appears to be capable and truthful," when in the circle, anyway, she silently added. "But that's not why I opened this door. Uncle, I can't tell you how much it pains me to say this, especially so soon after I have begun my endeavors here. But I must ask you for . . . advice."

"Splendid!" the mask in the mirror said. "And about time too. You need only ask. You know I cannot refuse you anything, my dear."

"It is unusual," Teysa said. "Are you alone?"

"A member of the Obzedat is never alone," Uncle replied. "But we are speaking privately."

"Good," Teysa said. She didn't believe him, but what choice did she have? "It's a question of—morality and business, I guess."

"You're joking," the mask replied. "What does the one have to do with the other?"

"It's an unusual case," Teysa said. "I have the capacity to end this plague. Probably within a few days. It cost me more than a little of my personal wealth. Yet this will only work if all of the cures are administered on the same day. And all my instincts tell me that this is the most valuable substance in this entire valley, which means I should sell it to the highest bidder. Yet to do so would be to waste it, as the plague will not be ended unless everyone takes the cure."

"And the Gruul that slew me?" Uncle said through the mirror. "You would give it to them too?"

"I have set the taj to the task, but I fear there may not be enough of them to kill them all," Teysa said. "Though once the plague is finished, we could see about a revenge contract."

"That is why I chose you for this, child. You do have a grasp of the long term. But it is a quandary, is it not?" the mirror replied. "Tell me, why do you *want* this plague to end?"

"Now you must be joking," Teysa said. "It's a *plague*. How am I to make this place worthy of recognition by the Guildpact in a year if I don't get rid of it? Wild claims of Selesnyan cures don't cut it."

"Well, the Selesnyans seem to think—"

"Uncle, please," Teysa said, "you can't possibly be suggesting I rely on those life churcher fools to be concerned with the timing here. And even if their Vitar Yescu does somehow wipe out the plague on its own, when Hauc gets the Cauldron up to full steam, I—we, the family—would be beholden to them for that."

"Ah, so your instinct *is* to make a few zinos," the mirror said. "You had me concerned. I must say, philanthropy is not a trait I would encourage if you someday wish to end up like me."

Like him. A ghost-lord. An immortal—as long as the zinos held out—patriarch of the Obzedat. For some reason, becoming the first matriarch on the council didn't appeal to Teysa as much as it used to. But he was right. The very thought of simply giving away the cure triggered physical pain in her Orzhov blood.

She'd never gone against the blood before. Not this much, anyway. Though she was surprised to hear Uncle so casually discuss sharing a cure for the plague with the Gruul that killed him.

They did kill him, didn't they? For the first time since she'd left the Simic doctor, her headache returned, mild but insistent. It was not accompanied by a fainting spell or dizziness, just a little bit of pain that said *something's not right here.*

"They will all find ways to pay for your cure," the mask in the mirror continued. "It may take some time, but, as you've often reminded me, you *are* an advokist. Contracts will need to be drawn, binding agreements made, payments arranged in due time. Interguild commerce is a sacred trust, my dear. It is not separate from the law. It is the law. That is how you solve this problem."

"So do it, in other words?" Teysa asked skeptically.

"Of course," Uncle said.

Could she trust him? Teysa wasn't sure. The pain in her blood and her head was telling her no.

"Something's not right here," she said, this time aloud.

"What makes you say that?" the masked face said.

"It's—" *you,* she wanted to say, *you and Melisk and this whole operation. The fact that I remember the Gruul killing you, but every time I try to picture it, my brain hurts. And the fact that the pain is worse than ever since the Simic gave me this new medicine.* But she said, "It's Melisk. I think he may be plotting. My blood is telling me something is . . . off with him somehow."

The mask in the mirror lost its smile and was silent for several long seconds. Finally, Uncle said, "You think so, do you?"

"Now more than ever," Teysa said. "It's not like you to not have an answer ready. What is it, Uncle? What do you know?"

The image of the mask became unfocused for a moment, and she thought she heard more voices, different voices, ancient and powerful, around the mirror's frame. After almost a minute of this, the mask became clear again, and the smile returned.

"If you really want to know, Teysa Karlov, then also know that this information will come with a price. Your allegiance, without question, to the will of the Obzedat."

Could the Ghost Council really do that, get her permanent devotion with a verbal agreement? She wasn't sure, but it could be true. And it was definitely true that if she didn't find out what was going on, she would go mad. Teysa had to know and had to know now. This time, the blood agreed, and it told her this was right. "My allegiance," Teysa said, "as always."

"All right," the mirror said. "Listen."

Teysa uncrossed her fingers and listened.

* * * * *

It took Kos and Pivlic the better part of the day to reach the edge of the flats. After another round of coughing almost knocked Pivlic off the back of the saddle and drew the attention of circling carrion birds, the imp had convinced Kos to at least tie a scarf over his face, which the old 'jek had done and found that though the coughing might be the first sign of infection, the dust was also part of it—the scarf did bring it under control.

Kos scanned the place where the de facto road ended, looking for the trail that Garulsz had pointed out. "There," he said, pointing between two rusty, jagged spires that looked like they had once been a single piece but had cracked in the heat and split down the middle. "Between those, that's where we need to go."

"Can this beast make it up that?" Pivlic said. "It is little more than a trail."

"No, I don't think she can," Kos said. Dromads were not good climbers. "Well, Garulsz did tell us it was a trail. I just hoped it might be big enough." He patted the dromad's flank and leaned forward to whisper in one flicking ear. "What do you think, girl?" The dromad whinnied. Kos sighed. His legs weren't what they once were, but he'd definitely have an easier time navigating that slim trail on foot. He didn't want to leave the dromad running wild, though—a walk back over the flats was something he might not survive. Not unless he wanted to bind Gruul fungus to his skin to stave off the effects of the *kuga*. He wasn't ready to go that far yet, assuming he could even find a Gruul with fungus to spare. Besides, he'd already developed a soft spot for the dromad mare.

Kos turned to the thrulls. The baroness had said one of them was smarter than the other, the one who looked like a freakish viashino. What had his name been?

"Bephel?" Kos said tentatively. The thrull with the spiky reptilian tail hopped over to him. The dromad didn't start at the thing's approach, that was a good sign. Now if it could take instruction as well as the baroness said. . . .

"What are you doing, Kos?" Pivlic asked as the old 'jek slid off the side of the dromad. "Oh, dear," the imp continued. "We *are* walking, aren't we?"

Kos lifted the imp off of the saddle and set him on the ground. "Yep," he said and turned back to the thrull. "Bephel," he repeated, "hold these reins, and keep this dromad here. Do you understand me? Can you do that?"

The thrull nodded and to Kos's surprise spoke in heavily accented Ravi. "Of course Bephel can! What, you think Bephel some kind of animal? Old man wounds Bephel!" With a shifty look, the thrull added conspiratorially, "Can I eat it?"

"No, *do not* eat it," Kos said, grateful that the thing could actually speak. He'd assumed that like the rest of its kin Bephel had no speech. He was glad to be wrong. "If you do, there won't be enough pieces left of you to put back together, I promise. Just keep it here and wait for us. We're taking your brother with us. You should be fine here, but if anyone comes out from one of those claims to give you trouble, then—" Then what? Kos asked himself. He didn't want the thrull to assault innocent prospectors, even in self-defense, not on his account. And the creature didn't look built for riding. "If anyone gives you trouble, lead the dromad back to your baroness."

"Baroness!" the thrull said, and its odd triangular face broke into a smile. "We should go see her now!"

"No, she told you to do as we said, right?" Kos said.

"Well . . . yes," the thrull agreed at last.

"So you'll only leave here *if* you're threatened," Kos said. "And when we return, we'll all go see the baroness together."

"You got it!" the thrull said, already eying the dromad's flanks.

"The other one—" name, name . . . Kos struggled to remember. All these thrulls' names were way too much alike. "Uh, Elbeph, right?"

"He doesn't talk," Bephel offered helpfully and spun a finger next to his ear. "Not good talk like Bephel."

"Right," Kos said. "But he can make noise, right? A few words? Can you teach him?"

"Oh, sure," Bephel said. "He's not smart like Bephel, but he'll listen. And he can jump!" As if on cue, the other thrull began to hop on his frog-arms, jabbering.

"Elbeph, you're with us," Kos sighed.

"Yes, this is going to go just flawlessly," Pivlic said.

"Hey, we're here to serve, Pivlic," Kos said. "Isn't that what you said? We're all Orzhov and all that?"

"Yes," the imp sighed. "Well, shall we?"

The trail was not as treacherous as it had initially looked, but it did turn out to be far too narrow for a dromad and two riders. Elbeph seemed almost impatient, hopping about Kos and Pivlic while the other two trudged along, calling out warnings when he spotted any treacherous-looking cracks that might drop away if you looked at them wrong. The only reason the trail was even here, it appeared, was because it sat atop rusted, fallen columns that looked as if a giant had laid them end to end in the distant past. The columns provided a sturdy backbone for the trail, but Kos was still wary of a few gaps in the ground on either side that probably went down for miles. The danger made him grateful for the thrull's occasional warnings.

"I should be flying," Pivlic said again after an especially difficult climb over a huge hunk of rock that had probably once been a pipe or culvert of some kind but was now just a corroded obstacle. "This suit is a purgatorial prison, my friend."

"One of us exposed to the *kuga* is enough," Kos said and pulled the imp up beside him. "Hold up, Elbeph," he called, bringing the froglike creature back to them. "I want to get a better—Oh, my."

"What?" Pivlic said. "What do you see?"

"I think," Kos said, "we just found them." He pointed at a section of the trail maybe a quarter mile up, where an upper torso and one head with wide, pointed ears appeared just over the crest. That would be their missing goblin, and right behind her was a big human covered in antigen fungus who turned occasionally to look back. At the rate the pair was going, they had to be running, which was not exactly safe in the Husk. You only ran in the Husk if you knew exactly where you were going or if something, or someone, was after you.

With a feeling of impending dread, he followed a line up the hill behind the running pair—the big one was definitely Vor Golozar, his distinctive tattoos made that obvious—and spotted more shapes. More Gruul, in fact, but pale, drawn, and hungry-looking. There were at least two dozen he could spot, climbing around and over the stone and corrosion like ants.

Kos checked the path before them. It looked like it would meet up with one of the runners following a few hundred yards away. It was indeed dangerous to run in the Husk, but right now they had no choice—those pale, mean-looking Gruul were going to reach their messenger first if they didn't go now. And since Golozar—one of the boldest Gruul Kos had ever met—was running from the others that quickly, there was no doubt what would happen to the messenger if the pale pursuers got to them first. He was surprised to find Golozar with the goblin but supposed he shouldn't have been. Golozar was honorable in his way, and Trijiro—whom Kos *did* trust, mostly—was too. Kos had other reasons to trust the Gruul raid captain that went all the way back to the City of Guilds, but it was not something many—not even Pivlic—knew about.

"Pivlic, you see that?" Kos asked.

"I'm afraid I do," the imp said wearily. "You're going to make us run, aren't you?"

Kos didn't answer because he'd already leaped down from the toppled column and was heading up the hill, carefully skirting cracks and fissures while holding the bam-stick steady on his back with one hand. The thrull bounded along behind like a happy dog.

"I should never have left the city," Pivlic said. He checked to make sure his own bam-stick was secure and set off after them.

CHAPTER 10

Deception does not come easily to an Izzet. From the most powerful magelord to the lowliest goblin devotee, their need to boast is too great. In dealings with their kind, make sure you keep your own secrets, for they will not.

—Patriarch Fautomni, *On the Lesser Guilds* (4211 Z.C.)

2 Cizarm 10012 Z.C.

Crix might have been more surprised than Golozar when the old man and the imp charged in to their rescue, but the look on the Gruul's face said otherwise.

"Kos?" Golozar shouted at the old man in the ill-fitting miner's suit, a scarf tied around his nose and mouth. The diminutive figure trying to keep up with the human had a black, leathery face beneath his domed helmet and ran like one far more used to flying. An imp, perhaps. But Kos? Crix had heard of Kos. He was—

He was about to run right into her. No, he was about to tackle her.

Crix and Kos slammed to the ground. The old man turned as they fell so that his shoulder took the impact just as a bamshot soared directly overhead. "Hello, Crix," Kos said, coughing. "Name's 'Kos.' Tenth Le—No, strike that. Just 'Kos.' People are looking for you."

"I'm—I'm Crix. Pleased to meet you, Mr. Kos," Crix stammered.

"You all right?" Kos said.

"Yes," Crix said.

"Good. I think that was a ranging shot. We've got to get out of here."

"Kos, what are you doing?" Golozar shouted. "This is not your place—"

"Spare us both the 'stoic Gruul' rhetoric, my friend," the imp said as he swung the bam-stick off of his back and snapped a shot into place. He lifted the 'stick to one eye and aimed at a rocky outcrop behind them. The imp, who looked like a human child in the miner's suit—or even a short-legged goblin—pressed one gloved thumb against the stud and fired. A tiny humanoid speck dropped from the outcrop a millisecond later without even a scream.

"A sniper," Golozar said quietly. "This is wrong. Aun Yom's group is not this large. There are too many heads."

"Maybe he's gotten some new recruits," Kos said as he got to his feet. "Where were you going, anyway? Why aren't you at your camp?"

"Trijiro asked me to get this goblin to the Cauldron. Believe me, the camp is the first place I'm going once I fulfill that promise," Golozar said.

"Just you?" Pivlic said.

"The others were killed," the Gruul said darkly.

"An accident, not Aun Yom," Crix supplied as helpfully as she could. She scanned the hills behind them and didn't spy any more specks—but several of Aun Yom's bandits were much closer. "Perhaps we can tell the rest of the story later. We're close enough to the Cauldron now that I think I can guide us there."

"Perfect," Kos said. "But won't you guide them there as well?"

"That," Crix admitted, "could present a problem. We've got to shake them."

"Perhaps—" Pivlic managed before the ground between their group and Aun Yom's bandits violently erupted. At first Crix thought it might be a geothermic vent—they were close enough to the Cauldron that such a thing was possible—but the reddish, scaly thing that burst from the crater in the Husk soon put the lie to that thought.

"Nephilim!" Golozar cried, pulling the stunned Pivlic back from the edge of this brand-new chasm in the middle of the trail.

"Another one?" Crix said. "But the last one looked nothing like this!"

"Each is unique," Golozar said, "ancient. . . . To the Gruul, they were once gods."

"Once?" Pivlic said, regaining his senses.

"Until we learned we could kill them," Golozar finished.

"Kill them?" Crix shouted. "You had to drop the last one into a pit! You said killing it was—"

"I never said it was a permanent death," Golozar said.

Crix could hardly believe that. This nephilim looked nothing like a construct. It was more like a tapered tube of raw, exposed muscle and tendons with a gaping, toothy mouth on one end that opened to the sky and emitted a keening roar. The sound was excruciating to Crix's sharp goblin ears, and she dropped to her knees clutching both sides of her head.

The nephilim clamped its jaws shut once more with a sound like a clanging bell. Two spindly legs emerged from either side of its glistening torso and pressed two disturbingly human-looking hands against either side of the crater it had created.

The goblin courier tried to get back to her feet, but Crix found she had completely lost her sense of balance. She managed to get vertical for half a second before tumbling over onto her back.

"I think I need help," she said.

Kos picked her up with both hands. "I think we need to carry her," the old man said to Golozar, who had already drawn a bead on the odd, skull-shaped scale over the nephilim's drooling mouth. The brain, maybe?

Crix was sure that hideous sound had scrambled her mind as well as her balance. Now was not the time for study. It was time to go.

"How are you with a bam-stick?" Golozar said, his face briefly orange as he let a shot fly at the nephilim. His voice sounded very far away. The shot ricocheted off the creature's tough hide, but it was enough to turn its attention to them.

"I don't think that matters," Pivlic said. "Look!"

Aun Yom's Gruul hadn't slowed their pace at all. They didn't even try to go around the nephilim. They just attacked it, like it was a simple obstacle to destroy and pass through.

"Those were terrible tactics," Golozar said.

"You think so?" Kos said. "You just did the same thing."

Crix could barely hear the rest of the heated words, both because of her temporary—please, let it be temporary—hearing loss and because she could not take her eyes off the scene before her.

The pursuing Gruul didn't just attack the roaring nephilim, they devoured it. Jagged blades hacked into the monstrous creature's flesh, sending greenish blood spewing everywhere. Well-aimed bamshots slammed into its open mouth and emerged from the top of its eyeless head, showering the ground with bone and slimy gray matter. Once the creature began to shudder violently and even began to pull in its legs as if it might retreat, Aun Yom's gang started to feed. They tore huge chunks of flesh from the creature's side and stuffed it into their mouths. Three of the Gruul fought over a long ribbon of flesh that looked disturbingly like a tongue, and one of the wiry legs was hacked free.

"That's as good a diversion as I think we can expect," said Kos as he lifted Crix onto his back. "Can you hear me, Crix? Can you hold on?"

The goblin tried to bring the world Kos had set spinning into focus, an effort that was finally beginning to show results. Kos's voice was clearer, too. "Yes," Crix said. "That way."

"You heard the lady," Kos said. "Let's get out of here. Golozar, watch our backs. Pivlic, keep your eyes open for gaps in the road."

"You cannot order me," Golozar growled. "I am not one of your deputy—"

"I don't have time for this, Golozar!" Kos said. "You and I both know you're no deputy anything. Just watch our damned backs while Crix here gets us to the Cauldron, would you?"

To Crix's surprise, Kos's words seemed to sink in. Golozar twisted the bam-stick and slotted another shot into place. "You lead," Golozar said.

"No, she leads," Kos said. "Me, I'm just the dromad."

Pivlic, the imp, was already ahead of them. "My friends, we must hurry," Crix said.

As they bolted down the path, Crix shouted to Golozar, "I guess the Gruul aren't the most dangerous thing in the Husk."

"Not by a long shot," the Gruul replied.

"They may be the hungriest, though," Crix added.

"That frenzy, I cannot explain," Golozar said. "But it worries me."

* * * * *

Zomaj Hauc stormed out of the *Pyraquin* and summoned the chief observer, whom the magelord had left in charge of overall Cauldron operations while Hauc was dealing with other matters in the City of Guilds. The goblin was more of a scientist than a labor foreman, but with the original foreman dead he was the most senior of the goblins and therefore had taken on the job of wrangling and managing the work crews at Hauc's order.

The magelord ignored the hails of greeting and praise from the devoted goblins, hundreds of them, who went to and fro pushing insulated carts of cooling lava into power sinks, adding attachments and modifications to the power plants and generators and performing other, simpler tasks, like polishing the brass—all crucial for proper functioning. A few were even standing, on break, apparently, gazing at the center of the Cauldron and the great ovoids that rested there. As Hauc passed, it seemed all of them at once clamored to get even a sliver of his attention—a glance, a punishment, a simple acknowledgment. Hauc had no time for the fawning workers right now, and the fact that they made such displays only added incrementally to his fury at the inefficiencies of the Cauldron project. They should be working, not cheering. He was only concerned with one goblin right now: the courier who, despite his efforts and those of his agents, was still missing somewhere in the Husk.

Chief Observer Vazozav scrambled up one of the many stair ramps that led to Hauc's personal observation-and-landing platform, suspended high over the Cauldron. The platform was dominated by the *Pyraquin,* which hovered over the platform on a cushion of antigravitic magic. The goblin had only grown more wrinkled over the last forty-seven years, and he huffed mightily as he stomped up the winding staircase. He was unused to running. That was going to change, thought Hauc. Vazozav would be run ragged by the time this was done, advancing age be damned.

"Chief Observer," the magelord said, with fire in his eyes, "what is the status of our operations?"

"My lord," Vazozav said. He bowed and scraped and tried to gather his breath in the thick, oppressive heat, all at once. "The panels have continued to channel the ectoplasmic energy, just as intended, and we've actually seen an uptick of about twenty percent.

There have been many deaths in the region of late, I believe."

"And more to come. The Schism is growing in strength. You have not diverted that energy into the power plants then?" Hauc said.

"Of course not, my lord," the goblin said, with a touch of injured pride. "Nor the windmills, which as you know are only for show. The plants are running at exactly the efficiency you requested, with all extra energy channeled directly into the—"

"I know what I asked," Hauc said. "That is enough. What about the workers? Have there been any additional incidents?"

"Not after those slackers were tossed into the lava pit," the chief observer said.

"Good," the magelord declared and looked up through a large, circular gap in the domed roof—a gap that was just a bit bigger than the *Pyraquin*—at the crystalline, blue sky. "Chief Observer, do you see those distortions?"

The goblin followed Hauc's arm up through the skylight and asked, "Distortions, my lord?"

"Look closely, Observer," Hauc said. "The ripples in the sky. Like clouds, but not like clouds. Focus your tiny eyes."

Vazozav squinted and eventually nodded. "Yes . . . I see them, my lord?" His tentativeness made the statement sound like a question.

"No, you do not," Hauc said, "for you do not possess the gift of great Niv-Mizzet. The dragon's gift is not given to those without vision."

The goblin looked confused, which did not surprise Zomaj Hauc in the slightest. "Yes, my lord," was the best Vazozav could manage. "I mean, no, my lord. No. Vision. I have no vision?"

"No, you—Never mind, Vazozav," the magelord said.

When Zomaj Hauc had been young, some three, four hundred

years ago—he sometimes had trouble remembering exactly how many centuries it had been—he'd received as a gift a trained blood-crested drekavac from one of the many family members who paid the dues for his academic and arcane education. He'd kept the thing for a week until he'd grown tired of it, the longest-lived pet he'd ever owned if he didn't count the beings in his colloquy, which in many ways were little more than pets themselves. The drekavac's killer instinct had been stolen by its trainers before Hauc ever got his hands on the creature, and so it was useless as anything but a specimen. Just before he vaporized the drekavac's skull with a blast of fire (from his own eyes—he'd just learned the spell at the time and wanted to impress upon his fellow students the speed with which he'd mastered it), the creature had looked at him exactly as the goblin did now. Expectant, faithful, with no clue of the doom lurking in its immediate future.

Hauc was sorely tempted to boil the chief observer's brain in much the same way, but he'd lost enough capable goblins. Sadly, this Vazozav was one of his brainiest remaining subjects.

Damn the Gruul for taking his messenger, and damn the Orzhov for not keeping her protected. The Guild of Deals had more zinos and raw assets than all the other guilds combined, yet he could not, it seemed, trust the Orzhov to get a courier from point to point without losing her. Crix was valuable for so many reasons, not least because she was one of the few creatures in Hauc's sphere of influence who actually possessed the ability to discourse at length about a wide range of subjects well beyond the greatness of Niv-Mizzet and the brilliance of Zomaj Hauc. This was by design, of course—his design. Crix was one of the few successes in the now-defunct goblin augmentation project, and her value was both monetary and personal. After a while, even an Izzet magelord tired of repetitive praise.

"Chief Observer, come here," Hauc said. "Stop looking at the sky and come here."

"Yes, my lord," Vazozav said. "What should I look at?"

"There," the magelord said and pointed over the platform rail past a network of pipes, tubes, and crackling bolts of electrical discharge at a pair of glowing figures lurking among the steamworks. The pair of hydropyric weirds—which, unlike the pyrohydric weirds, had exterior bodies of water filled with fire—stood placidly, obscured somewhat by thick, lingering fog around the lava pits, where most of the direct interaction between elements took place. "What are those two weirds doing?"

"They're guarding the lava pits, my lord," the goblin said.

"And those archers in the upper tier?"

"Guarding the power plants and the lava pits, my lord."

"And the djinn at the gates? The djinn standing and chatting with the weirds? That sleeping drake up there? I imagine they guard the gates, the weirds, and the nest, in addition to the power plants and the lava pits? Would that be correct, Vazozav?"

"Yes, my lord," the chief observer said. To his credit, he did not stammer in the slightest, though he flexed his hands into fists nervously. He, obviously, had not been a product of the augmentation project.

"Do I need to continue?" Hauc said.

"Perhaps if you would grace me with, er, a continuation of your brilliance, my lord? I am but a goblin and welcome enlightenment. My lord," Vazozav said and bowed his head to stare at his own feet.

Hauc continued not to kill the goblin, though the temptation grew stronger with every second. Fools. Surrounded by fools. Fools and inefficient wastrels. At least he knew they would be dead soon. He wouldn't need them once his courier came home and the Cauldron had served its true purpose. Then he would unveil his plan not just for the Izzet but for the entire plane. No others could possibly comprehend the greatness of what he was going to achieve, save perhaps the Firemind himself, but of course Niv-Mizzet was the only being that could *not* know. Not if Hauc was to succeed.

"Wake the drake, and get her in the air," Hauc said without rancor, which calmed the chief observer a bit. "Put the archers on rotating shifts, three per day. The head of each fire team will be rotated to the next one."

"From the twelfth team to the thirteenth, for example, my lord?" Vazozav said, eager to have grasped something with his small, unmodified goblin brain. That brain could cook easily with a gesture from Hauc, if he only gave in to the temptation.

"Yes, exactly," the magelord said instead of killing the chief observer. "The djinn and weirds will be put on labor shifts, as well as guard duty, and I want only one per gate and one each at every compass point inside this glorious structure." After a few seconds, he added, "Well?"

"Yes! I'll get right on it, my lord," the goblin said. "May I be of any other service, my lord?"

"No," Hauc said. "Keep yourself and everyone else off of this platform for the next hour. I will be in the flight sphere, in conference."

"Shall I assign guards to the steps leading to this glorious platform, my lord?" Vazozav asked.

"Chief Observer Vazozav, son of Joxotuxak," Hauc said. "If I need protection, you will already be dead."

The goblin's face went a little ghostly, and he almost tumbled down the steps as he backed away from the magelord. Then he turned, grabbed a rail, and virtually flew down to the lava pits, stomping toward the slacking guard elementals once he reached the work floor.

Hauc stood and turned his attention back to the skylight. The distortions were there. The Schism was spreading, even if goblins could not see it. He nodded in satisfaction that the mana-compression singularity bomb, at least, was performing exactly as expected. Hauc spun on one foot, strode into the *Pyraquin*'s open ramp, and pulled it closed behind him.

It was said by the ignorant that in Utvara there were no ghosts. This was not entirely true. There were ghosts in the Schism itself. Those lost souls provided the raw power he needed to complete the task Niv-Mizzet had set for him. The courier, of course, was needed to complete the related task Hauc had set for himself.

The mirrorlike pneumanatic device was already ignited, though colliding ripples obscured its surface. Someone was trying to communicate with him. He'd wasted too much time on the goblin. More delays, more inefficiency.

Not that he minded making his contact wait a bit. The Orzhov were demanding partners, but soon he wouldn't have to worry about them either. The urge to show them all who their true master was had overwhelmed him at times, but he bled it off with little jabs like this.

Hauc placed a small offering in the brazier; said a short prayer in praise of the Great Dragon and all that Niv-Mizzet the Firemind was, is, and would be; and ignited the token with a snap. The crystal hummed as it made contact with the aerial leylines, and the ripples in the surface smoothed to reveal the familiar white mask floating in a swirling black ether.

The mask was not smiling.

"Tell me," the magelord said without preamble, "that you have located her."

"Yes, my scouts have spotted her, but we may have other problems," the mask said. "She's beginning to suspect me. I'm concerned she might—"

"She who?" Hauc said. "Suspect what?"

"You know good and well," the mirror said. "I cannot speak her name here."

"I suppose I do," the magelord said. "Whatever you say. I forget how secretive you people like to be."

"You forget nothing," the mask said. "And as far as secrecy goes—"

"Yes, yes, your point is made," Hauc said.

"She is beginning to remember. It is getting more difficult to keep her in the dark."

"I suppose that's true too," Hauc said. "Your problem is not mine. Mine is the courier. Get her here. I would prefer for her to be alive, but that is not critical."

"I will do it, but keep your eyes open. My scouts tell me that the goblin is definitely not in the camp. She is moving fast in your direction and should arrive soon, with or without my help."

"Well, why in the name of the Firemind did you not tell me this earlier?"

"You seemed more interested in word games," the mirror said.

"And you seem obsessed with recriminations," Hauc replied. "Get that courier to me. I will be here, waiting."

"You cannot even take that contraption of yours into the air to give us some help?" the voice in the mirror said. "You could easily find and grab her, and I could set my scouts to the task for which they were intended—finishing the Gruul."

"This 'contraption' is the only thing keeping the one being that must not learn of our connection from seeing this communication. It will stay here until necessary, and I will stay in the Cauldron until our glorious end is achieved," Hauc said. "Your scouts have found the goblin. I'm sure they will retrieve her soon. Good-bye."

"Have it your way," the voice replied and disappeared behind a ripple of energy.

* * * * *

"This way!" Crix shouted. "The Cauldron is this way!"

"How do you know that?" Kos shouted, gasping for breath. The goblin pointed overhead to a fork in the trail that ran back up the Husk and, it seemed, away from the looming Cauldron to the west. "The other one looks like it heads straight there. I thought you'd never been in the Husk before!"

He'd been running for ten minutes straight, longer than he'd run for any reason for more than a decade. Having Crix on his back didn't help, but Golozar was taking potshots at the pursuing forces of Aun Yom, and Pivlic was scouting ahead, so the only way to keep up their speed had been for Kos to carry the goblin on his shoulders. Kos didn't believe in gods—he did believe in vampires, which was a separate issue—but if he did, he would have prayed that, no matter what, he wouldn't die like this, with a chatty, obstinate goblin clinging to his neck. He would have set her down, but even if she had recovered her senses her short legs would still slow them down. Pivlic's legs weren't much longer, but even in his miner's suit the imp was bounding ahead of them. Imps didn't weigh much, and their legs were made for launch. The same couldn't be said for goblins.

"Homing instinct, you might call it," Crix said. "Keeps us from getting lost. Couriers, I mean. That other trail is a false one. This is the right way."

"Which tattoo tells you all that?" Kos asked. He had to leap sideways to clear a fissure in the oxidized iron trail to get to the fork Crix pointed at, but he made it without losing the goblin or any limbs. His heart was pounding but not racing. He could tell the difference, and despite his hours-long exposure to the plague he knew that his heart wasn't going to kill him. Aun Yom's pursuit gang might, or the Husk itself, and most certainly the plague if he didn't get exposure to the pollen soon, but not his heart. Not now. He wouldn't let it.

"It's not like that," Crix said, "but I can't really tell you what it's like. Professional secret. But trust me."

"You don't know how it works, do you?" Kos said.

"I resent that," the goblin sniffed, "but, truthfully, no, not entirely. It's part of the job."

"I know what you mean," Kos said. "I don't know how the Guildpact works, but if it didn't, I'd never have been able to make an arrest in my life. Or so they told me."

"Of course. I forgot that you're a wojek," Crix said, ducking to dodge a black arrow that whizzed overhead.

"Used to be a wojek," Kos said. "This is my retirement plan."

"You don't seem very retired to me," the goblin said. "Nor do you look like an agent of the Orzhov. How do you know Golozar?"

"His zuriv chief is a friend of mine," Kos said. "But Golozar and I know each other from the city. You can ask him about it sometime. It's not my story to tell. But I try to keep my nose in everyone's business. Bad habit, I know."

"Kos! Quit yapping and keep running!" Pivlic shouted over a cracking sound from Golozar's bam-stick. Kos didn't risk looking over his shoulder—the path was too treacherous and growing worse the closer they got to the Cauldron—but he heard a meaty thump as the shot struck one of Aun Yom's bandits. There was no scream, but there was no sound of a falling body either.

"This is insane!" Golozar shouted. "I've shot seven of them. They barely seem to notice! How did you do it, imp?"

"What have those Gruul got that can stop a bamshot, friend Golozar?" Pivlic said. "I simply shot one in the head."

The crack of another shot, then Golozar said, "Nothing is stopping them. The shots are going right *through* them, and they don't even seem to care."

Kos cursed as he put what the Gruul said together with the savage feeding frenzy they'd seen. "You don't have many undead in the Husk, do you?"

"Not especially," Golozar shouted back.

"Aim for their legs," Kos said. "Knock them down. Or if you think you can deadeye them, go for their heads. I don't think those are Gruul, Golozar. I knew they looked too pale."

"Undead?" Pivlic said. "I hate the undead. With the notable exception of our beloved and holy Obzedat and all patriarchs who have chosen that path in lieu of—"

"You're not in an audience chamber. Just keep running, Pivlic," Kos said, "or start shooting."

"I can't," Pivlic said. "Golozar is using my bam-stick."

"What?" Kos said.

"The ammunition spheres are not infinite," Pivlic said.

"All right, Golozar, start aiming carefully, and when that one runs out there's one more on my back," Kos said. "And I mean *carefully*. We can't afford to run out of shots before we get there."

"Who put you in charge?" Golozar shouted.

"I did," Kos replied. "When those friends of yours killed our thrull, the collar came off. Are we going to start this again?"

"No," Golozar said. "Forget it. Just get us there."

Kos had to slow to a jog to avoid a fan of spikes jutting out from a rubble spire. Whatever the mizzium fence had once guarded had long since rusted away, but the twisted spikes still grasped at the fleeing group like claws. The Husk was littered with stray pieces of mizzium. It was one of the most sought-after substances prospectors and miners looked for, but prospectors never ventured into the Husk. The threat of Gruul raids was too great, to say nothing of the ever-present danger of things like the nephilim.

"Mr. Kos," Crix said, "we will not need to count our ammunition for long. Look at that."

"It's just 'Kos,' " the old 'jek said. He turned his head in the direction the goblin indicated and saw a dragon—no, a drake, he corrected himself, few had ever seen a *real* dragon—take flight from the center of the Cauldron's dome. Drakes were not true dragons, but they were close enough. This one looked big enough to roast the four of them alive if it chose.

The scarlet reptile wasted no time circling but spread its leathery wings and headed directly for them. It flapped in the hot, dusky wind and screeched a terrifying wail into the afternoon sky.

"Tell me why won't we need ammo." Kos said.

"Because," Crix said, "it's not coming for us, I believe—oh dear."

"Oh dear?" Kos said.

"Duck!" Crix and Pivlic shouted at the same time. The goblin leaped from Kos's shoulder and rolled into a ball before she hit the ground, while Kos managed to catch himself before he was impaled on the mizzium fence. Pivlic had actually shouted while he was *already* on the ground. The imp's survival instincts were without peer. There was an "Oof!" when Golozar hit the earth just after Kos did, and the sky went black as the drake—small compared to a dragon but still boasting a considerable wingspan—sailed only handsbreadths overhead. A wave of heat washed over them and the drake's cry was cut off by a blast of flame.

"Everybody alive? Was that one of us?" Kos shouted.

"No, it was one of them," Crix said, the first back to her feet.

"Nothing that belongs to Zomaj Hauc would think of eating his courier. Anyone else though . . ."

Crix didn't have to finish her sentence. The drake had already circled around for another pass at Aun Yom's group of bizarre undead Gruul, if that's what they were. Kos was almost certain now, but almost was not good enough for court, as the saying went.

Aun Yom was not bothering to fight the drake. Unlike the nephilim, the flyer had a distinct advantage here. Instead, the pursuers scattered, hoping, apparently, that enough of them could get around the drake to keep up the chase.

Golozar scoffed. "Shameful. They already flee! Aun Yom, you are no Gruul."

"I think that's safe to say," Kos said. The drake emitted a second blast of flame that immolated three more Gruul on the spot, and finally the scattering maneuver became a retreat. As they fled, Kos saw glowing light emerging from the wounds Golozar's shots had created. Now everything made sense—they were undead but not the kind he'd been thinking. These were corpses all right, but the thing that kept them moving wasn't necromancy. Not exactly. It was a form of ghostly possession.

"Can't believe my luck," Kos muttered.

"Yes, we were indeed lucky, friend Kos," Pivlic said from up ahead. "We will be luckier if that drake does not return to us after it finishes with them."

"No, I mean the bad luck," Kos replied, breaking into a jog as the small group hurried toward their destination. "I hate ghosts."

"Those weren't ghosts," Golozar objected. "Were they?"

"Look at those wounds," Kos said. "They're glowing. Those aren't ordinary zombies."

"Well, they're fleeing, anyway," Pivlic said. "And the drake is chasing. Would this be a fortuitous time to rest for a moment?"

"But we are so close," Crix said. "We must go on."

"I'm with Crix on this one," Kos said. "That drake is a patrol beast. It will be back, and like she said the rest of us are vulnerable even if she isn't." Despite himself, Kos hadn't felt this healthy, this strong, this *necessary* for more than a decade. You've been lying to yourself, Kos, he thought. You never should have retired, no matter how many dead you had on your conscience. The dead were still there, after all. Now he just had more time to dwell on them.

"They are fleeing toward Trijiro's camp," Golozar said. "My clan will finish them if the drake doesn't. I will not shirk my appointed task, but I admit I yearn to join them."

The temperature only grew more oppressive, the air thick with haze and plague. Crix was able to conjure some water to replace what they'd lost after they'd spent another half hour getting closer to the source of the steady rise in temperature. The goblin's homing senses grew sharper with every step, and finally Kos was able to set her down. Crix walked on ahead to lead the small group. With her help, they avoided any further mishaps and had reached the perimeter of the Cauldron by the time the sun started to cast long, serrated shadows before them.

Crix never paused at the edge of the boundary and walked out into the open. Amid the chaotic network of outflow pipes and support struts that made up the Cauldron's steamworks and power plants—a structured chaos, not unlike the great sigil built into the architecture of the City of Guilds—sat a gate big enough to admit Hauc's drake, with a single djinn standing guard. Its translucent form glowed with a harsh, orange light that looked an awful lot like a bam-stick ammo globe.

"These three are with me," Crix said. She strode boldly to the gate. "We are delivering a message to the great magelord Zomaj Hauc, may his flame never be extinguished." The djinn did not speak but stepped aside as the courier stopped in her tracks, waiting, and it silently nodded. Crix beckoned the other three to follow.

"Is this absolutely necessary?" Pivlic said. "We're here, right? Mission accomplished, as the wojeks say?"

Golozar stepped forward. "I swore to deliver this goblin safely. I'm going in."

Kos shrugged. "It will get me out of this air. Maybe they've got a spare helmet. You can walk back if you like, Pivlic. I'm sure the baroness will understand when you tell her you're pretty sure the courier got where she needed to go."

"You're responsible for my safety, remember," the imp said. "I could make you come back with me. But you make a good point, my friend. And the baroness would no doubt make many more."

The stone gate, which had looked like a solid block of granite when Kos first saw it, split along an invisible seam and swung inward. The short entry hall ended at a bend inside, and the entire entryway glowed with reddish heat from within that dueled with the torches to illuminate walls. A blast of warmth hit them full in the face, making Pivlic yelp in surprise.

Kos took a long pull on the water skin, hung it back on the belt of his torn, stinking suit, and stepped in after Crix and Golozar. Pivlic was the last inside.

"I'll watch our backs, this time," he said.

"You'd better," Kos replied.

* * * * *

Still seated in the privacy of the *Pyraquin*'s cockpit, Zomaj Hauc did not see the courier when at last she arrived. But he felt her step through the gates and into his immediate domain. He smiled.

At long last, it was that simple. He should never have worried.

Though she had never set foot in the Cauldron project, of course his faithful Crix would find her way, whether the Orzhov succeeded or failed. She was his creation. Most of her, anyway.

He would enjoy pointing out the Orzhov's incompetence.

Hauc decided to wait a while before notifying his masked accomplice. Why stop his partner from slaughtering Gruul, if that was his intention? Hauc certainly didn't need them alive, and their ghosts would provide far more use to him. Besides, the dragon's gift let him feel every exhilarated jolt of triumph from the drake.

Hauc smiled, and his eyes glowed a slightly brighter shade of red as he pushed himself out of the flight chair and pressed the release for the exit ramp. He couldn't imagine why he'd been concerned. His faithful courier had not failed him.

But these others would most certainly have to die for daring to follow her into the Cauldron. They would not understand what he was doing any more than Niv-Mizzet. The treasures he'd found in the Cauldron were his and his alone. And once they were free, the world would be as well. Freed from ten thousand years of unnatural order and abominable law.

The world didn't deserve it, but Hauc was doing it all for them. His reign would be glorious. Those who needed wiping out—like the Gruul and perhaps even the Selesnyans—would be eliminated. Those who needed his wisdom, his strength, his magnificence to lead them would sing his praises. The Guildpact itself would crumble, no longer necessary, when Zomaj Hauc set Ravnica ablaze beneath his fiery banner.

Hauc gazed out through the transparent sphere and smiled at his charges. With them at his side, no one could stop him.

CHAPTER 11

The Book of Orzhov—The Book of Deals—*is nothing more than a web of rules, regulations, and complications that can be interpreted by anyone to mean anything that individual wishes. We've made an excellent start indeed, but there is much room for improvement, fellow patriarchs. We have work yet to do. The Book is a living document.*

— Patriarch Enezesku, acceptance address to the Obzedat
(25 Paujal 9103 Z.C.)

2 Cizarm 10012 Z.C.

Teysa couldn't decide which feeling would win out in the end: anger or disbelief. With no clear victor in sight for the foreseeable future, she decided to embrace both. She'd been used, used by those she—well, not those she *trusted,* since an advokist, let alone a Karlov, never trusted anyone completely—but by those she had thought served the same purpose as she.

Her headache, at least, had vanished.

"Uncle," she said, struggling to keep her composure, "you can't mean that."

"Oh yes," the mirror said with a disconcertingly satisfied tone. "You did it. You cut your way through my chest and drove the Gruul blade into my heart. The pain was exquisite, and I thank you for the experience. A fitting way to end my physical life, was it not?" He laughed at his own weak joke.

"You think this is funny? I *killed* you," Teysa said. "And you took that memory from me. You both let me believe it was Gruul."

"It was necessary. For you to receive your inheritance, I had to die. It was the only way to make Utvara legally and completely yours. I would not spread that fact around, though, if you want to keep it—suicide is not approved of in these situations, and I believe a good advokist could make a case for it."

"Is that a challenge?" Teysa said, anger rising to duel with her shock. "You've manipulated me, and you've—"

"I can't understand your objection. You've taken the title of baroness, but given time you will be a matriarch, I believe." The voice in the mirror chuckled again. "If you do as we agreed and become our agent, the Obzedat's agent."

"I had no idea you were so flexible on these things," Teysa said. "A matriarch?"

" 'I am what I have to be to achieve what I want,' " Uncle said. "That was something the fourth matriarch said, recorded in the Book."

"What? Fourth matriarch?" Teysa said. "There are no matriarchs mentioned in the Book."

"The Book of Orzhov is something everyone ought to read," the mirror said, "the complete Book I mean, not that trinket of the mortal realm. You don't know half of our true history. And you won't learn it until you're dead. You wouldn't be the first matriarch, my dear, but you would be the first in a long time." The mask spread into a wide smile, and Uncle's wet, muffled laughter erupted from the mirror.

Why shouldn't Uncle be jovial? He'd gotten what he wanted. And he'd given Teysa what she'd—well, not wanted but accepted as a challenge. Her inheritance. The entire Utvara region. And all she'd had to do to get it was kill Uncle. And all he had needed to do was use Melisk to convince her it had been the Gruul. Was that really such a bad thing? He didn't seem to think so, and it chafed at Teysa that she'd had to learn now. If only they'd trusted her, she would have probably embraced the plan entirely. Now, she wasn't so sure. Teysa had a contrary streak that rose to the fore when others told her what to do.

Uncle and Melisk had taken away her memory of a great many other things, and kept much more information entirely secret. In the last five minutes, all of the memories had been restored and she'd learned why the Cauldron was so very important to the Obzedat, Uncle, and Melisk. But the first question she asked was the most urgent as far as Teysa was concerned.

"My spells," Teysa said. "The narcolepsy. That's how he took away my memories, right? Somehow, while I was unconscious—"

"Not exactly," Uncle's voice said behind the mask in the mirror. "He wasn't erasing your memory *during* your spells."

"When did he do it?"

"You don't understand," Uncle said. "Your spells were a convenient fiction. My dear, you have never had narcolepsy. That was Melisk doing his job for us. Think. When did the spells start? Now that I've released the memories, you should be able to find it."

Teysa drove through the new and unfamiliar hallways in her mind, opening doors that hid things she knew but couldn't quite place in the context of her life without careful examination. "They didn't manifest until he became my attendant."

"Are you sure?" Uncle asked. His tone made Teysa mildly squeamish.

"No, wait. Not when he became the attendant. They started when he and I first—" Teysa said. Oh no, she thought. I should have seen that one rounding the bend.

"I see you have remembered," the mirror said.

"I'm going to kill him. No contracts. I'll do it personally. Perhaps with that Gruul knife you two seem so fond of."

"You've already agreed to do that by agreeing to serve," the mirror oozed. "Of course you will kill Melisk. I—excuse me, *we*—leave it to you to choose the appropriate means."

"I didn't agree to serve yet."

"Oh?" Uncle's tone hopped from jovial to cold threat.

"No," Teysa said. "I crossed my fingers."

"This is not a playground, my dear, and we are engaged in a child's game."

"You'll have to prove that in court. But you've told me everything I need to know. And with these," she said, opening her cloak to show Uncle's mirror the plague cure she'd acquired from the vedalken doctor, "I'm going to stop it from happening," Teysa added. Her decision was made. "Uncle, I'm going to keep Utvara in one piece, and we're moving operations into the flats once this plague is gone. The prospectors can work for us, or alongside us for a percentage. Your deal is null and void as far as I'm concerned. You have negotiated in bad faith. Very, very bad faith. This place is mine now. I belong to no one."

"Now, wait, my young advokist," Uncle said. "You don't really think you can agree to abide by our wishes then do the exact opposite of what we say? I'm telling you it *must* happen, no matter what you think. You have no choice in this. You do not make a deal with a being like Niv-Mizzet and expect to just break it at the last minute. And now you are part of that deal."

"No," Teysa said, "I am not. I've been your tool, but no longer. The deal you made will destroy everything here. Everything, including billions, trillions of zinos in treasure. I'm doing this for myself *and* for the Orzhov. If this deal comes to fruition, it won't just be Utvara that ends up in flames. 'The Guild of Deals cannot thrive without a world to deal in.' Consider that my first matriarchal proverb."

"You will not command us," the mirror hissed. "You have no choice in the—"

"You would loose that upon the world?" Teysa asked. "The Obzedat has lost its mind. This is my place. *My* barony. It's not your call."

"Baroness," Uncle said formally, "you will be just as dead whether Niv-Mizzet decides to kill you for breaking this deal or the Obzedat has you assassinated."

"Let them try. Assassins don't scare me. I never made the deal," Teysa said. "You did. If your Great Dragon comes after me, I'll take him straight to the High Judges of the Azorius Senate. I still have friends there. And if he chooses to pursue punitive action against you, who knows? He might need a good advokist. Perhaps on that day I'll come out of retirement. You won't have a leg to stand on. Not that you ever stood."

"Now you overstep, girl." The mirror skidded sideways slightly from the vibration of Uncle's roar. "You are nothing without the—"

Teysa tossed her cane straight up in the air, grabbed it by the end, and swung the heavy, silver handle against the mirror with both hands. It shattered, sending tens of thousands of tiny, screaming portraits of Uncle scattering across the antechamber table. A few seconds later, the screams died off and the shards were nothing more than broken glass.

"Oh, I overstep all right," Teysa said. "And I'm going to overstep all over you for using me." She brushed the handle of the cane off against one of Uncle's favorite tapestries, then blew the remains of the mirror off the table in a sparkling cloud that settled onto the floor after a few minutes. By then Teysa was already out the door.

On the steps of the Imp Wing she saw the first appearance of the *kuga mot* that night. The ghostly, golden shape seemed to emerge from the rising moon to sail steadily southwest until it faded back into blackness, its journey barely begun. The third Grugg brother, faithful Phleeb, ambled out the door in his apelike way, leading the new Gruggs she'd made from his essence. She'd dubbed the new Gruggs Lepheb and Heblep. She'd grown them in a little under a minute, but already they were complete and ready for action. The Orzhov blood had many uses. Creating thrulls was one she hadn't used enough, in her estimation.

The Gruul considered the *kuga mot* a bad omen. Prospectors believed it a good one. But omens of any kind were myth, Teysa believed. The *kuga mot* was probably a completely explicable phenomenon like the Schism. The Schism was probably even responsible for the illusion, a reflection of the moon on the sky-fracture's magical fields, not one thing more.

Omens meant anything you wanted them to. One person's good omen was always bad for someone else. Tonight, the *kuga mot* was a very bad omen for her not-so-faithful attendant.

* * * * *

Crix and her assorted self-appointed guardians emerged from the tunnel and into a tangled, initially baffling network of stone, metal, fire, and life that made the convoluted architecture outside the Cauldron look tame by comparison. The steamworks certainly were orderly to a trained mind, set at perfect angles and degrees to embody the most complex equations and variables known to the Izzet, and then some. Crix's enhanced, analytical mind had little difficulty making out a few of the simpler calculations of fate here and there, as well as a tangle of pipes and energy-filled tubes that were a perfect depiction of Niv-Mizzet's Seven-Dimensional Geometromancy Proof. Others tickled her mind with familiarity, but she couldn't quite place them all. It looked as if the magelord had been toying with the equations, creating new ones and twisting the old, bringing them all together in a glorious collision that spawned something entirely new. Her heart burned just a little with pride, pride tempered by a curious anger she still felt toward her master over the unnecessary deaths of four Gruul that sat heavy upon her conscience.

If she ever became a magelord—a fanciful thought, to be sure—she would never kill indiscriminately. Of that she was certain.

It took the courier a few moments to realize that the goblins within were not walking on the configurations themselves but on ramps, ladders, and other dangerous-looking elevated walkways spanning the entire Cauldron. The place was filled with them, alongside towering fusion djinns and the silent weirds, many of whom labored as hard as the goblins, it seemed. Crix hadn't been sure what to expect, but being completely ignored had not been on the list. Yet no one paid them any heed, save a few wearily curious glances from the goblins.

There it was. One very long, cold look from a pyrohydric weird. Its fiery body flared in recognition, and it turned away from her. The magelord would know of her arrival soon, if he didn't already.

The tangles of brilliantly planned infrastructure, when viewed as a whole, looked like a bizarre metal-and-magic nest built around the more familiar cylindrical power plants and beetle-shaped pyromanic generators, positioned at the four cardinal compass points. Steamcores gathered energy from the generators, power plants, and the geothermic dome itself, then fed it back into the network and out into the world. They hummed with energy, filling the air, already hot as a furnace, with a buzz that the goblin could feel in her bones.

All of this would have been reason enough to praise the genius of her master, Zomaj Hauc, despite her minor disillusionment with the casual deaths that had affected her personally. But the things that made Crix stop so suddenly that an equally awestruck Kos collided with her were truly wondrous. The shapes inspired a primal, terrified awe in the courier's soul.

"Those are—Those, those are—" Crix coughed in the thick heat and smog that clung to these lower levels.

"They're what?" Golozar said. "They look like some kind of generators. That's what you call these things, isn't it?".

"Your education is surprising for a Gruul," Pivlic said with thinly veiled suspicion. "But I don't think the goblin would be reacting like that to mere generators. It's obvious what they are. Think. Even a Gruul must know who leads the Izzet."

"I think I have a pretty good guess, but if my guess is right, then I'm also pretty sure my heart's finally given out and you all are hallucinations. And I really would have preferred better hallucinations for the end of my life," Kos said. "Those can't be what they look like. They just can't."

"They are," Crix said as she finally regained her breath.

"I have to agree with the goblin, my friend," Pivlic said. "I can feel it. Can't you?"

One alone would have been wondrous, a miracle. Three was inexplicable, a sure sign that the Izzet were meant for the greatness to which they all aspired, individually and as a guild. Three majestic ovoid shapes mottled with gemstone patches of gleaming color: one red, one a faded blue, and the third a deep-purple pattern like spattered goblin blood. The ovoids were under bombardment, simmering—no, *incubating*—beneath a staggering amount of energy on all sides. That was why the equations had been changed. They were perfectly set up to split the energy the Cauldron was taking in and divert much of into the ovoids. Truly masterful sigil-work. At least half the power being produced by the Cauldron went into the nest, if Crix understood the calculations.

Indeed the whole Cauldron was a nest, and judging from the weathered, hardened igneous stone that seemed to grow into the bases of the objects, supporting them and balancing their weight, it was a very old nest. Clearly the gigantic shapes had once rested within the caldera of the geothermic dome beneath their feet, laid there long ago by a creature that certainly must have passed from the world before the Guildpact was ever signed.

"Those," Crix said, her voice little more than a whisper, "are dragon eggs."

"That's impossible," Golozar said. "There are no dragons. Not anymore."

"Blasphemy," Crix said, stunned. "Great Niv-Mizzet—"

"I should have said none but him," Golozar said. "But he is a *he*. You're saying he laid eggs?"

"My well-educated Gruul friend," Pivlic interrupted, "you would be surprised how many things I have seen in even my short time on this plane that I once thought impossible. Gradually, I have come to realize that nothing is impossible. There are only improbabilities, improbabilities that either are or are not."

"Those sure look 'are' to me," Kos said. "Those look alive."

"Oh yes," Zomaj Hauc said as he stepped to the edge of the suspended landing platform he'd turned into his central command center. His voice cut through the din easily, at least to Crix's sharp ears, and she saw recognition on the faces of her companions too. "Indeed, they live," the magelord continued, the crystal sphere of the *Pyraquin* looming behind him like a halo. "Can you feel their furious impatience growing by the second? They want out. And now that my courier is here, their wishes will be fulfilled." The magelord spread his arms wide, and his eyes burned with orange flame.

The nest began to move all around them, jolting Crix out of another of the day's shocks, which just kept getting more alarming.

The steamworks screamed as components twisted and bent into new shapes, and those shapes snapped off tubes and stone pipes as they broke free of the nest and surrounded the small band. The shapes were roughly humanoid and reminded Crix of smaller versions of that first nephilim she'd encountered, the junk monster.

These weren't just monsters. They were guardians, like the fusion djinn and the weirds. But these were controlled, Crix suspected, directly by the magelord. These things couldn't possibly have independent thoughts. They'd been part of the steamworks only seconds before.

"My lord," Crix said, "I have arrived. This is not necessary."

"Crix. Crix, Crix, Crix. My favored one. You were one of my proudest experiments," Hauc said calmly. The calm did not last, and his voice was already showing strain as he added, "You dare speak to me now? After you have almost failed me?"

"But my lord, I—"

"Crix," the magelord interrupted, "you are a tool. One of my favorites, I admit, but only a tool. Be quiet. You should not have brought these others into the Cauldron. It is not time for others to learn of this. Not yet."

"I would have thought he'd be happier to see her," Kos muttered to the others.

Crix had to agree. This was not the welcome she'd expected. This was barely even a greeting. She felt more like a prisoner here than she had tied up in the Gruul camp.

Golozar snarled a battle cry and raised his bam-stick, aiming at the nearest pipe-guardian. The metallic monster stood on two thick legs of fire and metal, with four arms ending in brass fingers of wire and bolts. It had no head to aim at, but the Gruul let fly a shot at the center of its skeletal, metal-frame torso.

"No, don't!" Crix shouted. "You can't—"

The shot went clean through without striking anything solid and pinged harmlessly against the bottom of the platform. The pipe-guardian knocked Golozar onto his back with one swipe of its arm and sent the drained weapon skidding across the floor. It teetered on the edge of a lava pit, and Golozar doubled over, writhing in pain from the blow and the searing heat so nearby.

"Come, courier," Hauc said, beckoning the pipe-guardians to close ranks around the four. "We have work to do. Because I like you, Crix, you may even survive long enough to see the purpose of the message you carry. I may even show them, if you obey me. But they will have to die, as will you. I must be able to trust my courier, Crix, and you are showing signs of too much independence."

Hauc's words hit Crix harder than any fist could. Her master, her magelord, the one being she served without question. And what had that service gotten her?

From here, it looked like a fiery death, that's what.

* * * * *

Teysa spotted Wageboss Aradoz first and decided he was as good a place as any to start distributing the cure. The guildless were the least likely to take free medicine at face value, especially from an Orzhov, so getting them to join her should serve to hasten the formation of her makeshift alliance, her own Guildpact, as it were, to fight Hauc's mad plans.

Part of her mind still had trouble wrapping around Uncle's revelation. The Cauldron was only partly artificial. It was built upon an ancient nesting ground in the range of an even more ancient race of beings, and it had been buried for a reason. If not for the deal the Obzedat had struck with the dragon Niv-Mizzet, it would have stayed that way. But Niv-Mizzet wanted them hatched, and he'd managed to ply the ghostly patriarchs with enough of something—gold? Souls? Something she couldn't even imagine?—that they were willing to risk the end of Ravnica itself. Utvara would be the doormat for the apocalyptic power the Obzedat seemed happy to set loose.

Three new dragons in the world. Utvara had enough problems without *that*. Teysa did not consider herself the world-saving kind, but she did not see how anyone could benefit from releasing those creatures. Perhaps the Obzedat themselves would be safe, being ghosts, but what was the point of surviving in a world on fire?

Obviously, a madness had infected the Obzedat, as surely as the *kuga* had infected her barony, a barony that would be a bowl of ashes soon if she didn't find a way to unite these people. Teysa was counting on the cure to win their initial loyalty, and she had plenty of other resources yet to fall back on if needed.

The trio of Gruggs followed a few paces behind, Phleeb watchful, the other two jabbering in random, meaningless syllables. Fresh thrulls always took a few hours to settle down, but they were immediately obedient, at least. Once she made a stop at the construction site in the slums, she would send them on another mission, assuming everything went as planned with the wageboss. If Teysa couldn't buy the half-demon, the entire plan was likely to fail, but she had faith in her own judgment. To an Orzhov who knew her business, Aradoz was a diamond in the rough, ready to be shaped for her purposes. A diamond she knew just where to cut.

The half-demon spotted her as she rounded the new path his crews had sliced from the slums. A few buildings had been left standing, those that still had aesthetic appeal, and Aradoz seemed to have an excellent eye for architecture. A few workers came and went from these structures. Obviously they'd also been saved to serve as housing for the wageboss's laborers.

She'd made a sound choice when she pinned this one, Teysa reckoned. She'd given him nigh impossible goals, but he was finding ways to meet them, financially and ahead of schedule. She was pleased. Finally something was going exactly as Teysa had planned.

Wageboss Aradoz hopped with surprising agility from the second story of the mansion's growing framework and landed in a crouch before them on the path. He straightened and bowed with the exaggerated formality of one who rarely, if ever, bows before anyone.

"Baroness," he said, rising to face her, "an honor, once more. Truth be told, I had expected you earlier, but as I told your attendant, we broke ground not four hours after I met with you. I would have journeyed to your tavern to report, but I feel I'm better used here, keeping us on track. There is little time to waste."

The towering half-demon wageboss exuded fealty, and to her surprise she couldn't find a trace of insincerity in it. Eagerness, even. Yet he wasn't telling the whole story, that much was clear. It would have been clear to a blindfolded first-year advoklerk. The wageboss must have found a treasure vein while laying the foundations. It was the only thing that made sense.

So be it. Teysa would get her cut later. Right now she welcomed his eagerness to help. She needed all she could get. She nodded to Aradoz and turned on her cane to take in the breadth of burgeoning structure. She could almost make herself believe she would end up living in it. "Well done. Wageboss, I'm also pressed for time, so I'll dispense with pleasantries for now. First, I want you to add a little something onto the work order."

The half-demon bristled, but the genial expression fought its way back to his visage before he said, "More work. At the same . . . rate as we discussed earlier?"

"Here's the renegotiation," Teysa said. "You can take it or leave it, and if you leave it, well, the polar factories always need wagebosses. You know, the mortality rates and all." Aradoz nodded and failed to quell a scowl.

"I'll take it, I'm sure," Aradoz said.

"Knew you were smarter than you looked," Teysa said. "You'll get me four of the biggest, toughest bruisers on your work crews. I'll pay you the market share for them, and they're going to go with me to the Cauldron for an important conference with that Izzet. When we're done, if they're alive, they'll be free to hire on at equitable rates as bodyguards or other positions suiting their abilities. If they seek it out, I will sponsor their petitions to become dues payers." The wageboss's eyes widened, and his spiked jaw clacked against his metal tool apron.

"Guild membership?" Aradoz said. "Baroness, these are just laborers. Are you sure they deserve such a rich prize? You must need them very badly."

"Don't spoil my generous mood with haggling."

"You wound me. I merely—"

"Aradoz, I'll make you a deal. Let me finish and I will let you keep both of your horns."

"My—Yes. Dues payers. I'm sure I have just the people."

"Now here's the part you should have waited for before you started in with the haggling. I can't rightly give them membership unless I buy them from a licensed Orzhov agent. Therefore, you are now dues-paying member as well, effective immediately, by my power as Baroness of Utvara." The wageboss's eyes widened, and he stood frozen in shock as she stepped forward and pinned a small stone to his collar. It matched the one on his chest and marked his full and instantaneous status as a senior dues payer. "Congratulations."

"Thank you, Baroness," the wageboss managed. "This is the most profound—"

"Listening, Aradoz. It's the single most important skill you can ever learn. Master it and you'll go far in this guild. Now show me who you've got for me."

"Right now? I need to go over the manifests, sort by seniority—"

"Not right now you don't. I'm in a hurry."

"Of course, Baroness, but I will need at least a few minutes to gather them together. Despite appearances, not all of these ones are fighters. Those ogres over there? They can crush rock with their bare hands and bend struts with their foreheads, but they're no good in a throw down. Too many blows to the head. But they're tough. If you just need cannon fodder, they're perfect."

"The best fighters you've got, and they've got to get along and take orders," Teysa said. "No cannon fodder. I made an honest offer. And before you go, one more thing," she added as a seeming afterthought, laying on a dash of number nineteen: Why, this just occurred to me. "I want you to hire up any and all guildless you've got left. Sign them to standard contracts. I'll seal them later. Put them to work rebuilding the surrounding structures. They're going to need places to live, places they can go home to after a hard day's work pumping zinos into the economy."

"Instant citizens," the wageboss nodded.

"You catch on quickly, Aradoz. Now these workers of yours," she continued, pointedly failing to call the workers 'slaves,' "will be very busy in the coming months and years turning this valley into a shining new city, one where their progeny will live full lives under the house of Karlov. If they have the strength for it."

Teysa knew that many of the guildless were exiles and castoffs from the Rakdos and Gruul, and the challenge of strength was something most of them would have trouble resisting.

"When do you need these four fighters?" Aradoz asked. The leering fool she'd first met had completely transformed, and an efficient businessman had taken over.

"Now, Wageboss," Teysa said. "Get to it."

She turned to the Gruggs. "Brothers, come here." The thrulls ambled over obediently on all fours, knuckle-walking like gorillas. Gorillas with wicked, gold-plated claws, not a stitch of fur, and frog's heads to match their amphibian legs. She needed a second Bephel, and his brother would have to do. She placed a palm on the lead thrull's forehead and said, "Phleeb. Speak."

"Phleeb speaks, Baroness, great, sweet, Baroness, she who—"

"Speak when spoken to," Teysa clarified, and the thrull clamped his wide mouth shut. "Listen. Take your new brothers and head north to the Husk. You're looking for Kos and Pivlic. Do you remember them?"

"Took other brothers, they did!" the thrull said, eager to get as many words in as possible as long as he had this new power of speech. "Can find them, for sure! Sure! Brothers still alive!"

"Good to know," Teysa said. "Then go find them, and if that courier's with them, bring them back. If the courier's not with them, help them find her—female goblin, blue robes, red topknot, with an arm that glows, you can't miss her—and bring *her* back. If she won't come back, kill her. And kill anyone who tries to stop you. Do you understand? It's very, very important that you can find her even if something has happened to Bephel and Elbeph. You understand me?"

"Yes! Blue robes! Bring back! Won't come back, she gets the claws! The claws! Got it!" Phleeb said. "Bephel and Elbeph, they'll be there! Gruggs hard to kill!"

"I'm counting on that," Teysa said. "Good luck."

The thrull trio cleared the edge of town by the time Aradoz came back with his picks from the laboring masses: a pair of minotaur siblings, male and female, who had more brands than skin, and mizzium rings through their noses that marked them as one-time Izzet workers. Good choice. They would be eager for payback. The third was a goblin who stood a head taller than any she'd seen before, tall enough to look her in the eye without raising his chin. No, not completely goblin. Those eyes and teeth showed some troll ancestry, which also explained his height. The fourth was an elf, Devkarin from the look of her, eyeing Teysa like a cat examining a mouse. The Devkarin looked away when Teysa met her gaze with her own. Nobody did cat on mouse like an advokist.

"Aradoz, introduce us and get to work on the other matters we discussed," Teysa said.

"Gladly, Baroness," the half-demon said. He pointed at the minotaur male and said, "That's Sraunj and his sister Enka. Found them at a Gruul camp. They'd killed everyone there, but the plague had knocked them down. The pollen works wonders. The fellow with the teeth is Dreka-Tooth. Guess why."

"No," Teysa said. "Hello Sraunj, Enka, Dreka-Tooth," she added, nodding to each in turn. "Welcome to the team."

"All right, all right, pressed for time, my apologies, Baroness," the half-demon said. He'd gone from the stunned phase to giddiness in record time. "The lady on the end is Nayine Shonn. Say hello, Nayine."

"Hello," the Devkarin said. The elf smiled, showing glistening teeth capped with mizzium points. Her black eyes reflected the moon beneath tangled, green dreadlocks matted with dye and clay. Teysa had heard of the tooth-capping custom among those Devkarin who still ate raw flesh, a practice that had been in decline for several years, but she'd never heard of mizzium being used in the process.

"Has the wageboss told you what's happening?" Teysa said.

"You need fighters," Nayine said. She seemed to be the speaker of the group, or at least one the others deferred to. "You own us. We help you, we go free. We can even sign up for your chump guild. Am I leaving anything out?"

"No," Teysa said. "But remember who's in charge."

"Of course, Baroness," the elf said with brazen insincerity Teysa chose to ignore.

"Release their shackles, Wageboss," she said, and the half-demon did as she asked. Teysa pulled one of the tubes of the plague cure from her robes and approached the minotaur. "Hold still," she said and pressed the end of the tube against the brute's shoulder. When she'd done the same with the other three and the wageboss, who sputtered an objection but held still just as the others had under the power of the blood, she handed the tube to Aradoz. "This must get to every one of your workers within the next day. It's a cure for the plague. That should be enough to for you to get the job done, but it's got to be done fast. If I find out you've charged a soul for any of this, you'll be out of the guild permanently."

"I—" the half-demon's jaw dropped all over again. "Yes, Baroness."

"Good man," Teysa said. "Follow me, you four. We're making a few stops before we get to the fighting." *If* we get to the fighting, she added silently.

CHAPTER 12

All over Ravnica, the ledev guardians patrol the roads and keep travelers safe. Everywhere but here. Why? What are they afraid of? Perhaps the rumors are true. Perhaps the Selesnyan Conclave's power is finally fading, and we bold pioneers must step into the void and protect ourselves. For if we don't, who will?
—Editorial, the *Utvara Townsman* (11 Golgar 1009 Z.C.)

2 Cizarm 10012 Z.C.

Teysa's small group had grown to a small army by the time they reached the edge of the Vitar Yescu compound. She'd gained the temporary allegiances of a dozen of Dr. Nebun's tough, resilient virusoids. They were misshapen creatures composed of the raw components of disease itself, or so the Simic had told her. She didn't need a verity circle to believe him on that count. They didn't have names as such, but she'd assigned them numbers, and the doctor had been kind enough to etch the numerals into their chests with acid. They would answer only to her until the doctor told them otherwise, and he would be hard at work in his lab. Teysa made sure of that with a few outrageous demands she knew the vedalken would find challenging. She'd turned down the proffered services of Uvulung the frog aberration.

The thieves' guild had assigned a trio of shadewalkers to her for forty-eight hours, after which she'd promised to pay triple for their services as needed. She assumed they were following along at the position she'd assigned them but was glad she couldn't make them out against the shadows. That meant they were doing their jobs, watching over the rest of them and ready to strike anyone who threatened her. The thieves were not a true guild of the Guildpact, though there had long been rumors that they answered to the master of the Dimir, the vampire Szadek. The rumors had struck most sensible people, Teysa included, as ridiculous, at least until the Dimir master had reportedly appeared at the Decamillennial Convocation only to be arrested by the very man she'd sent with Pivlic the imp to track down Hauc's courier.

Whatever its members were and whomever they served, Teysa knew the thieves' guild considered contracts to be as sacred as any Orzhov did. Their operations would collapse if a thief's word could not be trusted. Nor did they confine themselves to mere thievery. Many were private investigators of sorts she'd used herself during more than one important case.

There were no useful Rakdos in Utvara. The Gruul had long ago wiped them out during the fallow period—the two "tribal" guilds were bitter enemies. But she had gotten a quartet of hulking Golgari ogre zombies. Half-plant, half-dead flesh, they were not much smarter than the virusoids but would do the job. They would be due back at the farmsteads in forty-eight hours as well. If she hadn't succeeded in forty-eight hours, it would all be pointless anyway. They marched beside a pair of Haazda, the two sober ones she'd found at the station. The two men volunteered for the promise of free drinks at the Imp Wing for life, but they didn't get a nip until she released them from their promise to serve her. Haazda were not like wojeks, their oaths not as binding. They were probably the least effective members of her multiguild force, but their presence added to diversity, and therefore the strength, of her own personal Guildpact.

She only had three more guilds to take under her wing—the Selesnyans, the Gruul (assuming they were still alive, with the taj tearing the Husk apart looking for the courier), and finally any

Izzet who chose to abandon their insane magelord.

"Shonn," she called, and the Devkarin stepped up to her side. "Stay here with the others. This will only take a moment." Teysa still didn't trust her, but the elf was effective at helping her manage her "troops." Watching Teysa throw around her zinos this evening, she suspected Nayine Shonn had begun to see the potential benefits of the baroness's goodwill in ways mere words hadn't gotten across. The cure, distributed for free, had seemed to work wonders too. It was very un-Orzhovlike of Teysa, the Devkarin had said after the baroness paid off the thieves' guild, which was of course what the baroness was counting on.

Teysa took a deep breath and almost immediately sneezed as she inhaled the pollen-rich air. The small group jumped almost in unison, though she couldn't be sure about the shadewalkers.

"Everybody wait here," Teysa said. "I'll be right back."

She walked down a path of stone cut into a small, bleak field of mottled grass and thin, unhealthy-looking trees with cracked, oozing bark. The Golgari had more success in the metallic soil that bordered the flats than the life churchers. Only the Vitar Yescu was anything close to healthy in their compound. If it had been a structure, it would have been ten, twelve stories tall. There were spiraling ramps and stairs hitched to lookout posts where stood the first ledev guardians Teysa had seen since arriving in Utvara, but most of the Selesnyan population was there to protect the giant tree, not live on it. Instead, the various monks, acolytes, and high holy types made their homes in a small forest of fast-growing veztrees.

Teysa noted the Golgari had been only allowed a small portion of the structures, but that didn't surprise her. There hadn't really been enough Golgari for them to completely displace the Selesnyans, despite her order. The Vitar Yescu looked healthy as near as Teysa could tell, so apparently the nearby undead had not affected it. Not that the Vitar Yescu would be necessary, not unless the plague somehow mutated yet again.

One of the benefits of the two Haazda: They were as honest as one could hope for in law enforcement. The path forked just where they'd said it would and opened into a more complex web, with spiders the size of small dromads clinging to the veztrees. The arachnids spun long cables of glistening silk that the Selesnyans harvested for all the purposes one might expect—armor, weapons, construction, and art. Glowglobes hung from thick web lines, illuminating what the web-filtered moonlight couldn't.

The path ended at four veztrees that had grown together to form a small fortress of wood, stone, and steel. That was where the First Acolyte Wrizfar Barkfeather of the Selesnyan Conclave, Holy Protector of the Vitar Yescu, Knight of something, would be found, the Haazda said.

The spiders didn't disturb Teysa in the slightest. She'd walked under the legs of a solifuge golem that would barely have bothered to step on these creatures, and arachnids couldn't have been less frightening to her. She was not prey, and the spiders seemed to know it. They gave her a wide berth, some skittering away to their nests, awaiting an easier meal.

Teysa cleared the spider tunnel and stepped into the shadow of a living edifice. Unlike the other veztrees, these four—a subspecies, perhaps—boasted huge boughs bearing thin, waxy needles. The thick bark was almost completely covered in distinctive Selesnyan architecture. The homes, libraries, guard posts, schools, barracks—all of it grew upon and into the structure. One of the boughs had been coaxed to grow downward and form a wide ramp leading to the first elevated level of the Conclave of Utvara, where a set of redwood double doors some thirty feet at their arched peak stood open to the night sky. Teysa marched up the ramp, to the surprise of a few straggling parishioners who avoided her gaze. The doors swung inward, and Teysa involuntarily cringed when the wave of welcome and comfort washed over her. Emotional ambushes were a Selesnyan specialty, in her experience.

Church was in session. In session, and under heavy guard.

A wide central aisle separated two large groups that represented a jumbled cross-section of typical life churchers. Centaurs kneeled on their forelegs, their heads bowed in meditation. Silhana elves in white and emerald robes of varying styles that all somehow looked of a piece, sat cross-legged, equally lost in the gathering of minds that the Selesnyans, in Teysa's opinion, mistook for communing with life itself. There were wild-looking humans, too, young dryads fresh off of the Unity Tree, and even a hulking family of loxodons. A sextet of centaurs in ledev battle armor flanked the aisle in two lines of three, poleaxes sharp and gleaming in the greenish light of the Selesnyan globes. All paid her little heed as she strode toward the pulpit.

One of the Selesnyans certainly did notice her walk in, the only one whose eyes had been open from the moment Teysa had crested the ramp. "Wrizfar Barkfeather," she said, willing to risk disrupting a few wholly unproductive meditations on the wonders of existence. "I am Teysa Karlov. May we speak privately?"

The elf untangled his legs and rose to his feet effortlessly. He nodded once, and his face belied no other emotion in any way. She could use his cooperation, but didn't expect to get it easily. Her mistreatment of him had been foolish, a miscalculation that had only served as petty entertainment.

The old elf, who had long ago gone wrinkled and bald except for a heavily braided beard, raised a finger to his lips. Teysa nodded in return. Barkfeather crooked that finger and beckoned her to follow him up a spiraling inner staircase to the next level up, and Teysa followed. It was slow going. Apparently, respect for life in all its forms didn't extend to giving a woman with a cane a handrail, but she managed.

Barkfeather led Teysa through several winding tunnels grown into the tree's trunk and past several empty rooms. "You don't seem to be full up yet," Teysa remarked. "Recruitment down?"

The elf shot her an expressionless look over one shoulder just long enough that she placed a hand over her mouth and mouthed, *All right, already*. Expressionless, but not without meaning.

Their silent walk ended at a seemingly random door that bore no distinguishing marks as far as Teysa could see. Almost nothing in here did, the complete opposite of the ornately decorated, some might say gaudy, fixtures and doorways of an Orzhov structure. The door opened into a high-ceilinged room lined with books on one side and huge, segmented windows on the other. The moon looked huge and distorted in the haphazard Selesnyan design.

"The moon is not distorted," Barkfeather said. "It is something else causing that, something your kind bought and paid for, I think. You call it 'the Schism.'"

"Everyone calls it 'the Schism,'" Teysa said, somewhat relieved to find this entire exchange would not be conducted in pantomime. She walked to the only piece of furniture in the otherwise empty room, a large perch next to an open section of the window. "You don't strike me as a falconer, Barkfeather, but with a name like that I shouldn't have been—hey. Don't read my mind."

"Then do not think so loudly," the old priest said.

"I don't think—Never mind. What do you know about the Schism? Short answer, if you please. I've spoken to a lot of cryptic types today, and I'm a little weary of it, if it's all the same to you."

"I know it is why this place has no lingering ghosts. Well, except those taj of yours. They are remarkable, but they're a special case, aren't they?"

"Taj?" Teysa said.

"Your ghostly servants. Your attendant is with them, and you will meet him soon, I think, if you stay on your current path. What do you want from me, Teysa Karlov?"

"I wouldn't mind knowing how *you* know so much," Teysa replied. "I didn't come here for my fortune. I'm not here to argue with you either." She opened her cloak and pulled out a pair of plague cures from her dwindling supply. She offered them to the elf, who looked at them but did not move. "This is why I'm here: a chance for us to eliminate this plague now. End the *kuga*, Barkfeather, now, immediately. With this. And before you object, yes, it's Simic. I'm aware that the Simic and the life—the Selesnyans don't always see eye to eye, but this will work."

The elf still hadn't moved or changed his expression from one of constant contemplation. "How do you know it will work?" Barkfeather said.

"I put Nebun in a verity circle. He wasn't lying. It will work. But only if we all take it within twenty-four hours."

"This is extremely suspicious," the elf said. He took a few steps toward her and plucked one of the tubes from her hand like it was a poisonous snake. "Simic magic is based on unnatural beginnings. Their cures are often worse than their plagues."

"Just answer me this," Teysa said. "If everyone carrying the plague became immune, would that leave enough pollen to finish off what's airborne? Could it mutate again? The Simic can create these things, but you know how they behave once created."

"Could it? Would it?" the elf finally displayed an expression, one of mild surprise, for only a moment. "I think yes, the Vitar

Yescu could at that," he said. "The plague could also mutate. There are many possibilities."

"Many possibilities? Is that the best you can give me?"

"I am afraid so. But it interests me. I still fear there may be side effects to this Simic 'cure' we may regret later, but I misjudged you, Teysa Karlov. I had not thought you the type to try to save this place."

"And I treated you rudely," Teysa said. "That's just bad business." She placed the second green cylinder in his hands, and he looked at them with strange curiosity, like a child allowed to pick up a sword. "You, all of you, need to take this. The two tubes there are enough to cure everyone here, but speed is the watchword." Without waiting for his reply, she grabbed one of the cylinders back and pressed the end against his neck. Barkfeather gasped, and his eyes widened. "That's how you do it. Simple."

"It is—It is working."

"Of course it is," Teysa said. "Now it's up to you to take care of the rest. You must, Barkfeather."

"And why must we do this, Teysa Karlov?" Barkfeather said, his voice rising in volume and dropping in pitch as he straightened, his gentle eyes now creased in anger. "Who are you to command those whose only master is life itself?" He placed a hand against his neck as if he'd been bitten by an insect that had only now begun to itch.

"Because if you don't we don't have a chance of stopping three newborn dragons from burning us all alive."

Now the elf *was* shocked. It was so sudden Teysa couldn't help but break into a small smile of triumph herself. "Excuse me," he said, "three newborn *whats?*"

* * * * *

Teysa shifted the sling to keep her cane from slapping against her legs as she rode. The dromad huffed a bit but continued at an agreeable pace down the thoroughfare. The beast was a gift from Barkfeather and his church. The old elf had naturally insisted that the dromads were choosing their new masters, Obzedat forbid any being should possess another. The church had been able to spare enough mounts for anyone in her entourage who could ride. The others were keeping up as best they could, but the dromads were speedy.

They charged past mining claims, some of which were operating on into the night, though most were abandoned for the evening except for the night watch sitting in crow's nests built into the rigs. She reined in the galloping dromad when they reached a narrow trail that effectively ended the ride. This had to be the right way to the Gruul camp. At the very least it was the way Kos and Pivlic had gone. That much was clear from the slaughtered pair of thrulls and the dead, bloated dromad lying between them. The dromad was Kos's. She'd seen him take it out of the stable, and the thrulls were Bephel and Elbeph. Elbeph's body was spread over a mile's worth of trail, in fact. There was no sign of Phleeb or his new brothers, but then Teysa was no tracker.

Aside from the mounts, the Selesnyan had made one more major contribution to her forces, a golden falcon that squawked into her ear. "These were allies of yours," the bird said in the voice of the First Acolyte, or the nearest approximation an avian throat could muster.

"Yes, Barkfeather," Teysa said. "But don't weep for them. Well, weep for the dromad if you wish. But not the thrulls. Now don't hold on too tight. Those claws are sharp." She slipped off the side of her dromad, grabbing her cane from the saddle on the way down. She raised a hand to Nayine Shonn, who brought the rest of the odd gang to a stop.

"I can see what you're doing. I cannot be so close to necromancy!" the falcon screeched.

"Relax, it's not necromancy. Well, not exactly," Teysa said. Then again . . . "Actually, it is necromancy. Why don't you go keep your eye on the Husk? See if you can find any trace of Pivlic or that human Kos. See if you can find the Gruul. Just don't look down here if you're going to go all squeamish on me."

"Gladly," the falcon said. It launched from Teysa's shoulder and circled overhead, passing in front of the moon with a cry.

"Shapeshifting show-off," Nayine muttered.

"Quiet, for a moment, please," Teysa said to her motley assemblage. She stepped to Bephel, the nearest dead Grugg. Bephel had probably been killed more often than all of the other Gruggs combined, but that had only made him bounce back more quickly. She picked up his head, what was left of it, by the ear, and pressed it against the stump atop his reptilian neck. "Bephel," she said and released the head.

Against all logic, the severed head stayed put and began to grow new flesh. She then took his tail and a severed leg and did the same, repeating "Bephel" each time. An arm, another arm, and the thrull was complete again. "Rise," she said at last, and thanks to her Orzhov blood Bephel Grugg did just that. "Bephel. Speak."

"It's terrible!" the thrull said, as if complete resurrection was something people did every day. "The attendant—he's already been there, and he's doing bad things. Lots of bad things. It was fun to watch, but then he did bad things to Bephel and Elbeph. Elbeph, who was already injured! He was just trying to get back to me! Elbeph coming back soon?"

"In a minute," Teysa said. "The attendant has been where?"

"The pathetic camp of those Gruul primitives, of course," Melisk said, stepping from the shadowed overhang that jutted from the edge of the Husk like a natural barricade against the flats—the teeth of the Huskvold. The moment the attendant moved, the rest of the hills moved with him. Drawn, pale Gruul bodies possessed by the taj emerged from every crack, fissure, and outcrop in the area. The ghostly agents had been busy, spreading through what looked like at least thirty individuals by Teysa's quick head count. Thirty taj against her hodgepodge "Guildpact army," and the attendant himself, a power in his own right even without the blood. Or so it appeared.

"I have to admit, Melisk," she said, "I sort of hoped it would happen like this."

"What would happen like this?" the traitor sneered.

"That you'd bring the taj," Teysa said, "that you'd be too frightened, you pathetic, traitorous, mind-raping pig, to face me yourself. You're smart, I'll give you that. And damned devious. You've got a problem, though."

"Really," Melisk said. "And what would that be?"

"You aren't as smart as you think you are."

"These are the taj, my lady," Melisk said. "They have destroyed the Utvar Gruul in their homes and will hunt down the rest with ease. They destroyed an entire lokopede filled with Orzhov when there were only ten of them. You haven't got a chance."

"Where did you study, Melisk?" she asked.

"What are you talking about?" the attendant replied. "What does that have to—"

"Where?" Teysa repeated. "Don't bother to answer, because I know as well as you do. You studied in the same halls I did, learned from the same masters of law, of business, and of the arcane arts related to them."

"Of course I did," Melisk said. "I grow tired of this stalling. You can't talk your way out of this, 'Baroness.' I've been waiting too long, and you can't stop me now. The taj are mine."

"Then attack me," Teysa said. "Unless you want to know why I'd ask about your education, of all things, right now. Aren't you curious, Melisk?"

The attendant looked unsure of himself for the first time in as long as Teysa could remember. "Tell me."

"There are areas of study open only to those with the blood," Teysa said.

"This is ridiculous," Melisk said. "I am not a child, to be spoken to in this way." He looked genuinely surprised that Teysa wasn't already nodding along with every word he said. He was trying to trigger a "narcolepsy" spell. She rapped a knuckle against her forehead.

"Found a new doctor," Teysa said. "He fixed me up. You won't be getting back in here again, Melisk. You're not going to take anything else from me. And you're not going to take them either."

"Them? I don't know what you're talking about." Melisk smiled.

"The taj," Teysa said, "They answer to you?"

"As you can plainly see," Melisk said, but his voice was already betraying doubt.

"These three stones, Melisk," Teysa replied. She leaned onto her cane with her left hand and thrust her right into the moonlight. Her sleeve slid down to expose her forearm. "You don't have any idea what they really mean or what the blood means. Nothing created purely of Orzhov magic can resist it. Ever."

"I have enough taj at my back to—"

"Do you?" Teysa said. "Or do I?"

The attendant's eyes shifted back and forth. There were more than thirty taj backing him—or there were thirty taj surrounding him, from another point of view.

"Taj," Teysa said, her trained voice ringing clearly as a bell in the moonlit night, "kill Melisk. And don't leave any pieces larger than . . ." she smiled at Melisk, who had gone completely white as he tried to back away in every conceivable direction at once. "No pieces larger than an egg," she finished.

Teysa had never truly enjoyed what passed for vengeance among Orzhov the way she enjoyed the screams of the traitorous attendant that floated through the haze as her dromad galloped into the thick, humid air and echoed off the metallic hills. When the last note of terror died out long after Melisk had, Teysa called, "You can come down now, Barkfeather."

The baroness could just make out a wispy, translucent shape that left Melisk's dismembered corpse and wafted into the sky toward the Schism, curling like smoke as the falcon flew threw it beak-first.

The bird's flight path shattered the fragile ghost, and it began to flicker, failing to find cohesion. Melisk's soul dissipated like the smoke it resembled, and the falcon fluttered down to alight upon her shoulder.

"An auspicious first battle," the shapeshifter said.

"We didn't do the real work yet," Teysa said. "Let's get back to the dromads. I don't think these trails are going to get us to the Cauldron in time."

It was hours before dawn, but the sky was growing brighter by the minute. She knew little about what that meant for the Schism, the source of the new light, but it was bright enough to drown out the light of the setting moon.

"Shonn," she called as she sped back to her motley group.

"Baroness," the Devkarin called back. She was astride a dromad and led Teysa's beside her. "Your dromad awaits. Where to next?"

"Already counting your rewards, Devkarin?" Teysa asked as she pulled herself into the saddle again and secured the cane. "I'm impressed. You could have stolen that bam-stick easily enough." She pointed at the weapon that hung from the saddle below her cane sling.

"You'll need that more than I will," Nayine Shonn replied. "You're worth much more alive to all of us, in the long run."

"Good enough," Teysa said. "Tell me, does the Schism glow like that often?"

"Not in my experience. Then again, I have been jailed for extended periods by idiot Haazda with no senses of humor. Don't have too many windows, those cells."

"May I ask why they jailed you?"

"A little of this, a little of that. Murder, public drunkenness, public drunken murder. And robberies. Group raids on passenger traffic, temples, banks—the usual."

"But what exactly made them lock you up?" Teysa asked and sniffed the air. "Are you drunk now?"

"On what, the milk of Orzhov kindness?" Nayine said with the look of a woman telling a child how the gods pushed the sun into the sky every day.

"Smells like something . . . improvised," Teysa said with a bold effort not to wrinkle her nose. "But it doesn't really matter. I don't care. Listen—we're going in to the Cauldron, whether the Izzet like it or not. There's likely going to be some resistance to our entry when Hauc learns I had Melisk killed."

"Is that how an Orzhov gets around to saying you want me to help you figure out how to coordinate these losers into a raid gang to take on a magelord in his home? In *that?*" Shonn pointed at the Cauldron, glowing in the Schism light. It crackled with energy as the Schism brightened.

"Sure," Teysa said. "The way I see it, the first thing we need to worry about is—"

"You want my help, you listen to me first," the Devkarin said, "and we renegotiate the deal of my release. Again."

"You want a raise already?"

"You want your own little army?"

"Yes," Teysa said. "So let's get to work. We've got to get rid of that drake first."

"That's easy enough," the Devkarin said. "Can you hit anything with that bam-stick?"

"At a distance?" Teysa said. "Can't say I've really tried."

"I'll admit I've only fired one once, but I can pick a frog off a zombie's head with a longbow at two hundred yards with the north wind in my face. Let me carry it, and I'll take care of the drake."

"What about the exterior guards, the weirds, and the djinn?" Teysa asked, ignoring the request for now.

This did not pass unnoticed. The elf stared hard at the Cauldron for a few seconds, then turned in the saddle and said, "I think we can take care of them. Can any of us other than your parrot there fly?"

The hawk leaped from Teysa's shoulder and landed on the ground as Barkfeather in his elf shape. "You presume," he said, "that I can only call on the form of a hawk." His green eyes sparkled, and he grinned. "What did you have in mind, Devkarin?"

CHAPTER 13

Mizzium is an impossible metal, yet there it sits: impervious to the very agents that forged it. Or is it? I put to you that the dragon's metal is not immune to the extremes of temperature that are within our abilities to create.

> —Magelord Mindosz the Heretic,
> immolated by the Firemind on 8 Xivaskir 3203 Z.C.

3 CIZARM 10012 Z.C.

Kos had read enough zib-store novellas on late duty at the Imp Wing and decade after decade of slow night shifts at the Tenth to recognize one of the cheap entertainment's iconic figures: the maniacal magelord with a plan to consume the world with fire, floods, frost, or some combination of all three. The magelord always revealed his plan to the heroes once he'd captured them and strung them up in various awkward positions.

The retired 'jek never thought he'd actually meet such a character, or find himself in such a position, but Zomaj Hauc looked prepared to play the part to the hilt. Kos hoped he wasn't fooling himself. His ability to read people was a bit rusty, and the man was obviously insane. But here they were, strung up like an audience as Hauc paced the "stage" of his flight sphere landing pad.

Of course, life was not a zib-store novel, and escape seemed a dim hope at best if even Crix was bound up here with them. Mizzium and silver pressed painfully against Kos's body in a hundred places, but that was nothing compared to the throbbing discomfort at his shoulders and knees as he hung facedown over the Cauldron's interior. Hauc had ordered the four to be stripped of their gear and most of their clothing (in Golozar's case, they'd mostly taken weapons) and placed his prisoners at the four compass points. There they hung, suspended above him.

Kos had seen many things in the City of Guilds, but not since the great fertility festival of '87 had he seen such a dense concentration of goblins anywhere, let alone in Utvara. For better or worse, these goblins weren't concerned about the propagation of their own species. The Izzet goblins worked like industrious insects, without a break, to birth three new members of what might be the deadliest species on the whole plane. From Kos's angle they seemed to cover the breadth of the Cauldron's wide base and crawled upon all the struts, supports, transfer points, and power tubes that ran between the generators, the walls, the ground, and the nest at the center of it all. Smog occasionally blocked his view of the lava pits on the far side, but he could certainly smell them. Kos noted that most of the glowing, glassy white pipes and power from the east side of complex seemed to feed directly into the trio of eggs.

The defenses of the place—the workers could only count as defenders if they chose to fight instead of continuing to work, and they seemed preoccupied—included perhaps a dozen elementals that Kos could see; djinn monitoring the ramparts; and a few archers, goblins, mostly, perched on a ring above Kos. The translucent form of the famed *Pyraquin* scattered orange light chaotically over the entire area.

The Cauldron narrowed near its domed top, meaning Kos—at the north point, nearest the sleeping watch-drake—was no more than a hundred feet away from Golozar, to what Kos was pretty sure was the south. The old wojek guessed that the tangle of metal holding him up was at least six feet from the actual inner wall. Pivlic was to Kos's right, at the western point, and the goblin courier Crix hung on his left. They were all at least fifty feet from the landing platform where Zomaj Hauc stood, regaling them with the details of his plan. Or trying to. Kos couldn't decide what made his current situation worse—what Hauc was planning to do or listening to Hauc describe, around the many tangents, what he was planning to do.

Izzet magelords were legendary for their arrogance. There was a reason all those zib-store villains sounded the way they did—an Izzet with enough power simply could not contain the urge to boast about it.

The interesting part, to Kos anyway, was that Golozar had done most of the prodding that got Hauc talking. If the Gruul had shown such skills in the days Kos had known him back in the city, he might well have stayed on long enough to complete his academy training. Golozar might even have ended up his partner, and that might not even had been a bad thing.

"My lord," Crix said, interrupting Kos's ruminations, "why do you do this? I have traveled so far to bring you the message. You gave it to me yourself, said to give it to you here. Well I'm here, and, my lord, it was not easy. You must take this burden from me. Why do you wait?" Kos couldn't help but feel a little sorry for the goblin on top of all the other fear, dread, and panic fighting it out for his attention. Crix had become an uncertain, questioning child before a parent that didn't seem to want her.

"Give it up, goblin," Golozar growled. "So you're uncomfortable. Everyone I ever cared about is probably dead. We've all got problems. Take Hauc here. He can't possibly channel enough power into those eggs, and even if he does there's no way an idiot like him is going to manage to control three dragons."

"My discomfort is not—" the goblin began, then said, "Your whole tribe? Even that centaur?"

"Are you listening to the same magelord I am?" Golozar said.

"This is bad," Pivlic said. "This is really, really, really, bad, my friends." He wriggled in his polished, silver bindings. The imp was strapped upside down to a roughly human-shaped mizzium rack. The rack and three others like it had, a few hours earlier, been walking around long enough to pick up Kos and his three companions, climb the inside of the Cauldron at the four compass points, and merge back into the twisted tubing. There, the pipe-guardians had twisted and reconfigured themselves into perfect personal prisons.

But why had Hauc's pipe-guardians taken Crix as well? Kos had gotten the distinct impression that the goblin's message was urgent, as had the courier, obviously. Yet Hauc had been perfectly happy to let Crix hang there with the rest of them.

Kos stared down at a pulsing pyromanic generator that blasted heat at his face and upper body. It sat atop a beetle-shaped power plant drawing and expelling power and magics Kos did not rightly understand, except that they all combined to turn the air into something just this side of an inferno. And everywhere, goblins. Goblins who ran in place inside barrel wheels mounted to the sides of steamcores, goblins who turned cranks with wrenches that were taller than they were, and goblins who pulled levers by leaping upon them from the next level up. Goblins, all of them keeping the whole contraption going. Weirds and djinn poured molten stone and metals into the steamcores and a little less into the generators.

From his vantage point Kos could look down on Hauc's platform and see two of the three mammoth dragon eggs sitting beneath it. Kos was no engineer, but he'd be willing to bet that platform wouldn't survive the first hatchling.

Not that he knew a damned thing about dragons, really. Who did? There was only one dragon left, and he hadn't been seen in public for decades. Drakes, though similar, were just large animals. Dragons were something bordering on the godlike, but that old bastard Niv-Mizzet was a recluse who ruled an entire guild just to stave off boredom. He was famed for that. People wrote satirical plays about that. Niv-Mizzet was a folk hero in some circles, a god in others, but always representative of wanton, massive destruction.

The dragons of old were terrible creatures and were one of the reasons the fledgling guilds first considered uniting into the Guildpact. He'd learned that much at Mrs. Molliya's one-room school. Three brand-new dragons? Kos figured he wouldn't last long enough to know for sure, but odds were there wouldn't be much Utvara or Ravnica left to spend the rest of his life in anyway.

Fate's tricky solution seemed to involve shortening the rest of his life to accommodate. It wasn't a solution Kos was crazy about. Thanks a lot, Fate.

Crix was right side up like the rest of them, bound in much the same way as Pivlic, though she had one arm free for readily apparent reasons—the tattoos on her courier arm glowed brighter whenever the magelord drew close to her as he paced through his monologue round the platform. The arm hung useless. The goblin's nerves had obviously gone numb. Kos knew the feeling.

"My lord," Crix repeated. "The message. Don't you want the message?"

"Crix," Zomaj Hauc said, interrupting what Kos figured was a record for silence since he'd met the magelord—thirty-five, forty seconds, easy. "I will extract that in time. First you no doubt wish to know what the message contains. The curiosity must be killing you. All of you. I don't want curiosity to steal my thunder."

"The curiosity is bad, but this angle you have me hanging at is the worst part, all due respect," Kos said. "I think my shoulder's almost out of the socket, and the rest of my hair's going to burn off at this rate. It's never going to grow back in time for my funeral. And if I ever did want to have children, I'm no longer quite sure it would be physically possible. But sure, tell us. You know you're going to." And maybe, just maybe, let slip a way to stop it.

"The contents of the message mean nothing to me, my lord, and are only the business of the recipient," Crix said by rote. "Only the safe delivery to my master. I trust your wisdom in—"

"Why, thank you! Your wisdom is to trust in my wisdom." Hauc said. He began to pace a large circle around the edge of the platform, his voice booming in the weird acoustics of the Cauldron. "Your trust was the last piece I needed! Hooray! At last my plan will be complete. I have Crix's trust, everyone!"

"My lord, I only wanted to do my job. That's all I ever wanted," Crix said. "I don't understand your rebuke."

"Quiet, I was—Never mind. Crix," Hauc continued, and in the time it took to speak the goblin's name he went from frenzied to fatherly. "Dear Crix," he repeated, walking to stand directly beneath the goblin. The courier's message tattoos shone in response to the magelord's proximity. "The message is safe. I will accept delivery soon, but the time is not quite right. You did do your job, eventually. If the knowledge you possess passes back to me too soon, the wrong people may find out and may try to stop me. Neither of us wants that, I think. And I can't have you or your new playmates running around getting in the way of our operations."

"The Firemind," Crix said, her voice a whisper. "You would move against Niv—"

"Do not speak the name," Hauc interrupted sharply. "Not yet. His attentions must remain away from this place."

"Your operations are going to level 'this place,' " Kos said, "and every other place. You can't control three dragons. And I speak as someone who really only plans on using it for another year or two no matter what you do to it."

"You don't know *what* I can do," Hauc replied. His eyes flashed red and twin points of light sizzled across Kos's forehead. They grew hotter, and Kos could swear he smelled smoke.

"Magelord, from what you've told us," Pivlic jumped in with his best negotiator's inflection, "the Orzhov are your partners in this endeavor. It just so happens that I am the senior Orzhov negotiator present, and I believe there is no need to keep me pinned to this wall any longer." The imp looked dangerously vulnerable from Kos's angle, especially after getting used to seeing Pivlic in the bulky suit. His wings were splayed and gripped by dozens of hooks and clamps.

"Pivlic," Kos said.

"No need to keep my valet pinned to this wall any longer, either. He's a bit of a dullard—took one too many blows to the head in the brawl-pits. But I still owe back taxes on him." Pivlic elaborated smoothly. "Surely you can sympathize."

"You have interrupted my train of thought!" Hauc roared at Pivlic. Twin beams of white-hot energy flashed from the magelord's eyes and sizzled into the clamps holding the imp's arms to his side. The silver started to glow orange as Pivlic screamed. They bent and stretched as Pivlic writhed under the magelord's gaze. Kos caught sight off the fingers of Pivlic's left hand counting down: four, three, two, one, then a fist.

"Enough," Kos barked, hoping this was what Pivlic had in mind. "Just start over! You burning him alive!"

"Yes, but of all of you, he is the most worthless. I'm not too concerned about what the Orzhov think, let alone this interloping bartender." He stroked his chin thoughtfully even as he continued the assault on Pivlic. "But I don't want to burn Rack Seventeen any more than I have. Some of my servants still respect me." The magelord's attack ended as abruptly as it had started, and he turned his literally smoldering eyes on the old wojek. Pivlic moaned and whimpered, but from the corner of his eye Kos saw the imp press against the melted clamps—silver was a flashy but foolish choice for the bindings on "Rack Seventeen"—even as Pivlic put on his noisy show of pain for Hauc's benefit.

For the first time, Kos also spotted a small glassy globe directly behind Pivlic, glowing brightly as it absorbed the heat. The red water boiled like hot blood within, and a tiny crack appeared in one side.

I hope you know what you're doing, Pivlic, Kos thought.

One night on the road into Utvara, cornered by Gruul and fairly certain they would die, Pivlic had walked, slowly, through an open bonfire—twice, and each time over the course of half an agonizing minute—and emerged unscathed with his and Kos's weapons. They'd driven off the bandits, and Pivlic had been none the worse for wear. It took a lot of heat to even begin to make an imp take notice, let alone feel pain. Hauc, apparently, didn't know this, or thought he'd exceeded even an imp's pain threshold, because he grinned wickedly as Pivlic carried on.

"I don't get how you're supposed to just cook those eggs and expect them to hatch," Golozar interrupted, still doing his best to draw the details out of the magelord.

"You wouldn't, Gruul," Zomaj Hauc said. "But I'll try to put it in small words so you can understand." His eyes still rested on Kos as Pivlic worked one arm loose. "The Schism feeds on ectoplasmic energy. This energy follows those transfers there," he indicated the white, crystalline structures leading from the east wall to the central nest, "and incubates the new ones. This process is close to complete."

"You mean souls," Golozar snarled. "Dead souls feed your new ones."

"I believe I just said that," Hauc snapped.

"Golozar, let him talk," Kos said. "It's a . . . brilliant plan."

To Kos's surprise, Crix joined in. "Yes, my lord, you are correct. I do want to know the content of the message." It didn't sound particularly convincing to Kos, but he had a century of lie detecting under his belt. Hauc positively beamed. "Surely we can learn its import before you immolate the others?"

"Crix, I knew I could tempt your curiosity," the magelord said. "Well done. Calm and direct. If you weren't going to die soon, I'd consider putting you in for an observership. Now, *as I was saying*, the mana-compression device is at its heart a concentrated nothingness, a dimensional vacuum. Nothing is an unnatural state. The void cannot abide its own emptiness, and it cries out to be occupied. This particular device I created cried out to be occupied specifically by life itself, by living things. Initially, that is. It is a multistage mana-compression singularity bomb—can you believe it Crix?—and it is working perfectly. The initial detonation removed all unnecessary creatures. The second stage has been going on ever since. Soon, the third stage will release all the remaining energy at once into the new dragons. I will awaken them from their slumber, and they will serve me completely."

"You're awfully patient for an Izzet," Kos said.

"An initial outburst, or inburst, I suppose, then a slow build," Crix said with real awe Kos spotted easily. "You needed more energy than you could get with a single-stage device, but you could never build this place if anything that walked under the Schism was devoured as well. The calculations must have covered a mountainside. You are a genius, my lord," she finished sincerely. With a barely detectable shift in gear she asked, "And the effect on the dormant plague—how did that benefit your overall strategy?"

"The *kuga mot* brought the plague," Kos said, "and the *kuga mot* was your creature once, Hauc."

"I'm speaking," Hauc said and gestured at Kos without turning from the goblin. Kos's rack released a spring somewhere and a single red-hot needle lanced through the retired 'jek's left shoulder, exiting with a narrow jet of blood just above his collarbone. The needle was superheated to a dull rusty glare, but it was more than enough to cauterize the wounds. He hoped.

The needle entered some key nerve and began to tug ever so slowly upward. It was a strong contender for the single worst piece of agony Kos had ever experienced.

"Ever been filleted?" the magelord said. Kos struggled to keep his eyes focused. Hauc turned back to Crix. "The plague is for the brood. My brood. To them it is the breath of life, and they have been asleep for a very long time. The world was a different place the last time one of their kind first saw life. A place of fire and acid rains, and the great peaks still belched the core of Ravnica into the skies."

"Why not just start a bonfire?" Golozar said. "I'm sure you could get it started if you gave it a little effort."

"Only dragon fire can create such smoke," Hauc replied, "while the *kuga* will be in every breath they take from the first moments of their lives."

"You trusted a Simic to help you get your special air just right?" Pivlic asked, his tone carefully balanced to suggest just enough awe to keep the magelord explaining. Despite their ridiculous postures, Kos was now reminded much less of a zib-store novel and more of the interrogation rooms in the Tenth Leaguehall.

Kos could see Pivlic's free arm still at his side, but Kos thought he saw a silver shard in the imp's fist. Then the rack jerked the blazing needle out of his body and Kos went momentarily blind with pain. He barely heard Pivlic add, "Simic are crazier than Izzet, present company excepted, my friend."

"Yes, I am your friend. Someday you'll see that. Someday it will work," Hauc said. "Your small mind underestimates my abilities. Imp, I have studied every shred of Nebun's work. I've confirmed it independently. Nebun is a rank amateur compared to me—he did attempt to insert a ticking clock into the plague, something that would kill it after a few centuries, but I found that and removed it. The plague will remain for the brood as long as they want it. Ravnica herself has blown the cursed pollen back into your township and away from here, so that life churcher tree won't cause them any harm."

"Dragon fodder?" Crix said.

"A crude analogy but yes, essentially. There are other benefits as well. Utvara, as you might imagine, has the highest mortality rate on the plane, what with all the disease, heat, and general discontent in the hills. Ectoplasma does not come from nothing, and this place has the richest supply of ghosts on the planet. I calculate at least fifty thousand have fallen into the Schism already."

"Why all the dead?" Golozar bellowed. "What purpose did that serve? What have you—My village. What did you do to them?"

"Odd that you should ask the most pertinent question," Hauc said. He spun on one foot and clapped his hands deliberately, a professor praising a shallow student. "And we return—again—to the ectoplasmic relays," he said, waving at a vague area over Kos's head. "They are so very old, these new dragons. These new gods. They are not the parun's progeny. He is old, but they were meant to be his contemporaries. Contemporaries to the dragons that burned the world into being," He sneered. "I required Orzhov help confirming that they did indeed live, barely. But the raw, fresh

233

essence of life, captured at the brink of death, would ensure they would continue to grow."

"Well, that and heat," Kos coughed.

"Lots and lots of heat," Pivlic grimaced.

"Yet you're moving against—against the parun of our guild," Crix said. "How? Why would he set you to that task?" A light seemed to appear on her face, which wore a sudden, horrified look. "Firemadness. My lord, I am sorry."

"Firemadness? What's firemadness?" Pivlic asked.

"The Firemind eats away at—" Crix began.

"Crix, perhaps you don't have as much vision as I thought," Hauc said. "The parun cannot see all, not if we use simple precautions that keep him from focusing too closely, not when I shield us within mizzium. This entire place is lined with it to the core. But there are gaps in this shield." The magelord looked meaningfully upward at the circular skylight in the center of the domed roof. "I could not risk his learning from my own mind that I planned to betray him. That is where the message comes in and why I sent it in the first place," Hauc said, rounding a long bend to finally arrive at his initial point. "That is the key, the final part of the spell that will trigger stage three and make the brood kin recognize *me* as their true equal, no, their true master, when they emerge. The great one has long since lost real interest in the guild that bears his name. It is time for a new Great Dragon—for the Izzet and for Ravnica herself!" Kos found himself waiting for maniacal laughter and was rewarded a few seconds later with a long bout from the magelord.

The outburst gave the imp just the opening he was looking for.

"That," Pivlic said, "is not going to help property values at all, my friend. You must think of simple businesspeople such as myself. I am afraid as the sole Orzhov representative, it's my duty to register a complaint."

With that, the imp thrust a shard of silver blindly backward, shattering the cracking power node behind him. The glass exploded, and Kos half expected it to ignite and consume the imp whole, fireproof skin or no fireproof skin. The rack holding Pivlic in place went dead, and the silver clamps around his wrist popped open.

The proprietor of the Imp Wing Hotel and Bar, long since freed of the confining miner's suit, spread his wings and soared directly across the open space over Hauc's head. He looped twice to narrowly dodge twin blasts from the howling magelord's eyes then flew out of Kos's narrow field of vision.

* * * * *

Crix, still reeling from the revelation that the magelord she'd served her entire life planned to move against great Niv-Mizzet, didn't see the barreling imp until Pivlic was just a few feet away.

"Lean right!" the imp shouted, and Crix did the best she could to comply. "No, no!" Pivlic shouted. "Sorry! My right, your left! Good! Now close your—"

The imp didn't get a chance to finish before he reached the goblin. Pivlic hooked one hand under Crix's left arm—the one without the message tattoos—and slammed the improvised silver weapon he still clutched into the power node of the rack holding Crix in place. The node had not overheated, but apparently the imp's momentum was enough to do the job. Hot, acrid fuel showered briefly against the goblin's back, and she felt the clamps holding her in place detach. Before she could drop the twenty-odd feet to the platform below—assuming she could even aim for it and didn't drop all the way down to the lava pits—Pivlic, wings straining in the heat, managed to lift her away from the wall.

"Kos!" the imp shouted and swooped nauseatingly to dodge a shot from the magelord, who was calling his guards. "I can't reach you!"

"Get the Gruul free," Kos said. "You're closer."

"I can't carry any more than two, I'm not an infernal—" Pivlic sputtered.

"I'll make it to the platform," Golozar shouted. "Just get me loose!"

"Hold on, goblin," the imp said, and Crix did her best to wrap her numbed limbs around Pivlic's arm and left leg.

They would have made it, but Hauc would not keep missing forever. A blast of burning heat struck the goblin's arm and Pivlic's simultaneously, and the next instant Crix was falling. Falling past the *Pyraquin,* past the platform, and toward the open top of a lava-powered pyromanic generator. Just before she reached the rim of the house-sized cylinder, she heard a crash of breaking crystal as Pivlic, somehow, reached the Gruul. The last sound Crix heard before the heat made her pass out—she'd clenched her eyes to keep them from popping already—was Kos's voice.

"Pivlic! Leave us, damn it! Get back to town and warn them!"

CHAPTER 14

The Guildpact Statutes shall only extend to those zones designated "civilized" (see Corollary 0.315) by at least seven of the document signatories or their duly appointed representatives.
— Guildpact Statutes, Corollary 19.72
(the "Reclamation Clause")

3 Cizarm 10012 Z.C.

Was the sky just a bit clearer than before? It was hard to say in the weird light the Schism was sending into the night, but the haze seemed thinner, the air less oppressed with the tang of plague. Teysa's efforts with the cure were already bearing fruit, it seemed. Except for the Cauldron and any Gruul survivors, the Simic medicine had gotten around to everyone in the valley—even the prospectors—and now that it didn't have to keep as many people alive, the Selesnyan pollen went to work on the *kuga* winds themselves, as Wrizfar Barkfeather and Dr. Nebun had said it would. And everywhere the cure went it came with word of who had provided it.

Botany, magic, and medicine worked in strange ways, and Teysa really understood only one of those subjects. Neither was medicine or botany, but she trusted her verity circle, and her zinos. Teysa was in the process of bribing an entire township, plus the surrounding areas and transients.

It was too bad the Selesnyan Conclave and the Simic Combine seemed so diametrically opposed in their philosophies—Teysa suspected that if Barkfeather and Dr. Nebun ever got their heads together, they could do great things. Great, profitable things that would probably fetch a lot of zinos for the baroness who held the leases on their accomplishments. Once this crisis was over, she'd have to look into that.

Twenty-four of the taj had joined Teysa and the others on the last leg of their nighttime journey, and by the time they neared the Cauldron, the moon had almost completely set. The taj and Melisk had confirmed what she suspected: That messenger was probably already inside the Cauldron. It would still be a few hours until dawn. She'd dispatched the other six taj to the hills with inviolable orders to distribute the plague cure to any remaining Gruul. She doubted there were many, and the six who left had assured her they should have no trouble tracking the ones that were hiding. Melisk had made sure the taj tracked the survivors as they fled, with the apparent intention to finish them off once "his" taj had eliminated Teysa.

Teysa wished she didn't have to send the taj to save the same people they'd just been trying to kill—it wouldn't make the job any easier—but those Gruul were going to get that cure whether they wanted it or not. The taj could do that just as easily as they could kill the rest of them, even if it wouldn't be pleasant for those Gruul survivors. Pragmatism was called for. And if the Gruul then destroyed those six taj, it would be no great loss. The taj were even more resilient than thrulls.

She patted the remaining tubes of Nebun's cure—the last three—inside her cloak. Surely that would be enough. It was unfortunate that any Izzet inside who refused would have to be forced to take the cure, but Teysa's impressive regiment was ready for the fight, as far as she could tell.

The truth was, though, that Teysa wasn't sure what kind of resistance to expect from the Cauldron. She had one chance to avoid a fight, but she doubted it would work: Even if he hatched the new dragons, they'd destroy the magelord as well as everything else. She was not a military tactician, just a political and legal one. Hauc seemed to be following neither school of thought, and Teysa wondered if it were true that magelords sometimes went dangerously senile, then truly mad, from too much of "Niv-Mizzet's gift."

Could such madness mean the loyalty of his forces was questionable? She figured—hoped, really—that the workers wouldn't put up a fight if one happened, but there was sure to be trouble from the djinn guards, the weirds, and the sleeping drake perched between two of the floating sky reservoirs, one eye open for sudden movement that would awaken the reptile instantly.

Nayine Shonn had planned on taking the shot at the drake herself, but Teysa had ordered one of the shadewalkers to requisition a bam-stick and take care of it. The baroness could see parts of the weapon, if not the sniper, perched atop the last remaining column in a line that had fallen over like dominoes.

They couldn't afford to take this shot more than once, and the best way to ensure they didn't have to was taking it from as close to the target as possible, Teysa had insisted. Only the light-bending shadewalker could do that without alerting the drake to its presence. Teysa hadn't mentioned to Shonn that she didn't trust the Devkarin with a bam-stick just yet. Someone this helpful was just the tiniest bit too good to be true.

The other pair of shadewalkers armed with explosives had already been carried into position atop the water reservoirs flanking the red drake by a small, golden hawk that still rested on Teysa's shoulder, conserving strength for the upcoming fight. Shadewalkers barely existed in the third through second dimensions, or some such thing. They were light, from what Teysa understood, but solid when they needed to be. They were a little different from the taj but had a similarly silent, obedient angle going for them that Teysa appreciated.

The taj had split into small groups of five and six and moved stealthily near the rim of rusted hillside abutting the craterlike seat of the Cauldron. Some of their borrowed Gruul bodies were beginning to show signs of age, and many showed clear signs of obviously mortal injury that spilled white light. That didn't matter to Teysa. No one had to think they were Gruul anymore. Melisk's deception was over—now they were soldiers. Quick, deadly, ghostly soldiers. At Shonn's suggestion, the taj would stay until summoned by Teysa—or, in the event she was unable to summon them, by Shonn—when they met enough resistance to warrant the taj stepping in. It made sense to Teysa, and she'd readily agreed: Showing your entire case in the opening statement was not a good idea.

The charge would be led by Teysa, on dromaback. The virusoids would flank her on all sides. They would be able to withstand quite a bit of the heat they were likely to encounter and weren't as slow as the Golgari zombies assigned to bring up their rear. The minotaurs and Dreka-Tooth were the spear of the charge, while Shonn rode beside the "raid captain," as the minotaurs insisted on calling her. The Haazda, who were the most physically vulnerable, would break off from the charge at assigned points. There they could convey orders from Teysa, who planned to be inside the Cauldron soon after she launched the charge, to the taj and shadewalkers outside as needed. Their ultimate objective was to stay alive. If they went down despite the belt-loads of teardrops they carried, the taj would launch the second wave as a fallback, without the order.

Teysa flipped her cloak over her shoulders to reveal the dazzling Orzhov officer's armor she'd found in Pivlic's stores. It was a relic the imp said he'd acquired in an auction on Tin Street, and it fit Teysa well enough. The armor itself was a reflective obsidian black embossed with a gold Orzhov sigil—cut in a stark military style—upon the breastplate. She hoped it wouldn't come to combat on foot; her reduced ability to maneuver could easily be a disadvantage in that situation, but better safe than sorry. Besides, it helped her make herself believe she was really about to do this insane thing she was aiming to do.

Shonn rode up on one of the dromads, a stark white beast mottled with silver patches that reflected the looming Schism light. "Everyone is in position," she whispered. Teysa could tell her elf's instincts bristled at the lack of attention the Cauldron guards had paid them thus far. It was suspicious, Shonn had said. And it was, but there was little she could do about it.

Teysa had one chance to stop this entire thing from happening, without any fighting at all. And in that hope she had ordered everyone to let her advance on the Cauldron alone.

It was a little insane, but if she could pull this off, the sniper would not have to fire, the Cauldron might actually survive intact, and, most importantly, Teysa would be able to get back to the business of making this place something other than a blight, an insane gamble on prosperity.

"All right," Teysa whispered. "The open palm toward you means stay back, I'm parlaying. I'll wave you on if they reject me outright."

"And if they just kill you?" the Devkarin replied in kind.

"You have to ask?"

"You got it, Baroness," Shonn said and sidled over to give Teysa room. Her army parted before her and she rode out, into the Cauldron crater and down the oxidized road that led to the east gate.

Only two guards stood on either side of the iron doors, at least only two that Teysa could see: a glittering pyrohydric with four arms and a mizzium pike, burning with a light that rivaled the Schism, and a reddish, oily djinn. After being ignored so long, she was startled when one of them, the djinn, finally moved. He turned to face her and raised a hand in greeting. The weird stepped in front of the doors, moving just behind the other guard's shoulder. Each of them towered above her.

Teysa fought the urge to get her cane from the saddle. Sweat soaked her tunic beneath the black armor, but Teysa maintained a coolly neutral expression—number thirteen: I admit nothing—and reined the dromad to a halt. To its credit the beast also kept its cool, for now. Barkfeather stepped from side to side on her shoulder, the only display of nervousness Teysa hoped got across to the bemused djinn. Like those of most every race on Ravnica, the djinn had long ago been mixed in with humans. The true, gigantic variety—those who had rivaled dragons like Niv-Mizzet for power in the pre-Guildpact days, according to legends and histories—were long gone, for the most part. The remaining few were enslaved at the polar water stations—a badly kept secret.

The main difference between this djinn and a large human (other than the body that moved like living oil) was his lack of legs. The guard floated on a whirling cloud of wind that reached to his waist. Beyond that he was more or less solid. It made djinns slippery opponents, she guessed.

"We were wondering when you were going to attack," the djinn said. "I had a bet with my friend Vulka here about the size of the force you would use. Looks like we both lost. Neither of us thought you'd be crazy enough to ride up alone."

"I am Teysa Karlov, baroness of Utvara and the leaseholder for this business," Teysa said formally. "Your landlord. This tenant has violated at least seventeen sections of the Guildpact Statutes and stands in violation of pending laws to be enacted in the coming months. If he wishes to avoid costly and extensive legal action, he must show himself immediately to accept this subpoena." She snapped her fingers, and a small scroll appeared in her hand. She held it out to the djinn as the weird actually seemed to snicker.

If a snickering elemental was the worst that happened in the next minute, Teysa would count herself very lucky. "You'll find this document has been authorized, notarized, and sealed by the senior legal authority in Utvara," she said. "Me."

The djinn burst out laughing. "Sorry," he said. "I thought you said you were hear to serve a—what was it? Subpoena?"

Teysa sighed with practiced impatience. "Yes, a subpoena," she reiterated. "If Zomaj Hauc does not present himself in the next five minutes to receive this document personally, I and this duly appointed posse will deliver it ourselves. Will you bring him out? I'll ask you one last time."

"Do you have any idea what Hauc would do to us if we let you in? He strung up the last four in the nest," the djinn said. "Look, I'm sure you and that piece of parchment there think you're very important. But do yourself a favor and turn that dromad around. Go home. Things are going to get really hot around here soon, and I don't think you or any of your pathetic friends out there—hey, Dreka-Tooth, long time, no see—are going to want to be around for it."

"Pathetic?" Teysa said. "Is that your last word?"

"You heard him," the pyrohydric said in a bubbly voice. "Go home. You don't wanna die early, do you?"

"I was afraid of that," Teysa said. "Barkfeather?"

The hawk launched himself from her shoulder and flashed between the pair of surprised guards, who jerked back instinctively as the shapeshifting elf screeched. He kept screeching as he changed in midair back to an elf then in another half second grew ten times his normal size. By the time the second transformation was complete the screech was a bellowing trumpet from an elephant's trunk, and Barkfeather landed with a boom and kept on charging. The elephant ducked his head and aimed for the gate. Barkfeather struck it at full speed, shattered the latch, and effortlessly knocked the heavy iron aside.

The moment the hawk left Teysa's shoulder, several other things happened around her all at once. At Barkfeather's high-pitched call, the sniper shadewalker loosed a single bamshot that struck the sleeping drake in its open eye to emerge from the back of its scaly head in a small cloud of grayish scarlet. The blood-red reptile didn't even have a chance to make a sound before the single concentrated projectile carried most of its brain along with it.

The drake toppled over backward against the Cauldron's dome and bent a quarter of its surface inward with a crash. Simultaneously, the other two shadewalkers stationed on top of the water reservoirs triggered the jury-rigged bombs they'd constructed out of ammo globes. Twin explosions ignited the magically compacted liftspheres that kept the reservoirs improbably in the air, and the enormous, open-topped basins tipped over slowly, picking up speed as the water shifted within. Thousands of gallons of artificial rain fell in an instant deluge amidst the smoke and flame, dousing the two guards and the Cauldron itself.

The pyrohydric weird disappeared into the water, absorbed in a thousand-gallon rush. Meanwhile, the djinn melted like a wax candle under the downpour. A great explosion of steam shot out of the top of the Cauldron and Teysa reared back on the dromad as it fought instinctive panic. She guided it away from the roiling steam and the flood that washed over its ankles and into the tunnel ahead.

She turned back to Nayine Shonn, who to her credit had kept her forces from charging early, just as Teysa heard a trumpeting call from within the Cauldron. Barkfeather had made first contact with those inside. Teysa held up her hand and beckoned the first wave to follow.

"Charge!" Teysa called hoarsely at the top of her lungs.

When the spearhead of the strike had reached her, she dug heels into her dromad's flanks and it bolted forward. The air—clearer now than it had been even a few minutes earlier—was filled with the roars of Teysa's army and the splash of heavy feet on steaming, wet metal.

She had almost managed to stay atop her mount when a ball of black leather with wings slammed into her, screaming in terror. Pivlic struck Teysa squarely in the chest, and the two of them tumbled off the back of the dromad in a ball before she'd even made it much past the entryway.

Teysa pushed herself to her feet and managed to wrest her cane free from the panicked dromad as all three of them tried to avoid the virusoids and zombies who followed.

"Pivlic?" she demanded. "What the hell is going on?"

"My baroness," the gasping imp said, "You're—you're here?"

"Of course," Teysa said. "Utvara is my responsibility."

"Then you know—"

"The dragons? You saw them?"

"In a way. They have not yet hatched. But the magelord isn't just looking to hatch those things."

"What else?" Teysa demanded.

"He's going to take direct control of them," Pivlic said. "And he seems to think he can do it." The imp looked nervous. No doubt he expected her to send him back into the fray, but, eyeing his wings, she had a better idea.

"Take this," she said, handing Pivlic one of the precious green tubes. "Press one end against your neck—it's the plague cure," she said. "That's enough for several hundred people, but I need you to get it to anyone left in town or the flats who hasn't gotten it yet."

"That's all?" Pivlic said. "Good. I thought you wanted something impossible."

"Just do it, Pivlic," she said.

"How will curing the plague stop those dragons?" Pivlic asked.

"You'd be surprised, but there's no time to explain," Teysa said. "Don't worry about the dragons. We'll take care of them."

Or they'll take care of us, she failed to add aloud.

* * * * *

Kos watched Pivlic spiral downward, dodging potshots from guards and Zomaj Hauc himself, then disappear somewhere below the old 'jek's feet. He hoped the imp made it out and managed to get help from town. He wasn't sure what else they could hope for at this point.

Considering all he had seen in more than one hundred twenty years on Ravnica, Kos half-expected something to disrupt the action. Surely a brave soul would step forward, or the cavalry— some kind of cavalry, he wasn't picky—would step up soon. Pivlic could fly quickly. Still, Kos was fairly surprised by the form the interruption took and how quickly it came. He doubted this was Pivlic's doing, quick as the imp was.

A dead drake slid over the edge of the blood-slicked dome atop the Cauldron, dropped through the opening, and crashed onto the landing platform.

Hauc bellowed in a pure rage as he threw himself to one side, narrowly avoided the plummeting reptilian corpse. The landing platform shook and shrieked under the weight of the drake and sent a ringing hum through the entire nested framework and, by extension, Kos's skeleton. Support cables snapped, and the platform dropped with a clang on one side, rising just as much on the other. The magelord had to hook his fingers into a grate to keep from sliding over the edge, but his transparent flight sphere stayed hovering in more or less the same place, suspended by magical fields.

Kos pulled hard against the clamps pinning his arms, but the collision had not broken anything on his rack, unfortunately. He could only watch. He'd completely lost sight of Crix, who he thought had stopped just short of hitting a lava pit, and saw Golozar was no better off than he was.

If the dead drake was a mild surprise to an experienced former wojek like Kos, the deluge that followed really did take him completely off guard. A pair of metallic thunks shook the entire Cauldron again, followed by at least a reservoir's worth of water. The flood struck the flight sphere and flowed around it—the magic field was tough—and washed over the surface like a sudden and improbable storm. Hauc, Kos could see, managed to keep his grip, but the flood was too much for the already precariously perched corpse of the drake, and it slid down the platform at the head of thousands of gallons of now-brackish liquid and dropped down into the chaotic network of tubes, wires, and glass below. On the way it took out two more of the platform's support cables, which triggered a slow chain reaction.

Unable to hold the rest of the platform's weight, the cables snapped one by one. Each broken sound jarred Hauc and forced him to dig in for dear life as the platform dropped. The drake continued its postmortem plummet through the nest of tubes and wires, sending sparks and flame shooting out in all directions and over the screaming heads of dozens of panicked goblins, all of whom had quite wisely stopped working when the chaos erupted. It cleared a rough swath directly below Kos and allowed a wave of heat to blast him from below. He bounced and twisted in the rack frame as the Cauldron shook and jolted.

The water chased the corpse and reached the bottom long before the drake did. Moments later everything below Kos save the tops of the eggs and the rapidly dropping platform was consumed by billowing steam—the deluge had reached the lava pits and finally come to the end of the line, but now he had no idea what was happening down there. From the heat, Kos guessed that had they been anywhere below the platform at this moment they'd have all been completely cooked.

The drake's fall finally ended atop a power plant with three heavy steamcores running at full capacity. The power plant began to whine and groan, as if preparing to burst.

* * * * *

Crix came to on her back. The sound of snapping cables echoed in an underwater cave, then metal grinding against metal, and a tremendous crash followed by hundreds of little splashes.

The goblin lay on the rim of the open-topped generator. The heat of the lava inside wasn't as fierce as it should have been, and the goblin soon saw why. It was the same reason she was soaked to the bone and hundreds of goblins were splashing and screaming instead of working and shouting. Goblins were terrible swimmers, and she hoped the workers could get to high ground.

A small lake of foul water filled with chunks of twisted metal and broken glass sent waves washing back and forth across the Cauldron from one inner wall to the other. The drake—dead, to Crix's chagrin—lay atop a crushed but still functioning power plant, billowing steam and smoke. A crusty, cooling stalactite of fresh, rapidly congealing lava clung to the edge, frozen by the water in the act of mindless escape.

Crix coughed as the smoke and heat finally got to her lungs in earnest. Her skin felt like it was roasting. The goblin rolled carefully onto her feet with what was left of her native agility and almost jumped into the lava when she again heard the snapping sound that had awakened her several times in rapid succession. She gaped as the edge of the flight platform dropped incrementally through the rising, blistering-hot steam clouds in jolting clangs.

The water wouldn't last long. Already it drained through the exit tunnels and onto the dry floor itself. What didn't run out would soon be vaporized by volcanism that was making breathing ever more difficult. The lava pits didn't stop producing lava just because the upper layer had hit water—they just produced a lot of blinding, hissing steam and required supervision and tending. The Cauldron would be bone-dry again within hours, Crix guessed, and if the labor left the place would probably be consumed by fire not long after that.

By some kind of fortuitous luck, or magic—who knew what kind of protective enchantments safeguarded a dragon egg laid in magma and incubated for thousands of years?—the platform stopped dropping before it hit the central nest. There it swung on couple of sturdy remaining cables and lazily collided with the wall and the mathematically aligned power tubes, destroying the artistic creations of hundreds of goblins. The collision released crackling static discharges that shot through the steam clouds like tiny lightning bolts.

Crix hoped the destruction of the sigils impaired the dragons somehow, but she couldn't count on it.

The platform had arrived at a forty-five-degree angle, almost a perfect one to Crix's eye, and to her surprise she saw the lower half of Zomaj Hauc dangling through the fog. His legs kicked for purchase and disappeared into the haze.

Crix pulled back her sleeve and studied the glowing figures on her arm. As a safety measure, a courier was forbidden to learn the text they carried. But she'd been given a gift from the magelord. She knew what the message was and what it would do.

For the first time, Crix entertained the thought of just thrusting her arm into the lava crust. That would end the threat, wouldn't it? Everyone was assuming that the dragons would destroy the world if loosed upon it, but what was the proof of that, really? Crix wasn't so sure. Niv-Mizzet hadn't destroyed Ravnica.

It made Crix's insides squirm to force the idea through her loyalty-wired brain: The magelord couldn't be allowed to control the new dragons. She had worshiped Zomaj Hauc for as long as she could remember, but no one should have that kind of power except those born with it. Or, as the case might be, hatched with it.

She could easily make out the three towering dragon eggs through the fog and the screams. They, too, smoldered in the humidity.

"Be free, new ones," she said solemnly, kneeling. She raised her message arm over the lava generator's side.

"Don't do that," said Zomaj Hauc as he dropped from the smog above to land on the generator's rim behind his goblin courier. He clamped his hand around Crix's wrist and hauled her into the air with one arm.

"No, master," she said. "The dragons can't be controlled by mortals. Not even—It's not—it's not right." It felt strange to say. "Rightness" was not a particularly Izzet concern in most cases, but Crix was not just an Izzet. She was a goblin who lived in Utvara—for now—on the plane of Ravnica. Zomaj Hauc had given her a sharp, powerful mind, too brilliant for the magelord's own good. Crix was a citizen of this world, and she meant to defend it as best she could. Not that her best seemed to be doing particularly well.

" 'No' is the wrong answer," the magelord said. With a snap of his shoulder he twisted Crix's arm and sent her spinning in an agonizing circle in midair. The spin snapped the adhesive clamps along the stump of her shoulder, and the arm detached from its courier, delivered at last. The goblin landed hard on her side, unable to get her remaining arm under her body before the metal cap at the shoulder joint smacked painfully into the stone. The jolt felt like it momentarily knocked her entire skeleton out of her body.

Crix pushed herself onto her knees at a popping sound from the center of the Cauldron and peered through the haze at the eggs. The one with the purple spots started to crack.

"Now that's timing, Crix," Hauc said. "Why don't you stay here and watch this. If you survive the next hour I may have a spot for you on the labor crews." The magelord smiled cruelly. "Then again, everyone will have a spot on my labor crews when Ravnica is mine."

Riding a blast of appropriately hot air he shaped from the steam, Zomaj Hauc shot straight up and into the haze on an arc that, Crix calculated quickly, would end at the still-hovering *Pyraquin*. The goblin coughed a bit of blood into her remaining hand. She still lived. She could still try to stop him. And she could follow him, if she did what no courier was ever supposed to do unless ordered to do so by her magelord. Crix hadn't even done it on her long journey to the Cauldron. Hauc had not thought to authorize it. She was supposed to be on a low-profile ride in with the Orzhov. The others were still bound, assuming they'd survived the flood, and the imp had gone. There was no other way. Her voice atremble, she spoke the nine-digit failsafe code that gave her the power to use her full abilities.

Crix's body flooded with cold, exhilarating fire.

She shrugged off her robe so it wouldn't ignite, gritted her teeth, and sent the mental launch command that activated one of the many functions Hauc had built into her solid mizzium legs during the operations she'd endured for most of her early childhood.

Crix wasn't half the goblin she used to be, but it would be the nongoblin half that saved her today. If anything could.

Mubb the Hapless: Where did the great Niv-Mizzet come from, Magelord?

Magelord: You cannot create a dragon, insolent cretin! You will be served at the feast of the great Niv-Mizzet himself! Weirds! Seize the cretin!

Mubb the Hapless: Hooray! May I borrow some flameproof formal wear?

—Rembic Wezescu, *Mubb the Hapless Attends a Feast*

3 Cizarm 10012 Z.C.

The rack wrenched Kos's limbs anew as it bent under the strain of the platform's rumbling descent. The thing's arms drooped even further, apparently unable to do much else unless Hauc commanded it, and the magelord was busy holding on to the shifting architecture inside the Cauldron. The rack swung Kos's upper half down so that he was perpendicular to the tilted surface, his head pointed squarely at the hovering flight sphere in the center, with the dead drake still directly below him.

Another cable snapped nearby and whipped out at Kos, sparking with raw magic. He tried to duck but the rack wouldn't give, so he closed his eyes and waited for his luck to finally run out as the thing lashed toward him. There was a whistle overhead followed by a loud crack.

The mizzium cable sliced easily through the pipe-guardian's freakish metallic arms, somehow missing the dangerously explosive power node at the center, and all at once his arms were free. Sort of. Kos dangled upside down over the corpse of the drake, held in place only by the clamps around his ankles, or more accurately around his boots. The rack's severed "hands" still encased Kos's own, like monstrous lockrings designed by a sadist.

Kos wasn't sure whether it was the extra weight of the metal around his wrists or if his feet had just lost so much blood that they'd shrunk a full size, but he noted with mounting panic that his ankles were slipping free of his boots. He drove his toenails into the leather and stopped the slide, but he couldn't stay that tensed forever. His tendons were screaming.

"Kos!" Golozar shouted across the Cauldron. "You're slipping!"

"Really?" Kos shouted. "Hadn't noticed!"

"Just trying to—"

"Shut up! Can you get free? You carry rope, right? All Gruul carry rope. You have to—Oh, damn it, I'm slipping." Kos snarled in frustration.

"No, I'm still bound," the Gruul replied. "I don't have your luck. And yes, I have rope, but I can't get to it."

"I don't think you want my luck," Kos said. His toes continued to slip against the insides of his boots. No amount of tensing his toes could stop it now. The clamps had the boots and weren't letting go, but the boots were ever so slowly letting go of him. Kos instead tried to work his hands carefully free of the rack fragments and pulled his wrists apart as hard as he could, until the wires and jagged metal edges sliced into his skin and blood slicked his hands.

"That's not going to work! Try to land on the drake," Golozar said, "on your back. It might cushion your fall."

"Thanks," Kos said just as his toes lost the battle, and he dropped headfirst toward the floor of the Cauldron.

* * * * *

Teysa had managed to stay atop the dromad for the remaining charge, even as the deluge drowned the guards in the eastern quarter of the Cauldron and rose to the beast's flanks. The virusoids loped easily through the water, though she had concerns about the zombies keeping up.

The goblin workers weren't fighting much at all, and she'd already ordered her forces not to attack them unless the workers attacked first. As she broke into the foggy interior, she saw how wise that had been. Most of the workers had not panicked and abandoned their posts but scuttled all over the nest, fighting fires, closing off vents and sealing cracks.

The place was a mess. A huge platform listed to one side, suspended in midair. Steam and smoke mingled in great drifts, spewing from shattered pipes and who knew what else. Teysa almost didn't take notice of one of the goblins but did a double take when she realized the goblin only had one arm—and that it was shrugging off a robe identical to the one she had worn the last time Teysa had seen her, on a lokopede, moments after she'd . . . well, after she'd earned her inheritance. This goblin was the messenger. With her memories restored Teysa recognized her clearly.

Nayine Shonn wheeled her dromad and doubled back to Teysa's side. "Baroness, you may be able to tell your taj to stand down. We're not meeting much resist—" Teysa cut her off with a gesture, pointing at the goblin.

"The messenger," Teysa said.

The next moment Crix thrust her remaining fist into the sky and blasted off on twin columns of fire that shot from the soles of her feet.

"Did I really just see that?" Shonn asked.

"If she could do that, why didn't she—I mean, she could have been in the township in hours!" Teysa sputtered.

"Baroness, with all due respect, we have bigger trouble than that," the Devkarin said. "And you owe me ten zinos. We have a winner."

Teysa looked at the nest and saw her Devkarin lieutenant was right—the dragons had begun to hatch.

"You win," Teysa said. "Remind me to pay you if we live."

* * * * *

Kos only had a second or two to yell before he ran headlong into a flying goblin. Crix thrust her arm under Kos's shoulder and locked them together in an unexpected aerial collision. The jolt knocked the broken pieces of rack from his arms. They splashed into the rapidly draining pool below, just missing a few goblins struggling to keep a generator going, and took a great deal of the skin on his wrists and hands with them. Nothing seemed broken, however, and Kos could still clench a pair of fists, if painfully.

It struck him after a few seconds that they were traveling upward.

"Crix!" he shouted. "What are you—How are you doing this?"

The goblin got a better grip on Kos's arm—when had Crix lost one?—and muttered a few calculations the 'jek wouldn't have understood even if he had heard them clearly.

"One moment," the goblin said. "Need to adjust our vector if we're going to catch him."

"Catch who?" Kos said. He answered his own question when he saw the magelord land heavily on the upward side of the transparent flight sphere that bobbed in foggy air. "Oh," he said.

"To answer your previous question, I'm doing this by violating one of my most sacred oaths," Crix said.

"There's fire shooting out of your feet!" Kos said. "That's

violating more than an oath. There's got to be some kind of natural law you're—"

"Experimental courier augmentation. But I'm not authorized to use it without a direct order, unless my lord himself is in mortal danger. I'm probably going to be immolated for this. Now hold on, this is going to get tricky," Crix replied. "I'm going to drop you next to him. Try to keep him at bay until I can bring Golozar. Together the three of us might be able to stop him from reading those words."

" 'Keep him at bay,' " Kos repeated. "How exactly am I supposed to do that?"

"Brace your legs. You're going to land hard," Crix said. "Sorry. I'll be right back." As they passed over the magelord's head she unhooked her arm from Kos's with a whip-crack movement.

Kos struck the magelord in the chest with both feet, but Hauc saw him coming a moment too soon. He hooked an arm around Kos's ankles and let himself roll back, completely negating the impact and making the old 'jek's desperate off-balance uppercut miss by a mile. The magelord rolled and used his entire body to swing Kos down sideways. Hauc smacked the wojek face-first against the platform, but that gave Kos just enough leverage to drive his bare feet into the magelord's ribs. Hauc released Kos when he doubled over in surprise, retching and gasping.

Kos was an old man, but Hauc was not used to fighting like a street brawler. They both carefully got their footing on the platform, slick with mist and blood, mostly Kos's. The magelord gazed for a second at the glowing goblin arm and the glowing, fractured sky overhead and laughed in Kos's face.

Agrus Kos had come to Utvara in large part to get away from glowing things, especially glowing things that wanted to destroy the world.

He roared and charged the distracted Hauc, who turned too late this time. Kos slammed into the ribs he'd just kicked and drove another fist into the magelord's gut. There had to be a reason Hauc wasn't using his fire magic. Kos couldn't figure out why Hauc insisted on fighting like this. It wasn't the magelord's style at all. Entangled, the two skidded across the listing landing pad, Kos's arms latched around the magelord's neck while Hauc pounded at the old 'jek with Crix's arm. He stopped only when Kos managed to jam a bare heel into the gap between two bolted plates that had come apart at the seams.

The 'jek stopped short as Hauc kept going, but Kos brought him to a halt with an elbow to the groin. Hauc doubled over wailing, and that was apparently enough to get the magelord to remember that, among other abilities, he could burn holes in people with his eyes. Kos saw the flash just before it happened and shoved a palm against Hauc's chin, barely avoiding a pair of blazing beams that would have neatly sliced the top off of his skull. The fire ricocheted off of the flight sphere and into the platform, where it burned a pair of smoldering holes that sizzled in the moist air.

"Who are you supposed to be?" Hauc snarled.

"Kos," Kos said. "League of Wojek. Retired."

"What?" The magelord said, baffled for the briefest of moments.

"You asked," Kos said. They circled each other as best they could, but neither could reach higher ground than the other. "So why do you want to do this, Hauc? Niv-Mizzet hurt your feelings? This place just starting to get to you? Because I understand how that could happen. Sometimes it drives me crazy: the dust, the plague, that flower crud that gets in your nose and ears. But come on. You don't want to burn it up, do you? Turn those things off. Don't do this." Kos extended one hand.

It was enough of an opening for Hauc to swing the severed arm and connect with a mind-jarring *clang* to Kos's jaw that knocked him back against the side of the hovering sphere. The severed arm was not made of flesh and bone. It was metal, but not as heavy as iron or even mizzium. The lightweight material was probably the only reason the blow didn't cave in the side of Kos's skull. The 'jek barely had the sense left to brace himself against the flight sphere with one arm before he rolled down the slope.

Kos spat out a tooth, one of his few remaining originals. "That hurt," he said. "Who am I? Who the hell are *you?* Twelve years I had here, twelve years of almost nothing to do but sit and relax. And here you come along and it's the end of the damned world again." On "world" Kos brought a knee around that caught the magelord in the side of the leg and sent him skidding underneath the sphere, where he stopped, caught in whatever magic kept the thing floating, Kos guessed.

"Why the beating, Hauc?" Kos said. "Where's your big, flashy magic? I expect big flashy magic if you're going to try and destroy everything. Do it with some class. Where's the assembly? The war? The armies marching through the streets and the hordes of hideous, gibbering things? This is barely a skirmish."

Hauc's eyes flashed, but Kos had enough warning to duck behind the *Pyraquin*.

"Is it something personal, mage? Hey, you don't know any of my ex-wives, do you?"

The magelord's eyes blazed. Kos pushed himself off the sphere just ahead of another blast. This time Hauc didn't hold back, and Kos wondered anew about the wisdom of acting as the diversion when he didn't know the entire plan of attack. The old 'jek wasn't quite fast enough to avoid a searing burn across his back, but it was a glancing shot that didn't get to the bone.

I really need a line of work where a wound that isn't bone-deep *isn't* the bright side, Kos thought dizzily as he went down on all fours, his body tingling with deep pain. Kos crawled up the slope, doing his best to put the flight sphere between him and the magelord.

"I'm wasting time," Hauc said, "and power. Nothing more to waste." He strode past Kos and gave the 'jek a kick in the stomach as he passed. Kos rolled, groaning, onto his side. Hauc strode to the very edge of the platform and raised Crix's arm overhead. From this angle, Kos couldn't see the egg beginning to crack underneath him, but he could hear it popping. It was unlike any sound he'd ever heard before, like a crumbling mountain that rang like metal and left an odd, lingering hum in the air that chilled his bones.

The magelord started to read the spell that would grant him dominion over the first dragon hatched on Ravnica in at least fifteen thousand years, but Kos spotted something more interesting from the corner of his eye. There was movement overhead, and through the haze he could make out the last of Golozar's clamps coming apart under a concentrated blast of flame from Crix's left foot.

"Now there's something you don't see every day," Kos said. He coughed up some blood and hoped that Hauc's incantation would not be too short.

* * * * *

Teysa had her hands full. Fires had erupted on all levels of the Cauldron's interior, fed by broken pipes spewing volatile gasses and magic, which burned through more pipes, which started more fires . . . and everything, it seemed, was connected to the nest in some way, because as the coils and tubes came apart, so did the rest of the place. Pieces of the Cauldron dropped into the pooling water around her dromad's feet and narrowly missed the Izzet goblins who were everywhere, some working to keep what wasn't burning from catching on fire, others trying to keep what was functional running, and a few just screaming in panic and fleeing. The wailing deserters splashed through the smoldering pools and out into the Schism-lit morning, but Teysa did not order any of her forces to pursue. Not that she had as many forces left as she used to.

The goblins were no threat, but there were other holdouts. Her immediate problem was a band of hydropyric weirds, their liquid exteriors unharmed by the deluge Teysa had arranged for their fiery kin. The watery elementals had torn the living daylights out of the virusoids and left two of the ogre zombies in pieces—the weirds could harden parts of their bodies at will, and turn liquid with a thought. They always had a weapon, and you couldn't hit them with anything. The hydropyrics stood between Teysa and the three problems she would have to deal with soon—the eggs. The red and blue mottled ovoids now showed signs of fissures, and the purple one was already missing a few chunks completely. Skin like wet leather was exposed to the air in three places. The skin pulsed with life.

The baroness was down seven virusoids so far, and nothing they'd tried seemed to harm the hydropyrics in the slightest. Weapons went right through them and out the other side without visibly harming them. The water obviously hadn't worked, and the zombies were only igniting their fists driving them through the weirds. Fire didn't work. They simply absorbed it into their blazing cores. Teysa wished she had some idea where the shadewalkers were but had to trust that wherever they were they were doing what she'd ordered. Shadewalkers did not violate agreements, and all they had to do was cover her forces from outside. With her now were the last two Golgari zombies, a few faceless, voiceless virusoids, and Dreka-Tooth.

Unfortunately, she'd had to set the minotaurs and Shonn to the task of distributing the cure to the goblins—the minotaurs running interference, the Devkarin administering the cure whether the patients wanted it or not—and that left Teysa with only Dreka-Tooth as a bodyguard and a dromad that grew more skittish with each passing moment.

The taj were the only thing she hadn't tried against the weirds. The taj were more ghost than alive. Maybe their spirit nature could be effective. What she had in mind might be as bad for the taj as it was for the weirds, but she was running out of options. As if to illustrate the point, a weird took an eighth virusoid apart with a liquid arm that ever so briefly became an ice axe. She made a snap decision.

"Dreka-Tooth, fetch the taj," Teysa commanded. Now she wouldn't even have Dreka-Tooth, but he was the only one who could deliver the message to the Haazda communication line. And she needed the taj. She would go herself, but the others would surely break and flee without her leadership. Her "troops" were simply too stupid, by and large, to be trusted with a fight like this unsupervised.

Besides, she'd come this far. Turning back now, even to fetch reinforcements, felt utterly wrong to Teysa. She didn't dare take her eyes off the eggs or the magelord who appeared at the crest of the tilted landing pad and held an arm—Crix's severed arm, from the look of it, which barely surprised Teysa—over his head and began to shout ancient, blunt syllables aloud.

Dreka-Tooth patted her dromad on the flank, whispered a few calming words in the creature's ear, and bolted back toward the entrance to deliver Teysa's call.

She didn't turn to watch him go. Another chunk of purple eggshell dropped away, and Teysa was fairly certain she saw a yellow, catlike eye gazing at her hungrily. The eye was big enough for her to stand between the lids and still have room to stretch. It blinked once, and Teysa got the unnerving impression that it gazed right through her.

The dragon's eye shattered whatever remained of the dromad's nerve. It reared and tossed Teysa backward in a short arc that ended in an abrupt and wet stop just behind the beast. It turned on its hind legs and bolted back out the east entrance, making noises she didn't know a dromad could make. It almost collided with the raging, elephantine Barkfeather on its way out. Teysa was surprised. She hadn't expected the Selesnyan to last this long in a fight, but even elementals had trouble with several tons of elephant in close quarters.

From her prone, half-submerged vantage point she found herself gazing through the gaping circle cut into the domed roof, its edge roughened and bent by the effects of Teysa's first unofficial military command. But the roof wasn't what drew her eyes to the gap—it was the sky itself.

The Schism had continued to grow unabated while she'd been occupied and must have been changing every moment. From where Teysa sat, it turned the sky into a cosmic stained-glass window as life itself, stolen at the moment of death (or close to it) flowed unimpeded along its fractal seams. The white ectoplasmic tubes—which Teysa recognized as an Orzhov design—pulsed more strongly than ever and poured invigorating energy into the dragon's nest. With every syllable from Hauc's mouth, the Schism released the accumulated souls of almost fifty years, and the Cauldron, damaged as it was, had been designed to absorb much more than that.

A shadow helped her get to her feet, and another handed her a cane found floating in shallow water nearby where it had slid free of the rearing dromad's saddle.

"We are here. What would you have us do?" The voice came from one direction but had three distinct layers. The shadewalkers had returned after all, which must have meant that the reserve forces no longer needed to be covered. Dreka-Tooth had gotten through.

Teysa looked over the elementals' heads as they faced off against the last of the Simic members of her retinue. The landing platform was clearly visible now, and it hung precariously over the edge of the nest.

"I doubt you can do anything to the weirds either," Teysa said, more a question than a statement.

"You did not just see us try?"

"No, but I don't really see you now," Teysa replied. She pointed to the remaining cables and the single beam that were the only things keeping Hauc's landing pad in the air. "I would have you get up there somehow. In two minutes I want that thing dropped," she said, pointing to the suspension work. "Cut there, there, and there. I think should do it. Those eggs must be destroyed."

"It will be done," the curious voices replied.

"Wait," Teysa said. "Make it three minutes, and get those goblins out from underneath it first."

"How? We are but three," the shadewalkers said. "Even we cannot move that many in so short a time."

"You're invisible assassins," Teysa snapped. "Scare them!"

"We will." Without a splash the shadows disappeared completely. A few seconds later, a cacophony of ghostly warnings filled the air, sending even more goblins screaming out of the Cauldron through any exit they could find. She doubted it was all of them—goblin engineers could be dedicated to the point of mania—but she'd done all she could for them.

Teysa jumped out of her skin when a low, raspy voice floated over her right shoulder. "We are here, O Baroness. What do you ask of your taj?"

* * * * *

Zomaj Hauc had forgotten the sheer beauty of the words. The language was the original tongue spoken by the first dragons when Ravnica was a world of jungles and monsters. True Draconic required years of training to learn, and Zomaj Hauc was one of the few beings on this world that could speak it. He'd last spoken it when he finished the enhancement to the Orzhov device, the mana-compression singularity bomb, almost half a century ago.

His entire world was focused on the mizzium-alloy courier's limb, and it glowed at his attention. The human was beaten, and Hauc had managed to do it and still conserve more than enough power for this most critical task. Zomaj Hauc walked to the edge of the platform and gazed down at the eggs. All three showed signs of life, life he had saved after Niv-Mizzet had left them to die thousands of years ago. The Great Dragon did not deserve them. Hauc had found them, cared for them, and nurtured them with souls.

The ghostly sounds in the air and the nattering wojek were nothing. The only words worth speaking were the glowing figures carved into the arm. It had not been easy burning them out of his mind so the dragon would not find them. Crix had taken good care of the words, but her betrayal stung.

"Vsyo dovzer zsya mene, drazzac, drazzavh, drazzaugh," he recited precisely. *"Tiyava silz naya, ti silya nayana—"*

Several hundred pounds of angry Gruul cut him off in midphrase and knocked him against the sloping mizzium floor. The savage beast-man roared in his guttural, apelike dialect and pounded his chest.

"You should not have done that," Hauc said, eyes flashing. "I have just enough power to spare for you."

"You should do something about your tunnel vision my lord," Crix said as she swooped down from above and snatched her arm back from the distracted magelord. She sent a blast of flame into his chest before she launched herself over the nest and disappeared behind the dragon eggs.

"Crix, you cannot have them!" Hauc shouted. "And I did not authorize you to—"

"Shut up," Golozar said and slammed the magelord's face against the mizzium flooring. The world spun around Zomaj Hauc as the Gruul pulled him up by his collar and tossed him over the side. Hauc's back struck the blue-mottled egg hard enough to knock away a hexagonal plate of shell.

Hauc looked up at the blue egg, and the occupant of the egg looked back.

"No," Hauc whispered to the egg's occupant, "not yet. Wait, just wait!" He pulled himself up and scrambled through the ankle-deep water in the direction Crix had disappeared. He had to get that arm back or the brood would be lost to him. Lost forever. He had to get that arm back or the world would never be united under the benevolent and wise Zomaj Hauc. And the world needed him.

* * * * *

Teysa hoped she'd never hear anything scream like the hydro-pyric weirds again, until she heard the screams of the taj who sacrificed themselves to kill the elementals. Those were even worse.

The taj were in essence ghosts, trained to possess soulless corpses. They were fast, deadly, and impervious to harm, but they fought with steel like most warriors, steel and a few half-empty bam-sticks carried by battered and abused Gruul corpses. The hydropyrics were completely immune to such weapons, Teysa already knew.

But the weirds were, in their way, alive. The only way to stop them was for the taj to leave their bodies and try to take over the hydropyrics themselves. Fire and water against cold, final death.

And it worked—it only took a few seconds, in fact—but the cost was even more of her shrinking "Guildpact army." The taj who left their Gruul bodies behind consumed the essences of the weirds, but the weirds in turn burned away the taj. The result was explosive, took out two more virusoids, and left lingering screams in the air.

Teysa finally opened her eyes as the screams faded. The platform was still in the air, she could see through the haze, and there were five taj still standing. Where the hydropyrics had stood lay pieces of virusoids and zombie bodies, dead—truly dead—Gruul bodies, and rainbow pools of oil that were all that remained of Hauc's elementals.

She could hardly believe it. They'd won the ground fight, and the workers were finally getting the idea that they should evacuate. She might just pull this off, if the shadewalkers dropped that platform out from under Hauc soon. She could hear Barkfeather, now an elf again, shouting for the goblin workers to follow him to safety.

"Come on," she said to the remaining taj while eyeing the magelord, standing tall at the edge of the platform. "Get clear. This is going to be—"

Crix the goblin shot down from the ceiling, threw a hulking Gruul at the magelord, and flew off to the other side of the Cauldron. Teysa saw the Gruul pick up the magelord by the top of his skull and throw him over the side, then he stooped to help Pivlic's security man to his shaky feet.

At that second, she knew with absolute certainty that three minutes was almost up.

Teysa's warnings, obscured by the clamor of dying power plants, cracked steamcores, and screaming goblins, did not reach the platform in time. With a trio of loud metallic snaps the platform's supports gave way and it dropped, one end still snagged in the metal nest. They dropped onto the purple egg just as a black, scaly head cleared the edge of the shell.

The platform crushed the dragon's head flat with a wet crash, showering the immediate area with blackened brains and charred bone. The dragon died, suddenly and without warning. Fifteen times fifteen thousand years in the making, and Teysa had killed it.

Now *that* was power. But she and her shrinking forces were by no means out of trouble yet.

"Dreka-Tooth," she said, "did you see where that Izzet magelord landed?"

"That way," the mercenary said, pointing beyond the crushed egg to its cracking neighbors.

"Right," Teysa said. "Two more to go. Taj," she said, turning to the last few assassins she had left. "Go with Dreka-Tooth—this fellow—and find that magelord. If you can't find him, find the flying goblin. Hauc can't get that arm back. But if those eggs crack open, get out of there. I'm going to see if I can get to those two on the platform and get them out."

"We live to serve. We die to serve," said a taj.

"Easy for you to say," Dreka-Tooth grumbled, but he followed.

"And I just have to take care of everything else," Teysa said. Cane in hand, she half-hopped, half-ran to the collapsed platform and the two figures atop it who hadn't moved since it came down.

CHAPTER 16

Applicants for the licensed title of ADVOKIST must demonstrate fluidity in a minimum of five modern languages and three ancient ones in addition to Ravi. Does APPLICANT so swear? Check I for 'yes' and II for 'no.'

—Application for license to practice advokism
(revised 10009 Z.C.)

3 Cizarm 10012 Z.C.

"I know exactly where you're hiding, Crix," Zomaj Hauc called. He wasn't taunting either. She was close enough now that she could actually pinpoint the magelord without seeing him now that she had her arm back. Unfortunately, its violent removal didn't allow her to simply snap it back on—the clasps were scrap. So she clutched one arm of metal in a hand of flesh and bone and focused on the recipient of the message.

There. Hauc's head was visible just over the top of the red-mottled egg, the only one that was merely cracked. The purple one was smashed, and the occupant's brains were dashed over the igneous rock—an unbelievable sight. Of the remaining two, the blue one was making progress, but Red was a slowpoke.

Crix yelped and Hauc froze when the goblin, backing away from the magelord, stepped on another goblin who'd been lying faceup in the water. Crix knew this goblin. It was Hauc's chief observer, Vazozav. The chief observer awoke with a start and coughed up brackish water.

Hauc turned and looked Crix directly in the eye. He didn't burn her, or even smile, he just disappeared around the side of the red egg.

"Chief!" Crix said. She scrambled to the choking goblin and helped him turn onto his side and cough out the rest of the water. "You've got to get any goblins left in here out. Come on. You with me, Chief Observer?"

Vazozav blinked. "You—You're that courier."

"And I've got a message for you. The Cauldron is going to be in very bad shape very soon. Get any goblins left out of here."

"Except—" the old scientist coughed, "except you, I take it?"

"Right," Crix said. "I've got to keep this away from—the enemy."

The old goblin grinned as he rolled to his feet. He spit out a bit more water, and Crix was reminded of the old Izzet legend about the saboteurs of the great Sigil of Ravnica.

"Keep it away from the enemy," the old goblin grinned. "I'll get our people out."

"Take them to the township for now," Crix said.

The magelord rounded the edge of the red egg, which loomed over his head like a god-sized halo. The floor of the Cauldron shook with dropping chunks of masonry and the thunks and pops of the cracking eggs. The shells broke apart with claps of thunder.

"Go, Chief!" Crix shouted and heard the goblin stagger off as fast as he could.

It was hard for Crix to concentrate. Using the lifts drained more than just the pyromana stored inside her artificial shinbones. She'd used a lot of emergency energy and didn't want to risk a flight that might end in a long fall just yet.

Besides, if she tried to fly out of this she'd be an easy target for Hauc. Crix tucked her courier's arm under her remaining arm and ran. She heard a whoosh and a splash behind her, and the magelord vaulted over her head in a somersault. Hauc landed directly in her path and crossed his arms. His scarlet face grew frightfully grim around his burning scowl.

"Crix," Hauc said over the thunderous sounds of hatching dragons, "I need that back."

"My lord, I—"

"The message, Crix. Deliver the message."

"I did," the goblin said. "I'm taking it back. You shouldn't have this."

"You are telling *me* what I can and cannot have, little creature? Goblin vermin?" Hauc said, his short temper shattered. "Return it to me."

Crix did the only thing she could think of. She clutched the arm to her chest, ducked her head, and ran. Hauc put out a hand to stop her, and she slammed the end of the severed message arm into his knee as hard as she could—but the magelord, his power saved for this day, was supernaturally fast. He latched one hand around the end of her improvised weapon and immediately resumed his chant. Crix pulled with all the leverage she could get, but the magelord just stood there, reciting the spell, frozen in a weird sort of bliss. His grip on the arm was like a vise.

"Vaykena hadsya yasyz," Hauc said carefully, *"Liynwryza drava, drava ti selya, xizzaya Zomaj Hauc ditezzya."*

The magelord completed the last word just as the top of the blue-mottled egg shattered and sent a shower of sharp debris flying into the air. Crix covered her eyes against the deadly fragments, some of which were as big as sentry shields. She opened her eyes again when she heard the magelord scream in shock and surprise, and she tumbled over backward, the sudden winner in the impromptu tug-of-war match.

A thick chunk of dragon shell had cleanly severed Hauc's right hand at the wrist. Hot, red blood poured from the stump into the murky water at their feet.

"I will not deliver the message!" Crix said. "I won't let you do this. One guild—one man—can't have that much power."

Hauc clutched his bloodied stump. "You would presume to lecture *me?*"

"Not any more. I presume to stop you," Crix said. Fire blazed in her soul as she added, "I quit."

Hauc's eyes flashed, and Crix waited for the burning lances that should have been her severance. Instead, the magelord aimed the beams at the stump of his hand and cauterized the wound.

A shiny blue-black dragon's head rose behind Hauc like an enormous hypnotized snake. Thick obsidian plates on its throat pulsed as it drew its first long breath. Then it roared in the din and eyed the magelord with one massive orb. Most of its body was still in the egg, which made it look serpentine.

"You," the dragon said. Its voice blanketed out all other sounds or concerns. "Zomaj Hauc."

"Yes," the magelord said and bowed his head. He'd seemingly forgotten completely about Crix and his missing hand. "I am Hauc. I am your master."

Crix found she could not move. Even if this magnificent thing was about to kill her, she would regret every second she did not take in its magnificence. She had only seen great Niv-Mizzet from afar and heard his voice distantly, for the great one desired privacy.

Not like the blue dragon. This creature was simply alive, and it was beautiful. Crix felt a part of her heart break when it lowered its great head and rested its chin in the muck to allow Zomaj Hauc to climb aboard its neck.

"Blue," Hauc said, "do you see the sky above us?"

"Yes," the dragon said. It sounded . . . sad, somehow, grief stricken. Crix could only imagine what enslavement felt like to such a creature, but it made her anger flare even greater at the magelord.

And yet still she could not bring herself to move.

With Hauc astride its neck, his hand clamped around a spiky horn, the blue dragon looked up.

"Take us to the sky, and take the breath of life, my finest servant," Hauc said. Crix was amazed at his pomposity.

"Yes," the dragon said and spread its wings. The rest of its eggshell prison shattered, finally breaking the goblin out of her daze and sending her fleeing for cover. From the shelter of a toppled wheel she saw the blue dragon take flight. It tucked its wings at the last moment to slip out of the Cauldron with ease, roaring into the fractured sky.

Then Crix heard another thunderclap as the last egg cracked, the dragon inside clearly itching to join its kin in flight. Hauc's spell was supposed to control them all, wasn't it? Crix wasn't sure, but then the dragon's ghostly white snout pierced the cap of the egg.

The arm was glowing again as more of the albino dragon emerged from its shell. The color of the dragon's snout was identical to the light the engravings emitted.

"No, I can't do this," she said aloud. "It won't work. She's going to hatch, and she's going to eat me and kill us all because he's the magelord. I'm just a courier. This won't work."

The figures on the arm were similar to some ancient languages she'd studied. She *might* be able to pronounce some of it phonetically. And who could say it would even work twice, or for anyone other than Hauc?

Crix certainly couldn't, but she was out of ideas.

She started to sound out the first syllable in her head. The albino's red eye emerged from the egg and regarded her with intense curiosity. She wasn't getting it, and cursed her limited education. Surely the magelord had been keeping knowledge from the goblins. She could see it clearly now. She needed someone with an extensive education.

Crix spotted a shape in black robes climbing the toppled landing pad and supposed it was worth a shot.

* * * * *

Kos was fairly sure he'd been in more pain than this on at least
one or two occasions, but he couldn't have named any of them now
if he'd tried. The landing platform had given way just as Golozar, coming out of nowhere to toss the magelord overboard, had
helped him to his feet. Kos guessed the thing just couldn't take
the extra weight, but he could hardly blame the Gruul. Golozar
had saved his life.

It might have cost the Gruul his own.

Kos made a quick check and found nothing broken, though
Golozar was badly cut and seriously bruised. He hoped the blood
he was spitting out was only from the missing teeth and not symp-
tomatic of worse injuries he couldn't see.

He patted the back of his belt. It was still there. The lucky
'drop. It would be the last one he ever used, when he had no other
choice, and that hadn't happened just yet. Kos knew the teardrop
would almost certainly kill him, but he also figured he'd have a
few good minutes before the end.

It looked like Golozar might need the 'drop much worse. The
Gruul had tried to stay standing on the platform when it fell,
unlike Kos, who'd dropped as soon as the first cable snapped.
The impact had thrown Golozar against the deck hard, and he
wasn't moving. From this angle Kos couldn't even tell if he were
breathing.

The old 'jek finally regained his footing, ready for the platform
to shift again with every step he took toward Golozar. There was
an explosion of shattering shell on his fourth step that almost made

him fall, but the shower of plates and fragments didn't reach them. Kos watched slack-jawed as the goblin courier grappled with the magelord for control of the message arm and won, thanks to an errant piece of eggshell. His relief at that quickly deflated when the magelord staunched the flow of blood, climbed onto the dragon, and launched into the sky.

"Well?" Golozar said weakly. "Did we do it?"

Kos offered the Gruul a hand. "No. You going to make it?"

"Nothing broken," the Gruul said, grimacing as he popped a shoulder back into place with an agonizing snap. "Nothing important, anyway."

"Kos!" a voice called, and they both turned to see the baroness clamber over the side of the fallen deck. She hauled herself up before they could reach her, and she waved away their assistance with the end of her cane.

"Baroness," Kos said. "We found the messenger. Did Pivlic—?"

"He made it out," Teysa said. "Never mind him. Look."

The last dragon cracked through to top of its shell, its bone-white scales and reddish eyes glowing in the mist. Crix held up the glowing arm as if offering it to the creature.

"What is she doing?" Kos said.

"I think she means to take that dragon for herself," Golozar ventured.

"She'll never pull it off," Teysa said. As if she could hear the Orzhov baroness, the goblin closed her mouth and turned back toward them. She waved the arm in the air.

"Baroness," Crix called. "Help!"

"Gruul," Teysa said.

"Golozar," the Gruul growled.

"Golozar, then," Teysa said, "I hate to ask this, but time demands it. Will you carry me?"

* * * * *

"Vsyo dovzer zsya mene, drazzac, drazzavh, drazzaugh," Teysa said.

"Is she reading it right, Crix?" Kos whispered. The dragon's head was not completely clear of the shell yet, and the sides of the egg were bulging and cracking against the pressure of its wings and tail.

"I think so," the goblin replied. "I'm something of a linguist, but this tongue is—"

"Quiet!" Golozar hissed.

"Tiyava silz naya, ti silya nayana vaykena hadsya yasyz."

A bit more of the albino showed, wicked-looking horns jutting from its jaw. The spikes ripped away more of the shell, which clattered noisily to the floor. The noise rang weirdly in the sudden quiet inside the Cauldron. "Baroness," Kos said, "I think you need to hurry."

Teysa glared at Kos as if to say, Do you want to try this?

"Liynwryza drava," Teysa said carefully. *"Drava ti selya, xizzaya Teysa Karlov ditezzya."*

The albino dragon pierced the sides of the egg at last, and the pale, glistening creature spread her wings for the first time. She didn't roar like her brother but looked curiously at Teysa, Crix, Kos, and Golozar in turn.

"Hello?" Teysa said.

"You," the dragon said, her voice like a choir of snakes, "Teysa Karlov. You are this one's master?" The dragon, her head big enough to swallow a drake whole and her face like an ivory mountain, still managed to look slightly puzzled. "This does not feel . . . right," she said. "But it is so."

The dragon lowered her chin just as the blue one had and

looked at Teysa. Its red eye blinked once. "Shall I carry you, Master?"

"Now the tricky part," she said to the others. "Anyone here know how to ride a dragon?"

"I think I could manage it," Golozar said, his gruff voice belying true awe at the mammoth creature. "There used to be wild drakes in the Husk. Before they were hunted out we used to capture them. Showing off. I think it wouldn't be that different."

"All right," Teysa said. "You're with me, Golozar. Give me a hand up?"

"Lady, I barely know you. Are you out of your mind?"

"Quite possible," Kos muttered.

"Gruul, I don't have time to argue. *We* don't have time. Either you help or you don't. I can ride a dromad—this can't be that different."

The conflict waging war within Golozar's conscience raged plainly across his face. "My people may be dead," he said quietly. "I must return to them."

"They will definitely be dead if we can't stop Hauc," Teysa said and offered her hand.

After another few seconds of raging indecision, Golozar took her hand and shook it. "All right," he said. "You've got a point."

"What should we do?" Crix said. She looked even more awe-struck than Golozar, staring into the albino's glowing, red eyes. Even Kos seemed to be having trouble not staring.

After the Gruul had helped her settle in behind the albino's head and heaved himself into the seat behind her, the baroness answered.

"What about that?" she said, pointing to Hauc's flight sphere, still hovering in the air above the platform. Whatever kept it aloft must have been internally generated, Kos guessed. It had stuck to the platform like glue. It had never occurred to him they might be able to use it.

He still wasn't sure they could.

"Crix?" he said. "That's impossible, right?"

The goblin looked thoughtful. "No," she said, stroking her chin, "I don't think it is impossible. I know a few tricks with locks, and the control layout should be standard. If there even are locks. One doesn't normally just walk away with a magelord's personal property. It's just not done." She grinned at Kos. "But I think I'm past things that 'just aren't done.' What do you say? Ever flown in a 'sphere before?"

"I can't say I've ever wanted to," Kos said honestly.

"You'll love it," Crix said. "My grandfather took me up once. It's nothing like a zeppelid. It's more like—"

"Crix," Kos said.

"Yes?"

"All right, let's do it. Just stop talking about it or I'm going to lose what nerve I have left."

"Good luck," Teysa said. "We won't be able to communicate once we're up there, so try to keep an eye on us." The dragon lifted its head. "Dragon," she said, "take us through the roof if you can."

"I can," the dragon sang. "Hold on."

Kos and Crix were knocked over by the wave of hot air the dragon's wings kicked up as it launched itself through the interior of the Cauldron and through the rooftop exit. Its wings clipped the sides and sent off sparks then they were out of sight.

"Kos, we should go," Crix said. "If we can't get into that sphere, we're going to have to get out of here before the generators start to spill over into the plants."

"Why? What happens then?" Kos asked.

"Ever seen a geothermic dome erupt?"

"Not for a long time."

"Were you standing on top of it?"

"No," Kos said.

"You don't want to," Crix said.

The old 'jek nodded. "Good point. Well . . . Who wants to live forever?"

* * * * *

Zomaj Hauc soared over the flats and relished the warm rays of sun that struck his face when he gained enough altitude to see the rising orb to the east. He could feel the blue dragon's heartbeat against his legs.

"You shall be called Hauc's Blue, I think," he said. "Over time, as you prove your loyalty, I will consider giving you a true name, something fittingly historic. But for now . . . it's got a certain ring to it, does it not?"

"Yes," the dragon growled, "Master."

Hauc took a moment to draw a deep breath and relish flying under the open sky, with no mizzium plating or magical fields between him and the winds, free of any dread that Niv-Mizzet would find him. If the Firemind dared to challenge him now, the old guildmaster would get much more than he bargained for.

Something didn't smell right. Specifically the air. At the same moment he detected the heavy presence of pollen in the air, he heard the dragon wheeze a long, slow breath. White petals from the Vitar Yescu floated by.

"Master," the dragon said, "the air. It does not—" the dragon drew another ragged breath. "It is hard to breathe."

The magelord tried not to panic and fought to keep his flaring temper in check at the same time. "Can you continue?" he asked Blue.

"Yes," the dragon replied, "if you wish it."

"I wish it," Hauc said. "And I think I know a way to clear the air as well. Do you see that accursed tree at the southern end of your new range?"

"Yes."

"Burn it."

"Gladly, Master."

Hauc let out an involuntary shout of triumph as the Great Dragon, his dragon, began its assault on Utvara, beginning with the Vitar Yescu and the mewling, pathetic Selesnyans inside.

The Vitar Yescu grew closer by the second. "Now, Blue," Hauc barked.

The dragon's jaws flung wide and belched an explosion of blue flame that engulfed the Vitar Yescu's willowy branches in seconds. The blaze clung to the Selesnyan tree like gobs of oil and sent petals of flame coursing through the breeze. Screaming life churchers poured out of every orifice of the Vitar Yescu and into the surrounding veztrees. Black smoke bubbled and billowed into the sky, and Hauc bid the dragon to inhale deeply as they went past.

"Better," the dragon said.

"Good," Hauc said. "Who needs plague winds when you've got dragon fire? Again, Blue."

"Yes," the dragon replied and wheeled around for another pass at the burning Vitar Yescu.

The screams of the Selesnyans filled Hauc with an unreal sense of joy. Such pain as legends caused. Zomaj Hauc was going to rewrite the history of Ravnica, and if that whithered relic Niv-Mizzet or anyone else tried to stop him they'd burn just as easily.

* * * * *

Teysa whooped in surprise as they cleared the Cauldron dome and went from stifling, oily heat to cold dawn air in a flash. The sun now dueled with the Schism for the sky, but the Schism looked as if it had begun to fade again.

The blue dragon, Hauc astride its neck, soared away from them as they continued to climb.

"What are we doing?" Teysa shouted over the winds. "He's going that way!"

"We need to get some height on him," Golozar shouted back over his shoulder, "take him by surprise. We want to end this quickly. No offense, Baroness, but I have no desire to be cooked alive, and I doubt you do either."

"You don't talk like a Gruul," Teysa said.

"How many Gruul do you know?" Golozar asked.

"Counting you? One."

"Figures."

The dragon reached a height satisfactory to her pilot, and Teysa's stomach lurched upward when Golozar coaxed the albino to level off and begin a long, slow dive, building speed, toward Hauc.

The blue dragon had changed course slightly and now headed directly for the Vitar Yescu. It launched a searing volley of blue fire at the Selesnyan tree, which was beginning to cave in on itself.

"Barkfeather," she said, "you suppose he was in there?"

"Who's Barkfeather?" Golozar asked.

"A—" A what? An ally? A friend? A temporary ally, at least. Maybe there was something she could do. She needed every ally she could get until this was over. "We've got to go faster," Teysa said. "They haven't destroyed it yet."

"The plague will end, you said," Golozar said. "Why do you care?"

"There are hundreds of people in there," she replied. "And they're about to owe me. Faster."

"Yes," the dragon said, her voice rising with the wind along her broad, pale wings. The dragon's breath sounded labored.

"Dragon?" Teysa said. "Are you all right?"

"The air is thin," the dragon said.

The plague. She hadn't anticipated that she herself would be relying on one of the dragons.

"Ah," Teysa said. "Wish I'd remembered that part. Dragon, will anything help it?"

"Burning things," the dragon replied.

"I'll take us over the Vitar Yescu," Golozar said.

"No ordinary fire," the dragon rumbled. "Dragon fire."

As she watched Hauc's blue dragon send another inferno at the Vitar Yescu, Teysa said, "Don't think that's going to be a problem."

* * * * *

"This is too dangerous," Kos said.

"It's a ramp," Crix said. "You'll do fine."

"Not the ramp," Kos said, examining the flight sphere *Pyraquin*.

He was about to rob an insane magelord, and he'd come to grips with that. He was going to have to fly out of here in that death-ball if he was going to escape a fiery doom when the generators went up, assuming the chunks that kept falling out of the ceiling didn't crush him first. No, his problem was simpler than that, simpler even than not believing the goblin really knew how to fly the sphere. It had nothing to do with the bulbous flame pods packed with liquid pyromana that could probably just as easily blow you off the map as work properly.

If Kos got into the sphere, he'd be alone with only one other individual. In the last twelve years, Kos had made sure that never happened, ever. It was, he realized now, one of the reasons he'd stayed so long at Pivlic's. There were always people coming and going. Even on late, slow nights there would be at least one drunk at the end of the bar, Pivlic behind the bar, and Kos standing—or more often sitting—watch over it all.

Being alone with another was how the lurker got to you. He rarely dwelled on it, but Kos lived in constant fear that someday, somehow, those writhing, wormy tentacles would find him again. Find him, kill him, and take over his life. Kos would be gone, dead, but no one who knew him would even realize it. He'd seen many wojeks who had turned out to be impersonators exposed at the Decamillennial, along with a lot of others, and all had been good people once. Kos would die before he let that happen to him.

"Kos," the goblin said, "I can do this myself, but if you don't make up your mind soon you're not going to get out of this place in time. I can fly this. I promise."

"I know," Kos said. Come on, you old fool, he told himself. How could Lupul impersonate rocket feet? "Let's go."

He had to duck at the top of the ramp. Crix had moved into the pilot's seat and said apologetically, "I'm afraid you'll have to try to wedge yourself in over there. And don't touch that. Or that. In fact, don't touch anything."

"I thought you were sure you could handle this," Kos said. "Maybe there's another way to get out of—"

"I am sure," Crix said, but the wojek thought she sounded like she was trying to convince herself. "Hold on to those straps there.

We'll be taking off in a few seconds." The goblin buckled a pair of belts across her chest.

"Just hold onto the straps," Kos said. "Any other advice? Shouldn't I have a chair?"

"Maybe," Crix said. She waved her hand over a brazier that rose from the console as several crystals, dials, and glass bubbles of odd-colored fluids flickered to life. "Let's see, I should still have an offering left . . ." the goblin muttered. She fumbled at her belt and produced a few pinches of dust, each pinch a different substance, and tossed them into the brazier. Then Crix spoke a few words of offering then declared, "Ignite!" The brazier flared and the glowing controls hummed with life.

"Looks like we're fully fueled," Crix said, "I think. Either that or we've already overheated and I haven't even started the flame-pods yet."

"You haven't?" Kos said. "What's that noise?"

"Just the systems," Crix said. "She's a really beautiful artifact, isn't she? Only one of her kind, the *Pyraquin*."

"I'm honored," Kos managed. He tried not to dwell on all the different ways he was probably going to get burned alive in the air and instead tried to focus on how he was going to be destroyed in the Cauldron if they didn't leave. It didn't really help.

"Here we go," Crix said, gripping a prominent, red lever in her hand.

"Wait," Kos said. "No offense, but don't you need two arms to fly this thing?"

"Don't think so," the goblin said. "But if it turns out I do, keep yours ready, would you?"

Crix wrenched back on the lever, and the flame-pods roared to life. She jammed it forward again, and Kos was thrown back against the floor. Then the transparent invizomizzium ball shot straight up through the exit atop a column of fire, which grew into a conflagration as the nest of generators and power plants finally went off in a series of spectacular explosions that tore the Cauldron apart.

CHAPTER 17

Fined—Zomaj Hauc, magelord, a sum total of five thousand zinos per day until safety codes are met on Power Project U-001012. Fine levied in absentia.

—Public notices, the *Utvara Townsman*
(31 Paujal 1012 Z.C.)

3 Cizarm 10012 Z.C.

Pivlic was down to the last remnant of cure when he reached Garulsz's camp, but it was enough for the ogress and her crew, with a bit left over. He had to hand it to the Simic, the stuff went a long way, though no one would really know if it worked for at least another day, assuming some fool went wandering around the flats tomorrow without a sphere suit.

Pivlic had intentionally gotten to Garulsz last. He didn't particularly want to tell the ogress he'd left their mutual friend Kos to most likely die a horrible death, and his head still ached from his last visit to this particular mining claim. Garulsz had shown surprising restraint in Pivlic's estimation and only broken a single pick that didn't even come close to hitting the imp.

"So we go back to help, right?" Garulsz said after ruining a few more tools and sending her partners running for the mining rig lest she turn her frustration on their livelihood. This was exactly what Pivlic had hoped he wouldn't hear.

"Actually, I was thinking we might all retire," Pivlic said. He needed to stall. Either Kos and the others would succeed, or they wouldn't. Out here on the flats, a strange, alien heat beating down on his leathery skin, Pivlic didn't feel particularly confident about

Kos's success. Success at what? Keeping the dragons out of Hauc's control but watching them hatch anyway? What force on Ravnica could stop the new dragons now that they were on their way into the world? "Yes, we should retire, my friend. To the Imp Wing. Drinks are on the house."

"Me only drink dindin juice," Garulsz said. "Kos was telling me about some of that imp rotgut you sell, and—"

"Fine," Pivlic said. "I have plenty of—Oh my word."

A blue dragon emerged from the dome atop the Cauldron and roared into the sky on wings that momentarily blotted out the first rays of sunrise before wheeling overhead and flapping off toward the township.

"Or maybe we stay here," Garulsz said with the exaggerated caution of one not used to expressing caution at all. "Looks like bar might be getting cooked, imp."

"Why don't you just cast a hex on the place while you're at it?" Pivlic said. "Don't speak evil or evil comes back to you."

"Me don't know what that means, but—"

Something exploded inside the Cauldron, and Pivlic lifted into the air with a start when the brick and stone ground of the flats rocked beneath his feet.

"Quiet," Pivlic snapped. "Look!"

"Another one," one of Garulsz's miners shouted.

"Back to work," Garulsz shouted back, then added, "Look, imp. Another one!"

"I see it," Pivlic said. The second dragon looked a little bigger than the first, though it might just have been a trick of the light bouncing off of its ivory scales. The albino climbed straight up to gain altitude on the blue dragon, then leveled off and flew overhead after the blue dragon. Pivlic noted no one ducked this time. They just stood and watched, awestruck.

As the albino turned to follow the blue one's course, Pivlic caught a glimpse of the riders and almost dropped from the air in shock. The baroness and a savage Gruul sat astride the thing's neck.

"Who that?" Garulsz said.

"Beats me," Pivlic lied. "But I think there's going be a fight, my friends. And you know what that means." He turned to the ogress and her small mining crew and added, "Anyone want to place any—" his words caught in his throat when a third shape rose from the Cauldron. Of course, there had been three eggs. A silvery flash crested the center of the dome, and Pivlic prepared to mentally figure the odds if another dragon was thrown into the mix.

But this was no dragon. The translucent sphere cleared the dome and blasted off on a straight line after the albino. Just as the *Pyraquin's* flame-pods engaged, the Cauldron exploded in a spectacularly volcanic display. The shock wave knocked them all about and a hot wind washed over them, even at this distance. Pivlic was blown backward into Garulsz, who absorbed most of the impact.

"That no dragon," Garulsz said, pushing herself into a sitting position before the others. Pivlic, also sitting up whether he wanted to or not, nodded. A few more explosions went off somewhere in the Cauldron and new fires started along the structure, outmatching the flames clinging to the Vitar Yescu.

"No," Pivlic said, and pushed off of the ogress and back into the air with a flap of his wings. "As I was saying, any of you fine ladies and gentlemen want to place any bets? I'll extend credit to all bettors who can make their mark on a piece of parchment." He clapped his hands together.

Finally back in something close to his element. There was a fight going on, and fights naturally drew an audience. "It's a three-way race, near as I can tell, my friends," Pivlic said. "The blue, the albino, or the brave souls in the crystal ball? How many can make it? Who will survive? Come now, gentlemen and ladies, do not be shy."

Might as well make some zinos, Pivlic reasoned, just in case. He gave Kos better odds than he probably should have, but his old friend could probably use all the luck he could get.

* * * * *

The blue dragon burned a great gouge from the side of the Vitar Yescu, and Hauc was in the process of guiding the blue around for a third pass when a blazing column of white flame blasted across his flight path. He wrenched on one of the blue dragon's horns and pulled down just in time to avoid the albino dragon—*his* albino dragon—as it cut through the heavy air above with a roar. He caught a glimpse of the escaped Gruul prisoner and behind him that foolish child, that self-styled Orzhov baroness who had been causing him grief since she came to Utvara.

"Down!" the magelord shouted to his less-than-enthusiastic steed. "The Vitar Yescu, now!"

The blue dragon was under his control, but there was a difference between control and command. He could feel Blue fighting him and resolved to fight right back. Hauc was the master, not the dragons. Not the blue one and not the stolen albino. Not even Niv-Mizzet. Zomaj Hauc.

Unfortunately, master or not, he was not entirely flameproof, not against the ancient, magical fire of a dragon. He told the blue dragon as much and ordered it to do its best not to endanger him. He thought he heard the dragon chuckle at that but chose to ignore it. It loosed another blue-flame blast that took out a swath of the sturdy Vitar Yescu, but still the towering tree, though completely awash in flames, refused to fall.

Just so long as it burned. The Vitar Yescu was as good as dead.

Hauc craned his neck to get a bead on the albino, which he'd lost when it flew straight into the eastern sunrise. It emerged, bathed in a halo of orange rays, circling around the far side of the township.

"Smart, Gruul," Hauc said. "Give me a chance to pick another target, then strike when I do." He could tell the albino was lost to him. He felt no connection to it whatsoever. So be it. It had to have been the baroness. It explained the Gruul's presence—the dilettante needed a pilot, of course. Of the fools he'd left to die in the Cauldron, only the baroness could possibly have learned the ancient dragon language. It would be typical of the overeducated Orzhov.

"Blue," he said, "your next target is the albino."

"You would have me attack one of my own?" the dragon said. "You would do this and still expect me to serve you?"

"You will do worse than this," Hauc said.

"Someday I will be free of this magic, Zomaj Hauc," the dragon said, "and on that day I will burn the flesh from your bones and crush them between my teeth."

"I doubt it," Hauc said. "Now kill the albino."

"Yes," the blue snarled, a sound that bordered on a furious roar, "Mas—"

A glittering transparent ball shot from above, slammed into the side of the dragon's head, and ricocheted off to the west, ten flame-pods blasting at once as it tumbled, slowed, then leveled off.

"The dirty thieves," Hauc said as he struggled to keep the dazed dragon in the air. "Thieves!" he repeated, screaming. *Pyraquin! Til yin destrovo!"*

Hauc spat with fury as he shouted the words. He would miss flying in the *Pyraquin*. But now that he had Blue, he no longer needed it. Damn those fools for forcing him to trigger the self-destruct.

The dragon recovered quickly, only a bit bloodied, from the look of it, and resumed its course for the albino, which was finally coming around and heading back toward them. He paid the flight sphere no more mind. Perhaps he would have another one built someday but probably not. It would no doubt be stolen just like this one, like his albino.

Now the albino had to die too.

* * * * *

"What just happened?" Crix demanded.

"You're asking me?" Kos said. His arm had become entangled in cords and wires, and it was agony to keep holding on. If he let go, though, it would be worse. Crix seemed incapable of flying in a straight line. "It looked like we smacked into that dragon and bounced off."

"I know that part," Crix said.

"Sort of a dangerous strategy, don't you think?" Kos said. The cuts on his hands and wrists from the rack had reopened, and blood poured down both arms as he struggled to stay in one place as the flight sphere spun around. The spinning stopped abruptly when Crix slammed her fist down on a blue switch. No, it was still spinning, Kos corrected himself, but the cockpit wasn't thanks to multiple hulls. Nice trick. Crix leaned back in the flight chair and looked up at Kos.

"It's not the collision I'm worried about," Crix said. "The sphere can take it, and without weapons it's the only thing I can think of. You didn't suggest anything."

"I suggested—ow—that we not do this," Kos pointed out.

"Then we'd be dead in the Cauldron," Crix said, "but you're still missing my point."

"Which is?" Kos asked.

"That switch I hit just now?" the goblin said. "I think it's the only control on that board that's responding, and it's mechanical. My grandfather showed me how they worked. It's a clamp and release, swings the interior free of the—"

"Never mind," Kos said. "If you have no controls, how are we staying in the air?"

"Momentum," Crix said, "inertia, and residual magic fields. I think we're going to return to the surface in under a minute at this rate."

"Thanks for at least looking worried," Kos said. "What are we going to do?"

"There's nothing I can do," Crix said. "That was a risk—we knew it was his sphere. He must have used a ley command when we buzzed him just now."

"You sure it wasn't your brilliant 'slam them in the head with our flight sphere' tactic that did it?" Kos said.

"The sphere's pure, refined invizomizzium," Crix said. "That didn't hurt her in the slightest. The crash probably won't hurt the *Pyraquin* either. I don't know if I can say the same for us."

Kos cast about the inside of the sphere for something, anything, he could try. He couldn't accept that after these last few days he was going to end up a smear on the inside of a giant ball. He saw something that looked like a crank, something with a handle, anyway. It led to a section of something pulsing and covered in tubes, connected to the flame-pods, no doubt. The flame-pods that weren't working.

"Crix," Kos said, "is that tank or generator or whatever—is it supposed to look like that?"

Crix craned in her seat to see what Kos was looking at. The color drained from her reddish face. "Oh no," she said. "He didn't just switch off the controls."

"What? What did he do?"

"That's the pyromana tank. It's feeding back in on itself, and it's going to ignite. Now, see that hatch over our heads?" Crix said, pointing.

"Sure," Kos said.

"Open it," Crix said. "We've got to get out of here."

"I know, but how are we going to—"

The explosion of the pyromana tank cut off Kos in midsentence. To his relief, it exploded outward, jolting the entire vessel into another tumbling spin. It failed to immolate the occupants, hardly did more than heat them up a bit. He couldn't believe his luck and reached up turn the manual crank that would open what looked like an exit hatch. That was when he noticed the pain.

His arms would not move. He looked down at his chest and saw a bent mizzium cylinder protruding from the tank housing, still blazing hot from the explosion. It had entered his right arm just below the elbow, passed clean through his abdomen between his ribs, and, he gathered from the oddly numb feeling in the left half of his body, punctured his spine along the way before pinning his open hand to the inner surface of the cockpit.

"Help," he croaked. Warm blood began to pour from Kos's mouth, and he could not lift his jaw.

"Great Niv-Mizzet," he heard Crix say, her voice receding as his consciousness started to fade.

" 'Drop," Kos managed. "Belt."

"What?" Crix said, echoing dreamily in the old man's brain.

* * * * *

"He's watching us," Golozar said, "circling." He took them near the edge of the western Husk and guided the dragon northward.

Her nose swung round to face the blue one.

"It looks like the others are out of it already," Teysa said. "Dragon, do you have a name?"

" 'Dragon,' so far," the albino replied.

"How do you feel? Can you breathe?"

"I am managing," the dragon said.

"Can you hit the magelord without hurting the blue dragon?" Teysa said.

"Why would she do that?" Golozar said.

"Why would I do that?" the dragon echoed. "He is another dragon. This is my range, is it not? If he will not flee, he will die. Unless you tell me otherwise."

"I thought—You *want* to kill the other dragon?" Teysa said.

"Indeed," the dragon said. "I am no sentimental male. Shall I do it?"

Teysa only considered the question for a moment. "After them," she said through clenched teeth, then wrapped her arms around the Gruul's waist as he spurred the dragon with his heels and jolted forward on a collision course with Hauc.

She let one hand slip from Golozar to turn halfway around and scan the sky for the flight sphere. Teysa caught a glimpse of a trail of black smoke and a flash of something that might have been the *Pyraquin* still above the horizon. Then it was gone as Golozar guided the dragon around an outcrop of exposed mizzium infrastructure, bent by time and volcanism.

When she whipped back around, the blue dragon was much closer than she'd expected. Hauc bellowed commands from his perch, but his dragon seemed to be slow to respond. The blue one turned to face them, and she saw why—a sliver of translucent invizomizzium from the hull of the sphere had driven into its skull behind the right eye, which had gone from golden to scarlet, filled with blood. That must have been what sent the sphere off course, and it was probably going to kill the blue dragon on its own, in time.

Unfortunately, she didn't know how *much* time. It looked mortal, but who knew with a dragon? The blue dragon roared, its baritone bellow tinged with a scream of pain and a little confusion as it tried to comply with its rider and its instincts simultaneously. Finally, Hauc won out and the beast belched another blast of blazing indigo flame.

The jet missed them, but clipped the edge of the albino's right wing and burned it away to ash. The dragon roared in pain and, without being ordered to do so by Teysa, fired a return shot that caught the blue dragon in the neck and might have hit Hauc as well. They went past too quickly to say for sure.

"Dragon," Golozar said, "your injury. Can you stay in the air?"

"He burned my wing!" the albino roared. "My *wing!* I will stay in the air as long as that coward does. Count on that."

Teysa was a little concerned at how quickly the dragon's vocabulary was growing. It had been able to speak as soon as it was out of the egg, and was hatched with knowledge it couldn't possibly have gained personally. There was strong, ancient magic here she couldn't even begin to understand. She wondered how strong, really, a secondhand, repeated spell could be and what, if anything, she could do if she lost control of the creature while they were so high above the ground.

"Back around," Teysa said to Golozar. "Dragon, kill the human first. Then the blue mount he rides."

"We'll see," the albino growled.

* * * * *

" 'Drop," Kos managed. "Belt."

"What?" Crix said. The blasted pipe had completely impaled the old human, and blood poured from Kos's wounds and mouth. No one could survive this, not without medicine like—

"There's a 'drop!" she said. "On your belt!"

Kos blinked, his head lolling to one side.

"Hold on," Crix said. She undid her restraints and spun the seat around, then climbed on top of it. She reached around Kos's waist and found a lone leather pouch against the small of his back, and her fingertips revealed the telltale shape of a teardrop. Careful not to fumble it in the spinning flight sphere, she pulled it out of the bag and gripped it tightly in her fist. She leaned up so Kos could see her face and said, "This won't work unless you get free of this pipe. I'm going to pull you free, then administer this. I imagine it's going to hurt. Are you ready? Never mind, don't answer. Just get ready."

Crix hooked her arm around him, still clutching the crystalline teardrop of concentrated magic, placed her feet on the chair at an angle she hoped wouldn't do any more damage to Kos's insides than necessary, and hauled back with all the leverage she could gather and strength she could muster.

Kos let out an agonized, gargling wail as he slipped wetly from the pipe and toppled over onto the flight chair. Crix maneuvered around behind him, snapped the tip of the teardrop off with her thumb, and jammed it into the gaping hole in Kos's side.

The goblin risked a look down through the transparent floor at the rapidly approaching ground. Thirty seconds if they were lucky. She willed the medicine to heal the old human quickly.

As if in response to her silent plea, the 'drop shrank in her palm, pouring into the wound and rapidly accelerating the healing process. In another few seconds it was gone, and Crix pulled her hand back.

The skin had sealed almost completely, but there was no telling how much damage remained. It was only one 'drop, but one 'drop could work wonders. They were powerful, but still Kos lay slumped over the chair, unmoving. The flow of blood from his mouth had stopped, at least, but was that because he was healed or because he was dead?

Crix checked on the ground. Fifteen seconds.

Kos coughed, spitting more blood. "Heart," he said. Then he looked up and blinked. "Crix? Am I—"

"Abandoning ship," Crix said. She hopped up to the armrest of the chair, gave the hatch seal a twirl, and slammed her palm against the transparent metal. With a hiss and a pop the hatch opened through three layers of hull, exposing open sky. She looked down at Kos, who pushed himself up from the chair. "Hold onto my waist," she said, "facing me. Don't want you to get burned."

At that moment, another small piece of the *Pyraquin* exploded. Crix was thrown back against the console and slumped face-first into the pilot's chair.

Kos hooked one hand over the rim of the hatch and pulled his aching body up, panic taking over as the 'sphere filled with greasy smoke. Yet he still had the presence of mind to spare a look over one shoulder at Crix, who had saved Kos instead of leaving him behind. The contrast was immediately and shamefully apparent.

His conscience did the rest. If Kos got out of this, he'd get out with the goblin.

"Crix, wake up," Kos said. "Wake up!" He reached down without losing his grip on the lip of the hatch and slapped the goblin across the face, then pulled her up by the collar. "We have to leave."

"Right," Crix said, still quite dazed. "Leave."

Crix hooked her arm under Kos's and closed her eyes. Four seconds. Fire the pyromanic lifts. Two seconds. Firing.

A half-second before the *Pyraquin*'s final flight ended with an abrupt stop that created a brand-new crater in the middle of the Utvara Flats, goblin and wojek blasted from the center of the sphere and into open space on a column of sputtering smoke. A second after impact, the remaining flame-pods on Hauc's vessel detonated in a series of accelerating chain reactions that carried the pair much farther than Crix's feet could have.

Kos slipped a little when Crix swung her feet around to slow their inevitable descent. She willed the last of the pyromana from the lifts, gritted her teeth, and tightened her grip on the old human's arm.

The fuel gave out at the end of their arc, and they dropped the last bit, landing in a heap on a rusted hillside.

* * * * *

Twice, the dragons and their riders charged, and twice did the beasts, their breath faltering in clear winds no longer choked with plague and dragon smoke, blast sputtering streams of fire at each other's wings and flanks. And twice, to Teysa's alternating relief and frustration, the blasts missed both sets of riders entirely.

"Damn him!" the albino roared.

"You're too evenly matched," Golozar said. "Stop trying to burn him. You have claws and teeth. You're not a cannon, you're a dragon."

"And we need to injure him quickly," Teysa said. "You're hurt, dragon."

"I will," the dragon said, wheezing, "I will survive this. The blue one will not. The machine injured him first, but I won't let the machine take the credit." The dragon gasped deeply twice and continued, rasping bitterly. "Yet . . . I tire," she admitted. "The fire—I need time to recharge."

"Tooth and claw," Teysa said. "There's no time to rest. I'm sorry."

"You are in charge," the albino said with little sincerity. The dragon spread her tattered, scorched wings and brought her forelimbs up, talons exposed like a bird of prey. Hauc's blue dragon, readying another blast of flame, didn't see the albino's change in tactics until it was too late. The silver claws of the albino dragon sank into the neck of the blue one, which screeched and roared in terror and strangled pain. Teysa's mount closed its claws around the other's throat and abruptly changed direction. It pulled hard to the left, wrenching the blue dragon's neck around like a corkscrew with a popping, sickening crunch.

Zomaj Hauc, on the other hand, continued on the blue dragon's flight path sans dragon, screaming all the way. His journey—and his life—ended with a messy headfirst impact against the side of an iron cliff. Teysa heard him cursing her name the whole way.

One threat down. Very, very down. Her heart burned with bitter, vengeful satisfaction, but there was not time to celebrate. They weren't out of trouble yet.

"Hauc's gone," she shouted to Golozar, and leaned forward to whisper so only he could hear. "The dragons have to go too. Both of them. They're too dangerous."

"I know," Golozar said. "Hold on, I'll try to cushion our landing as best I can."

The Gruul might as well have attempted to wrestle a flatland cyclone, for the albino chose that moment to go completely mad, consumed by a blood frenzy. Its silver teeth tore into the dying blue dragon's flanks and ripped away chunks of flesh that it tossed aside. It clamped its rear set of claws around the blue dragon's tail and ripped the appendage from its foe's spine with another snap and pop.

All the while, Teysa felt Golozar, muscles straining to guide their difficult mount, slowly force the dragon to veer as it ripped into the blue, lower and lower. The albino was flying blind, trusting Golozar to steer while it dived headfirst into its kin.

The dragon—neither dragon—saw the jagged mizzium outcrop in time. Teysa herself almost didn't see it, and, with a hideous pair of harmonic screams, the outcrop skewered both dragons at once.

The next few minutes were a blur. Teysa was pretty sure she blacked out because the next thing she remembered was lying on top of Golozar, who was in turn piled against the twisted, crushed, and bleeding albino dragon. She could feel the slow rise and fall of the Gruul's chest. He still lived. The blue dragon was almost unrecognizable as anything but a mass of scaly, raw meat.

Teysa felt sadness and relief battling for supremacy in her heart as the albino dragon's red eye gazed at her with silent accusation, flickered, and went cold.

She returned the stare for a moment, but then her gaze was drawn to something that appeared in the sky over Utvara with a thunderclap. It wasn't a dragon.

But it did have wings.

* * * * *

Kos blinked. He thought he saw the *kuga mot* for a moment, and it was crystal clear—not a ghostly ball of light but a solid sphere with bolted windows and a hull forged from brushed, bronze-tinted mizzium.

Then the sphere disappeared and agony returned. The Schism remained. It was bright, brilliantly bright. Brighter than the sun, brighter than he'd ever seen it. It was beautiful, and he felt it pulling at him. Pulling at his spirit.

His heart began to pound, faster and faster, against the inside of his chest. He coughed, and Crix told him they were landing and to hold on. Kos could barely think straight. The pounding drowned out her voice. He struck the ground first, never taking his eyes from the Schism, and skidded before coming to rest against the rubble.

"Kos," the goblin coughed, "are you all right?"

Kos didn't answer. He couldn't feel anything below his waist, and his left arm was screaming for attention. It felt broken, shattered against the stone. In reply he raised his remaining hand and pointed at the Schism.

"Bright," he whispered. "It's so bright."

"What's bright?" Crix said. "The Schism. Yes, it's been—Wait, Kos, listen to me. Stay here. Don't look at it, it's—"

"It's beautiful," Kos said. "I can see her. She's come back."

"Who?" Crix said.

The Schism burst apart, shattering like a plate of glass struck by a stone, from the center outward. The dawn sky appeared to fracture as well, but behind the falling glass was the same sky—just clearer, sharper to Kos's eye.

From the center of the fracture emerged an angel. The sight brought what few tears he had left brimming to the surface.

"It's her," Kos said.

The flying figure grew larger, drew closer, and became more and more distinct as she soared toward Kos and the goblin.

Kos waved when Feather came into view, but the pounding of his own heartbeat drowned out even his own voice as he called out his old friend's name. He waved to her once, but then his arm became far too heavy to lift.

For a moment, the driving drumbeat in his ears ceased, and he reveled in a short eternity of blissful silence as Feather drew closer and called back to him, her voice making no sound. Her angelic eyes were wide with horror, and she was saying something. He could make out the shape of the words. They were "Kos" and "no," in that order.

Before Feather finished the second word, Agrus Kos was dead.

Here lies Agrus Kos, noted protector and faithful public servant
3 Paujal 9895–3 Cizarm 10012
   —Epitaph of Agrus Kos, lieutenant (Ret.), League of Wojek

5 CIZARM 10012 Z.C.

Pivlic didn't shed tears easily. True, that was mostly because imps didn't have tear ducts, but even if they had Pivlic wasn't the kind to weep over the loss of anyone. He'd once run a place where the customers killed and ate each other (after signing appropriate releases absolving the imp of all responsibility) back in the city. Death was no shock to him. Not usually.

But in honor of his friend Kos, he went to the trouble to put in drops that would give his beady, black eyes a touch of sympathetic moisture.

Feather, it seemed, did have tear ducts and had been using them recently from the look of it. The two of them led the two rows of solemn pallbearers, Pivlic holding his hands overhead to support his corner while the angel held up her end by stooping slightly and hooking her long fingers through a handle bolted to the side of the stretcher.

Behind Pivlic walked the ledev guardian Fonn, who had arrived that morning on a private zeppelid with the pallbearer opposite her—the Golgari guildmaster Jarad. They looked far friendlier than he'd last seen them. Affectionate, even. Behind them walked Crix, doing the job much the same way Pivlic was, flanked by a somber Garulsz, who had put on her brightly colored "city clothes" for the procession.

Kos's body lay on a shallow wooden pallet, arms crossed over the insignia on the wojek dress armor Pivlic had found in storage. Baroness Teysa Karlov quietly slipped into the procession at its head, dressed from head to toe in glistening black satin and wearing a shimmering silver veil. Vor Golozar, chief of the surviving Utvar Gruul, stepped to the rear, eyes downcast. Golozar wore the finest ceremonial hides his tribe—reduced in number, but more fiercely proud than ever—could provide. A gleaming new black pin on his collar that signified his unexpected appointment as Teysa's Minister of Security.

There was no dirge—a short and not-terribly-helpful last will and testament the imp had dug out of Kos's footlocker had asked for no particular music, so Pivlic had decided silence would be best. The others had agreed.

The long walk, the longest of Pivlic's long life, ended at a stack of dry, bristly wood and broken timbers. Wood was not easy to come by in Utvara. The pyre had required the help of most everyone in the township and eventually had grown much larger than was needed as more and more grateful denizens added to it.

At the base of the structure, Feather and Garulsz took over. They gently lifted the pallet atop the great pyre.

Before the fire was lit, Feather, who had kept the name Kos gave her decades ago, stepped before the pyre and faced the crowd. Pivlic desperately wanted to know where the angel had been, but Feather refused to answer any questions until Kos's memorial was finished.

"Agrus Kos," the angel began, "did not want this memorial. But we who remember him do. And it is my hope that somewhere his ghost, or at least his spirit, will forgive us for bestowing this last honor."

* * * * *

Miles overhead, a memorial of a different sort took shape, slowly, on a scale of time bordering the geological. Like nearly all the spirits of the dead that had tried to leave Utvara since the creation of the Schism, Hauc failed. He had snagged on the shattered sky amongst a multitude of ghosts then slipped over the edge into the precipice of the void, his spirit stretching out like bread dough. Then the sky broke like a window punctured by a bamshot. The shards of sky fell apart and the still-vibrant Schism effect locked everything in place as his spirit scattered across the heavens.

Hauc had gone to pieces, pieces that mingled sickeningly with raw, terrifyingly reptilian thoughts that comprised the shattered souls of two dead dragons on the disordered edge of the mana-compression singularity bomb's event horizon. Two dead gods, frozen just as he was in the fractured sky. There were others, too, thousands, Great Dragon, millions of them. None had been "used" or "fed to the dragons," but they all knew him and knew he was the reason they were there. They repeated his name, all crying at once, a pointless exercise as he could not remember it himself.

HaucHAUCChauchaucHAUCHaucHauc.

He did not know it was his name, but he knew the sound was morbid, incessant, and for some reason frightening.

He knew he would escape, of course, even if he couldn't quite remember that he was called "Hauc." There was nothing that could possibly destroy him forever, of that he felt curiously confident. It was only a matter of time before he remembered his name, and then the . . . thing that would let him get . . . get . . . over, get . . . where . . . get . . .

Get. First he had to get his scattered thoughts together, which couldn't possibly take more than a decade or two. Assuming he could find all the pieces.

THE KAMIGAWA CYCLE CONCLUDES!

WRITTEN BY SCOTT MCGOUGH,
AUTHOR OF THE MAGIC LEGENDS CYCLE TWO

OUTLAW: CHAMPIONS OF KAMIGAWA
Book One

In a world of mysticism and honor, a war is brewing. Spirits launch attacks against humans as, in the shadows, a terror lurks just beyond sight. Michiko, the daughter of the warlord Konda, must brave the dangers outside her father's fortress and stop the war that is about to sweep the land.

HERETIC: BETRAYERS OF KAMIGAWA
Book Two

Now in the employ of Princess Michiko, Toshi Umezawa tries to honor his commitments while pursuing his own ends. As the Kami War threatens to engulf Kamigawa, a spirit beast menaces the world. At the center of the battle is the Daimyo whose sinister crime gnaws at the world's heart.

GUARDIAN: SAVIORS OF KAMIGAWA
Book Three

Guardian brings to a close the explorations and adventures in the new and mysterious area of MAGIC: THE GATHERING first introduced in *Outlaw*. This novel previews the newest trading card game expansion set to be released in 2005.

MAGIC: THE GATHERING, and its logo is a trademark of Wizards of the Coast, Inc. in the U.S.A. and other countries. ©2005 Wizards.

DIVE INTO THE WORLD OF MAGIC!

PLAY MAGIC: THE GATHERING

NEW EXPANSION SETS

Saviors of kamigawa

MagictheGathering.com

MAGIC: THE GATHERING, CHAMPIONS OF KAMIGAWA, Betrayers of Kamigawa, Saviors of Kaamigawa, WIZARDS OF THE COAST and their respective logos are trademarks of Wizards of the Coast, Inc. in the U.S.A. and other countries. ©2005 Wizards.

FROM *NEW YORK TIMES*

BEST-SELLING AUTHOR

R.A. SALVATORE

In taverns, around campfires, and in the loftiest council chambers of Faerûn, people whisper the tales of a lone dark elf who stumbled out of the merciless Underdark to the no less unforgiving wilderness of the World Above and carved a life for himself, then lived a legend...

THE LEGEND OF DRIZZT

For the first time in deluxe hardcover editions, all three volumes of the Dark Elf Trilogy take their rightful place at the beginning of one of the greatest fantasy epics of all time. Each title contains striking new cover art and portions of an all-new author interview, with the questions posed by none other than the readers themselves.

HOMELAND

Being born in Menzoberranzan means a hard life surrounded by evil.

EXILE

But the only thing worse is being driven from the city with hunters on your trail.

SOJOURN

Unless you can find your way out, never to return.

Forgotten Realms and its logo and Drizzt Do'Urden are trademarks of Wizards of the Coast, Inc. in the U.S.A. and other countries. ©2004 Wizards.

ED GREENWOOD

THE CREATOR OF THE FORGOTTEN REALMS WORLD

BRINGS YOU THE STORY OF

SHANDRIL OF HIGHMOON

SHANDRIL'S SAGA

SPELLFIRE
Book I

Powerful enough to lay low a dragon or heal a wounded warrior, spellfire
is the most sought after power in all of Faerûn. And it is in the reluctant
hand of Shandril of Highmoon, a young, orphaned kitchen-lass.

CROWN OF FIRE
Book II

Shandril has grown to become one of the most powerful magic-users in
the land. The powerful Cult of the Dragon and the evil Zhentarim want
her spellfire, and they will kill whoever they must to possess it.

HAND OF FIRE
Book III

Shandril has spellfire, a weapon capable of destroying the world, and
now she's fleeing for her life across Faerûn, searching for somewhere to
hide. Her last desperate hope is to take refuge in the sheltered city of
Silverymoon. If she can make it.

www.wizards.com

FORGOTTEN REALMS and its logo are trademarks of Wizards of the Coast, Inc.
in the U.S.A. and other countries. ©2005 Wizards.

FORGOTTEN REALMS®

DRAGONS ARE DESCENDING ON THE FORGOTTEN REALMS!

THE RAGE
The Year of Rogue Dragons, Book I
RICHARD LEE BYERS

Renegade dragon hunter Dorn hates dragons with a passion few can believe, let alone match. He has devoted his entire life to killing every dragon he can find, but as a feral madness begins to overtake the dragons of Faerûn, civilization's only hope may lie in the last alliance Dorn would ever accept.

THE RITE
The Year of Rogue Dragons, Book II
RICHARD LEE BYERS

Dragons war with dragons in the cold steppes of the Bloodstone Lands, and the secret of the ancient curse gives a small band of determined heroes hope that the madness might be brought to an end.

REALMS OF THE DRAGONS
Book I
EDITED BY PHILIP ATHANS

This anthology features all-new stories by R.A. Salvatore, Ed Greenwood, Elaine Cunningham, and the authors of the R.A. Salvatore's War of the Spider Queen series. It fleshes out many of the details from the current Year of Rogue Dragons trilogy by Richard Lee Byers and includes a short story by Byers.

REALMS OF THE DRAGONS
Book II
EDITED BY PHILIP ATHANS

A new breed of Forgotten Realms authors bring a fresh approach to new stories of mighty dragons and the unfortunate humans who cross their paths.

FORGOTTEN REALMS and its logo are trademarks of Wizards of the Coast, Inc. in the U.S.A. and other countries. ©2005 Wizards.

A brand new title from *New York Times*
**bestselling author
Lisa Smedmen, and other great
Forgotten Realms tales!**

VIPER'S KISS
House of the Serpents, Book II

NEW YORK TIMES BESTSELLING AUTHOR LISA SMEDMAN

Fleeing a yuan-ti princess who has designs on your soul is bad enough,
but needing her help to retrieve a dangerous artifact that could enslave the
world can really ruin your day.

THE EMERALD SCEPTER
Scions of Arrabar, Book III

THOMAS M. REID

The final installment of the Scions of Arrabar Trilogy brings Vambran
back home to settle once and for all the question of who will inherit the
power of the great mercenary Houses of Arrabar.

MASTER OF CHAINS
The Fighters, Book I

JESS LEBOW

The first title in a new Forgotten Realms series focusing on the popular
Dungeons & Dragons® game character class of Fighters. Each title will
feature characters with a different exotic style of fighting. In Master of
Chains, the leader of a rebellion is captured by bandits, and his chains of
bondage become the only weapons he has with which to escape.

GHOSTWALKER
The Fighters, Book II

ERIK DE BIE

Each novel in The Fighters series is written as a stand-alone adventure,
allowing new readers an easy entry point into the Forgotten Realms
world. This novel is a classic revenge story that focuses on a man in black
with ghostly powers who seeks vengeance upon those who caused his
death many years ago.

FORGOTTEN REALMS and its logo are trademarks of Wizards of the Coast, Inc.
in the U.S.A. and other countries. ©2005 Wizards.

THE TWILIGHT GIANTS TRILOGY
Written by *New York Times* bestselling author
TROY DENNING

THE OGRE'S PACT
Book I

This attractive new re-release by multiple *New York Times* best-selling author Troy Denning, features all new cover art that will re-introduce Forgotten Realms fans to this excellent series. A thousand years of peace between giants and men is shattered when a human princess is stolen by ogres, and the only man brave enough to go after her is a firbolg, who must first discover the human king's greatest secret.

THE GIANT AMONG US
Book II

A scout's attempts to unmask a spy in his beloved queen's inner circle is her only hope against the forces of evil that rise against her from without and from within.

THE TITAN OF TWILIGHT
Book III

The queen's consort is torn between love for his son and the dark prophesy that predicts his child will unleash a cataclysmic war. But before he can take action, a dark thief steals both the boy and the choice away from him.

FORGOTTEN REALMS and its logo are trademarks of Wizards of the Coast, Inc. in the U.S.A. and other countries. ©2005 Wizards.

STARLIGHT AND SHADOWS IS FINALLY GATHERED INTO A CLASSIC GIFT SET!

BY ELAINE CUNNINGHAM

"I have been a fan of Elaine Cunningham's since I read *Elfshadow*, because of her lyrical writing style."
– R.A. Salvatore

DAUGHTER OF THE DROW
Book I

Beautiful and deadly, Liriel Baenre flits through the darkness of Menzoberranzan where treachery and murder are the daily fare. Seeking something beyond the Underdark, she is pursued by enemies as she ventures towards the lands of light.

TANGLED WEBS
Book II

Exiled from Menzoberranzan, the beautiful dark elf Liriel Baenre wanders the surface world with her companion Fyodor. But even as they sail the dangerous seas of the Sword Coast, a drow priestess plots a terrible fate for them.

WINDWALKER
Book III

Liriel and Fyodor travel across the wide realms of Faerun in search of adventure and reach the homeland of Rashemen. But they cannot wander far enough to escape the vengeance of the drow, and from the deep tunnels of the Underdark, glittering eyes are watching their every move.

FORGOTTEN REALMS and its logo are trademarks of Wizards of the Coast, Inc. in the U.S.A. and other countries. ©2005 Wizards.